Please don't tell my parents

YOU BELIEVE HER

Richard Roberts

bestselling author of *Please don't tell my parents I'm a* **SUPERVILLAIN**

CURIOSITY QUILLS PRESS

A Division of **Whampa, LLC**
P.O. Box 2160
Reston, VA 20195
Tel/Fax: 800-998-2509
http://curiosityquills.com

Cover Art by Eugene Teplitsky
http://eugeneteplitsky.deviantart.com

ISBN 978-1-94809-923-3 (ebook)
ISBN 978-1-71944-027-1 (paperback)

CHAPTER ONE

Setting forth to battle super-powered evil, it is important to remember not to be trapped in a robot body missing one arm. So, yeah, I failed that one already, but by the steel heart beating in my otherwise hollow chest, Penelope Akk would not give up. Right now, the parasite that had taken over my body was in my home, confessing just enough to my parents to make them think she was me.

Going home and confronting her was not going to work. I would do it anyway. Step by step, I would beat her and take back my life.

Literally step by step. The parasite left the teleportation bracelets on my robot body. In the courtyard of Upper High, I tried to use them and walked smack into a wall. They still worked, but using arm-mounted technology when I was carrying one arm in the other hand... I couldn't aim. I could teleport, but couldn't control where I ended up. After my third attempt landed me on top of the fence behind the school, I decided not to risk it again.

Also, I fell off the fence and landed on cobblestones so hard I worried for a second that my mechanical body might break some more. It really stung, too.

Pushing myself back up, I found that no, I was in no worse shape than before. The stuff my shell was made of might look and feel like porcelain, but it was tough. Grim satisfaction, that, but any satisfaction in a storm.

So, step by step, I walked home, up the street to the base of the hills, then along Los Feliz to the cozy little side street where my family lived.

Nobody bothered the broken robot girl marching irritably up the sidewalk. Hardly any cars were on the street, and no pedestrians. Fine by me.

As I passed the house next to us, Mom stepped out of the kitchen door, and walked up the driveway to meet me.

I couldn't help it. I rushed up to give her a hug.

To my lack of surprise, I didn't get to. She caught my outstretched hand, still holding my broken arm. Her other hand reached out to lay on top of my head, stroking my hair back to the base of my pigtails.

That gesture gave no comfort. Her face and voice set in the Audit's carefully crafted blankness, she said, "Of course. The copy would be convincing."

I'd expected this, but it still hurt. A lot. My metal heart ached, and my eyes stung from phantom tears I couldn't shed. "You believe her."

"The probability of her super power being as strong as it is gave me some trouble, until she shunted the kitchen table into hyperspace. Sometimes the million to one chance happens."

Glaring at my mother, I shot back, "You know what I mean. You believe that she's me."

Mom crouched down in front of me, balanced on the balls of her feet so that she could meet me more or less eye to eye. "I believe that my daughter Penelope is inside with her father right now, and I am talking to a robot double that sincerely believes it is the real Penny Akk. Taking this conversation as slowly as possible makes it less painful for both of us. If you are willing to keep your voice down, I will give you a chance to convince me otherwise."

Frowning, eyebrows pulled in tight, I asked suspiciously, "Why keep my voice down?"

"Because Brian hasn't figured it out yet, and this will break his heart when he does." Was that a hint of tightness in the Audit's impenetrable emotionless mask? A hint of wobble in her voice?

If Mom was hurting this bad... I couldn't shout and do that to Dad.

I wanted to—wanted to drag this out in front of everyone—but I couldn't do it. What good would it do? Ultimately, Mom was the parent I had to convince.

So I looked her in the eye. "She must have told you I've been trying to confess to being Bad Penny for half a year. To make myself confess, I built a robot and copied my mind into it."

Mom nodded. "That is the story she told. What happened today, after the public confrontation? This is your chance to tell me in your own words."

The words came rushing out. It took all my effort to not yell them! "The robot betrayed me. She wanted to be me. I messed up, making her so moral she went crazy. She tried to use the mind transfer machine to switch our bodies, but something went wrong. My body woke up without me in it, and instead she was... like an evil twin. She blew me up with a bomb, and left me to die, but I'm not going to." Those last few words came out in a snarl, but I managed a quiet snarl.

With a nod, her own voice quiet but still detached, my mother said, "The physical events you described match closely with the story she told us."

That was the last thing I expected to hear. "What? She admitted it?"

Her mouth twitched, and again, she took my hand, this time clasping it between both of hers. "What sounds more likely to you, Penelope? That your empty body betrayed and attacked you after a transfer you don't clearly remember, or that you made a fresh copy of yourself by accident, and your memories are so clear, you feel so you, that the original seems like a fake?"

...

I knew that my parents would be more likely to believe the parasite, but I hadn't expected the truth to betray me. Her explanation made so much sense. What if—

No. I was me. The original Penelope Akk. "She admitted that I was the original when she woke up. She blew me up with a bomb. She tried to kill the copy that betrayed me. Look! I would never do that!" Leaving Mom holding my broken arm, I pulled out the heavily dented Heart of Gold.

She looked at the Heart, but her continued impassive expression told me she was not sold, before she even spoke. "Penny's confession held a few surprises for me, but it was no shock to learn that she loves the drama of a villainous rant. You have her memories. Understandably angry with each other, you fought. You know about eye witness testimony."

I did. This wasn't just an Audit thing. Any police officer, lawyer, or psychologist would tell you the same thing. Begrudgingly, I recited, "No two people describe any event the same way, especially a fight. The evidence will tell a different story than either of them." That led to an inevitable follow-up. "You think I'm lying to myself."

"I think that reading expressions and tone differently, missing a few words or remembering them wrong because you were so emotional at the time, can make a situation seem the exact opposite of what it really is."

My shoulders twitched, sharply, because my whole upper torso had to move to do that. Putting the Heart of Gold away, I held up my wrist. "The Machine obeys me, not her. That's proof which of us is real."

"That is, by far, the best argument you have, but no one knows how the Machine takes orders, and the history of other particularly mysterious inventions suggests it's as likely it would find a robot version of its master more convincing as it is that it would only follow the true Penelope Akk."

She kept her cool, professional Audit demeanor through all of that. Then, suddenly, it disintegrated. Mom leaned forward, wrapping her arms around my head and pulling it to her chest. Her voice sounded only a touch hoarse, but that was... unprecedented. "Penny should never have made you, but not for the reason you think. A perfect copy means that there are two of you, now. You deserve to be taken into my home, raised and loved as my daughter, but I can't—not unless you accept that she's the real Penny."

My fist clenched so hard, it trembled. "I'm the real Penny. I want my body back. I want my parents back. I want my life back."

Her hands tightened on my shoulder. "It would be a poor copy of my daughter indeed that would say anything else. You know where that leaves me, and you know the results of accepting you into our lives while you believe that."

She was right there. I could not live in peace with the thing that stole my life, even if she let me. The parasite was evil, even if Mom hadn't seen that yet.

She would. Eventually. I couldn't wait for that, or trust it.

When I remained silent, Mom loosened her hug and leaned back, merely resting her hands on my shoulders. Oh, Tesla. Her eyes were bloodshot. She really was crying. Crying or not, her voice had gone steady again. "You enjoy being Bad Penny. You are the smartest, most sophisticated and yes, responsible fourteen year old I've ever met. You have made friends on the villain side, and maybe on the hero side. Go be Bad Penny, and when you've worked out that the Penny inside is the original, come back to us. And until then, don't trust Spider."

I didn't know what to say to that, either, so I stood there as she put my broken arm back in my hand, straightened up, and walked back inside the house.

The only good news was, that had hurt so much I couldn't feel it yet. It also wasn't a surprise. Okay, the details were different, but I'd known it wouldn't be as easy as convincing my parents. They had a flesh and blood kid and a robot duplicate. Who were they expected to believe? And the better the AI, the more likely it goes nuts, right?

I'd expected this defeat, but I had to try.

So... now what?

Charging in and trying to fight would only make things worse. My only home was right in front of me, and I couldn't get into it. I needed a base. Allies. Some place to start my campaign to get my life back.

Some place alone and safe when the emotions from this conversation hit.

If it had been the weekend, I would have gone to Chinatown. Now, the only villain I could expect to find there was Spider, who would love to help me—for a price. Mom was right about that.

If I stood on the driveway long enough, Dad would see me through a window. I couldn't do that to him. Not if he still wouldn't believe that I was the real Penny.

Back to my lair. That was at least a place. I could scavenge equipment, and think of something. The parasite had my phone. Maybe I could shut myself off until Friday.

I walked back up the sidewalk thinking gloomy thoughts like that, and as soon as the hedges blocked the view of my home, the Minx dropped off of a telephone pole in front of me.

She actually fell only the last ten feet or so, with her grappling hook reeling back in to its wrist holster. Landing in a deep crouch, one hand on the crooked pavement, she looked up at me with an amused smile. "I used to be able to do this in high heels, but it takes constant practice to keep ankles that strong."

If the heels on the boots she had on didn't count as 'high', I didn't want to know what did. Not that she had on one of her flashy, skimpy Minx costumes, but Misty Lutra—aka Claire's mom—had the figure and natural grace that made a business suit look like a catsuit.

"*You* believe me?" I asked. Maybe I'd predicted the conversation with my mom would go badly, but this was the last thing I'd expected.

She shook her head, not in denial, but with amusement to match her naturally playful smirk. Rising smoothly to her feet, she gave my cheek the pinch she had a thousand times before, when that cheek was made of flesh. "I don't have to. Unlike poor Beebee, I don't have a daughter to protect. Don't expect me to take sides, Penny honey, but I don't see how a mechanical body makes you any less real than you were when there was only one Penny Akk. I hope you always believed I'd be here for you in a pinch."

"The question never occurred to me," I admitted honestly.

She waved a hand, tracing liquid designs in the air. All the old folks were showing off their costumed identities today. With Misty Lutra, it was the grace of the world's best cat burglar. "There are practical issues that I'll have to figure out. I only just found out about this situation, and haven't had time to work out the details, but with Claire out of town there's plenty of time. Thank goodness I have your parents bugged, that's all I can say."

I goggled. "You *what* now?!"

Miss Lutra laughed, long and relaxed and playful. "Penny, putting tracers and microphones on your parents has been my hobby for two decades. It's a game we play, and I wasn't going to stop just because we retired. Brian has your house rigged so they don't work inside, but Beebee hasn't found the latest set. When it all hit the fan, I heard. Come on. Let's head back to my place. Reattaching that arm has to be our first priority, don't you agree?"

I followed along after her. My feet knew the way to Claire's house and could walk it in my sleep. That left my entire attention free for the sudden explosion of even-by-Lutra-standards weirdness. "Okay, wait. You bug my parents. Putting aside the sheer creepiness" —she laughed, but I bulled on—"of that statement, you did it during your professional careers. Doesn't that count as 'getting personal'?"

She fuzzled the top of my head. "If you ever doubt yourself, sweetie, that was a very Penny Akk question to ask. Spying on other supers is a grey area. You can break into someone's base, plant a camera on every square inch, and that's just the job. Tracking an enemy to their base is tacky, but allowed. For tech thieves, it's an important tool. Officially, you can bug someone's home if they carry it back on their costume or weapons, and you can spy on civilians all you want and it's a super-powered crime to be fought like any other. Technically, then, you can spy on their private life and their super-powered life, as long as you keep them separate—but by that point, honey, you're juggling dynamite. If the community decides you're mixing the two, there are no second chances or appeals. First offense—" She drew a finger along her throat and made the spitty decapitation noise.

Hmmm. So the population of people crazy enough to take that risk would thin itself out quickly. I nodded to indicate I understood.

She took that as her signal to continue, her voice fluttering with a hint of laughter. "Not that that was ever a worry with Beebee and Brian. You can do to friends what you would never consider doing to an enemy.

There has always been a giant exception in the rules for if the victim thinks it's all in good fun."

We walked down Los Feliz some more. Ahead, I could see the Lutra home, fancier than ours, because Mom and Dad just weren't showy people.

For a moment, my hand tightened on my broken arm, until I loosed my grip again and gave Miss Lutra an awkward half-smile. "Thank you for trying to distract me."

Hey, I'd lived with my mom for fourteen years. I knew how people manipulated each other to help, rather than hurt.

Leaning down, she pulled me into a sudden, tight embrace. If I'd still been made of mere flesh, it would have hurt. Sad, gentle, and encouraging, she said, "You are strong, Penny, and you will get through this. Your parents feel trapped and unable to help you, but I promise they still love you. I may not be able to get involved in what's brewing between you and your twin professionally, but in your private life, I will always be on your side. You're not alone."

My metal heart relaxed. Tension I shouldn't have been able to feel melted away, all over my body. She was right. "Thank you. That helps more than I would have believed possible."

It really did. The stakes might be high, but I hadn't lost everything. What I faced now was a supervillain rivalry, and I was very, very good at supervillainy.

Letting go and resuming our walk, she smiled down at me. "If this gets overwhelming, come to me. If you need a place to stay, I'll make sure you have one. If you can't take care of yourself, I'll do it."

What a difference it made, just knowing I had someone to catch me! I tried to crack my knuckles, only to be reminded that gesture doesn't work with only one arm. Still, that just made the point further. "I don't need a bedroom. I need a base. I am going to win this. Like you said, first step, get my arm fixed."

Tilting up the broken end, Miss Lutra peered down into my hollow arm. Her eyebrows went up, with a smirk both amused and impressed. "If we can find someone who can fix this technology."

Smirking back, I said, "If there's one benefit of six months of sin and criminality, it's that I know lots of mad scientists."

Miss Lutra laughed, and shook her head, platinum blonde curls bouncing around. "You never did get just how outrageous your super power is, did you? Look at this arm. No motors, no support structures, but you obviously have a full range of motion, plus a human sense of touch, provided by metal circuits printed on fabric. If you didn't have the arm to reattach, I guarantee no one in LA, even Brian or the Expert, could reproduce it—and Penny honey, there is no way I would let you walk into the Expert's clutches with robotics like this to tempt him."

Before despair could even begin to hit, she raised a finger. "Fortunately, Misty Lutra knows about an expert in neural circuitry whose work looks a great deal like this."

I pursed my lips. She was right, at least, that this was pretty exotic. Nobody I knew did anything quite like this. "Who?"

She grinned. She had the whitest teeth. Was it fair to the rest of us girls that the Lutras not only had a psychic power to bind men to their desires, but also physical perfection, so they hardly needed to use it? Sheesh.

Used to the jealous fuming of us less aesthetically-gifted women, Miss Lutra proceeded unperturbed. "That's what makes this complicated. Officially, I don't know who he is, where he lives, or that he's even alive. Getting personal can be complicated that way. Bugging your parents? Perfectly acceptable. Introducing you to someone I found out about by accident? We might as well put guns to our heads. Ah, but I have a plan. Climb in."

We had reached Claire's house at last, and Miss Lutra held open her car's passenger door for me.

Putting one foot inside, I paused before sliding in the rest of the way to give her a searching look. "What's the trick?"

"We sucker someone who does officially know where he is into making introductions. Besides, you'll love Pong, and she'll love to meet you."

CHAPTER TWO

We drove up the winding roads into the hills, where the really rich people live. The roads didn't just twist because it's hard to get up a hill. Everyone who could afford to live up here would be simply aghast to have a real street with real traffic going past their mansion. Along one of those bends, we pulled into the driveway of a house that remarkably had neither fence nor gate to protect it.

Miss Lutra demonstrated the necessity of such things by pointing down the slope and declaring, "Look, that's Jamil's house! You would not believe how much money I stole from him during my professional days. The hard part was convincing him to leave it lying around his home in cash."

That raised a separate question. These houses could afford to pay for super-powered private security. Was that a thing? And would it count as a hero or a villain?

Dismissive of any security of any kind, Misty Lutra half-led, half-dragged me to the front door, and gave it a knock.

An older woman in shorts and a loose sweatshirt (which had to be boiling her in the middle of summer) opened the door. On the short side, pear-shaped, white-haired, she looked classically grandmotherly, rather than a supervillain of any kind. Supervillain she had to be, though. Silver tattoos, like loosely-spaced celtic knotwork or maybe circuitry, covered her legs, the backs of her wrists and hands, and ran up her throat and cheeks. That was all the skin her outfit showed, but no doubt the tattoos went everywhere else.

I had seen markings like this before. In fact, I'd seen them earlier today, on two bikini-clad werewolves called Rage and Ruin. Ray and Claire called it 'the Upgrade.'

Exasperated and a touch sarcastic, the woman said, "Misty, this had better—"

It took her that long to register me, and particularly my broken-off arm. The tattooed grandma's mouth formed an 'o', and she lunged forward, pushing Miss Lutra aside. "You poor dear. Who did this to you?" Senior Super Citizen asked, sweeping me first into a hug (I was getting a lot of those today), then backing off to grip my chin in one hand and wave the index finger of her other hand in front of my eyes, like a vision test. I put up with it. We'd come here for this lady's help, and I could use all the hugs I could get right now.

All elegance and aplomb, Miss Lutra introduced, "Pong, this is... Bad Penny, I suppose, officially. Bad Penny, this is Pong."

"Come in, please," Pong urged me, pulling me into a front room as big as my house, with white walls that caught the sun blazing in from every window. Glancing up past me to Miss Lutra, she added, "And you too, I suppose." The dismissive contempt in those words was much too affected to be convincing.

Leaning forward into my peripheral vision, Miss Lutra explained, "Pong is one of the most successful supervillains of all time."

The old woman with the funny villain name let out a bark of laughter. "Most successful at holding onto my money, anyway, but that's not why Misty brought you to me. I'm a widely known sucker for transhumans."

Still over my shoulder, Miss Lutra told me, "That's someone who left their human body behind. It's taken from the word 'transhumanism.'"

Putting on my own 'jadedly amused' face, I answered, "Yes, I read science fiction, thanks." While both of the older women chuckled, I looked around at a second giant room, with huge, comfy pink furniture and wall-sized windows. There's no privacy like being a mile away from anyone on that side of your house. "This is definitely an expensive place."

Straightening up, Pong shouted, "ALABASTER! A broom!" The house tended to a lot of white as it was, but something the color of snow moved in the hall past the kitchen. It threw a plain, non-rich-people broom across the house, which Pong caught in one hand.

Like a magician reciting their favorite patter, the tattooed villainess said, "There are three ways to retire rich as a supervillain. The first is to make lots of friends on both sides. The second is to move far away, where no regular people knew you personally, and no one with powers knew you professionally. The third..."

Plucking a straw from the end of the broom, Pong held it out between thumb and forefinger. Pink light flashed, the straw disappeared, and a bang like a gunshot rattled my hollow body.

"...is for everyone to be afraid of you," she finished.

Following the line from her fingers, I saw a little round hole in one of her windows. No cracks, just a neat hole the width of a straw, like the damage you sometimes got in the vortex of a tornado.

I had to admit, I would not want to fight that. If I absolutely had to, stealth would be critical. Even giving her a chance to aim could be disastrous, and what about the other powers, the ones I knew nothing about? This soft, wrinkle-faced little old lady was one of the powerhouses of Los Angeles, years—probably decades—after retirement.

The Upgrade might have something to do with that.

Pulling me over to a worn, pink arm chair, she said, "Have a seat, please, Bad Penny. Relax. You are welcome in my home. How long has it been?"

"A few hours," answered Miss Lutra, leaning on the back of the chair as I settled into it. Criminy, this thing was comfortable, like falling into a huge, pink marshmallow.

"She can answer for herself, Misty. Turning into robot didn't make her mindless," Pong scolded.

Setting my detached arm in my lap, I held up a hand, wagging it from side to side in commitment to not committing. "I can, but she's also being nice. The day I've had is not... easy to talk about."

The old woman's eyes widened, tattoos pulling away from the

center of her face. Voice suddenly soft, she said, "Against your will. I'm so sorry. I should have guessed, with the damage. Don't worry, it will be okay. Misty brought you to me because my son, Emmett, had to be transferred into a robot when he was nine. His power was rotting him from the inside, and it was the only solution we could find before it spread to his brain. I know the transhuman experience as well as anyone flesh and blood can. How are you feeling? Not emotionally, and not the arm. Physically."

"Uh..." Truthfully, I'd been so busy with the first two issues, I'd barely paid attention to the robot body itself. I reported the one thing that leaped out at me. "I don't have phantom limb syndrome, but I've got a bad case of phantom entrails syndrome."

Pong smiled. "Hold onto that. It's a good thing. Alabaster! Robot refreshments, please!"

Something moved into the kitchen, easily visible from here. 'Something' was the best I could do. It was a white, more-or-less human silhouette. That was it. The changing shape as it moved around suggested three dimensionality, but all I could see was featureless white, immune to shadow.

Pong took my staring as a cue to keep talking. "You're a robot, so this wasn't a body-switching spell that will wear off in twenty-four hours."

"No. I have to take my body back," I answered.

She winced. "You're too young for a feud like this."

"It came to me anyway."

The white shape, Alabaster, walked silently up to us, setting a silver tray on a coffee table between my chair and the couch. It poured what looked like a cup of tea in a china cup, and set next to the cup a plate of three of the waxiest, flattest, most mass-produced looking chocolate chip cookies I'd ever seen.

I waved a hand in negation. "I don't have a stomach."

"Try them. Trust me," Pong urged.

Well, she did have a robot son, and seemed to know what to do. I picked up the cup, and took a sip.

TESLA'S TASTE BUDS!

The flavor hit me so hard, I barely kept hold of the cup. I hadn't noticed until now that I didn't have a sense of taste, and my sense of smell was vague, muted, and wrong, like in the middle of a really bad cold. The taste of tea crashed into that emptiness, and I swallowed automatically. That was another thing I couldn't do, lacking a throat, or even the muscles to fake it, but by reflex I tried, and the liquid disappeared from my mouth. It must have evaporated, but it felt like I had actually swallowed.

Reeling, suddenly desperately hungry and thirsty, I finished the cup and stuffed a cookie into my mouth. It might taste like a cheap cookie from a grocery store pack, but I could still make out the sugar and butter and chocolate. I chewed awkwardly, because my face might mimic human expressions beautifully, but my jaw didn't have a full range of emotion. Like the tea, the cookie disappeared into nothingness just in time for me to try to swallow.

Leaning back into the chair, I panted for breath, hand over my belly. "I can feel it in my stomach."

Pong gave me a warm and encouraging smile. "Your mind remembers. It wants to believe, and plays the sensations by habit. Do you know if this body can sleep?"

Still dizzy from the wonderful, warm feeling of having food inside me, I stammered, "Uh... I'm sure it doesn't need to."

"It doesn't, but you do. Make sure to keep sleeping. If you have to, have an off button installed and rig it to a timer so you deactivate for eight hours every night. Nothing will help you hold onto your humanity better, and the longer you feel human, the easier it will be to stay sane. Losing that human identity wrecks people."

I nodded. "You've got that right. The first time I woke up in this body, when I was just a copy and knew it, I... I... Sorry. My memories are... confused."

'Confused' did not begin to describe it. I remembered activating the Heart of Steel, watching it go maniacally insane, and having Ray pin it in place until it could be shut off. But I also remembered being pinned by Ray, the giddy laughter of knowing I wasn't like the flesh and blood people who'd made me.

For a moment I trembled, trying to put my face in my hands, and only succeeding with one. My gorge rose, and the nausea washed away the confusion, giving me peace again and curing itself. That Penny hadn't felt human, didn't believe it was the original. This one did.

But did that mean I was wrong? I had memories I shouldn't have.

No. Heart of Gold transferred me into the Heart of Steel, and that already held a copy of me. We'd merged, since we were the same person anyway. I picked up a few memories, and a sense of self that the copy didn't have.

Miss Lutra and Pong were both watching me with evident concern, but I lifted my head and held out a hand to reassure them. "I'm fine. I'm fine."

The old woman regarded me with sober admiration. "You're a strong girl, Bad Penny. The rumors said so, but I never trust them. You made it through your first identity crisis better than anyone I've seen or heard of."

"The refreshments helped," I replied honestly.

She chuckled. "That's what they're for. That, and enjoyment. I'll see if my provider can handle another customer. If not, you can visit any time for more. You can stay here, if you want."

Above me, Miss Lutra propped an elbow on the chair's back, and her chin on her fist. "I tried, but she's determined to get started on her quest for revenge."

"I would, in her position. So would you," the tattooed villainess said with a nod.

"Oh, that reminds me!" announced Miss Lutra. I twisted around to watch as she pulled out a little pink phone, dialed, and after a few seconds spoke into it. "Hi, Lucy! It's me, Misty."

She stopped, evidently cut off, and her smile grew even more sly than usual. "Oh, really? Then I'll make this quick. The Robot Penny situation has taken a turn for the weird. Can—"

Another silence, obviously cut off, and Miss Lutra's eyebrows rose. "But what will Gabriel say?"

From out of the phone, I could clearly hear Lucyfar yell in a parody of Gabriel's voice, "I'm not your boyfriend!"

That got Miss Lutra and Pong both laughing, and I managed a little snicker. Airily, Miss Lutra told Lucyfar, "Fine, fine. But contact me later, before you talk to either Penelope, okay?"

Lucyfar must have agreed and hung up, because Miss Lutra turned off the phone, and handed it down to me. Smugly maternal, she said, "This is for you, by the way. It's one of Claire's old phones. I cleaned its memory and set it up on my phone plan for your robot double, but now you need it."

This hadn't even occurred to me, but it would have, as soon as I was alone again. I used my phone all the time, and the parasite had it.

The perfect—even at the age of forty—Lutra face pinched in concern, and she added, "But take my very strong advice. Don't call Claire or Ray until they're back in town, and you can see them in person. I know you'll miss them and it seems like giving the other Penny an advantage, but contacting them too soon will make it harder to get them on your side. Take it from an old hand at manipulation."

My fist tightened, until I had to force myself to ease off because I might have the strength now to break the phone. She was right, of course. Mom made it clear all the time that painfully counterintuitive techniques like that were the rule rather than the exception in human psychology.

Sighing, I said, "I'm hoping to have this resolved before they get home anyway."

Above me, Miss Lutra said, "Speaking of which, I'm glad Bad Penny has you as a transhuman resource, Pong, but that's not why I wanted to introduce you."

Leaning back on the couch, the senior villainess gave the merely middle-aged villainess a skeptical stare. "This is going to be about money, isn't it?" She did not actually sound upset.

"No, it's about contacts. Bad Penny tends to overdo it on the Tier Three technology, and I was hoping you could put her in touch with someone who could fix that unusual arm of hers."

Pong just scowled. Her wrinkled old face was unusually expressive, and as much as she had a glowing smile, her frown radiated distaste. "Ridiculous. I don't know half as many mad scientists as you know in the biblical sense."

Lutras know no shame, of course. Rather than looking embarrassed at the mention of her romantically enthusiastic career, the Minx preened. "You know one that I don't. Look at the circuitry inside. Doesn't that remind you of an Upgrade?"

Pong stared for a while, her expression more troubled than angry. "I got these forty years ago. He could be dead."

Feeling like I ought to take more of a hand in my own fate, I said, "Rage and Ruin got their Upgrades four years ago. Whoever does them, he's still alive. Do you know how I could meet him?"

The hard, calculating stare of a supervillainess cut the 'plump grandma' image as Pong sat, silently considering my argument. Miss Lutra and I let her.

Finally, the tattooed supercriminal sighed and gave me a nod. "I'll give you his address. Don't show it to Misty, and go there alone. Don't expect him to just let you in, either. He's as likely to make you pass a test or get past a parade of traps as he is to welcome you. Once you do... well, he has a soft spot for teenagers in trouble, although you may not believe that when you meet him. And you tell no one, ever, who he is or where you met him."

I nodded, and jumped to my feet. "Fine by me. If he has a test, I'll pass it."

Her mysterious mad scientist could bring it on. This was my war. It was wonderful to know I wasn't alone, but I needed to take charge of fighting it.

CHAPTER THREE

Miss Lutra pulled up next to the Red Line station. The passenger door flipped open, and I half expected an ejection seat to throw me out of the car, which was totally unfair to Claire's mom. Instead she leaned over and kissed me right at the top of my bangs, such as they were. "This is as far as I go. Remember, sweetie, I can't takes sides with one Penny against another, but I'll give you all the personal support your parents wish they could."

I climbed out, and gave the stairway-lined pit that led down into the subway a resigned stare. "I wish you could support me by driving me the rest of the way. It would save a couple of hours." Letting out a long sigh that irritated me because these artificial shoulders wouldn't slump, I added, "But I'm not going to betray Pong's confidence."

She laughed, and gave me a fond, impish smile. It was creepy the way she had all the same mannerisms as her daughter. I had a robot double. Maybe Claire didn't know who her father was because she literally did not have one? Some kind of clone weirdness? Dimensional crossover? Alien shapeshifter that picked Miss Lutra to copy? Aliens did love Claire.

Waving to the older of the identical blondes, I descended into the bowels of the Earth, and faced the dread guardian of its hidden ways. Fortunately, along with my teleport bracers, Parasite Penny forgot to take away my Inscrutable Machine credit card. I didn't know how much was on it, but enough to buy a TAP card and put enough money into it that I could take public transportation for granted until I got my body back.

I was so getting my body back. What a crazy day, and it was nowhere near over.

Hmmm. Also, Note to Penny: Go back to the lair and loot it as soon as you have a place to put the stuff.

Taking the Red Line as a robot was no different from taking it as a human. I spent the time poking at my new phone, which was a bit slow and limited compared to the ones Dad makes, but fine. It had a good map, and that told me to take the Blue Line next, so I climbed up from the deep pits to the light rail stations.

Nobody noticed or cared about sharing a subway car with a robot, but on the train, three kids a few seats down kept nudging each other and looking at me. Well, 'kids'. They were older than me physically, but I was feeling mighty mature and weighted with adult issues about now.

The girl got out her own phone and took a few photos, angling to try and get a shot inside my gaping, hollow shoulder. One of the boys stood up, took a few cautious, halting steps towards me, and asked, "Do you have laser vision?"

With as much mechanical stiffness as I could fake, I turned my head up to look at him, and just... stared. After several seconds, he cringed, and crept back to his seat between the other two.

Ha!

"HA! AH HA HA HA HA!"

Wait, that wasn't me. I didn't have a second voice speaker I didn't know about, did I?

A thump on the roof of the car confirmed that I was not the source of this round of maniacal laughter. A woman's voice, rich and velvety and mocking, called out, "Your determination is simply adorable, boys, but you must give it up. Your plans are foiled, and *Gallus gallus* once again rules the day!"

Thanks to the train itself being in the way, I had no view of our mystery woman, whether she was a hero or a villain, and who she was running from. She did have a proper dramatic flair, and kept her voice loud enough to be heard over the rumble of train and traffic as she asked, "Victory assured—let's check if our services are needed here, shall we, darlings?"

And then...

Okay, I don't know what I was expecting after that, but it wasn't a chicken wearing suction cup shoes walking down the window opposite me. A chicken I got, however, its head tilting this way and that curiously as it peered at the occupants through tiny metal goggles.

At least the chicken didn't talk. The woman's voice still came from above us as she proclaimed, "Oh, my! Aren't you stylish. I can't do anything about the arm, but once you're fixed, if you need a good tailor to help you mend that magnificent steampunk costume, just ask for Diamond Pullet. Thanks to you, this public conveyance passes minimum fabulousness standards. It could still do with a few chickens, but for now, away, my pets!"

The chicken, flapping its wings in the wind—and wearing a small but dapper pinstriped vest—climbed back up onto the roof. Presumably its owner left. I heard nothing else unusual for the rest of the trip. The kids across from me took a lot of photos out through the window, but I was betting more out of hope than because there was anything to see.

Oh, Los Angeles. If anything could cheer me up, it was the reminder that all around me, other super-powered people were having equally weird adventures.

Eventually, I got off at Slauson. This was a busy traffic area, not the kind of place I expected junkyards—but right there across the street I saw the sign of an auto junk lot. Not the one I was looking for, even, which the map said was a couple of blocks down.

So, I crossed the street and walked those couple of blocks. I immediately passed yet another junkyard right across the street from the first one. Neither looked anything like I expected. One at least had a neat stack of brightly-colored cars with the wheels taken off. Other than that, no... well, junk.

I was almost at the corner I had to turn when a guy passing me looked up from his phone, saw a one-armed robot in front of him, and jumped a good three inches in the air. He could not be an LA native.

Or maybe he was, because when he recovered from his surprise he didn't look amazed. He leaned over me, frowning in concern. "Hey, are you okay? I mean, obviously you're not okay, but do you need help?"

"You want to help me?"

My own surprise must have sounded skeptical, because he winced, and rubbed his shaggy brown hair. "I know I'm probably asking for super-powered trouble, but I can't let a kid with her arm broken off fend for herself."

D'aw. I gave him a big, grateful grin. "Thanks, Mister, but I'm going to get the help I need now."

He sighed in relief, but didn't actually look much less anxious. "Okay. But if you need anything, you can have my number. Robot or not, a kid your age shouldn't have to go it alone."

Tell me about it, but... "I'm not. People are falling all over themselves to help me since this happened. It's doing wonders for my faith in humanity. Don't worry about me."

"You sure?" He gave me a searching look, a little scared, but meaning that question.

"I'm sure," I answered with a nod.

Another sigh, and he flapped a hand weakly. "Good luck, little girl. Seriously."

He started walking, and I started walking, and I left the random good Samaritan behind. Just as well—I had reason to believe I'd reached my destination. Instead of a building, at the street corner I passed a tall, chain-link fence with a green tarp behind it, and a not-quite-flat coil of barbed wire across the top. When I actually did turn the corner, the fence went on for quite a ways until it reached a gate, much bigger than the other junkyards. It kept going after the gate, too. This place was the size of a shopping center.

As for the gate, well, it was solid metal, had spikes along the top, a chain and padlock over the handles, and a sign.

CLOSED, Come Back Tomorrow

Nothing indicated actual opening hours. The sign looked reversible, so I slid it out of its display box, and read the back.

Don't Be A Smart Aleck, Kid.

Oh, yeah. This was the place.

How to get in? A small hole I could see through would be enough to teleport, but with my control problems I'd land on my face, possibly behind me across the street.

Eh. I'd take the easy route. Might as well get some use out of my condition.

Tucking my broken arm into my pouch belt, I jumped up and grabbed the top of the fence. The barbed wire probably poked through my leather gloves, but couldn't do anything to my artificial fingers. The stuff making up my 'skin' was more like hardened brick than porcelain. Much stronger and much lighter than I was used to, I easily pulled the rest of me up, and vaulted over the top into the yard itself.

Oh, yeah. This was the stuff. What a mess. Bits of car everywhere. Doors, steering wheels, mufflers, axles, engines. Not just cars, but all kinds of appliances. I spotted the front half and the back half of a washing machine across from each other in different piles. Not only did rusty metal layer the ground, it was built up in big heaps.

A tidy blue building in the back of the lot sported a logo in blue letters: 'Junkment Day.'

This was as far as my directions took me. Somewhere in this graveyard of technology, a mad scientist was hiding.

Besides me, I mean.

The actual building was the obvious place to start, and also the least likely. Whoever lived here took being an eccentric seriously. Still, I hiked across the lot, picking my way through the uneven footing, and peeked in one of the big glass windows.

Empty. Seriously empty. Stripped, but not abandoned. The interior wasn't dusty, and lacked the holes in the walls or sections of uneven paint that suggested refurbishment or disuse. It just contained nothing. Aside from a few (empty) shelves in the big auto-mechanic room, this building contained not a stick of furniture. No tools. No trash or litter. No decorations. Just white walls and gray floor. And yet, shadows in the light fixtures on the ceiling suggested they still held bulbs. The lifting jacks embedded in the floor shone, ready for service. A giant compressor lined one wall, radiating danger. The owner might have seen me coming, stuffed everything into a bag, and hidden under the floor.

I put that as the third likeliest possibility, right behind there being a secret door inside, but more likely than the contents being invisible.

Best odds said that the whole building was a decoy, and possibly a trap. Some of the junk piles could easily hide a bus, and the smallest could hide the hatch for an elevator. I went poking around.

One thing became instantly clear: When I got my superpower back, I would buy this lot and build my own lab on it. So. Much. Raw material. Scrap electronics. Pumps. Things with lenses. Huge chunks of steel in the form of car parts, some conveniently shaped into pistons and axles, ready to be used.

Hello. A mad scientist had been here already. Those heavy, pinching clamps ten feet away didn't belong to any piece of standard technology I could imagine. Too goofy. On the other hand, they could easily have been torn off of a low grade robot. And what was that thing with the lenses and the wires? Telescopes didn't need that much electronics. Cameras wouldn't be tube shaped. Was that a robotic eye? Or the barrel of a beam weapon?

A much bigger cylinder stuck out of a nearby heap. Inside, I could just make out the blades of a fan. Fan, or turbine? Yeah, that was a jet engine.

While scanning the detritus for more treats, I spotted the door. At first, it looked like an upright slab, but pulling away the lawn mower, muffler, and folding table stacked in front of it confirmed: Door. Nicely arched, and set into walls that disappeared back into the heap. I had no clue what the gray-brown stuff it was made of could be, either. Super-smooth stone? Metal with an odd color and wavy, mottled patterns?

And of course, slabs generally did not have keyholes. This door sported three, all big and clunky and positioned as part of the decorations.

Bas-relief carvings covered the arched... uh, stone. I'd go with stone, for now. Divided into quarters, each one depicted a figure, three with their own keyhole. Top left, a guy with the broadest shoulders ever stood with both hands on the hilt of a wide two-handed sword. Okay, technically a suit of armor holding a sword, but presumably someone would wear that armor. Somehow. It wasn't just wide, but sported thick shoulder, elbow, and knee pads, and spikes jutted out... everywhere. For bonus points, the armor had a bazooka-style weapon strapped to its back, and... yes, the sword blade had jagged edges. A chainsaw two-handed sword. Nice. The keyhole fitted in where the hilt joined the blade.

The upper-right quarter boasted some kind of ghoul. Hunched, clawed hands, stringy hair, skin stretched over a skeleton and not much more. A loincloth protected my virtuous eyes from what would be the grossest nudity ever. Unlike the suit of armor, this character didn't sport much detail or decoration —a few bugs, which would make zombie-style sense if they were flies. Instead they looked like grasshoppers. The keyhole took up almost the entirety of the ghoul's shrunken belly.

Lower left I liked. A person of indeterminate gender in what might be a suit of leather armor, wearing a hooded cape and a mask with a huge, pointy raven beak. Between outstretched hands hovered a biohazard symbol, with the keyhole in the center.

Finally, lower right. The Reaper. In case I'd missed that the first three were War, Famine, and Pestilence, this could not be anything but Death, in a robe and carrying a traditional curved scythe. Admittedly, an awfully squat Death. Wearing sneakers. And the robe was kinda more a dress, ending just below the knees, with non-skeletal calves. Death as a little girl.

I knew this one. Whoever carved this door had chosen the super-powered terror Psychopomp to represent Death. Penelope Akk Full Disclosure: I only recognized her because I'd finished a computer game based on her excessively murderous story a few days ago.

She did not get a keyhole, no doubt for some deeply symbolic reason, or maybe because this was an actual person, or maybe the keyhole would appear once the others were unlocked. The whole thing could not more obviously be a puzzle. The War, Famine, Pestilence, Death theme were clues that would lead me to uncover keys in the junkyard to unlock this door.

Fortunately, I didn't need to do any of that. Thanks to Alexander the Great and his Gordian Knot, I knew the solution to this puzzle already. Scraping my Machine off my wrist with the broken lawnmower, I swung him around until his legs began to wave, set him against the door, and said, "Eat."

He did just that. Ha! So much for the hard sciences. Those who study history are able to repeat it!

"Just the door," I told my wonderful little creation when he reached the frame it had been set into. The six-inch-thick door. By the time he finished, my Machine had grown into a pony-sized pillbug. So, I sat on his back, and pointed down the hallway just revealed. "*Hyah*, mule!"

He *hya'd*, scuttling on dozens of little metal legs down a featureless arched corridor of the same mystery substance. It must be metal, because the only not-really-features decorating the length were occasional ridges with bolts set in.

As for 'length'... Tesla's Unexplained Distortions. The hallway went well past the length of the heap of junk, without angling down. Glancing back, I made sure we were actually making progress. Yeah.

Wow. You heard about 'bigger on the inside than the outside' tech, but I'd never seen it, or heard of any actual examples. Or we might have just passed through a teleportation gate so neatly set across the corridor that I couldn't spot it. Either way, it was time to revise my opinion of the owner of this lot way, way upward. This person had access to hardcore mad science.

The hallway didn't stretch on forever, or anything. Just long enough to make it clear we had left normal considerations of space behind. That point made, when we reached the doorway at the end, what lay on the other side didn't surprise me *much*.

Fitting neatly into the arched doorway normal to such a building, the hall emptied into a church, of the old-fashioned Gothic cathedral kind. A multi-story empty space rose to complicatedly vaulted ceilings, with walls of gray stone bricks. The cross shape of the building suggested Christianity, but the giant statues lining the nave did not look particularly biblical. Of course, the only one that wasn't broken off somewhere depicted the big armored chainsaw two-handed sword guy.

Broken statue rubble filled some of the space, but emptiness filled a lot of the space. Workbenches held small, but obviously high-tech pieces of inventing equipment. One resembling a plastic blender looked suspiciously like a bioengineering device I had known and very thoroughly vaporized. No red alien cloning goo, though. Nowhere did I see a bed, or a kitchen, or anything that wasn't mad science related. Presumably, there were other rooms. Whether we were under or above-ground, I couldn't tell. Light shone through abstract, stained glass windows from all directions.

A thin, fit, but heavily-lined old man stood waiting for me, holding a ball-pein hammer that did not look appropriate for the delicate instruments on display. He wore overalls and a flannel shirt, both clean but worn. Short, white hair stuck out in all directions with the wildness of long-endured cowlicks.

He had quite a scowl on him, too, glaring down on me as I rode in on my own piece of mad science.

"Go away, machine," he said, nose wrinkled in angry disgust.

It took me a second to realize 'machine' meant me. I didn't let that stop me, although I did try to look and sound respectful as I bowed my head. "I need your help."

He gave me a sneer, not proud, just disgusted. "Why should I help you?"

"Because I passed your test."

If anything, he glared harder. "Eating my door doesn't count."

Keeping a straight face was getting really, really hard. My synthesized voice definitely sounded a bit amused to me. "Anyone who makes kids take a test to get in appreciates an original answer."

"Robots aren't kids. Maybe I was just trying to keep you out." He was way better at hiding that this was a game.

But a game it was, and verbal banter might be my favorite. My smile had to be breaking through as I struggled to sound serious and intimidated. "You'd have used a different door. Don't try to tell me that you don't have better ways to hide your lab ready."

I won that round. His scowl settled to merely irritable, and he gave me a long stare before asking with guarded caution, "Do you know who I am?"

"Not a clue, but you helped Rage and Ruin." Technically a lie, but correct in spirit. I was positive somebody had mentioned who gave Rage and Ruin their Upgrades once, but the name wasn't coming to me now. It would just be a name, anyway.

And this guy definitely gave them their Upgrades. As I mentioned their names, the same thin, silver circuitry tattoos appeared on his skin. A few seconds later, they disappeared, as if receding under the surface, only to be replaced by a different pattern of thicker lines. That kept happening. Whatever he'd given them, he'd given it to himself, squared.

He'd been great at pretending to be angry. He was lousy at pretending to not care. "How are they?"

"Enjoying life," I promised him. Not a lot of people enjoyed life more than those two villainesses.

"Cassie?" He did keep his tone flat and emotionless. Maybe it was only growing up with my mom that made that wave giant red flags about how how important those three were to him.

Trying for my own entry in the totally not embarrassed or bothered competition, I answered, "Got a crush on me. Don't ask, it's too weird."

He grunted, a tiny little noise in the back of his throat. Then he grabbed my head.

Like Pong, he didn't lunge. He took my cheeks in both hands with smooth confidence, then gripped my chin. Just exactly like Pong, he tilted it from side to side, then waved a finger in front of my eyes.

Maintaining the minimum frustration in my voice, I asked, "Okay, why do people keep doing that?"

He'd watched my face carefully while he did it, but his focus drifted, and he sounded thoughtful, almost like a teacher giving a lecture. "It's a test. It shows me that you're human."

I hoisted an eyebrow. "What, because I can track motion with my eyes?"

And, finally, he let go of my head and smirked. "No. You reacted to me invading your space. As a human, you care about being touched, and you know you're supposed to watch my finger. An artificial intelligence has no reason to have emotions about something like that."

That sounded like the backhanded way psych tests worked. And more importantly... "So you believe I'm human? Will you help me?"

Instead of answering, he said, "You really don't know who I am?" We had exactly the same disbelieving tone and stare.

Feeling irrationally apologetic, I spread my hands. "I don't keep track of retired supervillains. I'm only guessing you're even a villain."

His scowl and gruffness came back in a snap. "Maybe you should. They'll keep track of you. Not even many heroes care that there's a human mind in a piece of technology as temptingly advanced as this."

Had I actually touched a black and withered old heart, here? Seizing that momentum, I asked, "So, you'll help me?"

"Against them?" he asked, scowling again.

Pulling my broken arm out of my belt, I held it up. "With this."

His scowl deepened. The old man pulled his hammer back out of his belt, and gave it a sharp flick. "I'm a cyberneticist. I deal with organic-inorganic interfaces, not pure machines."

Retreating to the respectful head bow, I continued offering my arm, broken-off end first. "These do look a lot like Upgrade circuits."

He stood there, silent and grouchy, for a couple of seconds. Then he took my damaged arm in both of his, holding it carefully as he carried it over to one of the work benches.

Guessing that this guy probably did not want me staring over his shoulder, I waited. He kept doing stuff, which I figured meant I hadn't been rejected.

After a couple of minutes of peering and prodding, the old man stomped back to me and held out my arm in one hand, and a little white tube in the other. The tiny kind, like industrial superglue or thermal paste comes in.

"This ointment regenerates synthetic neurons. Apply it to both ends of the broken circuits, and they'll reattach. That will restore full control and sensation. Everything else you'll have to find a roboticist for."

I took the tube, and delicately tucked it into one of my many pockets. Then I took my arm, and held it all floppy because there wasn't really any respectful way to carry around a limp arm. He was playing detached and professional, so I tried not to sound gushingly grateful. "Do I owe you anything?"

His expression changed. His face hardened, maybe literally—the suddenly complex network of Upgrade lines making his whole body look stiff and metallic. With his brows set in a line, for the first time he didn't look an old man playing 'get off of my lawn.' He looked like a supervillain, and the serious kind. "Yes. Tell no one where you got this, or who gave it to you, or that I exist, or about this place, or describe anything about me to anyone else. Understand?"

"Yes, sir. Thank—"

"DO. YOU. UNDERSTAND?" Criminy, the guy's eyes were glowing, little burning coals of red in the back of his pupils.

"Yes, sir!" I barked, at attention.

He pointed at the doorway. "Now get out." That didn't sound quite as harsh and threatening, just like I'd completely used up my welcome.

Kicking the Machine with my ankle, I goaded it out and back down the tunnel. Awesome. I'd charmed a crazy powerful but secretive old coot, and had the stuff that would fix what a regular robot doctor couldn't.

Assuming there was such a thing as a regular robot doctor. But I was on a roll, and felt it. I ought to be utterly exhausted after the day I'd had, but that was the good side of a robot body. Maybe I'd lost my mad science power, but I would exploit this untiring thing to the hilt.

Laying my arm in my lap, I got out the phone Miss Lutra gave me, and punched up 'Roboticists near me' in the search browser.

And lo and behold, I found a news article. "Eccentric Robot Designer West Lee Revealed As Mystery Santa."

Chapter Four

Here you go. At least I got my turn before you put me out of a job," said my taxi driver, marking the sixty-seventh robot joke since I got in the car.

I flicked him my credit card. "I don't have any cash, so I hope your gross meaty fingers can handle an electronic transaction."

A minute later, after I'd signed, tipped, and as I shut the car door, he said, "Man, I wish my super power was good enough for crime fighting."

And then he drove away, leaving me facing the lair of my next conquest, the mysterious man known as West Lee.

He had to be mysterious. In the middle of a Burbank block full of little businesses related to show business, on a street full of boxy concrete towers housing animation studios, he had an Elizabethan mansion. The house was practically a castle, three stories tall and riddled with turrets. The windows were uniformly dark, like they'd been painted with soot on the inside, revealing only hints of curtains and nothing else. Dark gray pointed roofs and purple-tinged gray wooden walls stood out like a sore thumb. Were those even legal in LA?

The building looked dusty, cracked, and abandoned, but when I walked up the steps to the porch, that proved to be an illusion propagated by color. This building was in fine shape. At worst, the wood surfacing might be a bit rough.

West Lee did not make me go through the entrance test gambit. The door opened before I could touch the door knocker.

Of course, nobody stood on the other side. Embracing drama was at least two thirds the point of being a mad scientist.

I did check behind the door on the way in. Nope, nobody there. The door swung closed by itself, with an appropriate echoing boom.

The interior continued the theme of the exterior. A double staircase ran up the back of the entrance hall, and aside from the worn, red carpet leading to it, the floor stretched to the walls in a black and white checkerboard. Together, they made me think of a computer game set. If I inspected the grandfather clock, would I find it missing the hour hand, with a code scratched into the wood hinting at what time I had to set to open a secret door?

No time for that. I heard voices upstairs.

Away I went, bounding up the steps and following that siren lure. The upstairs had carpeting, at least, in a faded purple. A mirror hung over a little display table, on which two diminutive wind-up robots held a floral-print vase. As a nice touch, the flowers were all made of metal scrap parts. They might even do something, if you wound them up. Way down at the end of the hall, a doll in a red dress sat on another table. The face of the china head had gone missing, and a metal, robotic skull with bulging eyes peeked out from inside.

Other than that, closed doors lined the walls, and not much else. Closed doors, and two open doors. One ajar, but dark. When I actually looked at it, I saw a mask peeking at me through the gap. It withdrew into the shadows immediately, and the door snapped shut.

Light spilled from the other open door, and voices as well.

"There's nothing I can do about it. I don't control every robot in Los Angeles. I barely control any of the ones I built. You can't even tell me what she looks like," said a man with a scratchy, high-pitched voice.

Another man, with a deeper, rolling voice, replied, "We do not know what she looks like. Other than that she is heavily-armed and covered in a fuzzy surfacing, we have no reports. The thief girl does not want to be part of the community."

"I hoped you had fitted out one of my babies with a new body, West," said a soft-voiced woman.

The higher voiced man said, "I don't weaponize anything, Raggedy. Is anyone missing who's human-sized? I don't—um—Juniper was as big as a child. Have you heard from her? Mr. Pickles is okay?"

Raggedy! That was the old woman with all the living dolls, who helped Robot Penny. And *that* made the deeper-voiced man Gothic, her... husband? Partner? Fellow artificial life enthusiast? It made sense that they would be here with a guy who made robots.

Following those voices to the door, I found a workshop. No surprise there. This one specialized in making skulls, with shelves lined with metal eye sockets, jaws, jars of teeth, masks, and metal shaping equipment on the desk. Plenty of finished robot heads watched us from the shelves as well, with lidless, staring eyes. A lamp shaped like a robot, or possibly a robot with a lamp built into its hands, provided most of the light. A couple of feet tall, with a willowy body made of intertwined wire, it stood on the work bench behind its creator.

West Lee proved to be a chubby old man in ragged black jeans, a black jacket with a lot of little tools in a lot of little pockets, and a T-shirt emblazoned with a picture of a bipedal robot, missing so many pieces that it couldn't be identified beyond 'bipedal' and 'robot', hugging a child in a red cape. Fluffy, snow-white hair sat on his head like an untidy cloud, with a matching Santa Claus beard.

Raggedy still looked like a little old homeless woman, wrinkled and smiling and dressed in gray... well, rags. Next to her, Gothic stood in the same stiff posture with the same skull-decorated suit that I'd seen in Chinatown. These two had a Look, and were sticking to it.

Only West Lee actually faced the door, so he noticed me first. He lifted a hand to his mouth, his face bunching up in concern. That made Raggedy and Gothic turn around. They gasped as soon as they laid eyes on me.

Raggedy rushed forward, with a high-speed, lunging hobble. She clasped my cheeks in both hands, and asked, "What happened to you, dear?"

Gothic didn't move, although he looked just as pained and worried as the other two. "West Lee, this is the Heart of Gold, who stayed with us briefly. She was engaged in what we were told was a pretend public battle with her creator."

"No, I'm not her," I protested.

"What?" asked Raggedy, even more alarmed.

Gothic frowned deeply. You could have used his eyebrows as a ruler. "Memory damage from the injury?"

"No, no. Look. Hold this." I dumped my broken arm into Raggedy's grip, which got her to let go of my head. These people loved robots, and this body wasn't flesh and blood or all that anatomically correct, so it wasn't too embarrassing to undo a few buttons of my shirt, fiddle with the catch, and open up the doors in the middle of my chest.

Raggedy and Gothic went cold and still at the sight of my Heart of Steel. "What did you do with the owner of that body?"

"I didn't do anything. Some... *thing* took over my body, stuck me in this one, and—" My hand closed over my belt pouch containing the Heart of Gold. It would be too cruel to show them the battered lump. "I think my good twin can be repaired, but I don't know when or how. She's not functional now."

That got West Lee's attention, and he stepped away from his table to give me a look of pained sympathy. "You were forced into a robot body?"

Raggedy passed Gothic my severed arm. He turned it over a couple of times, scowling. Mind you, various levels of scowl were the only expressions in this room. "The current biological Penelope broke your body and the Heart of Gold both?"

"And the first step to dealing with her, is to convince Mr. Lee to fix my arm." I held out my hand to Gothic.

Raggedy started to say something, but he gave her shoulder a squeeze. She restrained herself, outrage fading to solemn, detached concern.

As for the Pinstriped Mummy, he not only gave me my arm, but put a card in it. I was learning something today. Supervillains like business cards. "You have come to the right man, Heart of Steel. West Lee will help you. When he has, please come to us. Raggedy and I like to make all new robots feel welcome, and she can fix your costume."

"It might come alive if she does," said West Lee, with the fluttering hesitance of someone who's not quite sure if their joke will offend anybody.

Raggedy patted my hair with a wrinkled hand, and said, "We're always easy to find. We don't have to hide, because no one wants to rob or arrest us."

They walked out.

West Lee, old Saint Mecha-Nicholas himself, backed up against his desk as if I'd come to kill him. Same wide eyes, stammering voice. "They're—Raggedy and Gothic are good people, but—they—I'm not the right man. I don't know how to fix that."

Time to fight technology with magic. I applied the most potent incantation I knew. "Please?"

His mouth opened and shut several times. Gradually, poised to flee, he reached out and accepted my broken arm. Wide-eyed terror became a bewildered frown as he peeked inside. Then he leaned over to look down the gap in my shoulder. "Where did you find this? Who made it? Is this alien? It looks—I've seen—it's a little like the technology Neon Rider used. People said that was extraterrestrial." Shaking his head hurriedly, he added, "I can't fix circuits like these."

I passed over the tube from the armageddon-obsessed back alley cyberneticist. "Synthetic neural regenerator."

Delicately plucking the tube away, he retreated to his table. Metal folding tools didn't look right for my arm, but he ignored the clamps and presses anyway. Scooping a volt meter and a head-sized lens out of a drawer, he handed the latter to the wiry lamp. Proving it was a robot after all, it extended two more skinny arms, using those to hold the magnifying glass in place. He peered through it. He tapped things inside my detached arm with the volt meter. After a little fiddling with dials, he did that again.

My detached arm's fingers twitched, and I was definitely sure a regular volt meter could not do that.

More fiddling. My arm bent at the elbow, made a fist, did all sorts of things. West Lee got out a soldering iron, then something that looked like a soldering iron, but with a bright spark at the tip. More limb twitching.

Every eye in the room watched his progress. Not just his own and mine, but all the heads on the shelves, and even the unattached eyes.

It took awhile, and they had more patience than me. Eventually, my attention wandered. It wouldn't be fair to say this room was empty. It had the heads, some of which were animal- or monster-like, or had as many as eight glowing red eyes. It also had posters, pinned all over the wall behind the bench. They ranged from old B movies, to exhibits from theme parks, and even a faded poster for—

"Gerty Goat's Family Farm!" I shouted.

West Lee let out a squeal, jumped at least two inches in the air, and dropped his tools on the floor. Hands shaking, he bent down and picked them up, but stopped halfway to standing up straight again. "You know Gerty?"

"I love Family Farm! Okay, the restaurant is cruddy, but Gerty Goat makes up for it. She's clumsy and can't sing, but she's happy with who she is, and she doesn't care what anyone thinks. Even if you don't love her, she loves you. I wish everyone could be like Gerty Goat."

He blinked at me, twice, still crouched. His eyes widened, wrinkles forming all around them, and he stood up with a relaxed confidence he hadn't shown since I showed up. He still stuttered a little, but his voice got more enthusiastic by the moment. "Gerty is mine. I made her. I made all the animatronics at Family Farm. You know, the original Gerty is at the store right here in LA? I still have the biggest share of the company, I think."

My head tilted as I processed this. "No wonder she's so sophisticated. She's mad science! I, uh... I peeked inside at her workings once. I was bad."

That only made him smile. Patting the bench, he said, "Sit up here. I think I can reattach your arm. The goo seems to work, so you'll probably have control, but it's going to be fragile. I can't cleanly reattach enough of the actuator fabric, and my best glues will still leave fracture lines, like scars. You won't be fighting any battles with this arm. I can reattach, but I can't heal."

A quick push with my good hand hopped me up to sit on the edge of the table. "That's okay. I know someone who can heal inorganic objects, and she's a friend." I should have thought of Mirabelle immediately. Then again, the less she had to fix, the better. Nobody was all-powerful.

My lips pursed as that thought led to others. "I'll need to go to Chinatown this weekend to see her. I should do that anyway. Everybody's super nice to a broken robot, but I need to stop relying on the kindness of strangers, and take my life back, literally." That would be, let's see... it was Tuesday, so Saturday was four days away. But they set up on Friday night, right? So three days.

Nervous again, Lee said, "You can stay with me until then. I have tons of room, and my creations will like the company." Then very quickly, maybe to change the subject, he said, "This is going to hurt. I suggest you shut yourself off until I'm done."

Oops. "I... don't know how to do that."

Quick, Penny, test the obvious! System shutdown!

...

Nope, didn't work.

Getting his confidence back, Lee leaned around to look at my back. "Oh. Well, the techniques used to make your body are beyond me, but not the design philosophy. Mad scientists tend to think alike. That's why I'm able to help you at all. You should have a shut-down switch... here!" I felt his fingers dip under the fabric of my lab coat, feeling around my stiff 'skin'. When they reached the joint between my shoulders and neck, something gave, then clicked.

I shrugged, because that was all I could do. No, wait, I couldn't shrug, either. Criminy, these shoulders! Lifting a hand and dropping it helplessly back in my lap had to do.

He did his own version of the pursed lip thing. "I could force a shutdown, but with your tech, it would be dangerous."

"I'll deal with the pain."

He hesitated for a second, then took me at my word. After a delay no longer than "Where is my doll repair kit? Droopsy, did—oh, here it is," he got to work.

Personally, I couldn't see much of what he did. It included sewing, and gluing, and something that made sparks. Oh, and the neural regenerator, which turned out to be a shiny gold paste he applied with a sponge on the end of a stick. And yes, it hurt. A lot. Gritting my teeth, I sat still and put up with it.

The last thing he did was fasten a bandage with wire underpinnings around my upper arm, to keep it in place. By then, I already knew the repairs worked. I could feel my fingers again! When Lee gave me enough room, I waggled them, made a fist, then bent my elbow. Perfect.

"The glue sets fast, but wear the brace until tomorrow morning, just in case," he said, wiping his hands on his jacket.

I flexed my arm some more. So nice. Both severed sleeves and my left arm's teleport bracelets lay on the table next to me. Could I fit them on over the bandage? I might be fit to travel already. "Maybe I shouldn't wait. I could get started tonight."

"When did you get turned into a robot?" Lee asked.

"This morning," I answered, not really paying attention.

At least, I wasn't until he took hold of my left hand in both of his, and gave me a worried stare, right in my eyes. He looked *so* much like Santa Claus! "Rest. Please. You think you're doing well because you're not used to a body that doesn't get tired. Take one of my spare bedrooms, please. When your emotions catch up to you, you'll want to have somewhere quiet to rest."

How could I argue with that beard? "Well... okay. I'll go find a room and lie down, I guess."

Finding a room proved so easy, it looped around and became hard again. When I left this workshop, none of the other doors were completely shut anymore. Some, mostly on this side on the second floor, had more workshops, for assembling electronics, or hooking together rods of metal into fully fledged limbs, or moulding plastic surfacing. Stuff like that. The first floor had actual regular house things, like a dining room and kitchen. I found at least six guest bedrooms, but most of the rooms were empty, although 'empty' might not be accurate. They didn't have any furniture, but they sure had robots. Little robots, big robots, bipedal robots, bug-shaped robots, and whole rooms of action figures and dolls whose eyes turned towards me when I peeked inside.

Finally, I picked a bedroom in a tower on the third floor. Its round shape, prevalent pink color, and windows looking out on the street gave the room a surreal air that felt more comfortable to me than the blandness of the rest of the house. Of course, it had more posters, this time for what had to have been the worst claymation holiday cartoons in history.

It also had bookshelves. Pink bookshelves, sure, but bookshelves. Actually, all the rooms that weren't for building or storing robots had bookshelves. West Lee clearly loved to read. But this one had the comic books.

In fact... yes! Pulling out the complete set of *Sentient Life*, I lay down on the pastel bed, and pointedly ignored half a dozen watching plush toys as I flipped through the pages.

I'd read these graphic novels several times, now. Would my attention span be better or worse without nerves and muscles to twitch and distract? How does a robot handle repetition and boredom? Those questions stopped being important as I got swept up in the story of a bioengineered dolphin, who loved his creators and felt proud of being able to explore the solar system for them.

Every word and picture touched my metal heart just as deeply as they had my original, flesh and blood version. When Delph's ship passed the orbit of Mars, passed the last outposts of humanity and entered the cold, emptiness of deep space, I felt his isolation as deeply as if I were there myself.

My parents would be tucking a monster wearing my body into bed right now. Until I retook my body, I had no parents. I had no home. Any home I could find would just be a fake, a bed to sleep in while I missed the place that I truly belonged, and the people who loved me.

Curling up into a ball under the covers, I thought about my parents, and wished this body could cry.

Without fidgeting muscles, it did take a long time to get bored. Eventually, I reached my limit. The worst pain had passed, and I couldn't lie in bed any longer and stare out the window at darkness and occasional passing cars.

So I got up, and walked around the house.

And walked.

And walked.

I'd underestimated the place on my first tour. The rooms not devoted to robots were hardly bare. Memorabilia filled bookshelves and mantles. Posters and photographs, statuettes and plastic toys, books ranging from massive hardbound picture albums to advertising pamphlets. If it had robots, West Lee had collected its merchandise. Movies, computer games, theme parks—he loved robots, no matter what the medium. Crafting supplies also filled closets and lay abandoned in bathrooms, bedrooms, and the middle of hallways. Not just obvious robot stuff. A bag of yarn and a three-quarters knitted fox puppet resided in the arms of a man-sized plush fox.

I had no idea what time it was. I didn't want to check. It also didn't matter. That was the good part of being stuck as a robot. I could keep walking until the sun came up. All night, all day, until Friday, if nothing better came to mind. That would keep the sadness at arm's length.

A hallway behind the main stairs connected the dining room and the music room on the far side of the house. No lights were on, and here in the heart of the building, no windows brought in light from the street. Only keen eyes let me see rough shapes in the shadow, and see the thing that stepped into the corridor ahead of me.

No way was this thing human. Bits stuck out the wrong way. Its outline rippled. Tiny white dots lit up near the top. Eyes.

The first floor lacked carpeting, and footsteps sounded behind me. Lots of footsteps, but light—the tap-tap-tapping of tiny feet. Looking over my shoulder, I saw robots ranging from ankle to waist high shambling in my direction, arms out.

The giant thing at the other end advanced. It showed no dedication to the floor, spending as much time advancing with arms propping it up between the walls as it did walking.

Run? Fight? If I ran, it would have to be over the little ones. The amorphous monster took up most of the room on its side of the corridor, though if I ducked past it, I'd have the advantage of surprise. There was no third way to go, or place to hide. They'd picked the longest stretch of doorless hallway in the house.

No. West Lee seemed like too nice a guy to do this to me. Hoping I was right, I stood still and waited.

The first of the little robots to reach me wrapped its arms around my calf, and gave me a hug. Within seconds, I was the center of a mob of hugging robots, some metal, some with china doll coverings, some like plastic dinosaurs or army men. Even a wooden marionette and a nutcracker.

The thing arrived. Up close, and with the light of dozens of tiny glowing eyes to help me see, I could finally make out more than a general shape. Admittedly, what I saw didn't help much : the biggest robot I'd seen so far, its spider's nest of limbs stuck out in odd places and directions. Only the head, at the end of a long neck, had a plastic covering, that same mask I'd seen earlier. Now, up close, I could see it wasn't at all human, but elongated like a reptile. A reptile with a huge, goofy grin. The rest of the body lay bare in a metal skeleton, which was why making out any shape had been so tough. Let's see... the reptilian face explained the wide, heavily-braced hips and thick tail; the things that looked like umbrella struts might be wings without membranes. Regardless, it had too many arms, too many legs.

It used most of them to hug me.

More minutes passed. A light went on, and a giant skeletal robot I recognized as a Gerty Goat with only the fuzzy head cover led West Lee into the hallway. Gerty pointed at me. Not much of me could be visible, sitting on the floor surrounded and covered by hugging robots, and with the big one huddled protectively over me.

In a rumpled nightshirt, West Lee regarded this sight with obvious befuddlement, until his hand lifted to his mouth. With a guilty gasp, he said, "Oh, I'm so sorry. You can't shut yourself off. I'm so used to pure robots, it didn't occur to me. Going without sleep really messes up a human in a robot body."

"It can't be fixed," I answered, resigned. It was a lot easier to be okay with my situation buried in hugs.

"No, I think I can, and this is important. Come upstairs."

He beckoned, but I didn't get a chance to stand. Not exactly. Hugging arms let go in a rippling wave, although many of the little bots patted me sympathetically before stepping back. The half-made Gerty took one of my hands, and the spider-dragon-thing grabbed my waist and under my arms, lifting me to my feet. The goat-bot let go, but the multi-armed, affectionate nightmare held onto me as West Lee led me upstairs, right back to the head assembly shop where we'd started.

"I didn't realize they were intelligent," I said as I half-walked, half was carried up the stairs.

"Not many are. Even the ones that can think aren't smart. Kind and sweet and loving, but not smart. I don't make AIs, only bodies. Some of these have computers other people made in them. Most of these are built around cloth hearts Raggedy made. They can't talk, but they can love. It's a good way to make robots."

The crowd in question followed us all the way up, peering in at the door as Lee led me back to the work table, and patted its surface. "Droopsy, if you could help support her? Penelope—uh, that is your name, right?—this may hurt. It's definitely going to feel strange."

I climbed onto the table, this time facing the wall. Droopsy, the giant spidery thing, held my arms, my head, and the different joints of my torso in place. She had a strong but gentle touch.

West Lee unbuttoned most of my shirt, and pulled it and the lab coat down around my shoulders. I felt him fiddling with the button on the back of my neck. A few twinges of pain didn't bother me, but something clicked softly, and I felt wobbly, and a touch nauseous. 'Why' became clear as Lee set the plates of my neck down on the table next to me.

Thank goodness for Droopsy. Her grip felt very reassuring indeed, which I needed since… I really didn't want to think about my neck's condition too closely. In a very real sense, my spine had just been taken out. So many yikes!

"Well, I can see what's wrong," said Lee behind me. "There's a blank patch on the muscle fabric. Your 'off' button doesn't connect to anything."

That triggered a memory. "Oh, yeah! I ran out of gold while making this body. I thought it was the self-destruct function that didn't get completed."

"It might be. This wouldn't be the first time that the power switch and the destruct switch used the same button. You really made this? How? This is the most advanced robotics I've ever seen up close."

I chuckled. Droopsy tilted my chin down to make it easier for West Lee to do something I could neither see, nor feel. I did hear a lot of clicking. "Not a clue. My power works in trances. The more impressive the invention, the less I remember."

Above a scraping noise, Lee said, "Oh, yeah, I understand. My power is pretty weak. Ninety-nine percent of the time, I have a natural feel for robotics, and that's it. Every once in awhile, though, I have a fit where I black out and make something incredible. I still have no idea how Epimetheus works. How can anyone make a robot that evolves?"

"Is he…?" I started to ask, not sure if I'd misunderstood the name of the big spidery thing.

I got a sigh in reply. "The last I saw him, he was walking off into the sea. I hope he's okay. For a while he went crazy and thought he was Evolution. When he accepted that he wasn't, he got super depressed."

"Oh."

And lo, for she that does not asketh receiveth! That is, West Lee patted the plastic snout hovering over my head. "And Droopsy Dragon here was the same way. I wanted to add a new animatronic to the Family Farm cast. My power took over while building the prototype, and this is what I got instead. She looks a mess, but she's highly intelligent. She can even talk, but she's too shy. It all comes out sounding like quotes from a Family Farm show. If it were your birthday, she wouldn't shut up."

The plastic dragon face lowered a few minutes, little white dot eyes in black lenses watching me hopefully. I tried to shake my head, which needless to say did not work. "Sorry, Droopsy. That was a couple of months ago."

She licked my forehead with a stiff rubber tongue.

Lee's nervous tone came back. "Anyway. I'm sorry for babbling."

"Oh, no, it's great! I've never met another mad scientist who has fits like mine. It makes me feel understood."

He did something that felt prickly around the base of my neck, then hot. With a hint of growl, he said, "You have, trust me. Most mad scientists don't like to talk about it. Everyone likes to pretend they know what they're doing."

I started to laugh, and then went "Ah! Ooh! Ah!" instead, because it felt really weird and uncomfortable as he fitted my neck plate back into its socket.

I knew when he finished that, because Droopsy let go. A quick nod and roll confirmed that everything worked.

Scooting around, I hung my legs over the edge of the table and asked, "All done?"

He laid some tools in a drawer, and shut it before I got a good look at them. "All done! Your off switch should work now. Press it, and it will put you in a modulated turned-off state, with regular but very brief awakenings. That should imitate REM close enough that you'll feel like you slept. I think that you can decide how long you want to sleep when you press the button, but even if I'm wrong, I built a failsafe into the switch. After eight hours of sleep, it will reactivate you."

I hopped off the table, and stopped because Lee went into a case of severe fidgets. He winced, and scratched the back of his own neck, and looked around until even Droopsy leaned over and watched him in concern.

Finally, he said, "There's nothing stopping you from pressing it again when you wake up, if that's what you want. That's not my decision. I'm pushing sixty, and I haven't figured me out, much less what's good for anyone else."

Aw. Actually, I felt a lot less depressed. And then I gave a little jump. "That reminds me! I'm surprised you didn't do the head turn trick."

"Oh, you mean like this?" he asked, waggling a finger from side to side. "If you think you're human, that's enough for me. Raggedy and Gothic would rather you be just a robot, anyway."

I reached around behind my neck, and felt the little square button. Looking over at the little robots crowding the door, I asked, "If I turn myself off, you'll tuck me in bed, right?"

They nodded, spilling into the room and holding their arms up eagerly.

That made me laugh. "This is great. I could certainly use a robot army to get my body back."

West Lee shuddered. On that kindly Santa Claus face, anger looked out of place, but now he was definitely angry. He gulped at words, fighting with his shyness. "I. Do not. Make robots. To fight."

Holding up a hand, I laid it on his shoulder, then reached over and gave one of Droopsy's stubby, clawed hands a squeeze. "I admire that. A lot."

He let out a sigh, not just smiling, but sagging in relief at not having to be mad.

Well. Only one thing left. "Okay, guys. Catch me."

Pushing the button on my neck, I turned myself off for eight hours.

CHAPTER FIVE

I did sleep a lot, not to ease the pain, but because it was such a wonderful, pleasant relief. The off switch produced a 'lying in bed and feeling lazy' sensation, and after a day like that, I needed it.

Besides, every time I woke up, Droopsy would be there, clinging to the ceiling and watching me sleep. The presence of a giant, metal, spider-dinosaur skeleton hanging above me produced the same feelings of comfort and safety that would normally require a whole pack of affectionate German shepherds.

When sundown on Friday arrived, I tried to see myself out. As I approached the front door, an arm that looked an awful lot like one of Droopsy's unfolded from above the lintel, turned the knob, and opened it for me. So. One final mystery solved.

Then, reveling in my finally being able to wear my bracers right, I teleported across the street!

It stung. Ow. Pain lanced through the cracks in my arm, and my chest. They weren't worse than 'stinging', but each teleport carried the burden of however far I went in one step. My damaged body couldn't take that much shock.

I cut it down, and teleported half a dozen steps along the sidewalk, skipping ahead of a couple of people. No pain.

Sweet.

And now, to get moving. Chinatown was across the hills to the southeast, but a decent walking pace was about four miles per hour, and I could make six times that easily, without getting tired. Granted, it was a surreal journey, with the world constantly skipping like a strobe lit room, but it didn't take me long at all to pass the last street onto the hills themselves. Unlike a car, I could go cross-country. Unlike a human, 'uphill' didn't matter. Distance was distance, to my bracers.

Round about full dark, and whistling with the immense satisfaction of being a queen of mad science, I approached Chinatown from the back end. Unlike most parts of town, it had fences between and around buildings, shutting off all but the main entrance. I spotted a gap, and blinked through. Of all my inventions, these bracers were second only to my wonderful Machine. It was great to have them back. I couldn't use them when I was pretending to be good.

Of course, I was good. It was the other Penny that was evil.

No. I'm REAL. The other is a FAKE.

"Bad Penny!" shouted a guy sitting on a nearby rooftop. He waved his banana, and went back to eating it. It matched his suspiciously banana-like floppy yellow costume.

Mom had been right about one thing. These were my people.

This early on Friday, the storm of villains descending on Chinatown amounted to a mere drizzle. I strutted my way through them, keeping an eye out for familiar faces. I saw a few, but none I actually felt like I knew.

One face I specifically did not see belonged to Bull, thank goodness.

Ah, but every face setting up at the mad scientists' tables I knew. I'd be right over, but first, I was passing the dim sum buffet table thoughtfully spread out near the mall entrance. Leaning over a tray of soup with boiled eggs in it, I sniffed as hard as I could.

Oh, yeah. I could smell that, the sharp vegetable smell of the soup, and the rich sulfur eggity. Weak, though. I so needed to get some robot food from Pong.

Underneath the table, a squeaky voice said, "Hello?"

Leaning down, I lifted the tablecloth and peered underneath. Half a dozen mason jars filled the lower shelf. Five contained black goop. The sixth... a wrinkly pink and white mass, squished up against the glass.

Also some peach color, like really pale skin. Very much like skin, what with the hazel eye blinking up at me hopefully.

"Could you, uh... help me out, uh... here?" the girl's voice asked, audible thanks to the air holes punched in the lid of the jar.

Hey, I might be back to villainy, but I wasn't evil. "Sure. Watch my back." Someone had to do this to her, right?

I picked up the jar. I tried to pick up the jar. Criminy, it weighed at least as much as an adult person. Maybe I could lift it, but not at this awkward angle. So instead, I unscrewed the jar lid.

The contents of the jar squeaked, "Thanks. Sorry to run, but you know how it is."

I did know how it is. Enough that I experienced only mild surprise as hands and feet, squishy and tentacular and barely recognizable, wriggled out of the mass in the jar. Rocking, it turned the jar over, and scampered away into the night.

Good deed complete. Time to return to villainy!

In fact, time to make an entrance. Taking a step to activate the bracers, I teleported across the hall in front of the mad science vending tables.

Yeah, it was too far and my arm hurt, but so worth it when everybody stopped chatting and sat up with a jerk.

Red Eye pumped her fist. "Yes! I told you she'd show up this weekend."

"It's going to be great having a permanent Bad Penny," said the big guy with the beard. Mechanical Aesthetic?

I held up a warning finger. "Only until I get my body back."

"Of course," said the silver-haired Expert, who stood between the tables and never seemed to have one of his own.

A guy in spandex and wire harnessing leaned over his table of wire harnesses and little computer chips. "Is it true the original you has your super power?"

Giving him a hard look, I said, "I am the original. The thing that stole my body stole my super power in the process, yes."

Supervillains were terrible at hiding their smirks, and I smoldered with irritation at the obvious lack of anyone believing me here. Not that I'd expected them to, but criminy!

Mechanical Aesthetic looked at his comrades, and frowned. "Point of order. She is technically no longer one of us. Should Bad Penny be allowed to wear mad scientist goggles?"

Red Eye scowled. "We don't take them away from a mad scientist who loses their powers."

The woman behind her, with a table piled high with helmets, said, "She never actually had powers. Only the biological Penny does, and she's gone straight."

A middle-aged guy with a table labeled 'Custom Booby Traps' flashed her a sardonic grin. "She'll be back when she turns eighteen. Trust me."

The Expert stepped forward, and gave me a brief, stiff bow. "Forgive your colleagues for upsetting you, Bad Penny. You know how obsessed we get with details. Regardless of our banter, you remain our colleague and welcome in our fold."

"You just want to irritate Brian—" Helmet Inventress started, only to have Red Eye lean back and cuff her over the head.

The Expert rubbed the bridge of his nose, eyes tightly shut with exasperation.

Pretending my feelings weren't actually hurt, I said, "I don't have a pair at the moment, anyway."

"We'll bring you a spare," promised Mechanical Aesthetic, despite being the one to bring this up in the first place. He even flashed me a sincere-looking grin.

For better or for worse, these were, indeed, my people.

Before they could go off on any more tangents, I asked, "Has anyone seen Lab Rat?"

"He'll be in. He always is. What's up?" said Red Eye, still glaring at the woman behind her.

"I need a new lair."

Booby Trapulator (Yes, I totally made that name up), nodded. "Good person to ask."

Expert dipped his head. "Check back later."

I sighed, and turned away. "Yeah, I do have other errands while I'm here."

Lowering his voice, the Expert told my back, "Do not go see Spider."

The last thing I heard, as I drifted into the crowd, was Red Eye's scolding voice. "What is wrong with you guys? Yes, she's a great villain, but she's still thirteen!"

Le sigh.

After that erratic reception, loneliness crept up on me fast. Chinatown just wasn't as fun without Claire and Ray. Even if they believed me, they were at camp.

Maybe that's what this was. Supervillain camp. A month of chaos, sleeping in a different bed, and then going home is all the sweeter.

What's the first rule of not dying of homesickness at summer camp? Make friends your own age. That meshed perfectly with my plans, anyway.

So. Who would be around?

I struck immediate gold. Fast movement caught my eye, a teenage boy running faster than any normal human could, weaving around adults on the way to the buffet table.

I teleported in front of him. Step. Blink. Whack! He ran right into me! As I tumbled through the air, shoulder aching in a downright worrisome way, I reflected on my own foolishness. Will had only super speed, not super reflexes!

Fortunately, he did have that speed, and caught me on my way down. Gratefulness quickly turned to awkwardness at being held in the arms of a boy not my boyfriend, and I quickly squirmed back to my feet.

"Woah, sorry, Penny! Why are you so—oh, wait, sorry again. You're Robot Penny, not Meatbag Penny!"

My teeth clenched, but I would explain it to him later. Right now, he was an invaluable source of information. "Have you seen Cassie or Mirabelle around?"

Looking nervous now, he pointed to the far end of the building. "Not Cassie. I tried to ask Mirabelle if she wanted to come to my place and play video games, but her brother's around. I mean, she doesn't come here without him, but he's sticking close to her tonight."

Heading in the indicated direction, I waved behind me. "I'm not trying to get his sister alone for hanky-panky, so I should be fine."

No response followed me into the darkness. Okay, into the well-lit main hall occupied by chatting supervillains. But no response followed me into the metaphorical darkness, so Penelope Akk scored herself a point for banter, and payback for the Robot Penny mistake.

On the other end of the building, in the last darkened, emptied store, a girl sat in a chair reading a book. I identified Mirabelle by her sheer lack of visibility. She wore an ankle-length dress, gloves, and a hat with a brim so wide it completely hid her face when she looked down. The only person more covered up in this building was the odd creature named Schleimy, wearing its multiple layers of clothes and selling dubious magical items a doorway down.

At the sound of approaching footsteps, Mirabelle looked up. She'd been a classmate for months, and I still had trouble making out the details of her face. Made of pure glass, her transparency obscured the details. Other people with better eyesight assured me she was stunningly pretty, and looked human except for the cat ears and tail.

She also glowed faintly, which explained how she could read a book in a dark room.

Even I could make out her gentle smile, which went with her soft, happy voice. "Penelope? What a nice surprise."

"Thanks," I said, only to have awkward guilt hit me. I'd only come to her for help, not out of friendship. Some of things Remmy and Heart of Gold said to me hit home, there.

But, I did need her help. Critically. So I tugged one of my braids and went on. "Could I get you to do some healing for me?"

She was *so nice*, maybe because she lived a life intimately familiar with pain and fragility. She reacted to the request by pulling off her gloves and saying, "If it's within my power, always. I heard a story that you were hurt fighting yourself, but I'd hoped it was only a story."

The one thing I absolutely refused to do was drag Mirabelle into my battles. Yes, I needed allies desperately, but even a little adventure would literally, physically break her. That she could put herself back together provided cold comfort. Barbara, whose powers ate away her sanity, was also off the list. Sad, because of all people, she might be able to tell that I was the real Penelope Akk.

So, instead I undid the temporary clasps West Lee had used to attach my sleeves to my shirt and lab coat. The armored fabric slid down, giving Mirabelle a good look at my scarred robotic arm.

She gasped, hands over her mouth as if she didn't get hurt this badly on an almost daily basis.

...okay, wow, Penny. Seriously guilting yourself here, huh? Let the girl be kind!

Ahem. Reaching out for me, she said, "That's even worse than I heard. Let me look closer, please."

I sat down next to her chair, and laid my arm over her lap. Glass hands slid over my ceramic (or maybe plastic?) skin. That thought felt as strange as the softness of her see-through fingers. We were both inorganic right now. Maybe, when all this was over, I should spend more time with Mirabelle.

For now, her glowing hands spread warmth through me, deep into bones and muscles I only felt like I had. She smiled again, now reassuring. "You're in luck. Whoever set this did it well, and my power works best with breaks."

I fought down a whimper, which proved harder than expected because I couldn't bite my lip. Like my shrugless shoulders, my jaw didn't move as well as it ought.

My grumpiness over that melted away. Mirabelle's healing touch felt so good, like the best massage, and it reached past my arm and into the cracks in my chest. Prickly pleasure inside my arm told me the weird fabric that lined the shell was even sewing back together.

It took me completely by surprise when a man snarled, "What do you think you're doing?"

Mirabelle answered before I could recover from the total relaxation. "She's hurt, Entropy."

At this point, I looked up, to see the expected black-furred cat man in a well-tailored suit baring his pointed teeth. "That robot is neck deep in a war with the Akk family. I will not let you get involved."

I opened my mouth, but Mirabelle pressed her fingers to it. She met

Entropy's yellow-eyed gaze solidly, a sharp contrast from her usually shy, down-turned face. "This is my friend, and my decision."

His scowl just got wider and more animal, but Mirabelle kept her hand over my mouth, and Entropy did not actually do anything. She used the time to pull my sleeves back into place, and they raveled perfectly into the costume as if the bomb had never gone off.

As awkward as this was, one final issue weighed on me, even harder because of Mirabelle's kindness. Digging into my pouches, I pulled out a ten pound lump of gold, and dropped it into the crystal cat girl's lap. "Can you heal this?"

"Get. Out. Of. Here," snarled Entropy.

Mirabelle glared at him as if he'd, well, just threatened a friend. "Shush," she said, and then turned her attention to the Heart of Gold. Picking it up, she turned the small, heavy device over and over in her hands. They glowed brighter, and brighter still. Half a dozen clinks sounded, with no particular rhythm, and two of them accompanied visible dents popping back into place.

Still, when she handed it back to me, it remained visibly battered. "I'm sorry, Penelope. My power isn't perfect. It handles fractures well, but deformations are more complicated. Whoever's in there, she's alive and sleeping, but this is the best I can do."

One more thing to blame on the parasite. One more reason to wage this war.

Maybe Mirabelle could see my anger in my face. She clasped my cheeks in her hands, leaned down, and kissed my forehead. The outer of her body did feel as warm and pliable as skin, even if the texture was a little too slick. Pulling me up, she said, "Go, please. I need to be left alone with my brother, while we talk about how I get to have friends."

Entropy's fists tightened until his rings squeaked against each other. I got out, fast, ducking outside into the warm, summer nighttime air.

Only to get ambushed, grabbed from behind and yanked off my feet with Cassie's arms around my chest, and her squeal against the back of my head. "Pennyyyyy! Oh wow, you're so light! I love this robot body."

"Thanks, but I'd rather be human," I wheezed.

She swung me from side to side, dropped me on my feet, and twisted me around to face her with her hands on my shoulders. Her smile lit her face, and her eyes literally glowed with electricity. "Oh, I heard. Flesh-and-blood. You called me Tuesday evening and said you went completely insane and think you're the original and now you're determined to steal her body."

Well, criminy. "Ah." Seriously, what could I say to that?

Cassie didn't need me to say anything. I'd forgotten how she could gush and fangirl over me. She must have been really trying to keep it down until now! "I don't know if I believe her. About the insane part. Obviously you want her body. Who wouldn't? But I watched the robot you when we were in Chinatown, and I can't believe she would go that kind of crazy."

Hope returned so fast my heart hurt. "You believe I'm the real Penny?"

Her hair crackled, turning bluer by the second. She pulled me into a tight hug, cheek to cheek. "I don't know. As your friend, the right thing to do is to figure out which of you is real, and stand with her to stop the other. I'm just so happy to have two of you, I can't think straight."

No way I'd imagined this conversation covered the real thing. I actually felt guilty saying, "I need allies, Cassie, and I can't rely on adults."

She pulled back, shaking her head rapidly. "Oh, no way. Supervillains and heroes all have their own agendas. I have so many stories to tell you! Claire the Corrupt Cutie says your parents kept you super sheltered."

Technically, I should be mad, but gossiping about me and believing everyone was naive compared to her were the two most Claire Lutra things imaginable. If she'd said it, she meant it as praise.

Don't let Cassie's babble distract you, Penny! I pushed on. "If there's anything I can do to convince you, let me know."

"I will, I promise. Just right now let me enjoy it. Oh! Oh oh oh! You haven't seen!" In jeans and a T-shirt, Cassie didn't have many pocket options, but she still searched them in a desperate scramble until she pulled out a large, but otherwise average-looking bolt. Quivering with emotion, she said, "I have a second power."

With the bolt in one palm, she held her other hand above it. Slowly, wobbling all the while, the bolt floated up between them.

That made me straighten up and gawk. "Woah. Why do you get two powers?"

She rolled her eyes and made a *pfft* noise. "It's not like it's rare. Her Sullen Unstoppability Claudia has, like, fifteen powers. But I bet..." Reaching out, she held the hand not holding a bolt in front of my face, then moved it slowly down.

I responded by saying, "Aak! Eek! Stop that!" and dancing back out of range. What a sensation. Where her hand passed, it felt like being tickled from the inside!

My dismay only made Cassie pump her fist in glee. "Yes! So cool!"

At which point Cassie's sister Ruth stepped out of the mall, one fist full of beef jerky. A whole sheaf of beef jerky. Five pounds, easy. I had never seen so much in one place in my life. "What are you crowing— oh, no, you are not."

Grinning fit to burst, Cassie slung an arm around my shoulders, crowing, "Look who I found!"

Ruth did not grin. In her work clothes of ripped black leather, greased purple hair, and dark makeup, she glared like the end of the world. Grabbing Cassie with one hand, she hauled her little sister into the air and onto her shoulder. "I know who it is, and you're not supposed to be talking to her."

Cassie started to kick, but with Ruth's silver-tattooed arm around her waist, my blue-haired electric fangirl wasn't going anywhere. "What? No! She's my friend!"

Not bothering to talk to me, Ruth turned and walked down the street. "She's a deluded copy of your friend. I am not letting you get involved in their war. It is not going to happen."

Cassie kicked harder, flailing ineffectually in her sister's super-strong grip. "Ruth, come on! Don't you see what this means to me? She's unattached! This Penny could be mine!"

"If you shock me, so help me, I will use my claws. This is non-negotiable, Cassie."

"Come oooooooon!"

And that was the last I heard. Standing there, I didn't know what to think. I'd always liked Ruth and Rachel. Yes, they had a rough side, but they'd been so nice to me, until now. As for Cassie, would she be back? Would she be on my side? Could I deal with the guilt of pitting her against her own sister?

Finding allies was going to be trickier than I thought, and I'd thought it would be tricky. Criminy.

Also, did Cassie just say that she had a romantic interest in robot me?

Penelope, do yourself a favor. File that one in the 'Questions I don't want answered' category.

Well. If I stood here, I would get discouraged, fast. What next? Lucyfar would certainly believe me, if I found her, but was down around my last choice for exactly the reason Cassie named. Nobody had more ulterior motives than the unpredictable Princess of Lies.

However! Through the milling supervillains, I saw a skinny, hunched figure creeping up on the mad scientist tables.

Glorying in my ability to do it, I teleported right up in front of them again. "Lab Rat!"

He screeched, tossing a large cardboard box in the air. The mad scientists responded in a flurry of motion. Red Eye pulled out a gun that fired a red beam, which formed a red globe of light around the box. Mechanical Aesthetic's arm shot out, extending ten feet of copper stovepipe to catch the box in his hand. The guy with the wire structures threw one at the box, and the wires wrapped around it and glittered. An extra ripple in the air hinted someone else had activated still another device, but I couldn't tell who.

As awesome as my teleport bracers were, I so needed more toys.

The red glow and air ripple disappeared. Mechanical Aesthetic lowered the box into Lab Rat's waiting arms.

Said Lab Rat did not hold a grudge. He beamed at me with delight, stroking his box and babbling, "Bad Penny! So tasty to meet. Robot, yes? Will be Bad Penny forever, they say, and looking for me personally? Tasty, tasty honor."

It wasn't worth correcting him about my identity. Bracing my hands on Red Eye's table, I gave him my 'serious supervillain' expression. "I need a new lair, and you're the man who knows them all."

Dropping his box on an empty table, he bobbed his head. "It's true. So true. Vermin tell me many things. So many tasty things. Hidden places, forgotten places. But what will you pay?"

"I have money. Do evil vendors take credit cards?"

Red Eye shook her head, smirking. "He doesn't need money."

"Everybody needs money," argued the woman with the display of helmets.

The Expert flapped a hand. "Lab Rat makes quite a lot, and spends very little, but it's really up to him."

Lab Rat rubbed his leather-gloved hands together. His whole skinny body was sheathed in tight brown leather, with randomly spaced pockets and buckles. "Always thought Bad Penny's technology tasty."

Red Eye nodded emphatically. "Oh, yeah."

The helmet woman behind her gave Red Eye's head a poke. "You're no slouch."

"Not in her class. Have you seen these photos?" Pulling out her phone, she tapped a few buttons. I had a glimpse of her background screen, a human-shaped prism shining rainbows everywhere. Then it was replaced by a photograph of... me. Me, sitting on a train, with my broken arm and my gaping open shoulder. The ripped fabric lining the inside of my shell, and its golden circuitry, showed clearly.

The Expert nodded in his detached, professorial way. "Impressive, certainly."

The Dark Hatteress craned forward over her table to look. "Wow. Where are the mechanisms? There's no skeleton, no motors, no nothing."

Mechanical Aesthetic pulled out his own phone, staring at it with a hungry smile. Others started getting out their phones as well.

My mouth was hanging open, so I might as well say something. "You all have the pictures those kids took?!"

Red Eye patted the surface of her table close to me. "Relax, Bad Penny. That kid tried to post them online. Spider pays someone to keep watch for that. You can bet they scrubbed the pictures not just from the Internet, but from the guy's hard drive. Nobody outside the community gets to keep sensitive material like this."

I tilted my face down, and gave her an unimpressed stare over my— woah. I was so used to wearing glasses, I didn't realize they were gone until now. But anyway, back to sarcasm! "Just all of you."

"Hey, our interest is professional!"

I sighed heavily, and rubbed my face. Supervillains! "Well, I'm not selling a finger, and I'm short on other tech right now."

Lab Rat shook his head, violently, almost like an animal. "They are so silly. Ignore them. Yes, want Bad Penny's technology, but always willing to give tasty deal to friend. Recently abandoned lair exists, would like something from inside it, but cannot go. Only Bad Penny can. Will provide location, Bad Penny bring back prize, can have base."

Hefting an eyebrow, I gave him the Fish Eye. "And only I can do this why...?"

Lab Rat grinned hugely. He did have buck teeth, but not actually rat-sized. He also went back to twisting his gloved hands together. "Belonged to defunct heroine Miss A. Does not want it anymore, but big trouble if anyone try to take, yes? Ah, but Bad Penny is different."

"Deal. I'll go tonight," I said, before he could change his mind.

Miss A's real name was Marcia Bradley, and I very much wanted to meet Marcia. Nobody else had that perfect blend of craziness and friendship that made her likely to help me against the parasite. The base would be pure bonus.

CHAPTER SIX

T he beach. The Pacific Ocean north of Santa Monica. The long, long, how-long-can-a-road-get Pacific Highway stretching north along it, with a few little side roads running down the slope to the sand and water. Marcia's father had picked a lair for her with an incredible view.

Or at least, he would have if Lab Rat hadn't said the lair was underground.

Also, I wasn't supposed to know that Marcia's dad was the Original, supposedly a quite skilled hero until she sucker-punched him so hard that six months recuperation and the advanced healing available to heroes still might not have him back on his feet.

But I did know that, even if I had to pretend I didn't. Which meant Marcia's dad owned the beachfront mansion atop Miss A's lair.

Say that with me, now. 'Beachfront mansion.' Even Pong's home on the hills would be orders of magnitude less expensive than beachfront property near Los Angeles. Just how rich was her family anyway?!

From my perch on a street lamp a block up, the yard looked messy, and mostly dead. A table and chairs lay upended on the lawn. One window had a hole patched up with cardboard. These are not things I normally associated with houses that cost more than a hundred million dollars.

But hey, if the place was abandoned, better for me! Jumping down from the top of the lamp, I landed in a crouch, just to enjoy how strong and light my new body was. Might as well take the good with the bad!

Then I teleported to the lair entrance Lab Rat described.

In a chained-off parking lot, behind a closed management shack, stood a small garage.

"This is the part where Ray would say something serious about the practicality of a lair entrance two blocks away, and Claire would wonder if we can steal something with the Original's autograph on it." Closing my eyes and rolling my head back, I groaned at the dark late-night sky. "I have so got to get new sidekicks. At least until I can get my old sidekicks back. I hope that house isn't as abandoned as it looks."

Turning back, I stared out at the black ocean water, listened to the faint roar of the surf, and felt the sea breeze. "No, Ray would hold my hand and lean against me and say nothing. Penny, triple underline that need for sidekicks. And get your life back before a freaky parasite steals your boyfriend."

The garage door lifted easily. It wasn't locked, and the inside could be described as 'shabby, gray, and empty.' One thing stood out. Regular garages generally didn't have a ramp down underground blocked by a steel gate.

I owned the ultimate lock pick in the form of the Machine, but this time my baby would not be necessary. That weird little Lab Rat knew how to prepare, and I pointed the electronic car key he'd given me and pushed the 'garage door' button.

Sure enough, the gate lifted, and with a nice, smooth 'shoop'. Very classy and superhero professional.

I snuck down the spiral ramp, crouched low and hands out, in case anyone saw me and needed to know how stealthy I am. I couldn't see any cameras, or detect them with super special robot senses. Wouldn't super special robot senses be great? Would Good Penny have told me about them?

Super special robot senses, activate!

Yeah, nothing.

Maybe if I said it out loud? "Super special robot senses, activate! ...I so need new sidekicks."

The bottom of the ramp opened into another little garage, with sleek walls and floor, and much less dust. Fortunately, it had plenty of debris to replace the dust. Picking up a pink piece of curved plastic, I made a professional scientific judgment. "Marcia really hated that motorbike."

I'd never seen her driving one, but the shiny chrome bits lying around would be a small motor, and a bicycle's worth of struts, with lots of pink plastic coverings, all of it beaten and smashed into fragments. Ooh, and rainbow-colored tassles for the handlebars! Yes, post-psychotic-break-Marcia would destroy those just on principle.

Okay, well, all that was fun. Time for business. A very long passage stretched away toward what my keen sense of direction told me had to be the beach house. Light shone through a gate at the other end.

What would be the purpose of that featureless tunnel? "Let's see. Traps, detectors, alarms, more traps... skip it." I focused on the other side of the gate, and took a step.

Blink! From harshly-lit garage, to hideous pink antechamber! My body gave a little jolt from the effort, but it hadn't been too far. The gate now behind me meant nothing, because it had all those nice spaces between the bars. I had yet to figure out exactly what kind of gaps I could and couldn't teleport through, but a portcullis more air than steel? No problem.

Something had to be said. "My god. It's full of pink."

Marcia had not decorated this lair. Even pre-psycho-Marcia had not decorated this base. A father who thought he was doting but actually wanted a doll instead of a daughter decorated this base.

Oh, it had the proper base stuff. Trophy shelves, weapon racks, maps, bookshelves, a table with built-in microscope and other no doubt nifty detective gizmos. An entire wall of monitors and computers, which certainly made me grin to look at. Those would definitely be handy! Two closets by the door, a bathroom considerably bigger and more luxurious than the one in my home—jacuzzi, no less!—and a bedroom. No question, this place was practical.

It was also pink. Different shades of pink, from pale rose paint on the walls to bright bubblegum computers. Seriously, the covers on the computers were so pink they seared the eyes. Carpets, bed, everything actually part of the room, was pink. The bedroom back at West Lee's place had been themed. This was just child abuse.

Speaking of abuse, someone had sure abused this place. The bookshelves and closets sat empty, although a few torn pages littered the floor, and a pink ballerina-style Miss A sidekick costume hung next to the shelves, perforated by darts, a knife, and an axe, all of them sunk at least an inch into the wall. Trophies gaily bedecked every surface, bent or crumpled or ripped in half or shockingly intact, just out of place. Marcia seriously had a lot of trophies. Spelling bee trophies, dance trophies, swimming trophies, gymnastics trophies, archery trophies, even a few oddities that must come from supervillain loot, like cracked goggles and a shattered crystal ball. A sword hung in its own case on one wall, although the glass fronting was smashed. Well, sort of a sword. It looked to be made of the same white stuff as my shell, honed to an edge on the sides of the blade, and separated into two pieces—left and right halves of the blade itself, and a pommel, all with a round gap in the middle where some missing item would lock them together.

I would have to ask Marcia about it sometime, hopefully while we planned my taking back my body together.

Meanwhile, I had other weapons to find. This place ought to be teeming with grapples, smoke bombs, steel batons, and other Miss A equipment. I didn't see any. Not that I wanted them, but Lab Rat had asked me to find something... ah ha!

A cardboard box lurked in the shadows beneath Marcia's bed. (The sheets had a big capital A on them, in darker pink. Classy.) Pulling out that box, I opened it to find...

...my target. One box of junk mad science. Rocket shoe inserts, collapsible tool kits, guns powered by air canisters, and odder things like a blender and a miniature fishing rod. It all had a clunky, low-tech look, but no doubt worked wonders far beyond its meager appearance.

Behind me, something went *shoop*.

Turning around, I saw a section of wall had slid out of the way to reveal a staircase up into the mansion above it, and down those stairs trotted the girl I'd hoped to see. Marcia!

Our eyes met, and Marcia's face lit up with unholy glee, the only kind she felt these days. "Yes! I knew it would be you!" With that squeal of glee, she ran down the remaining steps and threw herself onto me for a hug.

"Glak," I replied solemnly.

She couldn't squeeze my breath out, but she did pick me up by her arms around my chest, and spun me around in a circle. "Oh, wow, you weigh practically nothing! I never dreamed you would break into my base, but when the alarm went off, who else could it be? I'm so happy you picked me. What does it feel like to have your body stolen by an evil robot?"

My heart leaped, and I swear I could feel it rattling against the wire cage that held it in place. "You believe me?" Could it really be this easy?

She returned me to my feet, standing back and flashing a huge, white-toothed grin. "Of course I believe you. Everyone tells me I'm crazy, but assuming everyone is wrong about everything has worked for me so far."

I drank in the glow of her friendship. Mmm, to be loved. Marcia looked so honestly, unreservedly happy to see me. Despite the mess outside, she must live in the beach house above. She'd clearly just gotten out of bed, with her short black hair an uneven mess, and dressed in a knee-length nightgown that might have been a big man's shirt a very long time ago. Now repeated dye jobs and the peeling of whatever logo had graced the front left the whole thing a patchwork of pink, gray, and worn white spots.

Confidentially, I felt considerable relief seeing that gown. Having seen some of the stuff her father dressed her in, I'd put even odds she slept in lacy lingerie and very little of it. Apparently the inappropriate dress-up-doll stuff was strictly for public, downgrading my impression of Marcia's childhood from 'skin-crawling nightmare' to 'miserably oppressive.'

Running my fingers back through my bangs and down one braid, I said, "I'm not going to argue with success. I need everyone I can get on my side."

"Ee-yee-yee-yee-yee!" she squealed, dancing around me in a circle, arms waving and thrusting and hopping around. She lolled her head grotesquely back and to one side to smile at me, which didn't disturb her dance at all. "This could not be more perfect. I'm a new me, and you're a new you. Finally, we can start over."

Her glee abruptly vanishing, she whirled on the spot. Standing at rigid attention, she clasped her hands together against her chest, eyes closed, frowning.

The frown deepened. Her mouth pulled tight. I took a couple of steps back, then a couple more as the first black sparks jumped off of Marcia's body.

Marcia's eyes opened, and her face contorted, teeth clenched in psychotic rage. She lunged at me, fist-first straight for my face.

She struck fast. She struck really fast. But I knew that already, which was why I'd put some space between us. One backwards step of my own, and I blinked across the room, leaving her to slam her fist into the wall.

Screeching in frustration, Marcia yanked her hand free, leaving knuckle prints through the pink plaster and into the rock beyond. Spinning, she threw herself at me again. Now I was across the central chamber, and it was most of the size of the house above. I had nearly two seconds to teleport past her to the other side of the room.

She crashed into the garishly colored computers, ripping them open and shattering one of the monitors. Criminy! I wanted those!

My relief turning to weary exasperation, I said, "Starting over, huh? With our first battle?"

"Yes! It's going to be awesome!" she shouted, charging me again.

I blinked to the far side of the room again, watching her. She smashed into the bookshelves, fell over, picked herself back up, and threw herself at me again.

And again.

And again.

Each time I teleported away, trying to do so early so that she wouldn't break too much when she hit whatever I'd been standing in front of. I also tried to keep to the clearer stretches of wall, in case Marcia had some kind of plan going.

Not that she would. I'd seen a whole semester of Marcia sparring.

I knew her strengths and weaknesses. Primary strengths: literal, I-did-not-want-to-get-within-arm's-reach strength, and an ability to heal anything that didn't instantly vaporize her. Primary weaknesses... well, number one, she fought in a screaming rage, which made for very little strategy.

Literally screaming. "Stop! Dodging! Fight me, you stuck-up! Irritating! Nerd!"

That last punch hit her computers again, although I didn't think that one could get any more broken. She did take out three more monitors.

I leaned against the wall by the trophy shelves, one foot raised and ready to teleport even as I let out a frustrated sigh. "I wanted those, but if we're enemies, I guess it's moot."

Staggering out of the smoking, spark-spitting mess, her nightshirt now covered in dust and soot, Marcia laughed, "Oh, please. Enemies? Who said we're enemies? I like you more than anyone else in the world, except maybe Sue. That's why I want to pound your face in!"

I let out another sigh, deeper this time. The problem with the crazy person believing me was that, of course, she's crazy.

Marcia wobbled half a dozen steps, eyes unfocused and dazed. If she got farther than the middle of the room, I would teleport over by the stairs.

Instead, she drew herself up straight, and repeated the hands together thing. Both the anger and glee faded away, leaving her face calm, serious, and intent.

This little trick would lead to a black lightning field throwing zaps at me. Rather than let her complete it, I picked up the nearest trophy and threw it at her head.

Direct hit! There was no sense in pulling punches with Marcia, so I'd thrown with all the strength my robot body had. She went down, with what looked like a dent in her skull.

Of course, being Marcia, she growled in fury, crawled back up to her hands and knees, and her head popped back into shape. Then she turned to me.

And I teleported away, before she could even charge. She looked around in a hurry, spotted me, and I blink out of her sight again. Three more teleports had her spinning in place, until she shouted, "Would you stop that!?"

I did, leaning against a wall again, foot raised, ready to disappear if she attacked.

She saw that, and paused, frowning not in fury, but in thought. Which meant Marcia's second major weakness kicked in, and she collapsed.

I didn't dare catch her, so thank goodness she managed to shield her head with her arms when she hit the floor. Poor Marcia. Oh, yes, I very much knew her weakness. She ran on anger and concentration. Make her stop and think, and her healing power deserted her, presenting a very painful bill instead. So, I'd run her around in circles until she had no choice but to try and figure out a new plan.

Violently shaking, Marcia pushed herself up onto her elbows again. I winced. She let out a low growl, shoulders tensing, trying to summon her rage back. Instead, she made a *blurp* noise, and clasped her mouth shut with one hand. Bug-eyed, she crawled clumsily towards the bathroom.

Criminy. Okay, time to abandon safety and be a friend, Penny. Hooking my arms under her shoulders, I dragged her to the toilet, and stepped outside while the horrible noises happened.

Eventually, the sounds coming from inside switched to running water and the buzz of an electric toothbrush. Shortly after that stopped, Marcia emerged, shaking, rubbing her face on a towel. A towel with a number of new stains, most of them red.

"Why do you do this to yourself?" I asked, grimacing. She still walked like someone whose legs might give out at any moment. It was hard to look at.

Her grin, on the other hand, could turn night into day. "For someone so smart, you *so* do not get it, Penelope Akk. Losing to you at the Science Fair is one of the worst moments of my old life. Now it's gone, and our first fight is me running around crashing into things and breaking them, like a demolition derby and a game of tag rolled together. I mean, I lost both times, totally, but this time I lost to a friend, and I did it as me, because I wanted to."

My mouth opened. My mouth closed. My mouth opened again. "Okay, that was unexpectedly deep."

She laughed, although her voice wobbled with exhaustion. Everything about her wobbled, even leaning against the door frame. "I was never shallow, Penny. People assumed the pretty blonde cheerleader didn't have thoughts of her own. Now they assume the crazy girl doesn't. This time, not only can I think, I get to act on those thoughts."

I nodded, leaning against the other side. "Makes sense. So. As totally serious super-powered people. I need new teammates to get my body back from an evil parasite that stole my body, and a base to operate out of. Are you in?"

Lifting a trembling fist, she touched it to my shoulder in a mock punch. "The base is yours. I always hated it. I'll go make a mess of one of Dad's other houses."

Reaching up, I took her hand in both of mine before she could pull it away. "Okay, but the teammate part is what I really need. I want you, Marcia. We could make beautiful banter together."

She lowered her face, and coyly fluttered her eyelashes. "Oh, stop. I bet you say that to all the super-powered lunatics."

Straightening up, I pulled her hand to my chest. "Only you, Marcia Bradley. Only you, because everybody else is too busy standing back like mature, reasonable people who understand that maybe I'm right, or maybe my evil parasite clone is."

Eyes smoldering, Marcia whispered, "Oh, Penny. I've always wanted to be someone's desperate last resort."

"Say you'll be mine, Marcia. Let me selfishly exploit you as a battering ram and distraction, because my regular teammates are out of town."

She shook her head ecstatically, hair flying. "Oh, yes, yes! I will be your disposable minion! Just as soon as we're caught up. I think we have three fights left to go. You would think I'd have numbered them, what with the months of stewing in resentment."

My jaw dropped. "Aw, come on!"

Extricating her hand, she pinched both of my cheeks, gave my face a wiggle, and then yanked her hands back. "Woah! Okay, that feels creepy. Like skin and rubber at the same time. Sorry, Penny. This is the path I choose, the path of the frenemy. The time of our uniting in the common cause of Justice is not yet!"

I jerked my thumb in what I hoped was an Easterly direction, towards our school and indeed, all of LA. "I thought we did that already, when the Other Claire mind controlled Sue and Barbara into kidnapping Ray."

For several silent seconds, Marcia stared at me. Then she let out a squeal, and threw her arms around my shoulders. Rubbing her forehead against mine, she cooed, "That one sentence is better than thirteen years of my life, but my mind is made up! I'm categorizing those experiences as 'the Interregnum.' When we're all caught up, I'll write it down so you can enjoy the adventure. Right now, I'm going to go wake the housekeeper at our place in Burbank, and tell her to run screaming into the night. Sorry about the monitors. They're mostly for spy cameras. My father loves spy cameras. Those are all broken anyway. I ate them."

Unwilling to betray unwarranted credulity or unwarranted skepticism, I let that claim pass. All I could do was pout and try the Sad Puppy Dog Eyes trick as Marcia, whistling "Ode to Joy" with perfect, delicate musicality, headed for the stairs.

Sad Puppy Dog Eyes did not work. I not only lacked Claire's superhuman adorableness, my artificial camera eyes probably couldn't even manage regular human adorableness.

When she reached the second step, she touched a button I couldn't see, making the wall slide shut. Not fast enough. I caught a glimpse of her wiping her nose and mouth on her sleeve, and leaving trails of red.

Point of order, Penelope. Could I have felt good about myself bringing a partner on board whose powers did that to her?

Moot now, and I was running out of potential allies, fast. Like, 'Can I call Jupiter and get Remmy to come back?' fast. Still, I had the base. I would run Lab Rat's prizes back to him, come back, and sleep in that goofily-colored but fantastically comfortable looking bed.

Tomorrow, I'd talk to Mourning Dove, and scout out a plan to steal the mind switcher.

Chapter Seven

Mourning Dove first. I sped through the noonday city, every step taking me to a new building, crossing LA at a speed cars couldn't hope to match. I could cover at least half a block per step with no strain at all, and my only limit was how fast I could make sense of the view in the shutter-show of rapid-fire teleportation.

Somewhere along the way I passed my school. That would be second, on my way back to my lair, in case I needed to take loot with me.

Hopping the rooftops of the tall, tall buildings in downtown went more slowly, not because they were hard to reach, but because I wanted to enjoy the wind, the sun peeking through the clouds, and the occasional high-altitude chicken flapping past carrying a book.

LA's neverending LAness would get me through this hard time without my parents.

Taking a deep breath that I could almost feel in lungs I didn't technically have, I braced myself. Time to descend upon my quarry.

This time, I broke into the Library in the most insidious and diabolical way. I teleported down to the front step, and walked in like everyone else.

The book detector just inside the door wailed as I stepped through it.

A security guard, his idle afternoon of harmless literacy interrupted, gave me a cautious eye. Yes, I might be short and fourteen years old, but in full supervillain costume. Stepping forward, I held open my lab coat. The shirt and pants and corset didn't have enough space to hide a book. My belt pouches might, but the book would have to be pretty small.

His tension did not relax one ounce.

Reaching out an arm, I waved my hand between the sensors, setting them to screeching. "It must react this way to robots."

A little old woman, whose blue dress, white blouse, and gray hair in a bun screamed 'librarian', hobbled up on a cane. "Yes. It does. We get a lot of super-powered trouble."

Scrunching my nose and eyebrows, I gave her a lopsided look. "Who would be crazy enough to attack the Los Angeles Main Branch Public Library? And I hope this isn't rude, but am I speaking to a librarian, or *the* Librarian?"

The security guard suddenly spoke, in the same little old woman's voice. "We are all the Librarian, little girl."

Criiiimiiiiiny. Holding out my hands innocently to either side, I said, "I'm not here for trouble, Ma'am. I only want to talk to the library's other defender."

The old woman eyed me like I might turn into a horde of ransacking Visigoths at any moment. "Mourning Dove is not in. You can wait in the pit and I will try the paging system."

In an impressive display of either the Librarian's power or the LA population's jaded disposition, no one reacted to that name. Kids and adults stepped past us, back and forth through the front doors, intent on the magic of the written word.

Bowing respectfully, I said, "Yes, Ma'am," and headed for the center of the building.

With the literary goddess out of sight, I could indulge in feeling stupid. Of course Mourning Dove didn't hang around all day. She would hardly ever be in the library at all.

On the other hand, she could teleport, and if that meant she could travel LA as fast as I could, this would not be a long wait.

Away from the Librarian's screening influence, I got a couple of stares as I walked past. One at my costume, one at my hand hanging at my side. The doll joints of my fingers were the only obvious sign of my robotic body.

Even with Dove not here, I'd contacted someone who could get ahold of her in the field. This had been the right decision. I satisfied myself with that thought as I rode down five floors of escalators into the lowest point of the building.

A new display had replaced the Orb of the Heavens and the soul-sucking silver mask. A mayonnaise jar filled with green goo and eyes floated on the platform, in a cage of crisscrossing golden beams. Much more prominently than the previous plaques, a sign at the front read:

This display is on temporary loan from the hero Mech.
Please do not touch or speak to the exhibit.

Whoa. This was the monster that had come with my cursed jade statue, locked in a container my dad invented. I did wonder if it survived the destruction of the statue. Apparently so.

Out of respect for the library, the warning sign, and my having plenty of trouble to deal with already, I did not touch or speak to the jar or its contents. Just to be safe, I didn't even look directly into those accusing eyes.

The janitor's service door opened, and Mourning Dove walked through it with a complete lack of drama.

She didn't even bother with formalities. "What do you want?"

Okay. Look: clean-cut, virtuous, honest, and full of integrity. Standing up straight, I looked into her yellow-stained, bloodshot eyes, and said, "Help."

"No." Not a moment's thought, or a flicker of emotion on her withered face.

I hunched up in wounded shock. "You of all people know I'm the real Penelope Akk!"

"You are a robot." No emotion, or motion at all. If I'd needed a reminder I was talking to a corpse, her ability to stand utterly still brought it vividly to attention.

Okay, that was drama. Don't let her intimidate you, Penny. Forget sulky, either. I gave her a defiant glare instead. "You warned me twice about the parasite in my head. You said it would betray me. It did."

She met my gaze without reluctance or passion. "I warned Penelope Akk that her power would turn on her. It has corrupted her, wearing away at the self-control and idealism she first displayed. If it continues to grow, she may even go mad. That does not make her any less herself, or you any more than a mechanical copy."

Gritting my teeth, I strangled down a yell to a hiss. "Look into my mind, the way you did then. You'll see I'm telling the truth. She stole my body."

Now, finally, her expression hardened, tightening with a touch of anger. "I do not need to read your mind. No one knows better than I that a machine is a machine, not a person."

I blinked, and then squinted at her as realization hit. "You can't. While my mind is stuck in this robotic heart, you can't read my thoughts."

She didn't answer.

I threw my hands up in the air. "Fine. I was really counting on you to at least believe me. You could have burned the parasite out of my brain. I'd have found a way back in somehow."

My stomach knotted saying that, but as much as I hadn't wanted to put it in words, this was going to end with destroying my super power. The thing in my brain needed it to pretend to be a person. Going back to being a powerless regular person would hurt, but I wanted my parents and my friends and my life back more.

Sighing in frustration, I started to turn away from her. "If you won't help me, I'll go it alone."

"No." She held out a hand, palm up.

I paused mid-step, surprised. Pity, from Mourning Dove?

Her impassive face turned into a scowl, and her raised voice croaked so badly my throat hurt in sympathy. "You are a machine who intends to hurt a living person. It would be irresponsible not to stop you while I have you in front of me. That is how I pay for what I am."

I raised an eyebrow. "You're the one who thinks I'm just a robot. Your life drain powers won't work on me."

"You are mistaken." The words came after black smoke poured out of her hand, sinking into me.

First cold, then numbness. I felt like I was falling. No, I was falling, my legs getting too weak to hold me up.

Fortunately, that brought my raised foot in contact with the ground. Focusing on a spot behind Mourning Dove, I teleported to the wall.

Strength flooded back. Mourning Dove looked around, but I'd instinctively landed facing her, and the stairs. As she caught sight of me, I took another step, blinking way up to the top.

Last time she'd known where I would teleport. This time she had to look.

Darkness seethed, and she appeared in it next to me, already reaching.

I stepped again, down the hall. She teleported off to my side and ahead of me.

We had a long, straight hallway in front of us to the exit. I took another step, focusing on a spot in the corner of my eye.

I blinked into place on the top floor balcony, right next to the door to the Reference section. Pushing that open, I hurried inside.

No puffs of darkness followed me. It had been instinct, a plan formed so fast I couldn't put it in words until now. She couldn't read my mind, so I went whole hog on misdirection.

If I didn't hurry, she'd find me anyway. Nobody ever said Mourning Dove was stupid. At least this was a library. Yes, I'd startled a lot of people, but they had all gasped in whispers.

Blink down to the catwalk. Blink across it to the windows. Hurry hurry hurry.

Okay. Now for the most dangerous part. The windows in the library didn't open by themselves. Unslinging the Machine, I twisted him into activation, and pressed his face against the glass. "Eat."

...and hurry, my favorite creation, because the Librarian was awake, and vandalizing a window would get right up her nose!

When I heard a cranky old woman ask, "What are you doing, child?" I prayed to Tesla the hole was wide enough, and took a step, focusing on the sidewalk outside.

Ow ow ow ow ow ow ow!

This time my knees did give out, and I fell hard onto my side on the pavement.

It took two seconds, tops, for the pain to recede and disappear. Nothing seemed to have cracked. What was that about?

Time to build a wild guess on a wild guess. I'd always figured my bracelets worked by dumping all the strain of running the teleported distance on my body at once. The hole in the window hadn't satisfied its mysterious need to pass through. Instead, it ran me the long way, all the way out through the front doors and around.

Pushing to my feet, I swung my arms. No aches. Hopefully no permanent damage. I could have Mirabelle check, but wasn't sure I was comfortable getting her in trouble with her brother for anything but a desperate situation.

Yes, yes, all well and good, Penny. Now get out of here before Mourning Dove sees you!

Blink. Blink. Blink. Up onto a building. Over to the next building. Around a corner behind a tall tower. Getting that far meant I'd lost Mourning Dove, and she probably wouldn't chase me. Probably. If I avoided her in the future, she wouldn't come looking.

Criminy, though! Another big disappointment! I'd been sure, *sure*, that Dove would at least recognize me as the real Penny.

Nothing for it. Luck had run my way when I needed it the most, after Parasite Penny blew my arm off. If the world decided to stop raining helpful strangers down on me now, I had no reason to complain.

Off to rob my old base, then, which would conveniently take me miles away from Mourning Dove.

CHAPTER EIGHT

O pen Sesame!"

The oversized electrical cabinet opened, says me! I peered down the magic elevator shaft into my old lair, which should still be my lair, but I just knew the parasite would dispute it. And lo and behold, a thin red ring circled the shaft, with a red blob on one side. Not super obvious in a shadowy vertical tunnel, but I'd been looking.

I bypassed the trap by teleporting to the bottom.

Shink-WHAM. A metal lattice swung up out of the floor around my landing spot. My other foot touched the ground just in time to blink me across to the far wall of the entrance hall, which I duly leaned against and wheezed. My body trembled as if I actually had nerves to overload. Behind me, right at the doorway of the elevator, tangled wires gripped one another in a mad knot.

You'd be in the middle of that if you hadn't built up mad reflexes from villainy, Penny.

Also, important lesson: The parasite has your brain, and all its devious thinking abilities. Assume treachery at every junction.

Speaking of every junction, would there be more traps?

If it were me laying them out, there would be one more, not in any obvious spot, but rather in one of the passages between important places in the lair. Fortunately, the labyrinthine layout meant I could take side routes around most of those.

Would I have thought of that, as the trapper? Even if I had, I'd have stuck to the main chance. These traps didn't have to succeed.

So, I circled around to the summoning chamber, and I walked. Yes, teleporting would skip past any traps, but it was much harder to react quickly when I was already trying to catch up to the perspective ship. I'd gotten lucky on the cage trap. The perfect position suggested the parasite remembered she'd left me with the bracers.

My energy-bending gloves would be nice. A lot of my tools would be nice. After I passed the second workshop containing none of the building machines, a suspicion built that I would get none of them. The parasite had anticipated me, and stripped the base.

Of course, the bulky mind switcher might not have fit through the exits, but I could teleport it out and into a hiding spot for collection, with no more damage than separating a few cables.

I reached the summoning room, and discovered that the mind switcher had indeed been too big to carry out. Parasite Penny had broken it instead.

Sure, that was the smart thing. Even the obvious thing. But also the sacrilegious thing.

Vile, pernicious parasite. How? How could you destroy such a rare and incredible invention, just to prevent it from being used against you?

I would definitely not be using the mind switcher against her. Debris lay scattered all over the chamber. Bits of soapstone, wires ripped apart, unidentifiable burnt chunks, metal boxes chopped into star shapes—even Mirabelle couldn't hope to fix this.

She also hadn't been able to move out the all-powerful remote control console. Of course, she hadn't broken that. Oh, no. In fact...

I leaned over, and squinted at the panel where I'd ripped out some wires to temporarily shut it down. Yes. Someone had attempted to make repairs.

What target had the remote control been set to last? Why, my current body.

Two could play this game. Where... yes. Like a lot of things in this base, the console needed electrical power, and a thick cable plugged it into the wall sockets. I would miss those wall sockets, hidden behind fake mossy brick surfacing. The builder of this dungeon had been such a gigantic poseur, he'd created his own new kind of style.

A gap in the metal surfacing allowed the power cable out. It had wiggle room. If I were subtle...

Unhooking the Machine, I told him, "Nibble."

Placing his jaws against the edges of that gap, I used him to eat the hole just wide enough that he could crawl inside. Sticking him in, I mimed a basketball. "There's a clock in there. Eat it, and this much area around it. Then regurgitate everything in an evenly mixed lump, and crawl back out."

About sixty seconds of crunching noises later, he emerged. I wrapped him around my wrist, and indulged an evil chuckle. "Turnabout is fair play, monster. If I'm lucky, it will take you weeks of trying to fix this thing to discover it's irrevocably trashed."

Oh, well. I'd left some deliciously valuable blocks of silver and other exotic metals down here last time. Had the parasite picked them up?

No. She hadn't. I knew, because I knew exactly what I would do. The metals were somewhere in this base, supposedly carelessly abandoned, in the middle of a trap I could not teleport out of.

Whatever. No weapons, and she'd destroyed my ace in the hole, but I'd destroyed hers. Round one of our duel: a draw.

Nothing else to do here. I left, and when I saw the cage trap melded back into the floor, I angled around really carefully until I got a safe peek up the shaft I could use to teleport out.

After that, I walked around Upper High to the street. Just walking down there had felt good. Something was wrong with the bracelets. They did their function just fine, but... I couldn't put my finger on it. Using them too much felt wrong. Addictive?

Immersed in those thoughts, I nearly walked right into Marcia and Ifrit.

Surprised, I said the first thing on my mind. "It is so freaky seeing a boy I know wearing spandex."

Marcia burst into the most undignified snorting giggles imaginable, and shoving her fists up against her mouth only made them worse.

Ifrit, in a skin-hugging blue-and-red costume, blushed and scowled. He had the figure for it, but if supervillainy could give squishy me muscles, there couldn't be many heroes that weren't physically fit.

I couldn't recommend the color choice on that outfit, though. The red and blue clashed so badly they left uncomfortable after-images in my brain, and I didn't even HAVE a brain at the moment.

No jokes, please, subconscious.

Their momentary paralysis allowed me to take control of the conversation. "Why are you two here?" I paused, letting out a groan. "This is fight number two. The one with Ifrit. You didn't bring Sharky or Gabriel, did you?"

Folding one arm under her chest, Marcia flapped the other. "Oh, please, why would I bother? All they did was stand around and flap their goober hatches."

Even keeping in mind Marcia was smarter than she let on, it wouldn't be hard to make her clobber Ifrit for me. She enjoyed her charging bull rage too much.

So, I took a few steps back in case she tried a sucker punch, and covered it by putting my hands on my hips and glaring. "And how did you know I would be here?"

She gave me the exact same arms akimbo stance back, but with smirking skepticism. "It wasn't exactly hard to guess. I didn't expect you to rob your old lair so fast. We just planted the alarms and hadn't reached Hollywood before they went off and we had to turn around."

"I thought you said you ate the—oh, no. You didn't."

She met my stare of horror with a gleefully non-innocent smile, singsonging, "I don't know what you're talking about!"

In an attempt to find a topic that didn't make me want to take five baths, I turned my exasperated stare on Ifrit. "I would have thought you'd be too mature to get caught up in Marcia's ridiculous revenge ritual."

His blush faded, Ifrit took a steadying breath, exasperation fading into a set-faced determination, eyebrows and lips flat on his dusky face. "I don't care what craziness she has in mind. I'm here to stop you."

He looked so serious about it, which only made me more confused. "Stop me? She told you I'm the real one, right?"

Ifrit sneered. "She did, but—"

Slapping my forehead, I finished for him, "She's crazy, so you don't believe her."

I looked back at Marcia. "Which is exactly what you wanted. Are you sure you won't join me now? Think of the uses to which I could put your ingenious dementia!"

Clasping her hands to her chest now, she leaned her head back and let out a huge sigh. "You are the sister of my heart, Bad Penny, but this cruel world of hero and villain pits sister against sister, locking those who should be comrades in an embrace of violence."

"Great. The robot is as crazy as she is." Frowning in the only real anger I could remember on his face, Ifrit pushed Marcia out of the way, and pointed a finger at me. "Penelope is a good kid, robot. Stay away from her, or I will roast you into ashes."

Stabbing my chest with my thumb, I snapped back, "I am the good kid. She's a parasite who stole my body! Did she put you up to this?"

He lifted his chin, indignant. "Penny isn't going around scrounging up people to help her deal with you. I'm a hero. We protect kids from murderous machines."

I gaped. "Am I going to be getting this from the whole hero community?"

"As far as we're concerned, the name Bad Penny is now where it truly belongs."

Swiveling, I pointed an accusing finger at Marcia. "I am going to get you for this."

She cackled, hopping on one foot and pumping her fist. "Our rivalry will shake the heavens!"

"I don't want our rivalry to shake the heavens. Submit, and you can be my brainwashed servant. You can't tell me that doesn't sound like—"

Fire roared up around me in a circle. To Ifrit's credit, that happened before he said, "This is idiotic. Surrender and I'll deactivate you and hand you over to Mech."

It was good flame. Lots of heat haze, scorched pavement, very scary. Alas, not opaque, so I sidestepped and blinked across the street.

I didn't have a quip or attempt to talk reason into him ready, so Ifrit took the initiative. Fire exploded, this time around himself, a whirling protective vortex at least a good six feet in radius. Marcia had to stumble backwards, slapping out sparks on her clothing.

Over the roar of wind his fiery shield created, Ifrit shouted, "I know you can teleport, robot, and I know how to stop teleporters from sneaking up behind me."

Well, I certainly wouldn't get a chance like this again. One foot forward, I blinked behind Ifrit just as he'd warned me not to. It was hard to see anything in the red, orange, and yellow inferno, but it didn't take much precision to grab the back of his head. With my artificial strength, I shoved him back and down, slamming the eighteen-year-old fire summoner onto the sidewalk.

Two unexpected things happened. First, I was not used to being anything but a scrawny nerd, and he hit hard. At least fighting experience made him try to lift his head. The crack when it smacked the pavement merely shocked me, without actually making me fear for his life.

Second, I was also not used to how ridiculously light I was, now. Leaving the Heart of Gold hidden under Marcia's mattress actually took off like a fifth of my weight! The violent movement and driving wind from Ifrit's flame shield catapulted me into the air.

Somersaulting in midair, I landed in a crouch, one leg off to the side and one hand flat to the ground. Marcia applauded, then made "Ow ow ow" noises, because she'd burned her hands.

With nothing to burn and their creator stunned, Ifrit's flames vanished. Stalking over to him, I nudged him with my boot. "You kept rubbing it in that I'm a robot, and it didn't occur to you that I'm fireproof? Go back to being a sidekick, little boy. No, first tell the parasite in my body that I'm coming for her, and *then* go beg Marvelous to teach you how to fight."

He didn't respond. I would trust Marcia to be smarter than she pretends. If he had a concussion, she'd get him help.

As for Marcia... she'd gone from clapping to making weird, bubbling noises.

I turned around, to find her clutching her own shoulders, and with her cheeks inflated like a hamster. She trembled, letting out gulping noises as she wrestled to keep her breath held.

"What?" I asked, suspicious.

Her shaking hand rose, pointing at my head. "Your hair wasn't fireproof," she squeaked, and then collapsed to the ground kicking her feet and shrieking with laughter.

I blinked. Then I lifted a hand, and slid it over my now smooth scalp. "Well, CRIMINY."

Chapter Nine

When I got back to the Fortress of Pink, I slept. For the first time since I'd been bodynapped, I felt tired. I wasn't even aware that was an option, but my body dragged with unnatural heaviness, and I collapsed on Marcia's pastel covers with release. One quick check that the Heart of Gold was still under the pillow, and I turned myself off for a couple of hours.

Oh, yeah. That hit the spot. Definitely freaky robo-exhaustion.

Fine. I would sleep until tomorrow. It felt good to sulk anyway.

My hair! My beautiful braids! Okay, they weren't beautiful. I had rat-colored brown hair, and sometimes jealousy poked at me for Claire's unearthly, natural, platinum blonde.

But not often. She had 'look at me, I'm in a magazine' hair, but my dull, brown, braided pigtails gave me style.

Or they did. Now all I had was a bald, ceramic white head. Or maybe it was plastic. Or some kind of freaky carbon weave, although not likely because those exotic materials were crazy tough and wouldn't break from a mere bomb.

So. Today's summary: Mourning Dove believed I was a deranged robot duplicate to be destroyed if convenient. Ifrit believed I was a deranged robot duplicate who kicked his incendiary backside. Basically the entire hero community intended to protect the parasite from me because they were Noble Defenders of Children.

Suddenly, I understood why Apparition once told me I was too understanding to be a hero. Criminy!

Looking straight up, arms folded behind my head, I said, "This, oh ceiling covered in phosphorescent star stickers I am positive Marcia did not choose or desire, is a problem. I need my hair replaced. Only mad science will do that."

The stickers reminded me that all the mad scientists I knew were villains anyway. Well, except for Echo and Mech.

I let out a heavy sigh. "I should write letters home. Dear Mom and Dad, today at super power camp was that day where you announce you don't like sports at the top of your lungs in the cafeteria, and now nobody wants to sit at your table except the kid who keeps trying to stick her fork in her ear."

On that note, I turned myself off for another round.

I awoke to a tinny voice singing, "Stacy's mom has got it goin' on!"

Supplying the chorus of, "AAAAUGH!" I jumped into the air, fell off the bed, and scrambled around until I found my phone.

I did not need to check the caller ID. Only one person would have set that as a ringtone for herself. "Good… uh, afternoon, Miss Lutra. To what do I owe the pleasure of this call? Please tell me Claire is home."

"No, although you should read the emails she's sending me." Her sly amusement turned to concern. "I wanted to check on you. How are you doing?"

Wow, another summer camp metaphor. First call from home! The one that makes you break down crying with homesickness.

Forget THAT.

Dropping onto the bed again, I stretched out and answered, "I'm holding up well. My arm is fixed. My success rate finding allies is running negative numbers, but if I have to, I'll win this alone. I'm better than her."

She digested that in silence for a moment. When she did answer, her voice radiated warmth and pride. "I always thought of you as Brian's little girl, but in your heart you're Beebee's daughter, aren't you? Strong as steel."

I glanced down at the hatch in my chest. "Yeah, pretty much."

"I had brunch with her this morning."

My steel heart clenched, a knot of sudden pain. "How are Mom and Dad?"

Misty Lutra's voice betrayed no sign of whether my moment of weakness had been audible. "I told her about your battle yesterday with Ifrit. People fall all over themselves to tell me the latest gossip, and all she'd heard was that you got in a fight. When I told her how thoroughly you won..."

Another pause, and Miss Lutra continued solemnly, "I thought she would break down crying from relief. She said this means you're as good as she thought you would be. You're brave and strong and skilled and intelligent and mature enough to succeed and get through this, until you and the other Penny finish your battle."

"She said that?" My mouth felt dry. It was dry, but now it felt that way.

"What she actually said was that she is now confident of the probability that you will be okay, and she said it with her face in her hands. You know what Beebee means when she talks like that."

I did. Miss Lutra had translated perfectly.

When I failed to find words adequate to my feelings, Miss Lutra want on. "If I know Brian, and only your mother knows him better, I'd say he's devastated, but is trying to hide it. They love you, Penny. I promise. They feel trapped. There's no research and no manuals for a situation like this, and they're as lost as any normal parent. Maybe more."

I held up an arm, spread fingers against the brilliance from the ceiling lamp, and studied the socketed, artificial joints. "I don't blame them. Maybe that's part of being a robot."

"It's part of being Beebee's daughter."

Okay, that made me grin. "Thanks, Miss Lutra. I guess you can't tell them I love them, but thanks."

"You can bet your mother knows I ran to tell you everything."

Ha! I grinned even wider. "Yeah, she could probably have written out this whole conversation verbatim." Which would mean she accepted, at least, that I was as much Penny as the thing wearing my body.

Ha again! Rolling upright, I said, "I'd better go prove my Mom right by going to get my hair fixed, before Chinatown switches back to weekday mode."

All warm and honeyed, she said, "Have fun, sweetheart."

"You know... I think maybe I will."

Just as I'd hoped, late afternoon at Chinatown meant a steady crowd of relaxed supervillains hiding in the mall and out of the public eye. A clustered customer base should mean lots of mad scientists ready to sell to them!

Instead, my luck continued to play. It was Mechanical Aesthetic, Expert, Red Eye, Cybermancer, and a man and woman I didn't know. They did have customers. Two women—both the same height, with curly brown hair, and just enough not-similarity that they looked like sisters, not twins—were studying Cybermancer's bombs. One wore a cowgirl costume, including a leather skirt, stetson, and three gun belts. Only one holster was sized right and had metal peeking under the strap to suggest a normal pistol. The others... well, Mad Science. Oh, and the skinny rifle on her back had to be a bb gun. Her sister wore shiny black pants as tight as spandex, a red-and-white striped sweater, and more belts. Where the first girl had guns, this one had slim, pokey things. Not knives. Screwdrivers, bits of wire, bent forks, a tin can, different kinds of pins in her hair, a lockpick set in a breast pocket... that kind of thing.

The mad scientists I didn't know had a customer, too, a woman—

Business, Penny! Don't get distracted gawking at how much fun being a villain is.

In fact, business ceased. The whole crowd turned to stare at me.

I let out an aggrieved sigh. "You heard already?"

Her face calm, but her voice lugubrious with anticipation, Red Eye said, "No, but we're about to hear something great."

"Do you know anyone who can do cosmetic doll fixes?" I asked.

Cybermancer supplied the names I expected. "Raggedy and Gothic."

I shook my head. "I don't think this is their kind of work."

Red Eye tilted her head forward, giving me a scolding, sideways look from her good eye. "We're going to need to know what kind of work, before we can help."

...

There was no way around it. Why had I even hoped?

I pulled off the big pink snow hat I'd scavenged from Marcia's not-quite-empty closet.

Nobody laughed. No one's expressions changed. The complete motionlessness of their faces and the prolonged silence eloquently spoke of how hard they were trying not to laugh.

Finally, Cybermancer said, "I take it we should see the other guy."

Thankfully unable to blush, I said, "He rued the day, yes, but it was literally a pyrrhic victory."

Cybermancer spread his gloved hands. "You know I'd help if I could, Bad Penny, but this is way outside of my field."

"I can help," said the Expert, looming behind the others like a vulture.

Red Eye jerked to attention. "What?! Don't you think..."

Everybody stared at her. The Expert really stared at her, like a principle scolding a kid in detention.

She raised her hands and lowered her head. "Fine, fine."

I wiped my forehead, which needed a lot more wiping than it did a couple of days ago. "Good. I did not want to have to ask Spider for help finding someone."

The Expert's jaw tightened in disgust at that idea. "No. That would have been a bad idea."

Snapping his fingers twice, Expert said, "Come, child," and set off across the mall.

I followed his long-legged stride. We headed across the mall, up the stairs, and into one of the empty shops, stripped of their merchandise every weekend, and presumably refilled sometime tonight to be ready for Monday morning. No sign of that, yet. Instead, the Expert slipped a key into the lock of a back room, and opened the door into a laboratory too big to fit into mall.

Not that it was huge, but the white-paneled room was bigger than the shop, and the walls of the mall didn't have room to contain that. While stepping inside, I checked the lintel. Dull brown metal gave way to shiny white metal on an exactly straight line.

The Expert noticed my interest. "In exchange for the technical work turning a collection of random inventions into a moon base, Spider granted me access to portals that allow easy access to my facilities."

"Runtime on the Orb of the Heavens? That's quite a payment."

"It was quite a bit of work, which very few with or without super powers could perform. Brainy was not available." He waved his hand at a chair. "Sit."

I sat. It gave me time to examine the room. The Expert liked tidiness. White tile walls, floor, ceiling. Shiny metal counters. Nearly arranged complex machines, all blinking lights and clear plastic cylinders. The place looked like my Dad's workshop, where he subjected mad science devices to every test imaginable to non-mad science in the hopes they could be reproduced by regular people. Lots of monitor screens, a big computer, rows of jars with printed labels on the shelves, that sort of thing. The chair, right out in the open, was fastened firmly in place and obviously there so that larger machines could be rolled up to the occupant. The padding on the seat, back, and armrests was also white, and thick enough to be comfortable.

As he puttered around behind me, tapping on keys and making things clink, the Expert said, "The obvious problem here is that most methods of adding hair would require removing your scalp. Not an option to us, even temporarily."

"... but you have a solution, or we wouldn't be here."

I couldn't see him back there, but he sounded a little bit smug. "I do. A couple of pieces of technology I've kept around, without ever being quite sure what I would do with them. Remember that lesson, Bad Penny. Mad scientists should be packrats."

His footsteps signaled him stepping up behind me. Fingers poked at the top of my head, massaging the stiff dome, for all the good that would do. For a moment the pressure increased, and then let up, followed by a thoughtful hmmm. "You react to the touch. I take it you have full tactile sensitivity."

I bobbed my head in a series of pleased nods, although not being able to shrug spoiled that a bit. "If I had to get stuck in a robot body, this one is pretty good."

His voice took a turn for the serious. "The downside of this superior technology is that the first stage, where the bonding element repairs your follicles so that new hair can be attached, will hurt. I suggest you deactivate while I work."

Not really thrilled by that idea. "I'll be fine. Having my arm reattached hurt, and I handled it."

"It will hurt a *lot*," he stressed. A whole lot of passion and grim warning went into that sentence.

"Ugh. Fine, fine!" I waved a hand, and reached up behind my neck.

The Expert assured me, in strained tone of someone not used to giving comfort, "Sixty seconds will be enough. That will get you through the first stage."

Sixty seconds. Okay. I pushed the button.

Awake! This sleep was so short, I didn't actually feel like I slept. The world merely blinked, and I found myself with my head lolled forward. Not far forward, because a collar kept it fastened to the back of the chair.

Tesla's Government Fiasco, really? Okay, yes, some kind of trickery with payment, that I expected from the Expert, but kidnapping?

Kidnapping it was, or at least imprisonment. Not just my neck, but my wrists and ankles were fastened to the chair as well. Together, that locked me in place pretty thoroughly. My body didn't compress or bend like the old one.

The cold pressure of my teleport bracers remained on my upper arms. I tapped a foot on the floor. Without being able to move my body in the process, the bracers didn't activate.

You know what pressure I didn't feel? The Machine. He'd removed my precious Machine!

Should I panic? I could panic. No. Bad Penny preferred sarcasm. "Sixty seconds, huh?"

Blithely, the Expert answered, "I do intend to fix your hair. I will probably even let you go, but I would be a fool to let technology like this escape without thorough investigation."

"So, you do this to all the robot girls."

It was hard to tell if my acid voice stung him or not, but his voice did heat up with passion. "You have no idea what you're wearing, Bad Penny. I saw those photos. Your circuitry is not merely advanced, it follows the same design as an Upgrade."

Part of me needed time to come up with an escape plan. The other part of me wanted to know more. I satisfied both by snarking, "You're not the first person who's said that."

He responded with a contemptuous growl. "I keep forgetting your mother's mad and futile desire to make you grow up a normal child. Do you remember the First Horseman?"

"Like of the Apocalypse?" I asked, trying not to let my suspicions slide together before the Expert filled me in.

My obvious ignorance goaded him into doing just that. "In 1992, the First, Second, and Third Horsemen appeared in Los Angeles, on an incoherent mission to kill as many superhumans as they could. If civilians died in droves, so much the better. In response, the community coalesced to kill them quickly and with extreme thoroughness. Most of it. The First Horseman knew a cybernetic technique that allowed him to massively increase other people's powers. It is called an Upgrade, and as far as I am concerned, it is technology more valuable than the Conqueror Orbs, because it can be copied. Someone deciphered how it works, and gave Upgrades to Rage and Ruin. I want that secret. If disassembling you will let me decipher it, that is what I will do. Fortunately, I expect that removing a finger will teach me everything that can be learned. If my examination is successful, I may even be able to reattach it."

"But it's Spider everyone warned me not to trust," I observed, pouring on a whole bucket of sarcasm.

The Expert leaned around in front of me, and I got to see his smirk as he examined my forehead. "Of course. If you'd spoken to her, she would have told you not to let yourself fall into my clutches. You are a prize the entire mad science community will be slavering for, and you would lose your value to her if one of us took you apart."

Something clinked behind me. The Expert's hand closed on my neck, his thumb reaching for the button back there. "But first, I'm going to actually fix your hair."

Ten seconds. He pressed it.

Ten seconds later, I woke up. This time I lay there. It was easy enough. My eyes hadn't closed, and my head lolled forward, but that was all.

It got a little harder when the Expert massaged some gunk onto my scalp. He was not kidding about it hurting. Exaggerating, yes, but woo, what a burn! If I wasn't clamped down and my shoulders unable to twitch anyway, I'd have given myself away. Plus, I could hold my breath indefinitely.

Burning paste gave way to what felt like that special dentist toothbrush, something that vibrated my head and scratched its way over my lost hairline.

While he did that, I tried to figure out an avenue of escape. I might be stronger than him. Would he be incautious enough to release an arm to get at my finger? Was the chair fastened to the floor? If I could tilt it forward, that might be enough to let me use my bracers. My eyes scanned the room, looking for anything that might help or inspire.

I found help in the least expected place. The Expert might be a duplicitous jackanape, but he at least was a geek. I approved of the computer game boxes stacked neatly in cupboards, and the line of superhero figurines in a row down the lowest shelf. Mostly superheroines, but that was how the figurine industry went. He even had a little statuette of my mother, whose sculptor had accurately captured her stiff gray suit, but had posed her in a flirty, hip-tilted stance Mom had probably never adopted in her life.

Mom's statue caught my eye because the one next to her moved. The tiny heroine, with fluffy hair, a crazy poufy dress, and an even crazier grin, climbed down to the counter top, picked up my Machine lying there alone, and twisted him around.

His legs moved. The statuette had activated him.

Its task complete, the figurine pulled herself back up to where she'd started, and became motionless again.

Well. Ain't that a thing.

And before I could ask the question, I knew what thing. That statue moved with the same careful grace I'd seen in another line of statues, on a shelf in Chinatown. It had been carved, or infected, or however his powers worked, by Gothic, a man with a clear motivation for saving helpless robots from being dismantled.

The Expert stepped away from my chair. I felt hair lying against the back of my neck, and a few strands hung in front of my eyes. Time to go, then.

"Machine, eat my restraints," I ordered.

The Expert's feet thumped. He walked back up to me, and pressed the button in the back of my neck.

Two seconds.

I didn't even notice that delay. It wasn't even enough time to miss the Expert stepping into view, picking up the Machine, and dropping him in a can.

Crunch crunch crunch. He ate his way out immediately, and resumed crawling across the counter towards me.

Taking a solid steel box down from a shelf, the Expert dropped my Machine in that. More crunching, and after a couple of seconds, my wonderful creation crawled through a hole he'd chewed through the side.

Frowning, not angry but analytical, my gray-haired captor carried the wriggling Machine across the room, opened up a wall safe, and sealed him in.

I had to say, that safe looked secure. Shiny metal, high-tech lock, thick door with visible layering of all kinds of no-doubt exotic materials.

Why, it took my baby nearly thirty seconds to eat his way out. He'd gained a fair amount of weight by now. Instead of lifting him, the Expert went and fetched a cube made of plastic struts along the edges, and no actual walls. I took considerable satisfaction that he went and fetched this new cage before my Machine escaped the wall safe. This once-proud mad scientist already knew he'd lost this battle.

As my pudgy millipede-shaped contraption emerged from the wall vault and dropped onto the table, the Expert set the plastic cube down over it. Walls of twinkling purple appeared, filling every gap.

They went out when the Machine crawled through the nearest, and his patient crawl became a scurry, accompanied by a loud bang when he jumped off the counter onto the floor.

Scowling, still more thoughtful than angry, the Expert stepped past my baby and pushed him back with one foot. The Machine took a chunk out of the mad scientist's shoe for his pains, but it did give the old man time to unhook my left ankle, then my right. Solemnly, he said, "I know that you're awake. It would be interesting to continue these experiments, but the outcome would be the same, and I have no desire to waste your time further. There."

The last lock around my neck opened, I stood up, and the Machine stopped. I had no more restraints for him to eat, after all. Picking him up in both hands, I cradled him to my chest and stroked his back.

Despite, or maybe in response to, my accusing stare, the Expert lifted a bread-box sized machine off a table at the back of the laboratory. When I saw the skinny, dangling mechanical arms, I recognized it. How and why had this guy ever gotten his hands on one of my dad's automatic hair braiding machines?

Regardless, he held it out to me, and I tucked it on top of my Machine. He finished with a little bow. "I agreed to fix your hair, and it will not be finished until it is braided. Under the circumstances, I could not ask you to do that here."

Not willing to give him the dignity of a response, I walked out the door. It opened onto a back street I didn't recognize.

I was tempted to return to Chinatown and talk to Spider just out of spite, but I had an obligation to take care of. Gothic and Raggedy had given me their business card way back when, and I owed them a thank you!

CHAPTER TEN

Iblipped across the city, building by building, trying to read my phone's map without accidentally teleporting onto it. That whole weird 'stare at the spot you want to arrive at' control scheme.

On a handy sidewalk, I paused to let my badly abused GPS catch up. Yes, this was the place. One shake confirmed that my beautiful new braids still flopped correctly, and let me look around. Of all places, Gothic and Raggedy made their lair in the heart of South Central, one of the most persistently 'bad part of town' areas, despite the superhero infestation I had to avoid along the way. Still, in this particular neighborhood the endless low houses were no worse than dusty. Shiny white vans with uniformed workers certainly did not radiate terror of crime.

Ah, there was the address. It took me a moment because, rather than the usual front door, the entrance to my benefactor's base slunk a half-floor down, at the bottom of a flight of cement steps. Not exactly common, and it hid the building number.

Hid the building number so well, in fact, that I only spotted it when cadaverous Gothic opened his front door, looked across and down the street at me, and waved at me in scooping motions. They looked urgent, not friendly.

I teleported to the top of the steps to find out why. This made the normally severe and reserved old man grimace in dismay. His hoarse whisper carried up the steps to me. "What are you doing? Evade! Escape! The capture squad is right behind you!"

The what now?

I looked around, but this time actually paid attention to the people on the street. All of them wore dress shirts of colors so pale they wouldn't hide the bright yellow smiling sun logo. Many of them held guns and cannons of unorthodox size and shape. Confusion reigned, with lots of pointing at me and arguing.

Their vans also bore smiley suns and the name Happy Days Toys For Children.

Criminy. These were henchmen, and I hadn't noticed.

Now I knew what the problem was with all this teleporting. Tunnel vision. Eyes darting from spot to spot as you caught up with each jump had a hypnotic effect.

One of the goons worked out how to use his cannon, pulling a lever and firing a net at me. Bad for me or not, I certainly was not going to abandon my best protection, and I teleported across the street. Another pointed a bulky flat-surfaced gun in my general direction, and when she pulled the trigger it threw a badly aimed fountain of ice.

Should I steal that? An ice gun could be useful. Although not one that also froze in a block around its owners hand, like this did.

So far, I was less than impressed. When the henchman with the clipboard pulled out a handheld detonator, I saw no sign of any bombs. I stepped out into the middle of the street, just to be sure.

He pressed the button.

Eight hours later, I woke up sitting on a pedestal in a room full of robots. The neat row of pedestals, fluorescent lights, and white walls and floor had an institutional look. A smiling sun painted on that wall and the message 'We Promise Not To Automate You*' made it pretty clear which institution.

A different worker with a clipboard shrieked when I looked up, and threw that clipboard to the ceiling.

This unarmed yahoo certainly wasn't a threat. I teleported to the door.

Hmmm. Thick, vault-like, with a little plastic window that blocked my bracers. With the diagonal yellow stripes obscuring the view, I wasn't sure why the door had a window at all. What the door tellingly lacked was a handle. Instead, a box with a slot suggested a key card reader.

Well, in a room for housing kidnapped robots, that made sense. I would just have to take the card from the minion.

I turned back to find the poor guy pounding his fist against a box with 'In Case Of Robot Uprising Break Glass' printed on it. When he saw me look at him, he scooped up his clipboard again, and banged at the box with that.

The glass cracked. A sign popped out of the top of the box reading 'The cost of this glass will be deducted from your paycheck.'

Could I just take the key card off his belt? I didn't see where he kept it.

While I scanned his pockets, the minion finally wedged his clipboard into the crack running around the edge of the box, and levered it open. Whimpering, he punched the candy-striped button inside.

Eight hours later, I woke up again, sitting on my pedestal. Alone, this time, at least.

Thank goodness for West Lee's sleep failsafe. I was already tired of robot deactivation signals. Granted, humans had to deal with mind control.

Okay, Penny. Time to shake off the tunnel vision. First, take a deep breath.

I was not taking any breaths at all.

Of course I wasn't. Robots don't.

"... forget *that!*" My voice echoed in the empty room, a reminder that whatever body I might be stuck in, I was definitely human!

First step. Breathe. The first couple of breaths were just making noises and moving my chest, but after that, I started to feel it again.

The beating of my heart helped, even if that heart was made of steel and technically contained me, with the rest of the body just a plug-in.

So. That was the real negative of teleporting. It focused me, slowed down my reflexes and thinking, and most importantly made me less human. I'd have to go easy on them, but no way could I give up my second most effective invention ever.

"Which I'm not wearing," I said aloud. No bracers on my arms. Panicky henchmen must have removed them after my first unplanned awakening.

Also missing were my clothes. Oh, criminy!

But forget being embarrassed. My Machine. They'd taken my Machine off my wrist!

Okay okay okay. One step at a time.

First, breathing good? Yes, still breathing.

I needed to get my clothes, then my Machine, then get out. The teleport bracers should be with one or the other, or all together.

Right now, I had to get out of this room.

No. Right now, I had to prepare for if someone pushed that stupid button again. Note to Penny: If you even think someone is going to, set yourself to sleep for only one second. In fact, do that now. Self, I have no idea if this will carry through, but the next time you're turned off, sleep for one second.

Okay, now to get out of the room. This was a Happy Days outlet, right? So there would be stolen or experimental weapons around. I could certainly use them better than the employees.

"Ah, Bad Penny, but are there any in this room?"

The room contained a lot less than I'd first thought. Not many robots at all. On the pedestal next to me sat a bot like a skeleton with wire muscles and a few chrome plates like haphazard stretches of skin. Very creepy. Probably filled with weapons. I had no idea how to get to them or turn him on, but worth keeping in mind.

On the next pedestal down sat... well, this was sad. It looked like an oil drum with jointless, stubby arms and legs bolted on. It had plastic googly eyes for pity's sake? A quick thump registered a hollow clang.

Happy Days must have these poor saps on a quota, and they were so desperate they'd started capturing fake robots just to make up their numbers. I mean, on the next pedestal they'd stolen a... a...

A Gerty Goat animatronic.

Up close, she was huge, and there was absolutely no mistaking her. Blue smock with little white flowers, apron, gray carpet covering. A rough patch under one foot even showed where she'd been broken off of her stage. They'd stolen a Gerty Goat animatronic. This was the definition of desperate.

Was she damaged? Did they hurt her? I couldn't help myself. Yes, she was just a restaurant display, but Gerty was my favorite. Despite my increased robo-strength, I couldn't get any of the seams of her smock open to check on the internals, but nothing looked damaged. A little old and shabby, yes, but not damaged.

The door clicked and hummed. I hid behind Gerty. A seven-foot-tall goat provides excellent cover.

In walked a big guy, not muscular, not fat, just big. With dark skin and short, red dreadlocks, he wore the Happy Days uniform with more ease than the others. Maybe he just had naturally good posture.

Okay. I would stay out of his sight, and slip through the door behind him when he left. Or before, if I could manage it.

Right now, he blocked my way, and did so quite thoroughly by rushing up to my abandoned pedestal. Gripping it in both hands, he exclaimed, "She's gone. Was she disassembled? No, she wasn't scheduled until tomorrow. I checked! Did Travis move her time up?"

He sounded increasingly panicky. He also sounded increasingly British. And increasingly familiar.

My eyebrows pressed together, and I leaned out enough to ask, "Are you... Byron Slade?" That was the guy's name, right?

He let out a yelp, grabbed his chest, then leaned one hand against the wall and panted for breath. "You're alive?" Oh, yeah. Listen to that hope and relief. I'd made the right choice to reveal myself.

"Yes. Do you mind not looking? I'm kind of clothesless here." Technically there was nothing to see on this body that could have passed for a mannequin, but that knowledge helped surprisingly little.

He immediately turned his back, and started complaining. "I knew this would happen. If we went around scooping up robots, sooner or later we'd kidnap a person who happened to be mechanical!"

"I thought you quit this place."

He stuck his arms straight down, fists clenched. "I did. I got a fun job at a hobby store. Two weeks in, it got bought out and became Happy Days Table Top Entertainment. They just wanted to use the game boxes for smuggling. I quit and took a job in a call center, right before they renamed it Happy Days Telecommunications Frontiers. The translation position at the Japanese television station was the coolest thing I'd ever done, until it became Happy Days Broadcast Content. I liked the pet shop job, and then I barely got out of Happy Days Beloved Companions Center after the chicken incident."

My disaffected savior shuddered, and thumped a fist into the wall. "Happy Days buys every single place I go to work!"

I blinked. "Wow. Do you think they're following you?"

He shook his head. "No. It's just my luck. Or maybe it's a lesson." He lowered his hands again, this time flexing and clenching his fingers. "I've had enough. I mean, I'd already had enough, but kidnapping a little kid robot is too much. I've had so much enough that I'm going to do something. I'm going to rescue you."

I covered an awkward cough with my fist. "Not to be ungrateful, but could you get my clothes first...?"

"I know where they are. I'm going there anyway. You go back to pretending you're asleep, please? Not that anyone will come in, but just in case."

He flicked his card through the door's reader, and left. I took his advice. He obviously meant well, and knew this place better than I did. Climbing back up on the pedestal, I let my head and arms hang, and waited.

That gave me time to concentrate on breathing, and listening to my heart. And to worry. Hopefully nothing would happen to him.

Was that a stomach gurgle? It was shocking how easy it was to stop feeling human. The smart thing to do would be to worry about this later, but that kind of thinking got me here. So, I twiddled my toes. Robots did not have toes.

The door opened. Byron entered, throwing me my clothes, which I caught gratefully and retreated behind Gerty to wear.

He put on armor. He already had most of it on when he entered, but instead of a suit, it was more like a pile of mismatched parts, and didn't go on easily. They did match in one way. Every piece was shiny and white.

With Gerty between us, I asked, "Where'd you get that stuff?"

"When I could not get away from Happy Days, I got more and more angry. Every time I quit, I would steal something. It's not like the company legitimately owns any of it. And now, I will stop dreaming and put it all to use."

Corset adjusted, I slid my coat over my shoulders and stepped out from behind Gerty. "Wow, Byron. That's pretty amazing."

He, too, fastened on his final item, a visor and white plastic headband that left his dreadlocks free. Standing up very straight, chest inflated, he declare, "That name is dust. I am no longer Byron Slade, wage slave. I am a superhero now. I am... Radiance!"

Something clicked, and the armor flickered with constantly changing rainbow lights.

I gave him a firm nod of approval, and ticked off on my fingers. "Okay. Now we get my Machine, get my teleport bracelets, and escape. And take Gerty with us."

He looked past me to the slumped, unpowered animatronic. "You can not possibly be serious."

"I'm not leaving my childhood icon here to be disassembled," I said from my lofty, nostalgic vantage point as a serious fourteen year old about to enter high school.

"Do you know how massively, unbearably heavy that is?" Radiance asked, incredulous.

Walking back over to her, I scooped my arms around the back of the machine. "About to find out."

The answer, it turned out, was 'too heavy.' I couldn't budge her. To his credit, Radiance didn't argue any further, just walked around the other side and helped lift.

The array of armor pieces included a strength enhancer. His arms got even more glittery, and he lifted Gerty... by about an inch.

"GOAT ALERT! GOAT ALERT! GOAT ALERT!" wailed an invisible PA system.

I propped a fist on my hip. "Seriously? A special alarm on the Gerty Goat display, but not me? I don't know whether I'm insulted, or impressed by their taste."

Radiance jerked upright, mouth drawn in a grimace. "Nobody told me about the alarm! That self-absorbed ninnyhammer Simon is supposed to record all—I shall get you out of here, Bad Penny, while the getting is good."

Backing away did me no good. He scooped an arm around my middle, and hauled me off the ground. Punching his armored chest, I yelled, "Not without my Machine!"

Swiping his card, he carried me out into a wide underground hallway, the kind used to haul freight. Robots could get pretty big, after all. "I'm afraid it's in the vault in the Ultra Hush Hush Company Property Room, and I have had no chance at all to break in yet. I normally do that while they're processing my termination paperwork."

A woman in a sun-emblazoned shirt whose lumpiness suggested concealed armor burst around a corner, pointing a pistol at us. Radiance waved his hand like swatting a fly, and a ray of light swept over her. She slumped, her gun falling out of her hand, then dropped down to a sitting position.

As we passed her and started up the stairs, she mumbled, "Sparkle sparkle sparkle."

I smirked up at Radiance. "I'd say you're fired."

"So is she. No conventional weapons on shift, young lady!" Pulling a little box off his belt, he pointed it at her and pushed some buttons. It beeped. "Two demerits."

I raised my voice, already pretty loud to be heard over the Goat Alert siren. "Okay, but now we go get my Machine."

"Out of the question! There is a small army of employees back there, almost as well armed as me. We were dreadfully overstaffed after the takeover."

"This is not open to debate. I am not leaving my Machine!" Bracing my hands against his arm and chest, I wriggled, pitting my enhanced strength against his even more enhanced strength in an attempt to slip free.

... and then we reached the top of the stairs, and I had to stop, at least momentarily. An absolutely huge room, multi-story with brick outer walls and high windows, filled most of the building. Conveyor belts, bins, pulley systems, and tables crisscrossed everywhere.

My mouth already hanging open, I asked, "Is this... a toy factory?"

His lip curled in disgust. "Until Happy Days bought it."

"And you worked here?"

Disgust turned to tight-cheeked wistfulness. "I did, indeed. My job was color-coding the sprockets. They need to be easily identified, you know, but also visually appealing when put in place."

Awed, I said, "You might be the coolest person I have... "

Noise drowned me out. Not random noise. Electronic beeps and hums. Music? Yes! A little like the electro-swing Ray liked, but even more synthesized. Words lurked behind the noises, processed into an incomprehensible mumble.

It did sound better than the 'Goat Alert!' it replaced.

"That unspeakable racket is not our muzak! Happy Days prefers their unspeakable racket much more drab!" Radiance shouted, dropping me to the floor so he could put his hands over his ears.

Yeah, this was loud enough it must hurt regular flesh and blood ears. It was a jamming attack, and a distraction. I'd used the tactic several times myself. Happy Days wasn't behind this, so who else had gotten involved? Echo? He was a sound-based hero, but not music-based.

The nearest wall melted into dust, carving out a hole big enough for a teenage girl to step through. A little bigger, because it had to accommodate her huge, round backpack. That looked out of place, too big for her wiry frame to carry, but at least the cat-eared headphones over her blonde hair protected her from the musical overload.

Ah, right. I did know a music-themed tech thief. Timely entrance by Ampexia!

I recognized the round thing clamped onto one gauntleted hand, as well. A sonic liquifier. Completely harmless, unless you were a rock. Cement, bricks, and plaster counted.

Pointing at the liquifier, I asked, "How is the inventor doing?" Last I'd heard, he was miserable without it.

A fact no doubt connected to Ampexia yelling back, "If you tell anyone I used this to save you, you'll regret it!"

Wait. "You came here to save me?"

"Come on, let's get out of here!" she shouted, jerking a thumb at the hole she'd made.

"We have to get my Machine!"

Ampexia squinted. "What?"

"Can you hear me?" I yelled.

Reaching back to her round backpack, which looked like a giant stereo speaker with a metal rim more than anything else, Ampexia tugged on a switch. The deafening music turned off.

Jamming deactivated, the PA system resumed blaring, "Goat Alert!"

I pointed at the stairs. "We have to... uh... are you okay?"

She did not look okay. Open-mouthed horror spread over the older girl's face. That turned into a pained grimace with a hand slapped over her face, and when that pulled away she settled on a look of miserable resignation.

Unhooking a cable with a suction cup at the end from her backpack, Ampexia growled, "I know I'm going to regret this," as she fastened the tip against the wall. She flipped open a lid on the back of one glove, and called into the microphone, "Wakey wakey eggs and bakey!"

The floor and walls shivered as the words echoed through them. It wasn't loud, exactly, just pervasive.

In response, men and women charged up the stairs, some with the bulging shirts that signaled armor, and the rest with yellow stickers on their foreheads reading 'Temporary Security Intern.' The latter did not look happy, and only a few carried the bulky, mismatched mad science weapons all the actual security guards had.

Radiance stepped protectively in front of me—or rather, he took a step forward and shoved me behind him. Same result. I gave Ampexia a raised-eyebrow stare. "Is this what you wanted?"

Scowling, shoulders hunched, she not-exactly-answered, "Just wait for it."

The Happy Days guards were even less happy to see us than we were to see them. A quick argument broke out.

"It's a hero! He's freed the Bad Penny robot!"

"I thought we decided it's an android?"

"Which hero? Man of Courage?"

"He's got to be a villain."

"Well, look him up in the manual!"

At the back of the crowd, a rumpled man did carry a huge softcover book, and flipped through it madly. Pulling out a box much like the one Radiance had used to give demerits, the guy announced, "Unknown super-powered assailant procedure. First fill out... I'll do that later... right. Initiate security lock down!"

He pressed a button. With a loud bang, metal shutters slammed closed over every door and window, including the doorway down into the stairway. They all had big smiling suns, and the painted message 'For Your Comfort And Convenience, Please Reduce Your Breathing Until Oxygen Flow Is Restored.'

"That won't make a difference," groused Ampexia, thumbs in the pockets of her battered cargo pants.

"What are you talking about, kid?" yelled the rumpled man. He pushed forward, giving me a look at his cap with the label Senior Junior Branch Facility Overseer. It was a big cap.

One of the minions pointed. "Hey, that's Ampexia!"

"The thief?!" yelped the manager. Spooked, he retreated into the crowd of employees, flipping through his book some more. "One second. We have a procedure page for her."

Bricks cracked. Metal banged. Heavy things crashed against other things. The shutter over the stairs exploded out of its doorway, as did a fair amount of the wall next to it. Through that gap stumbled...

Gerty Goat.

She held an oversized frying pan I'd seen in a hundred (well, at least a dozen) shows out in front of her, and with the spasmic, uneven motions of an animatronic, swept it to the side as she called out singsong, "Who called for eggs and bakey?"

The motion, too fast and awkward, flung two fried eggs and a strip of freshly cooked bacon out of the pan. They sailed through the air, hit the manager to form a perfect smiley face over his regular face, and then dropped off.

Ampexia backed up against an assembly line, sat down, and pulled her hoodie over her face.

Shock flooded through me, replaced by hope and joy so powerful I thought I'd float off the ground.

Gerty Goat was alive. She was real.

Letting out a whoop, I ran across the factory floor, shouting, "Gerty!"

Her head pivoted to look at me, then her upper body turned. Her permanent smile didn't change, but her plastic eyes fixed on me and her jaw flapped as she asked, "Who's a Gerty Girl?"

"I'm a Gerty Gerty Girl!" I squealed with glee, throwing myself into her open arms.

Rapidly, but stage by stage, her upper arms closed around me, then her forearms, then her hands, holding me up and against herself in a tight hug.

"It's awake!" wailed a Happy Days employee who did not appreciate the magic of the most pure and perfect mascot in restaurant history.

"Who has the Prospective Specimen Gentle Inhibition Digital Applier?"

The manager squeezed his manual against his chest. "The clicker is in my office, and I just locked that down!"

"No, I've got it," said one of the security guards, fishing around in his pocket.

Both of them fumbled, nearly dropping the little cylinder with a button on one end that looked so much like a detonator. When he had it securely in his grip, the manager said, "We'll deal with your demerit later. Right now—"

Half a second, Penny!

He pushed the button.

Then he pushed it again.

And again. And again. And again. I kept the 'half a second' setting in mind as the room flickered and strobed around me.

"Sh—not—ting—off!" someone shouted.

Closer to hand, Gerty wailed, "My—ty—rl—hurt! Som—fe—a sm—salt! Wa—r! Gr—ed bl—ck—per!"

Somewhere in there, I went from being hugged to cradled in Gerty's arms as she leaped and stomped and stumbled across the room. She charged right through the pack of employees, some of whom were definitely repeating, "Sparkle sparkle sparkle," so I had more than one defender.

About there, the manager dropped the robot shutoff device. Ampexia thrust out a hand, fingers spread. Her glove vibrated, then the clicker vibrated, and it flew across the room right into her grip.

It didn't reach its target. The manager jumped on it, grabbing on with both hands. A couple of security guards leaped on top of him, making a pile.

Radiance gave them a calculating stare, and lifted his hands over his head. They glowed brighter and brighter, and then he swept down one arm, rolling a ball of white light with blue twinkles around it into the group. The ball went right under the minions still fighting Ampexia's sonic pull, and disappeared.

Silent light blossomed up in a fountain, sending Radiance's former coworkers staggering out of the way. The clicker floated in the air for a second, and slowly crumbled into glitter that blew away.

Leaping out of Gerty's arms, I spread my own wide. "Ta da! I'm back! And thanks to the difficulty of replacing mad science, likely to stay that way!"

The manager gritted his teeth, opened up a panel in the back of his book, and pulled out a little computer game joystick. "That's it. I'm activating security protocol level Fuzzy Bunny."

"No!" shouted quite a lot of people. One of them was Radiance, who fired another dazzling light blast. No use. The manager ducked behind his troops, who took his sparkly punishment for him.

They slumped, then jerked back upright. Everyone who had an intern sticker on their face suddenly stood at full attention.

They at least had control over their mouths. Barely. Through clenched teeth, one begged, "Please don't do this, Simon!"

Simon, the Senior Junior Branch Facility Overseer, snapped back, "It's this, or demerits for not being team players." Then, joystick held in both hands, he gave it a jerk. All the interns took a step forward.

Radiance spread his hands like a gunfighter. The lights around him rearranged. Some pieces of armor glowed much brighter, and a sheen like the reflection off a soap bubble gleamed around him. "Fuzzy Bunny is dreadfully more dangerous than it looks, children. Prepare for a fight."

Gerty's upper body jerked, not just upright but slightly backwards. Aghast, she said, "A fight?! Do I need to sing the ' Pancakes Are Better Than Global Thermonuclear War' song?"

Ooh. Tempting. I'd never heard that one, and would bet Family Farm took it out of the show lineup in the 90s, before I was even born.

Practical concerns won over artistic temptation. Clutching the animatronic goat's apron, I looked up at her with wide, concerned eyes, and said, "Gerty, I don't think they know much about teamwork."

Her head swiveled left. Her head swiveled right. Her arms lifted, again stage by stage, to clasp her four-fingered hands under her chin. The towering mechanical goat's eyelids shuttered, and her voice dripped with sincere compassion. "But without teamwork, how can they understand friendship? Listen up, everybody, while I tell you how to work together!"

I got out of the way, post-haste, as Gerty lumbered towards the assembled henchmen. The actual security guards shot her with a variety of weapons. Cannonballs, energy globes, piranhas, lawn darts—

they all slammed into Gerty, only to bounce off without effect.

Peeking out from under her hood, Ampexia sneered. "Good luck with that, nimrods. You couldn't hurt the kitsch colossus with a nuc—"

I ran over and slapped a hand over her mouth. "Not that word! You'll distract her!"

Across the factory floor, Gerty's hands shot out of their sockets, trailing fat chains as they looped twice around the Happy Days employees, then yanked them all together into a knot. Pulling them to her, Gerty crowed, "Lesson one of teamwork is a big 'ol hug! All the best lessons start with a hug, don't they, kids?"

Voice as low as the still-running alarm would allow, Ampexia said, "You know how to control her?"

"You woke her up."

She shook her head in rapid denial. "That's all I know how to do, and she won't leave me alone!"

I grinned. "Well, of course. Gerty loves music."

An idea popped into my head. While Gerty had the guards distracted... "Can I use that wall resonance thing?"

"It's a—" Ampexia started to complain, then sighed, surrendering to my grotesque ignorance. "Yeah, sure." She held out her glove.

I shouted into the microphone, "Machine! Come to me, eat your way through any obstacle in your way, and bring my bracelets—but don't eat those!"

My message delivered, I looked towards the stairs to await my baby's return.

That also let me enjoy the show. Gerty now had the entire clump of henchmen lifted off the ground in her web of arm chains, swinging them from side to side in an increasingly enthusiastic hug.

The manager found enough breath to yell, "You—"

Breath or not, he didn't get any farther. A little turret popped out of Gerty's ear, squirting a glob of bubbly white soap right into the guy's mouth.

"I don't know what you were about to say, but shame on you for almost saying it!" Gerty chided him. The brief moment of seriousness disappeared, and in a gleeful tone she asked, "Would you like to sing a song now?"

"Nooooo!" wheezed half a dozen poor fools.

Gerty ignored them. Rocking spasmodically from side to side, jiggling her captives in the process, she chanted, "Oh, there's a goat in the kitchen / And I wonder what she's fixin'..."

Being brought to life hadn't improved Gerty's singing voice even a little.

It was a perfect moment.

Radiance felt it. He hadn't moved since Gerty started her teamwork lesson. He stood wide-eyed, overcome by awe as he watched the show.

Less impressed, Ampexia squeezed her headphones over her ears, trying to shut out Gerty's awkward lyrics and even more awkward voice.

The chain holding the Happy Days goons slipped. One fell out, then the rest, all in a tumble. Whirring, her hands withdrew back into their places, only to be extended in front of her, flexing one finger at a time. "Whoops! I'm a butterfingers. Butter is very important in the kitchen."

Running across the room, vaulting over a toy-making machine in the way, I jumped up and wrapped my arms around Gerty's shoulders, rubbing my face into her scratchy, carpet-upholstery fur. "I love you, Gerty Goat. Will you come with me and be my friend forever and ever?"

Her upper body swiveled, which didn't work because I turned with it. Then her head turned, which let her grin down at me. "I'm already your friend forever and ever."

I gave her an extra squeeze, slid down, and explained, "We're just waiting for my Machine, now."

"Which way is it?" the giant artificial goat chef asked.

Radiance, still stunned into silence, pointed.

Gerty spun around on one foot, and jogged through the wall in that direction. Jigged, in fact, bouncing from one leg to the other like a stop-motion sailor as she sang, "When you lose your favorite spoon, what do you do?"

She hit an important circuit along the way. Not that the electric flash hurt her, or even slowed her down, but a number of lights went out. Thankfully, so did the Goat Alert speaker.

The Happy Days employees moaned. None seemed to be in any hurry to fight. Radiance was still staring after Gerty. I wandered back to Ampexia. "Boy, am I glad I was here when you came to rescue Gerty."

Her kneels still pulled up under her chin, she scowled up at me. "No, I told you, I came to rescue you. I didn't even know the Weapon of Mass Friendship was here. She'd finally shut up and gone away, and that was fine by me."

Uh huh. Methought she doth protest too much, but it would be impolitic to press the point. Anyway, that just raised more questions. "Not that I'm not grateful, but why would you want to rescue me?"

She growled. She rubbed her scalp. Standing up, the taller teenage girl looked me right in the eyes. "I've got a problem, and I need help. Somebody who knows how to fight. I don't trust any of the grownups in this city. They all have ulterior motives, and the superhuman 'community' is like a big club where everyone gets drunk and challenges each other to the lamest dare they can think of."

A moment of silence, and Ampexia added, "Plus, I hear you need help. You help me settle my feud, I'll help you settle yours."

I nodded. "Okay, but I'm bringing Gerty."

She rolled her eyes. "You are such a dweeb. Fine, whatever. You don't have a clue how annoying that thing is, yet."

Squealing with glee, I pumped my fist and hopped around in a circle. "I have a supervillain team again!"

Increasingly loud thumps and crunches heralded Gerty climbing out of the hole she'd created, holding my Machine in both hands. It wiggled, but made no attempt to bite her. Proof enough for me that she was really alive.

Ooh, and my teleport bracers dangled from the Machine's front legs!

I threw myself onto her for another hug. "Gerty, I love you!"

"Who's a Gerty Girl?" the animatronic asked.

"I'm a Gerty Gerty Girl!" I shouted with pride.

The goat head turned to face Ampexia. "Who's a Gerty Girl?"

"Yeah... no," replied Ampexia, heading for the exit.

Without missing a beat, Gerty looked at Radiance. "Who's a Gerty Boy?"

Lifting a shaking hand to point at himself, he said worriedly, "I'm... a... Gerty... Gerty Boy?"

Dropping me to the floor, the goat bounded over and grabbed Radiance in a hug that made him wheeze.

With her attention diverted, I wrapped my Machine around my wrist. It felt so good to have him back, like being complete again. Sliding down my coat, I clamped the bracers into place on my upper arms, over my shirt. That would do until I could properly change.

Anyway... "I can't teleport back to my base. I'd leave you and Gerty behind," I told Ampexia.

"I've got a truck, a driver's license, and my own place," she said, jerking a thumb towards the outside world.

"I get to ride in the back!" shouted Gerty. Her arms swung up, then she lurched towards the exit. Her jerky, animatronic movements made for clumsy walking, but launched her into the air in a skipping run pretty well.

Okay, the run was also clumsy. She tripped over something I didn't see—maybe her own foot—and rolled through the wall, tearing out a big tunnel right out to the street. "Oopsy doopsy!"

Grinning enormously, hands in my pockets, I followed her out.

Radiance trailed behind us, lingering long enough to get out his little Happy Days button box, he jabbed its keyboard over and over. "And as a reward for being such nasty coworkers, I am giving all of you the maximum number of demerits! Enjoy!"

Cries of despair sounded inside the heap.

"I was about to get promoted!"

"They'll send me back to Sewing Apparatus Location Straw Pile Facility!"

"Hey... do you think we might get fired?"

"Oooooh, yeah!"

Ampexia did, indeed, have a large and battered pickup truck outside. Giggling with childish glee, Gerty crawled up onto the bed, and sat motionless, except for her head, which spun around in random directions, smiling at everything.

I gave my smile to Radiance. "Thank you for saving me."

He got down on one knee, which he had to do to look me in the eye. Taking one of my hands in both of his, he said, "Thank you, Bad Penny, for giving me the push I needed to become who I wanted to be."

Straightening up, he looked off over the Los Angeles skyline, towards the eastern mountains. "And now, there's still some day left, so Radiance shall save it!"

He jumped, and a rainbow appeared under his feet. He slid away up its curve, as smoothly as if he were sledding downhill.

Pushing open the passenger side door, Ampexia leaned her head out and called out to me, "Get in, already!"

"Wait!"

In a mad rush, I ran inside. The factory floor wasn't the only room Gerty's tunnel opened into. Ducking into an office, I grabbed pens and paper, and ran back into the truck.

Ampexia looked at my haul as I pulled the door shut, shook her head, and didn't say anything. As the truck started up, I wrote.

Hello Mother. Hello Father.

Greetings from supervillain camp.

Today, we had our first big competitive event. I thought I was in trouble, since none of the other kids like me. It turns out, there's always a friend to be found if you look! Me and two other outcasts made a team, and we beat them all.

I think camp will be okay from here on out, but I still can't wait to come home.

Penny

There. If Miss Lutra was telling the truth about how my parents felt, someday Mom and Dad would get to see these letters. Maybe before I defeated my parasite twin.

CHAPTER ELEVEN

Ampexia rubbed her gloved hands together, staring down the tunnel. "A seaside mansion. This is going to rock. My lair is only a sealed-up bookstore. It does have good soundproofing."

I grimaced, considerably less sure about this. "The mansion's not part of the base, but it's true that nobody's using it. First we have to get you in past the traps. By myself, I teleport."

She jerked a thumb behind us at Gerty, who loomed in the enclosed underground garage and spun her head in excited circles. "Use the battering ram."

"I'm not a ram, I'm a nanny! I love taking care of kids!" corrected the hulking animatronic.

Wishing I could hunch my shoulders, I said, "I couldn't live with myself if she got damaged."

"The juggernaut jughead doesn't get damaged. She doesn't even get stained. You saw when those meatheads shot at her."

Ampexia's disrespectful attitude towards the entertainment legend that is Gerty Goat bothered me, but she was right. The Original wouldn't booby trap his own daughter's base with anything worse than the cheap mad science weapons Happy Days gave its hoodlums, right?

Because he was such a good father.

Put your trust in goat, Penny Akk. Spinning around, I grabbed one of Gerty's hands, and gave her a beaming smile. "Gerty Gerty Gerty!"

"Penny Penny Penny!" she chanted back.

I pointed down the long, dark corridor towards the distant portcullis and its garish pink background. "Would you go fetch my teddy bear?"

She gasped. "You can't go to bed without a teddy bear! That's just not right!"

Gray arms in blue sleeves swung up and forward. In a series of lurches, no two joints moving in sync, she thundered down the hall ahead of us.

She'd gotten about a third of the way down when an alarm went off, way down in the base. "AAAA" yelled Gerty in alarm, her arms windmilling. At the top of their arc, they ripped a hole in the ceiling. Electronic parts fell out. Something else crunched under her next step, and the alarm went silent.

A few yards down, a metal shutter slammed down behind her. Ampexia and I were treated to about a half second of silence before Gerty staggered back through it, knocking the trap off its hinges and bending it in the middle. She waved her arms, which were covered in a purple plastic goop that sprayed out of a turret in the ceiling.

"You're a soda jerk!" Gerty accused it. Her mouth opened wide, and wind roared around us as purple gunk got sucked into her maw. When she'd swallowed most of what weighed down her body, she positioned her mouth under the turret, letting it spray right down her throat. That went on for several seconds of loud gargling, and then her head shot up on an extensible neck, slamming her jaws closed on the nozzle of the trap itself.

Gulp gulp gulp echoed up the corridor. Finally, the turret ran out of material, and with a protracted series of crunches Gerty ripped it free of the ceiling by pulling her head back into place.

"What was I? Oh, yeah! Teddyyyyy! Teddy teddy teddy! Gerty's comin' for ya!" Arms extended again, she charged through the other metal wall that was supposed to form a box. This one got a goat-shaped hole ripped in it.

That seemed to be it for traps. Gerty didn't slow down, and was about to impact the portcullis at the far end when we heard a wet noise, and she stopped, frozen in place. The air gleamed around her, as if it had become solid. Blue light shone around the wall, floor, and ceiling.

A stasis trap? Seriously? Okay, I'd seen one in Mech's hideout. Someone must make them. But you couldn't tell me it wasn't crazy expensive.

Even without my super power, I knew what to do. I'd have the Machine eat into the wall until it found the mechanism and broke it.

I had just reached the broken alarm panel when my plan changed. The shiny air cracked, shattered, and vanished back into regular see-through air. The blue glow in the wall turned orange, the color of melting rock. Gerty finished her charge, crashing through the portcullis and knocking it into what used to be Miss A's base.

Gerty stumbled to a halt. Her head spun around to face backwards, and she called out to us, "Oops. Maybe it's not broken. Maybe it's always open, because we're friends with the whole wide world!"

We didn't answer her cue, so she waited, silent and motionless, while we followed her. I wanted to applaud, but it was more important to watch my step.

Scowling, Ampexia stepped around harden purple splatters on the floor. "These traps are dumb. Superheroes are dumb for putting them in. They could hurt themselves. They probably do."

I thought about that for a few seconds. "You know, I bet you're onto something. I should have asked her, but I bet Miss A never used this hallway at all. She probably had a safer way in, and this is the lure for suckers. That would match what I've heard about the Original's paranoia."

Or maybe her dad figured that if Marcia got caught in a trap, she deserved what happened to her. It would be nice to think he cared more than that.

Gerty's head turned to watch us, mouth open and eyes blinking, as we stepped around her into the control room.

Ampexia got her first full look at the bludgeoning pinkness of Miss A's decors. Face tight, she said, "This is way too small for two supervillains. How do we get into the house?"

I pointed at a blank stretch of pink wall in an empty pink corner. "There's a stairway over there somewhere, but I don't know how you activate it. I guess... Gerty, do you want to play a game?"

"Do I?!"

"There's a secret door in that corner! Help me find it!"

She clunked across the room, crushing a couple of Marcia's old trophies. Robot hands patted the wall curiously. *Thump thump. Thump thump.*

Crunch.

Ampexia watched Gerty's attempts to free herself destroy what used to be a secret door. With an exasperated sigh, the blonde high schooler leaned over to me and said, "I try not to bash on what other people are into, but your robot role model is majorly stupid."

Gerty's head swung around. Then her upper body swung around. Then her legs thumped around. Proudly, she announced, "I'm dumber than a sack full of hammers on a clothes line in Februtember! But you know what's more important? That I love you."

She spread her arms, and I leaped into her embrace. Ampexia took a step back, only to get yanked by a projectile grapple hand and yanked in to join the hug.

Sympathetic to the fact that my new teammate was not into goat hugs as much as me, and also needed to breathe, I said, "Gerty, you know the game's not done, right? You have to find the door at the other end of the secret passage."

Her arms swung wide, dropping us, and she gasped. "I'll find it as soon as I wash this plaster off my hands. A clean cook is the only acceptable kind of cook, you know!"

Gerty tromped up the stairs. Ampexia followed, and I followed Ampexia. We passed through the broken wall my animatronic idol hadn't even noticed on her search for a bathroom, and into a library.

This place was a wreck, and had been a wreck before Gerty got here. Stacks of valuable old books had clearly been lined up and used for punching. A painting of a handsome, muscular man, his smiling wife, and their golden-haired little girl had been defaced with a black magic marker, which put a mustache and devil horns on the father, scrawled black holes for the eyes of the wife, and colored the girl's hair black.

Ampexia paid more attention to the living room on the other side of a wide doorway. "Cooool. That TV is huge. Look at all those game systems. And the stereo isn't total garbage. Is that seriously marble on the dining room chairs? Who would do that? This place is going to rock as a hideout. I am going to get all my things, and live here until they send an army to chase me out."

I jerked a thumb at the front of the house. "Don't come in through the doors. I bet they're trapped worse than the hallway downstairs. At least we know that's clear. You really don't mind the mess?"

She kicked a vacuum cleaner that had been broken in half, and had the imprint of Marcia's toes in the casing. "Naah, that makes it feel more like home."

I clapped my hands together. "So! With that settled, what's the job you need my help with? Know a place I can steal some weapons, first? Gerty is great for brute force, but I have doubts about her tactical—what?"

Ampexia gave me such a convincing look of suffering and exasperation that I actually did feel guilty. With exaggerated pointing gestures, she explained, "I am going to go get my laptop out of the truck, hook up to these speakers, and edit some nightcore. Then I'm going to call a friend. Because I have a life. I don't steal things every day. You need to take time off, too. This is not healthy."

Loud thumping interrupted us as Gerty stomped up the hall. Good thing this mansion was roomy. Water dripped off of her, leaving a trail of puddles. Some of it flew around from her extended arms, wagging up and down opposite each other. "I'm a Cleany Claribelle! I also washed the dishes!"

Rubbing her hand down her face, Ampexia growled, "And if you can shut that thing down, please do it, because I can't create music with her telling me I need to find a rhyme for 'udder.'"

"Udders make butter! Let's all have another!" Gerty singsonged happily.

I sighed, leaning forward since I couldn't slump my shoulders. Walking up to Gerty, I gently slipped an arm around her aproned middle, feeling the rough metal struts underneath of a body packed with machinery. "It's that time, Gerty. Mi mi mi miiiii..."

She recognized the slow, sad tone. Wagging from side to side, we sang in unison. "The man behind the curtain / Says it's time to go for certain / But I wish I had the time to bake a piiiiie."

Head tilted to one side, Ampexia watched us sing the song that ends a Gerty Goat show, her expression twisting into different forms of puzzlement.

"Come back soooooonnnnn..." At the last words, Gerty's voice slurred, deepened, and her eyes closed. She slumped forward, arms hanging, until with a clang something locked internally, stopping her from falling over.

I faked a deep breath, and stepped away. Now I could talk to my new blonde teammate seriously. Rapping my knuckles on my wrist produced a hollow clonk. "I haven't got a life anymore. A freaky brain parasite stole it with my real body."

"So?"

I scowled in anger, and then in thoughtfulness. She was serious. That was obvious.

With my parents unavailable, I'd assumed everything else was also gone, but... was that really true? Perhaps it was time that Penelope Akk turned her currently solid-state genius brain towards the most difficult puzzle of all—being me.

Chapter Twelve

Ducking behind a pillar, I fired desperately with my new weapon. Direct hit!

"But what is this? No! My puny Earthling technology is useless!" I gasped, pulling the trigger over and over, emptying my ammunition into my opponent, only to watch it all be sucked into her body.

Opposite me, Barbara scooped up a ball of water out of the fountain, and flung it at Jacky like normal kids would a snowball. Jacky must have had eyes in the back of her head, because a cavity opened in her gelatinous blue body, closing around the ball.

Actually, since her eyes weren't really eyes, I had no idea how Jacky saw, or in what directions.

What I did know was that she'd gotten awfully big, even in the puddle-shallow kids' play fountains next to Griffith Park. Awfully, awfully big.

I realized what was coming too late. My teleport bracers would have looked ridiculous on bare arms, and I had no real cover. The skinny fountain poles were a joke.

SPLAT. Jacky's body compressed, like a squeezed balloon. Barbara and I shrieked as waves of water crashed over us.

Then we did what any reasonable person would do, and doubled over laughing.

Shaking my head to clear water out of my braids, I stepped out onto the grass. My feet needed some shaking too. Water pooled inside them. Fortunately, wiggling my toes helped it drip out of the joints.

That gave me time to shake my puny robotic fist at the uncaring skies. "Curses! Foiled by my failure to anticipate that a slime-based hominid would absorb water!"

Giggling, we headed over to the picnic basket, while Jacky compressed down to a translucent blue girl shape, explaining with a hint of gurgle, "It's not safe for me to swim, so this was nice. I can get melty in the shower, if I'm not careful."

From out of the woven wicker basket, Barbara withdrew a neatly folded red-and-white checker tablecloth, which she spread out on the grass for us. Waiting under the cloth, I saw plates and tableware.

I gave her a smirk, leaning as heavily on 'friendly' over 'teasing' as possible. "A picnic traditionalist, I see."

Her ghost-pale cheeks flushed. "Goth culture is more about aesthetic than depression. Wait until you see my parasol."

The parasol was not a joke. It lay next to the basket, and even furled I had never seen so much white and pink lace in my life.

It would only be the icing on the cake. Instead of any ordinary modern swimsuit, she'd arrived vintage Victoriana, in a one-piece bathing costume of red-and-white stripes that covered from neck to wrists to ankles. Even her black hair, currently sporting one purple stripe, had been rolled up and tucked into a matching red-and-white cap. The outfit didn't go well with her soft figure. Barbara was already more hourglass than most adults. A more traditional bikini or one-piece would be worst. Whether you liked the effect or hated it, there would definitely have been too much Barbara and not enough swimsuit.

She fit in perfectly with the group. I wore a plain blue swimsuit, which suited my skinny frame as well as anything would, and showed off all the mannequin joints on my arms and legs. The ball joints on my hips were a little freaky, to be honest. Jacky the blue slime girl didn't need to wear anything. If she decided she did, I was pretty sure she knew how to shape and color change to fake it.

One of us alone might have gotten attention. Together, we became an LA thing and nobody paid any attention.

Hey, maybe they thought we were being filmed for a movie?

To dispel any hint of cynicism, I treated them both to a beaming smile. "Thank you both for coming. I wasn't sure anyone would want to hang out with me."

Barbara smiled back, more softly. Somehow, her black lipstick remained intact despite our splashing around. Magic? Mad science? Who would make mad science lipstick? "I like having more friends. After I started reading Abigail's books, I had to hide from regular people, in case I hurt them. Now that everyone knows about my powers..."

Jacky snickered. "The supervillains can't get enough of you."

Now it was Barbara's turn to smirk, and even roll her eyes. She did cynicism surprisingly well. "A pretty dress and healing powers are all you need to get a statue dedicated to you in Chinatown. I've heard the words 'Confidentially, I was fighting this fungus monster...' five times this week. My healing powers aren't even that good."

"You cure disease well. That makes you a marvel all by yourself," said Jacky.

Barbara's cheeks got pink again. "Says the girl who can't physically get sick. But the point is, they're not real friends like you two."

"I feel like the kids who knew Jack didn't know me, anyway," mused Jacky.

That made me blink. I didn't know what to say about it. I'd forgotten that before I met her, Jacky had to pretend to be a boy.

Barbara unpacked sandwiches which, true to form, had been wrapped neatly in wax paper. I opened up my plain brown paper bag, pulling out my own sandwich. The fake robot bread might be as hard as a cracker, but the taste of cheese and wheat when I took a bite made my head spin. The first bite evaporated, but on the second my reflexes kicked in, and I swallowed. The illusion of really eating completed a moment of perfect peace like I hadn't felt since I got roboticized. The sandwich came with a box of fake apple juice, complete with a fake apple juice box I had to punch a straw into. Hopefully the logo would keep regular people from drinking it. The box displayed a picture of a clunky gray robot drinking from a box with a picture of a clunky gray robot drinking from... well, and so on. This being the product of mad science, I assumed the recursion was infinite, and somewhere in there a quark had a picture of a robot drinking from a box carved into it.

As I lifted the straw towards my mouth, I heard a distinctive, rapid *chunk chunk chunk* in the distance. Barbara and Jacky both stopped and stared up the street behind me.

"What is that?" Barbara asked.

"I think it's a Gerty Goat robot," answered Jacky, amused and fascinated.

I turned around, not actually dreading what I would see. Sure enough, Gerty jogged up the road, bouncing in her spasmodic animatronic run. She made good time, anyway. Cars wisely gave her lots of room, but she wasn't slowing down traffic much.

Questions flooded me. How did she locate me? When did she wake up? How long had she been following me? I'd been all over town today getting things ready for this picnic!

However she detected me, I was definitely the target. As soon as she got to the no parking curb, she swerved off the road and galloped towards me, shouting, "Who's a Gerty Girl?"

There was only one thing to do.

Leaping to my feet, I ran over and grabbed her wrist. Pointing at people walking their dogs, I told her with wide-eyed concern, "Gerty! You're just in time! One of those dogs must be Sheepy the Sheep Dog. Can you watch them and tell me which one it is?"

She gasped. Her upper body swung forward and down like a drinky bird. Wobbling in the world's worst dog impression, she bounced off to inspect the real canines.

Had I just unleashed villainous chaos and destruction? Well, I did hear screaming, but it was two kids shouting, "Gerty!" and Gerty shouting back, "Who's a Gerty Boy?"

I looked back at Jacky and Barbara. The latter chewed delicately on a sandwich. The former had turned almost opaque, so we wouldn't have to watch her slime girl digestive processes.

Dabbing her lips with a handkerchief—which still didn't disturb her lipstick—Barbara said, "I'm sure some of the other kids from the club would love to hang out with you. I know Marcia would, but I'm not sure how to get ahold of her."

For a moment she stopped, her mouth tightened, and she continued with an apologetic tone, "I did pass the invitation on to Cassie. She said she would try to sneak out, but I guess she didn't make it. Her sister is only letting her spend time with the flesh and blood Penny."

"Sue still hates you. No loss there," commented Jacky, now definitely more sarcastic than I'd ever heard before.

So. Cassie was hanging out with the parasite. It was weirdly flattering. Cassie liked me so much, she would get all of me she could get, in any body. Not cool of the parasite to take advantage of that, but definitely not Cassie's fault.

My silence must have stretched, because Barbara said, "When school starts up, Ruth and Rachel won't be able to keep Cassie away from you."

Uh, woah. I sat back, feeling the illusion of my muscles all tightening up at that alien thought. "School? I intended to have my body back before then."

She shrugged, making me jealous. "If you don't, I know Upper High will accept you. Polly Vinyl Chloride, my stepmother, is a robot. She went to Upper High."

Jacky leaned forward, lifting a squishy blue finger. "If you do switch bodies and she becomes the robot, they'll let her in. Either way, you'll have to maintain a truce on school grounds." Then she smiled, looking over at our currently candy-striped goth picnic partner. "I'm looking forward to going to the same school as Barbara."

"For one year. I'm going to be a senior. After that..." Barbara's head lolled back, looking up at the sky. Her eyes were green—no, as I watched, they turned the same blue as the post-Gloom summer sky. "I don't know what I want to do about college. I have a career for life with my healing powers, but that doesn't mean I don't want a degree. A lot will depend on how Abigail is doing, I guess."

Nodding, Jacky leaned back on one hand, her arm compressing a bit before pushing her back up. The pool, an inch deep though it was, had left her more 'slime' than 'girl.' "I like history. It's a shame that's not one of the special programs at Upper High."

I sat up sharply. "History is my favorite subject!"

Jacky giggled, her eyes widening in eagerness. "Did you cover World War One this year, too?"

My grin had to be blinding. "It's one of my favorite topics, ever. Who knew that such a tragedy could also be so silly? Oh, hey, did your class go over Roanoke? All those mysterious statues?" I sank back onto a hand in imitation of Jacky's pose, my enthusiasm fading to speculation. "I wonder if Barbara and her sister might be the only two people who know what happened there."

Across the blanket, Barbara inhaled sharply. Jacky sat up, and warned me, "Asking questions like that is a bad idea."

Barbara, however, held up one of her hands, palm out, and gave us a weak smile. Her eyes had turned back to green, but a blank, plastic green, not any human color. "It's okay. What I like about having super-powered friends is that you understand. It's not just that you don't freak out I hear voices. You'll get it when I say that they're hard to fight because I know they're telling the truth."

Rubbing her hands over her face, she mumbled into them, "I'm so lucky my stepmother is immune."

I frowned. "Immune to voices?"

She shook her head, and took another slow breath before continuing. Her casual tone rapidly returned as she explained, "Immune to our powers. She says it's because our magic doesn't make sense, and she always makes sense. I know it helps bring Abigail back to reality."

Jacky reached over and squeezed Barbara's hand. "I know you were worried if She Who Wots didn't stop being a villain, Mourning Dove would go after her."

My upper torso twitched and wriggled. "There's a fight I wouldn't want to bet on."

Barbara grimaced, although it had no real emotion behind it. "Mourning Dove would win. Being all-knowing is useless when you can't think clearly about that knowledge."

The slime girl's brow suddenly furrowed, or at least pressed down in a thoughtful way. She gave her friend a sharp, curious look. "You're officially in the community, now. What is up with Marcia and Mourning Dove? I've seen them together."

I chuckled, wondering that myself. Then that thought split off another, a strange thought I had to say aloud. "Are we... gossiping?"

"Yeah, and it's great," answered Jacky, with a grin that literally stretched off her face. Freaky, but also charming.

I tried to think about that. In the distance, what sounded like a couple of kindergarteners sang a song about identifying sheep with Gerty. I'd never heard this song before. I was pretty sure she'd started making up new ones.

The corners of my mouth pulled up in a smile that felt like it happened before I even knew I was happy. "I didn't think I'd get to have this until I got my regular life back. Especially since nobody believes me."

"I do," said Barbara, and after the slightest pause turned defensive. "Not because of the voices. Just being your friend while this all went on, seeing it with my own eyes, the body switching story makes sense to me. I wish... I was sure enough to take sides. Attacking the wrong Penny would be horrible."

I shook my head quickly. "Oh, no, I'm fine with that. I didn't want to put you in danger of your powers anyway."

"More evidence this is the real Penelope," commented Jacky dryly.

Blushing again, Barbara tucked a lock of wet black hair back under the bathing cap. "Maybe I can't help you in combat, but I'm happy to be your friend, and put together a normal life while you work this out."

"Huh," I said to that. This was all a lot to put together.

Life didn't have to consist of revenge. I could take breaks. People wanted to see me. Buying a computer would be a good idea. If seeing people was an option, maybe spending time alone playing computer games was, too. Maybe this robot body had improved reflexes?

As I watched Gerty dispense sheep-shaped cookies to a confused family, I mentally prepared a letter to write when I got back to my base.

Dear Mom and Dad,

I miss you, but camp gets easier once you start making friends...

Chapter Thirteen

Full villainous disclosure: I was no expert with computer technology. Competent, sure, but with Ampexia, the difference between 'competent' and 'expert' became clear. She didn't have a super power, but my new gaming computer and the monitors and machines already in Miss A's base were turning into a rat's nest of wires.

"You won't get much use out of these, but you'll have all the monitors any girl could dream of, and access to the bug transmissions. Heh. That's so messed up." She snorted in amusement.

"What, the trackers or the cameras?" I asked, watching her hook up another wire. How did she find a motherboard with so many USB ports? I mean, I was there at the store, but I still didn't think they made them. Good thing I could actually spend my supervillain money now.

"All of it. I heard superheroes bugged people, but I didn't expect to see it."

I pursed my lips, and made wild guesses based on almost no experience. "I think only the weirdos do." Miss Lutra, after all, was legendary for her shamelessness, and Mom for having the kind of inhumanly logical standards that wouldn't mind. "From what I hear, the Original was a serious control freak."

'Was' might be the operative word, there. Even with access to super-powered healing, having your skeleton shattered was the kind of thing it was hard to recover from enough to still fight crime.

She tinkered some more, then gave me a suspicious look through her mad scientist goggles. "How are you feeling?"

Locking my fingers together, I swung my arms up above my head, bent my back, and stretched. It felt a little janky without proper shoulders, but my robot arms swiveled better than the human versions. "Better. Less pressured. I still want to get straight to helping you with your problem."

She sat back, turned the computer on, and stared at it until the monitors lit up in sequence, all with different startup screens. "Yeah. The longer it's not fixed, the worse it will get."

"So, what's up?"

She watched the screens, not looking at me, voice neutral. "An object was stolen from me. It is dangerous and has personal importance, and I have to get it back. The thieves are dangerous, our goofy goat-bot is useless against them, and they keep the object on their person at all times. I can't do this myself. I need a fighter, and not an adult, because they're all freaks in this town. You'll get opportunities to go full supervillain, and you love that."

I ran my tongue along my lips, voice dropping to a purr. "I've had some small tastes lately, but yes, I miss it. Do I get any more details about this job?"

Ampexia shrugged, still focused on the computer screen, as if arranging icons was difficult. "No point until you're equipped and ready."

That could not be a less subtle hint she didn't want to talk about it. I didn't want to make her uncomfortable by pushing, not until I had to. So, I changed the subject. "Despite my reputation, you steal tech way more often than I do. Any ideas on where I can find some mad science weapons without actually hurting anybody?"

Ampexia's slender face split with a sly grin. "Yeah. I do."

"*This* is the place?" I asked, staring across the parking lot in astonishment.

Look, I'd been around the evil block a time or two, but this was the first time that block contained an agricultural supply store. Yes, the store was huge, actually filling the block. Granted, it had a giant cardboard goat sign over the entrance, for no obvious reason since the name on that sign was 'Oh, No! Beans!'

Goats were rapidly impressing me as symbols of mad science. The giant robot goat climbing out of Ampexia's truck bed helped with that.

"Why would a store for farmers have mad science?" I asked, making sure to raise one eyebrow for that lopsided bewildered look.

"Because most super-powered weapons weren't designed to be weapons," my immaculately jaded blonde colleague answered.

Gerty provided her critical perspective. "Plants are food, and without food, you can't make breakfast!"

It is quite hard to miss a fourteen-year-old in a steampunk scientist costume, a sixteen-year-old with a speaker as big as the rest of her strapped to her back, and a lurching, squeaking, seven-foot-tall anthropomorphic goat. Prospective customers got back into their cars and drove away. Employees around the entrance put on a competition for most nonchalant exit. A few people just saw us and went in to shop anyway.

Stepping through the glass double doors, I threw my arms wide and declared, "Farmers, salesmen, and children of all ages. You have been blessed, for today your humble store is the victim of the newly reformed Inscrutable Machine!"

Behind me, glass crashed and tinkled, and Gerty asked, "Golly gosh, did you feel that? Is it raining?"

Most of the store went quiet as we marched down to the customer service desk. Man, this place was big. Agricultural supply stores looked a lot like hardware stores, with towering racks of machines and parts and tools, but with added bags. Bags, stacked on groaning shelves, filling whole aisles. In the distance, I saw a seriously big, garishly purple tractor looming over the customers examining it. In the farther distance, something mooed. My numb robo-sinuses must be missing quite a stink.

An older man and woman regarded us with wide, anxious eyes as we reached the desk, and I gave the service bell a series of loud whacks.

"Nobody ever raids us," said the terrified woman, in a low tone that clearly wasn't meant for me.

"But we paid our supervillain insurance, right?" asked the man, his mouth equally frozen and words coming from behind a nervous grimace.

"Yes."

"Oh, thank goodness." His demeanor changed, slightly. Leaning forward, he raised a finger and asked more loudly, "What can I do for you girls?"

Ampexia slapped the counter with her gauntleted hand. "Where's the high-tech department?"

His arm slowly rose, pointing a few rows over. "Power tools are in—"

Ampexia's groan cut him off. "What a bunch of dinguses." Twisting a dial on her wrist, she shouted into the gauntlet's microphone and her voice echoed around the store. *"You are all a bunch of dinguses!"*

Suave and leaderly, I flourished my hand in a circle. "We're shopping for something a bit higher-tech than that."

"I don't know what you're talking about," the man answered. Oh, what an obvious lie. He did such a good job of sounding sincere. If only the words himself weren't so obviously defensive!

I bowed my head obligingly. "Then I suppose we must do our own browsing. Gerty! I have a gift for you." Scooping up the counter bell, I tossed it back over my shoulder.

She caught it with a clunk. Her jaw hung open as she stared at it. Then her body tilted precariously to one side, and she chimed the little bell as she gleefully sang over it, "Ding ding ding! Listen to the pretty ring!"

Hopping happened. The floor thundered and cracked. Ampexia and I left Gerty to her song. She slid over the counter, and I vaulted it.

"Gotta be back here," Ampexia said, knocking on the back wall.

I peeked into the office behind the counter. It had its own bathroom door. And the next door down opened into a workshop for shaping wood and metal, with tools that would have been great if I still had a super power. "Not somewhere exotic? Inside a storage bin, or under the floors?"

"That's too fancy. These people aren't smugglers, they just have special merchandise for special customers. Not that I have a clue what qualifies someone as an elite farmer."

The older customer service woman scowled at us. "It's not about wealth, if you're wondering. I hate factory farms. The best farmers are the ones with skill and passion."

Ampexia lifted her goggles to give the woman a sneer. "In California's agricultural market? Yeah, right."

They glared death at each other, but any incipient battle was preempted by the other incipient battle.

"AaaaaaaaAAAAAAAAH!" In the distance, a scream dopplered from faintly audible under Gerty's lyrics to a mighty war cry. I turned around in time to see the superheroine arrive.

She had to be new to this. She was eighteen, tops; scrawny, with so many freckles that it looked more like she had brown skin spotted with white. Actually, that might be it, since her stiff, jutting hair was also brown with white spots. Brown-and-white vertical stripes on a skin-tight spandex bodysuit made her look tall, but Gerty still dwarfed her. This became apparent as the heroine zoomed down an aisle at high speed, vaulted over a pile of debris, and kicked my animatronic sidekick in the face. Repeatedly. This girl had seriously fast legs.

Paying attention to the back wall, I'd tuned out Gerty's performance. I'd had to. Clapping along and dancing would have interfered with the theft. Now that I was paying attention again, I could see the destruction she'd wreaked, collapsing the shelves in our area and spilling bags everywhere. Cracks lined the floor, and displays farther off had fallen over. A whole lot of people were also standing back at a safe distance to watch her show.

Now we had a new act, with the young superheroine circling Gerty in a passable display of super-speed, dispensing kick after kick that produced thumps and clangs but didn't budge the goat-bot in the slightest.

Gerty always grinned, but she looked particularly happy and excited as her head turned around and around to follow her attacker. About the fourth time the heroine came around to the front, Gerty's arms swung up and then out, and she shouted, "Who's a Gerty Girl?"

"AAAAA!" shouted the lanky heroine, stumbling backwards, falling over, staggering to her feet, weaving around dizzily, and then running away down an aisle. At the very end of it, she turned around and shouted, "I'm the Emu!"

"Emu eggs have blue or green shells, are as big as twenty-four chicken eggs together, and taste like chicken eggs too! Learning is fun! Stay in school!" Gerty announced to the lurking crowd.

"Ah ha! Death from above!" shouted the Emu. In the few seconds while Gerty talked, she'd managed to climb to the top of a row of shelving, and now she streaked down it and leaped from the end, landing on top of Gerty's shoulders.

A series of furious kicks to Gerty's face, neck, and jaw later, the novice heroine declared in despair, "Where do you have to kick this thing to hurt it?"

Gerty pondered this for about five seconds. "Let's sing the Leg Song!" she cried, pumping her arms in and out, and bending her knees to bob up and down.

By now, it was pretty clear the Emu was not sophisticated enough to go after the brain if she couldn't defeat the brawn. I got back to work. Ampexia had already abandoned the show, looking at a readout on one wrist while working her way down the wall, thumping it with her knuckles every couple of yards.

She was on her fourth thump, tops, when she pointed. "Reinforced wall. It's a vault or something."

Nodding, I stepped up to that spot, cupped my hands to my mouth, and shouted, "Gerty Gerty Goat! I hear you have the looooongest legs the farmyard ever did see!"

"I'm a tall drink of water!" she chanted back, not pausing her spasmodically rhythmic kicking. The foot lifted in my direction shot out on a telescoping rod, punched through the wall, and ripped a large section of it open before she pulled it back and returned to her kicking dance.

Myself, not wishing to take an animatronic boot to the head, I teleported onto Gerty's shoulder to wait out the strike. Precariously balanced on the other shoulder, the Emu let out a shriek as I appeared, and fell off backwards.

That caught Gerty's attention. As the heroine hit the floor and immediately rebounded to her feet, Gerty asked her, "Are you a tall drink of water, too?" Not content to wait for an answer, a hatch in the goat robot's chest popped open, and out ratcheted what looked an awful lot like the barrel of a cannon.

"AAAAAA!" shrieked the Emu. Her legs flailed, but it took a second for them to line up to actually go anywhere. That was time enough for a blast of water to drench the young woman.

The Emu had had enough. Eyes whirling, fists pumping, back arched, she ran for it, whipping down the aisle towards the front door like an arrow.

A voice came from Gerty, much more buzzy and synthetic than her usual. "Unhappiness detected. Arming long-range frown-seeking love missile." The fur carpet, blue smock fabric, and white apron string split on her right shoulder, opening up to reveal the crowded mechanisms inside. Out of that slid a rocket as long as my arm, covered in valentine's hearts, smiley faces, and 'I Love You!' graffiti.

Wise to the better part of valor, I blinked over to the customer service counter to watch. The missile leveled, and Gerty's uncharacteristic mechanical voice said, "Target locked. Fire."

It did, the missile streaking off in a blast of smoke after the Emu. She had already reached the front door, but the missile flew faster. Her attempts to weave through the parking lot did her no good, either, as the projectile turned in flight, and... well, she was too far away for me to get a good look. I saw a pink, sparkly puff, heard another panicky shout, and a distant scratchy recorded voice sang, "Daisy, Daisy, give me your answer, do..."

Hopping off the desk, I joined Ampexia at the entrance to the secret room. "I was expecting more resistance than that."

She smirked. "Yeah, it's not like we didn't stick out like a sore thumb on the drive here. The serious heroes must be busy."

We stepped through the hole together, and examined the secret vault.

Which, I had to say, did not really deserve the term. Ampexia had been right. This was just a big closet with a reinforced hidden door. On the shelves, with labels hanging from them on strings, were scattered oddball pieces of mad science.

One immediately caught my eye: A metal stick around the length of my forearm, with twistable rings and covered in mysterious etched symbols. It was the telekinesis device Claudia's mother Irene referred to as her Push Rod.

How had that gotten here? Last I saw it... Actually, I wasn't sure when I'd last seen it, but it had been in my possession. Did someone steal it? What other of my creations had been taken by tech thieves, without me even noticing? I'd used the Push Rod with a remote controlled robot. Had the robot been taken, too? Or did I build it into something?

Whatever, I would leave it here. It was a wonderfully useful device, but mediocre as a weapon. Let someone with non-combat needs enjoy it. I would play with new toys.

Let's see, the thing with multiple handles and saw blades on the front looked interesting. I heaved it off its shelf, only to discover it wasn't as heavy as it looked. 'Mega-Plow Hoe', the label said, and it even came with instructions! Yes, I could sure use this. And what was this thing like a gun with a big glass bulb full of paper? 'Kudzu-Eating Wasp Sprayer. Ship to Carolina Facility.'

Ah. No, that would be left here. There were depths of cruelty too evil for me.

The thing with the silvery, brick-sized sponge with wires sticking out of it, on the other hand, looked great. The label said it was for highly localized weather control and irrigation. Oh, yes, this would be perfect.

Ampexia barked, "Yes!" and snatched up what looked like a little metal lamp made mostly of wire. More excited than I had seen her before, she held it up to me. "Subsonic insect repellent! I've always wanted this thing. Watch this."

Either she had expected it to be here, or she really had always wanted it, because she had a place ready to fix it into the top of her stereo backpack. She punched some buttons on her gauntlet and crashing death metal boomed out of her backpack. Then she flipped a switch, and the music changed. It was still the same music, but now I could only hear it because it hummed faintly out of the walls and floor.

Clearly, other people could hear the music. The customer service reps we had terrorized yelped. The crowd in the distance let out a series of unhappy shouts. "My head... can't... so dizzy! Take it away!" whimpered the old woman.

Ampexia, flinched and grimacing despite her cat-eared headphones, turned it off. "Okay, that's going to take some work, but it will be awesome, especially with robot teammates."

I'd already gone through most of the room's inventory. It wasn't exactly an armory. I did notice a little plastic disk.

"Huh. Is that the sonic liquefier?" I asked out loud.

Ampexia gave me what looked almost like a guilty grin. "That's how I knew the mad science agricultural tools were getting routed through here. Leave it. I promised the builder it would be used for its actual intended purpose."

Out in the store, Gerty said, "Who's your little boy or girl? Is it their birthday?"

We had company.

A superhero strolled down the the bag-strewn corridor towards Gerty. He looked particularly harmless and unassuming, an old man with sagging wrinkles and thick white handlebar mustache that nearly hid his mouth. He wore a jacket too big for his skinny frame, made of something brown and fuzzy. Tweed? Was that tweed? Or mole hair? Fabrics were not exactly my specialty. Barbara would know. His slacks were made of the same stuff, and he walked with a folded umbrella as if it were a cane. His dress shirt was at least gray, but suspenders, tie, and leather shoes added more dull brown to the mix.

I had no doubt whatsoever that this skinny little man was a superhero. The clothes, while too big, were immaculately pressed. His tie might be made out of rock, it was so straight. Under fluffy eyebrows his eyes moved between Gerty, myself, and Ampexia with alert confidence. Most of all, it was the walk. That shriveled frame moved with a casual precision that made the rubble under his feet seem like an even floor.

He walked a little like Mom, which was not a comforting thought.

Ampexia was as professional as I'd always expected. She watched him for two seconds, and didn't question if he was really a superhero or dangerous. "Have you heard of him?" she whispered.

"No idea. Probably came out of retirement because he was here shopping," I whispered back.

"So we have no idea what his powers are. We have the loot. We can escape through the undamaged aisles."

I shook my head minutely. "He'll follow Gerty back to our base."

She grunted, since groaning would be too obvious and noisy. "This is why I wanted to ditch that thing."

Actually, he probably wouldn't. We didn't exactly count as the kind of hardcore threat to public welfare worth tracking across the city. We were robbing a glorified gardening store, for Tesla's sake!

But I didn't want to just give up. Especially not now that I had real weapons.

The first of those weapons swung her animatronic goat arms out, and clunked forward to grapple with the intruder. The old man's umbrella swung up and poked her in one hand just as those arms started to close for a hug. That effectively communicated he did not want to be hugged, and Gerty froze in place. Effectively communicating anything to Gerty was pretty impressive, and he'd done it with a gesture.

He spoiled the effect by opening his mouth and making the most unspeakable noise. 'Unspeakable' was the word. I couldn't have made it. I couldn't make it with this artificial voice box. The noise wasn't loud, but squeaked and screeched and stuttered and grinded. His lips wobbled like he was drooling oatmeal.

Gerty swung back up to straight from where she'd bent forward to hug. "Oopsadoops! You're right! Who's a Gerty Boy?"

He made the noise again. No, a slightly different noise, much less squeak and more scratch. Like an irregular duck call.

Gerty's jaw flapped with excitement. "Golly gosh and jeeparoos, no,

Mister Protocol! Not in ages and forever and ages! Since before breakfast, even!"

Ampexia and I shared a glance. Nope, she didn't know the name Mister Protocol either. There could be a thousand retired superheroes in this city. Most of them quit by thirty, right?

He gargled at the goat. Goat-gargled. Her arms swung down by her sides. Her upper body wobbled forward and back, and she exclaimed, "Safety is the only thing more important than waffles! Initiating full diagnostic."

And with that, she went into a sort-of song and dance. Her computery voice came back, and she raised one hand and bent her joints one at a time as she mumbled through a list. "My toesies are warm, my fingies conform, my knuckles show friction loss but within norm..."

Mister Protocol stepped around her, toward us.

I really should have attacked while he was busy with Gerty. Maybe it was the name, 'Mister Protocol.' Maybe I'd instinctively worried Gerty would give me a Time Out. Maybe it was just habit. Whatever, I'd obeyed unwritten and thoroughly stupid supervillain tradition and let him finish one duel before starting another.

Ampexia at least had the right idea. She flipped a switch on one glove, muttering, "He wants sonic attacks, huh?" When the glove started to hum, she raised it to point at the old man.

As her hand lifted, he made a bing-bong musical chime, and the glove went quiet. The LEDs on them and her backpack went out. So did the lights on her cat-ear headphones, and the faint, eternal scratch of their muffled music.

Growling, eyes wide, she flipped switches, stabbed buttons, fiddled with wires, but her equipment refused to turn back on. Her legs wobbled a little as well. That heavy backpack must have had a weight compensator in there somewhere.

Time to try the plow. If I understood how it worked, it should force him back and give me planning time.

Still toddling forward towards us, he looked straight at me and said, "You are not expected to understand this."

Shut down.

What? No.

Fatal error. Restart.

No, not going to!

Sleep mode.

Half second—wait, I couldn't be shut off by internal command anyway. Tesla knew I'd tried. You had to overload me or press the button.

While I argued with myself, Ampexia lost her temper, and stomped forward to try and kick the old man in his shin. He was at least as skinny as us, and not much taller. He looked like one solid kick would kill him.

His umbrella barely moved, swinging just enough to turn her foot aside once, then a second time. That one sent her crashing down on her back, looking like an upturned turtle.

Segment violation – core dumped.

Forget the voice in my head. It had no power. This old guy was coming after me, and he was way more physically adept than he looked, even if that wasn't a high bar.

Mister Protocol, huh?

I went with the stupidest idea I'd ever had, and asked him, "Would you like to play a nice game of chess?"

He stopped cold. "P – KB4?" From his pocket, he pulled a pile of paper with the title 'Request For Comments (RFC) 11938 – Network Chess Protocol.'

Then he started drawing a chessboard on the floor with the point of his umbrella, and I knew I had him. I'd guessed the theme of his powers and his obsession.

The only mad scientist who'd ever consistently defeated my Mom was a guy named Chaos Theory, whose seemingly harmless inventions did things that were always useful, but never predictable. Normally she would avoid a fight she couldn't predict and let someone else fight him, but that same chaos made her unable to avoid him. Thank goodness he never actually wanted to hurt her, and there were plenty of other heroes around. Dad, for one.

The point was this: while Mister Protocol drew a chess board for us, I completely broke the rules of courtesy, fair play, and good order by pointing the weather control sponge at him and squeezing it as fast and as hard as I could.

Fluids gooshed through the tubes from the small tank holstered onto my shoulder, the other half of this stupid-looking device.

The effect was decidedly not stupid. Water condensed out of the air so fast, a howling wind exploded from the target, and the thunderclap sent Mister Protocol sailing.

He hit the pile of mulch bags, hard.

Loud and petulant, I whined, "Gerty! I want waffles *and* hash browns! Let's go home!"

And then I yanked Ampexia to her feet, and ran for it.

She finally reactivated her equipment about ten yards down the aisle, at which point we ran for it a lot faster. Gerty's thumping, crunching footsteps confirmed I'd freed her from diagnostic mode.

I was pondering my victory speech when we hit the front doors, or at least what was left of them after Gerty's arrival. After all, this was the revamped Inscrutable Machine's first public victory, over two heroes, even.

Except the third hero was waiting for us in the parking lot.

This woman liked diamonds and feathers. Okay, the gemstones could be glass, or shiny plastic, but her spandex one-piece *glittered*. It wasn't quite the normal cut for the classic superhero costume, either. Yes, it was mostly skin-tight, but with lapels so wide they were almost a cape, and a short skirt only around the sides in back. Together they gave the effect of a dress coat, even if they were all one garment. Add the gemstones, and they gave the effect of chain mail, a suit of jeweled armor. Scarlet boots laced with a bow-tied ribbon nearly reached her knees, with thick but impractically high heels that must have required serious leg strength to walk in.

She probably had that. Not that I would have called her fat, but she definitely sprinted to the hourglass, and had trouble slowing down after she reached it. That soft-looking figure could easily conceal muscles like rocks. She stood with a tilted, flaunting posture that emphasized the curves even more.

A small, red-painted mouth in a sleekly oval face pursed, then smirked, and she said, "Tut tut, darlings. Did you think you could escape without facing a real hero?"

Criminy, that accent. She could be Radiance's sister. They talked alike, looked alike, and had the same scarlet hair, the color of this woman's lips and boots. In his case it had been an obvious dye job. In hers, it looked like that bright, unnatural color was, well, natural. It flounced as she tossed her head.

Well, if she wanted to be like that...

I smirked back, arching one eyebrow and putting a fist on my hip. "Haven't I already defeated one bird-themed poseur today?"

Oh, yeah, the feathers. Criminy, the feathers. Where her costume didn't have gems, it had feathers. Not in sleek lines, or long swoops. Fluffy crests of feathers, mostly in brown, but with a constantly shifting rainbow riot of highlights. Mostly they stuck out around her lapels, but they also trimmed the skirt, ran down a chest that didn't need more emphasis, accented her shoulders, and lined the tops of her boots. Oh, and she had a few tied into her hair.

Waving a hand lazily, she declared, "You defeated the Emu, children. A sweet girl who's trying hard, but emus aren't exactly birds of power and majesty. Now, you face Diamond Pullet, and you will learn the true glory that is the chicken."

And with that, three chickens fluttered down out of the sky. Two landed with a thump, but the third, large and pitch black, settled gracefully on her shoulder like a pirate's parrot. Except no parrot was that shining, ink-black. Even its eyes and legs and beak were black.

All three chickens wore little suits, which covered a lot less but were at least as shiny as Diamond Pullet's own.

Raising my chin proudly, I answered, "I see your chickens, and raise you a goat."

I lifted my arm and pointed at the exact moment that Gerty stumbled through the wall, shedding bricks. "Cheese and crackers.

Wasn't there a door here a minute ago?"

Diamond Pullet, iridescent red and yellow eyes never wavering from mine, snapped her fingers. "Girls. Barnyard dance battle."

The two chickens on the ground strutted, heads bobbing forward and back, to stand in front of Gerty. She stared at them. They stared at her.

Then the chickens spun in a circle and started sidestepping rhythmically and flapping their wings in what was clearly disco.

Gerty's lower jaw flapped with glee for a few seconds before she shouted, "Yay! New friends! Your name is Griselda, and yours is Princess Mighty Thews Mega-Fashion. Now let's all get down and funky together!"

I was probably the last person with the right to say this, but watching an animatronic goat try to disco in a high-speed version of its normal, one-joint-moves-at-a-time, stuttering pace was just weird. There was also no way I would get her to stop any time soon. I wasn't sure I wanted to.

Ampexia whispered in my ear, "Keep her busy."

Oh, I could do that. Good thing this robot face moved naturally, because it was time for my most arrogant sneer. "Your chickens are impressive, but this is a battle you cannot win. I have both youth and experience on my side. The name Bad Penny instills fear in man and woman alike. A trail of adults helpless before my evil lays behind me. Literally, in fact. You will be the next fool crushed in my robotic grip."

Holding up one hand, I flexed my fingers, then closed my grip, showing off the doll joints. Ampexia slid the sponge and its accessories off my arm first, making that easier.

She also helpfully set a little pocket speaker next to Gerty and the chickens, playing some particularly synthetic-toned disco for them to dance to.

She laughed, as bright and glittery and liquidly feminine as her appearance. It made me kind of jealous. My laugh sounded like a demented junior witch.

"Oh, darling, darling little girl. Like my noble and beautiful birds, I too have been underestimated time and again, and I believe the carpet of fools I have left pecked and scratched behind me is as long and luxurious as yours. It is my destiny to build a fabulous chicken world out of this sordid, crime-dirtied vale of tears. No one can stop me, although I do give you credit for that magnificent steampunk ensemble you have going there." She golf-clapped, and her shoulder chicken clucked in clear approval.

I gave her one, growly snort of a laugh, so as not to sound maniacal. That would beg for moving on to the fight. Jerking my head towards our pets, I said, "But are you as fabulous as you believe? Behold! Even now, my goat gains the upper hand over mere poultry. Admit your weakness, Diamond Pullet. And be swift, for I left a hero inside with a mild concussion, and should he rejoin us your heart will wither and perish at the horribleness of his suit."

My boast about Gerty was not in vain. Not that the chickens were bad dancers, but Gerty kept getting faster, and her stop-motion moves more complicated. She also had to be getting extra points for the blasters with big crystals in them that had emerged from her lower arms, only to rotate around and shower her with maddening rainbow colors. The weapons looked suspiciously like Red Eye's creations repurposed from war to friendship.

The voluptuous heroine watched me with flattened eyebrows now, which shadowed her already floridly mascara'd eyelashes. "Well. Aren't you full of surprises. I, the great Diamond Pullet, should know better than to underestimate anyone. Perhaps you, Bad Penny, will be the first to taste the succulent terror that is my full power. Vantablack! Show that goat what rhythm is."

"We could do that," shouted Ampexia from her truck, "Or we could escape, because I've loaded all our loot while you two were yakking. Bad Penny, get over here! Let the goat catch up!"

'All' our loot? There did seem to be more in the truck bed than I personally stole. Apparently my larcenous teammate went back for seconds. I approved thoroughly.

Diamond Pullet clapped, her languid, satisfied smile returning. "Oh, how that was clever. And you do rant so well, Bad Penny. It was a pleasure dueling you. Alas, that distraction technique was so brilliant, I wish I had thought of it myself."

She paused, and a fourth chicken darted out through the hole Gerty left in the wall, flapping madly as it flew up over the roof carrying a gleaming silver item of clothing. Hard to tell what as the garment whipped around, but clearly mad science.

"Oh, that's right! I did."

Had there been something like that in the vault? I'd really only paid attention to the likely weapons, and grabbed just enough to get by.

...wait. Was Diamond Pullet a villain?

She flourished her arms, releasing more fluffy feathers, and with furiously undignified flapping of her own rose into the air. She almost made it look good with her curved back, one knee lifted pose, but... no. Graceful or not, she called down, "Goodbye, children! Thank you for the good time, and the lovely gift," and flew away.

Well. That left me with one last villainous rant to perform before this caper ended. Swiveling sharply in place, I gave the store's silent, spectating customers and staff my most florid bow. "Ladies and gentlemen, the Inscrutable Machine thanks you for kneeling before our might. Now that we have liberated the hidden arsenal from this horticultural hidey-hole and defeated the heroes fool enough to try and stop Bad Penny, I must avenge my partner's mysterious injury by equally mysterious opponents unknown!"

"Yay, a guessing game!" shouted Gerty as she fell over onto the pickup truck bed, which was about all the climbing she could do.

"This is the dorkiest team I could possibly have joined," grumbled Ampexia.

"AH HA HA HA HA HA HA HA!" I laughed, and ran to join them.

CHAPTER FOURTEEN

Somewhere on the 405, Ampexia checked her cell phone.

With feathery gentleness, I reproved her, "Do you mind? I don't know if this car has mad science shock absorbers, but I know the other cars don't."

"I'll drive!" Gerty's gleeful enthusiasm was unmistakable.

Trying to sound equally apologetic, I answered, "Sorry, Gerty. You couldn't pass a breath test."

Heavy wind noises followed, but they did not seem strong enough to threaten anyone's driving. Good enough!

My remonstrances to my new partner were equally efficacious. "You're right. I just wanted to know if it worked."

My left eyebrow kinked up, I opened that eye wide, and leaned just a little toward her while tilting my head away. "Whaaaaat's going on?"

She made brush-off noises. "Eh. I slipped a phone into the dress, so I could follow it with the anti-theft GPS."

My other eyebrow rose to join its colleague. "The dress is that important?"

"No, I think it's just shiny and repels dirt. I knew it had to be what chicken lady was after." She wrinkled up her nose, and swerved us around a little blue car that must have been the only driver on the freeway not in a hurry to get somewhere. Gerty waved at them and did huff-and-puff breathing exercises in their direction.

I pressed my hands to the arm rest between us, leaning closer and grinning. "So it's Diamond Pullet you're after. She's the secret enemy you need help with."

As casual as I was eager, Ampexia said, "No, but she's connected and will lead us to them."

I leaned in a little more, until she had to lean away. But not much, because, you know, safe driving. "So let's follow her!"

Reclaiming her personal space, the dirty-blonde bonked her head against mine. "Immediately? What have I told you about learning to chill? She won't run straight to the real target anyway."

"Aw."

Ampexia's nose wrinkled again. "You're starting to sound like the goat."

"Yay!"

"Yay!" chimed in Gerty, flapping her arms up and down, although I'd bet she had no idea why we were cheering.

My partner groaned in much-abused weariness at our shenanigans. "I am going to dump my loot at our base, and go buy music gear. I want to score some pieces just for the repeller. You can come along, I guess."

So we did that, and an hour later, I found myself watching over Ampexia's shoulder as she pawed through a rack of unboxed electrical components that all looked the same. Well, no, that's not true. They all looked different, but in ways that didn't mean anything to me.

"I wouldn't think they'd have anything compatible," I said, as she compared things to the lantern-shaped sonic weapon.

"There are smaller stores for that. I'm here looking more for something I can upload tunes to and then use the gizmo as a speaker. Why waste a unique platform like this with music files compressed for a phone?" She pointed at a hole around the lower edge.

"You could just buy something in Chinatown," I said, as the person who had a dozen friends dying to sell her weapons but insisted on obtaining them the hard—and fun—way.

She shuddered. "No way. That place is full of freaks, and you can't trust any of them."

I couldn't deny that. It was why I liked the place! Ampexia, having exhausted the opportunities of this rack, ducked around to the other side of the aisle. We'd traveled about twenty. This store was gigantic, dwarfing even the agricultural store we'd just robbed. Surprisingly, nobody had panicked when we entered, but maybe two high schoolers in costume were a lot less scary without a seven foot animatronic goat.

She slipped back into her explanation. "Anyway, you can do a lot with just normal equipment. Only the super crazy advanced stuff doesn't try to be at all compatible with normal science. You may need to go adapter crazy with the old equipment. Sometimes you find one that takes a plug that got invented after the device."

Tilting the machine on its side, she pointed at a hole. "That looks like an RCA jack to me. I hope it's digital sound instead. Let's see what this does." Picking a cord off the shelf, she stuck it into that hole, then inserted a flash drive into the disk-shaped device on the other end of the wire. Its readout flashed lights, until it showed '01.' Then she pressed a button.

People screamed. I couldn't hear anything, but my metal heart vibrated in my chest, which was not a comfortable sensation. That stopped abruptly as smoke puffed out of the plastic disk, and Ampexia yanked her drive free.

"Time to go to one of those smaller stores?" I suggested.

She scooted around behind me, pushed a hand into the middle of my back, and pushed. "Yes. Now."

Nobody stopped us exiting, either. When we were out in the parking lot and away from prying ears, Ampexia eased up on the pushing. Her anxiety faded to a wry half-smile. "Don't spread it around, but that happens all the time. It's why I'm always stealing or buying new equipment."

"What? You're an expert!"

She rolled her eyes. "No way. Three quarters of what I do is just trying stuff until something works. You're the expert. How do you *do* that?"

Ampexia pointed at Gerty, sitting in the back of her truck, one foot raised, tapping her dull, knife-shaped toes one at a time. "Three point one cake cake cookie butter frosting pumpkin. Three point one cake cake chocolate chip cookie sundae..."

"Still counting to pie?" I asked my favorite goat as I circled around to the passenger side.

"I'm a good counter!" she answered, wiggling her toes one at a time. That particular foot had seven, now. I was pretty sure it had four when I'd left her here.

While we buckled our seatbelts, Ampexia picked up where she left off. "If I try to outwit her, she just runs off on a tangent and destroys something."

I tried to shrug and failed. Curse you, robot shoulders! But it was a good sign I kept trying, right? "Some of it's that I've seen all her shows. Most of it is knowing her obsessions. It's like in combat."

"You've lost me," said Ampexia, spinning the steering wheel and guiding us out of the lot.

"If you know what your opponent's going to do, you have the fight half-won. That's easier with obsessive people. I mean, let's face it, anybody wearing spandex tights and fighting crime is crazy. Normal people find something more practical to do with their powers."

That got a cynical grin, and a nod. "Preaching to the choir here."

I knew she'd eat that one up. Aside from her high-tech gear, in combat or regular life, Ampexia wore jeans with holes in them and T-shirts for bands I didn't know. Today's was for Boreal Network, with a logo I didn't recognize. Maybe a circuit board? No, wait, those were roads. A map!

Drag yourself back to the topic, Penny! "Look at you. You love music. Someone could probably guess what you're going to steal that way. It still wouldn't help them in a fight. If I could claim somebody in Orange County was abusing a chicken, Diamond Pullet would abandon the fight to go save it. Most heroes and villains are like that, if you can figure out what their button is. It really helps coming up with schemes to fight them."

Just to make my position clear, I repeated, "You love music. It's not like it's baked into your DNA. I haven't got a clue about music. I don't even know what genre your music is."

She scowled, her head tossing in mild irritation. "It's not a genre. I make what sounds good. Most of what I make lately is vaporwave, but there are a lot of micro-genres on the electronic end of the spectrum, and some of them blend."

"So, what even is vaporwave?" I asked.

She looked at me for a second, before realizing I was serious. "Okay, electronic music is about taking old music that was not meant to be serious and reclaiming it. Video game music, elevator music, corporate training video music, even smooth jazz. Vaporwave is nineties, synthwave is eighties. Future funk is disco. It's all about making the trivial meaningful. I like to make music that sounds like it came from a computer. You can communicate emotion in ways lyrical music can't if you throw away human language and show people how to feel like a robot."

I coughed into my fist. That is, I made a coughing sound into the curled, doll-jointed fingers of one hand.

Ampexia, who had been sitting up straighter, talking more passionately than I'd ever seen her before, slumped down again. "Sorry. Or maybe you get it better than anyone."

"No, but I'd love to learn. It's cool seeing you inspired, and it's a neat topic. Do you have any samples?"

She perked up again. "Do I? Kid, you just called down the thunder. The beautiful, beautiful synthetic thunder. Are you sure you want this?"

I nodded, honest and earnest. "Hit me."

Ampexia was already pushing buttons on the truck's stereo. For this, she didn't have to take her eyes off the road.

We had sidestepped into why Ampexia did or did not like individual heavy metal songs rather than having an opinion on the whole genre. I'd only been treated to half a dozen different songs. The topic had wandered fast. I'd been right about the lack of obsession thing, because while she might lean to one style when she made music, my teammate loved all music, or at least made no exceptions for style.

I had also been right about the experience being awesome. Bonus points, all signs pointed to Ampexia being able to talk about this nonstop for the rest of her life. In case of boredom, the Inscrutable Machine would always have a backup option.

No, what surprised me was when we pulled up into a parking spot on Melrose. It was weird enough that Ampexia found a place to park. This had been the last place I'd expected to find a mad science store.

My expression must have been something to behold. Ampexia switched off the stereo, and told me, "It's not like they sell laser cannons, or anything. You can sell mad science graphics cards and heat sinks from a storefront like anybody else, with the right precautions."

Those precautions would be the signs in the window. There were a lot of them. You could hardly see inside!

This technology does not meet any standards of anyone anywhere. Management takes no responsibility for what products bought here may do to your computer, or any collateral damage to persons, property, animals, or space/time.

We are serious. The stuff here is as dangerous as it is awesome.

Those two summed up the message pretty well.

"So the owner is a mad scientist?" I said when we were both out of the truck.

She nodded, her eyes gleaming with the anticipation of acquiring new gear. "With zero interest in crime, and zero legal obligation to ask me what I'm doing with his experimental products. Plus, he gets a lot of salvage from mad science wreckage. You haven't lived until you've seen a USB-compatible universal game cartridge adapter. And I mean *universal*."

I grabbed her by the elbow as she reached for the front door.

"What? Is it the goat?" she asked, giving me a puzzled look.

Looking her right in the eyes, I said, "You're stalling."

"Who? Me?" she asked, then sighed. "Okay, that might as well have been a confession."

"Why do you keep putting this off?"

She chewed on her lower lip, looking up past the top of my head rather than meeting my gaze.

I tried again. "I get it, this opponent or whatever they stole is embarrassing, but you know, you haven't made fun of my being stuck in a robot."

Her awkwardness snapped into a disgusted squint. "What kind of jerk would do that? This isn't a game for you."

I nodded, and tapped her in the middle of her chest. "And I am going to return the favor. Besides, you know whatever you're planning to do with that tracker, it won't work if you wait much longer."

Ampexia bared her teeth in a grimace. Her shoulders squirmed, and her head wriggled. Then they sagged, only to have her face snap back up and fix me with a sharp, challenging stare. "Whatever happens, whatever you see, you have to promise not to tell anyone."

"I swear."

CHAPTER FIFTEEN

We plugged the signal from the stolen phone into Ampexia's GPS, and followed it south, and then south some more, all the way down to Anaheim.

As the buildings got more pretty and white and modern, and the palm trees more lush, I wondered if bringing Gerty Goat to Disneyland would be the greatest thing ever, or absolutely unacceptable. She would break stuff. A lot of stuff. But Disney could afford it, and Gerty would make so many kids happy.

When the road sign at the intersection said to go straight for Disneyland, but the sly, quiet feminine voice of Ampexia's GPS told us, "Turn left," I knew my question would not have to be answered. Today.

We followed another pretty street Disney was no doubt proud to be seen next to, until the GPS said, "You have arrived at your destination, dummy."

We got out in front of a big, cone-shaped building. Maybe more trumpet-shaped, since it curved out to the bottom floor, and swooped inward as it went up half a dozen flights. Picturesque place for a super-powered battle, definitely. Not only was it oddly shaped, the bottom floor was all glass walls around the edge, while the upper levels had white stone surfacing and very few windows.

A sign above the entrance read 'FruiTastiCo!' A sign just below it read 'No Longer A Subsidiary Of Happy Days Sugar Substitutes, Thank Goodness.'

I peered over Ampexia's shoulder at her phone as we got out of the truck. The dot that we were following was actually outside the building. So...

"Her." I pointed.

As much as I like gloating, neither Holmesian deductive skills nor a genius with maps were required to make this judgment. First, the young woman I pointed at was wearing an obvious superhuman costume, of the 'spandex one piece, gloves, and boots' variety. Vertical white-and-orange panels stuck out in any crowd, as did her bone thin shape and bushy red hair.

Also as soon as she saw three supervillains pull up, she ran for it. That gave me a clue!

She sprinted into the building, arms waving, which is an appropriate reaction to seeing Gerty Goat go, "Oh boy, a squid hunt! Tallyho! Yip yip!" and charge across the pavement after you.

In fact, since I had nothing against this building or the company that owned it, I had to teleport in front of Gerty, one arm held out and the other with a finger to my mouth. "Shhhh! We're trying to be stealthy. This isn't just a chase. We're looking for clues!"

Her mouth hung wide open, and she jerked up straight. "Clues?! My sniffer is at your disposal! I can smell a pinch of oregano in a pound of paprika at twenty paces!" A hatch in the side of her head opened up, extending three magnifying glasses that hovered twitchily in front of one of her eyes. A couple of seconds later, a fourth extended to pose in front of her nose.

Bending forward like a drinky bird, she went down on all fours and lurched and wobbled along with me and Ampexia into the big, circular lobby. It had nice burgundy carpeting and a lot of gilt. Whoever designed this place definitely had aesthetics over utility in mind.

Forestalling Gerty from knocking out this building's supports gave our quarry time to duck out of sight, but the problem solved itself. My animatronic sidekick twitched her muzzle around as she crawled over the carpet, until she pointed towards some stairs. "A slime trail! I'mma getcha! All the world is my kitchen, and this chef knows where all her ingredients are kept!"

"Stealthy!" I reminded her. She nodded, straightened up, and started exaggeratedly tiptoeing up the hall. As she did, one of her eyes clicked, turned purple, and glowing spots showed up on the carpet in a trail leading upward.

People stayed out of our way, staring from doorways, as we followed the trail up to the third floor, around a circular hall, and to a women's restroom.

I went to push it open. Ampexia kicked it open instead, a vibrating glove extended in front of her.

At the far end of the washroom, the villainess paused in trying to ratchet a little window wider, and spun around to face us. Back to the wall, she squealed, "I just wanted a pretty dress with jewels on it! I figured it'd be fine if I stole it from another supervillain. Why do these things happen to me? This is worse than when the octopus woman got too friendly!"

"Where did you get the dress?" I asked, trying to sound calm.

"Energizing soy sauce!" announced Gerty, not sounding calm at all.

"Take it! Just take it! I don't want it anymore!" shouted the villainess. She pulled a glittery, tube-shaped dress out of her costume. Given her skinny frame and the modestly thick spandex, I really should not have been surprised she was able to hide it in there. Throwing the dress at me, she jammed her arms into the opening of the window, maybe three inches by twelve inches.

She fit. Her body writhed like a snake, compressing as she went through the gap. It looked pretty weird when her head flattened out to get through, but I saw no sign it hurt.

To be honest, I wasn't that surprised. She was a supervillain, so she had to have powers. Boneless compression? Why not? It did gave me a serious déjà vu feeling I'd met her before, but there were only a couple of hundred active villains and heroes in the city. I couldn't always be meeting new ones.

I caught the dress. The jewels, which couldn't possibly be actual diamonds, not that many of them, weighed it down quite a bit. I had to feel around to find the phone.

While I did that, Gerty shouted, "Nooo! My stir fry!" and ran right through the wall after the escapee.

Ampexia gave me a guilty look, one hand scratching behind her headphones, not actually meeting my eyes but instead keeping her face tilted down. "You were right. I procrastinated too long."

I waved it off. "Chicken lady doesn't exactly keep a low profile. We'll find her. Right now, let's collect my goat."

Since we were on the third floor, the hole in the bathroom wall looked down over a sloping roof, sharply angled near us but almost leveling out a floor down. Groove marks traced Gerty's path for about ten feet, then disappeared. The explanation for that presented itself as, far down near the edge of the building, Gerty sped along on roller skate-style wheels, accompanied by a championship level yodel.

Personally, I blinked to the edge of the roof, then blinked down to the ground in time to watch Gerty catapult off into mid-air. Gravity, which two tons of robot has a lot of, took over quickly. She smashed into a small park area, gouged a deep furrow in the turf, broke a metal bench and a lamp post, and skidded to a halt in front of a second bench—on which cowered our noodly supercriminal.

Curled up into a ball with her arms over her head, she whimpered, "I'm not tasty! I swear!"

Holding up both hands in a sign of peace, I stepped pointedly between Gerty and the girl. "We are not going to eat you, I promise."

A low, throbbing sound signaled Ampexia landing next to me, using the jetpack power of her giant speaker. She had one of those expressions so blank she seemed stunned, and the same quiet tone as she said, "She's not afraid of us. She's afraid of them."

I followed a pointing finger as five velociraptors in frilly dresses trotted out around the curve of the building.

The dresses were magnificent: extremely girly, so elaborate they clearly were intended as costumes rather than real clothing, and color-coded. Red, blue, yellow, black, and pink—each dress was different, but Barbara would have been proud to wear any of them. Short skirts bared a lot of tail—some skirts in stiff bells, others made mostly of layers of poufy petticoats. There were bodices, bow ties, and round, starched shoulder ruffles. The red dress gleamed like plastic, the black dress had gothic crosses, and the pink had tons of ribbon bows, especially at the tops of the thigh-high white stockings. The other velociraptors had to be content with knee-high stockings, which didn't cover that much since they had to end at the ankle where huge, sharp talons got in the way.

Frankly, the raptors needed the dresses. For long-tailed, razor-fanged, sickle-clawed murder birds, they were naturally drab. Their feathers came in brown with streaks of black. Bare, featherless heads had that wrinkly, scaly, gray skin of a particularly ugly vulture. Only the raptor in the pink dress had blue and red-and-yellow highlights shining in its feathers, which from my understanding of birds meant it was the only male.

Oh, and they all had big, plastic magic wands with musical symbols on the end.

The red dress raptor jumped on top of a statue of Buddha, which I hoped she would not defile in the way birds usually do. It gave me a sense of scale. The largest of her flock, my guess was the top of her head came up to about my shoulder, although that meant her mostly horizontal body would be heavier than even my original.

Her exaggeratedly massive claws clung to the statue's head, keeping her in a poised, confident perch despite the Buddha's legendary roundness. Opening her mouth wide, she squawked, "Who's a pretty bird?"

Pink raptor shook its arm-wings, then its leg-wings, and trotted up next to her. "Pretty bird!"

The blue raptor, crouched low to the ground, slunk up on the other side, looking up at its leader to ask, "Polly want a cracker?"

"Cracker! Cracker!" declared the red enthusiastically, bobbing her head up and down.

Okay, that was two identified. The red's name was Polly, and the pink Pretty Bird.

Yellow nuzzled Blue's neck, squeak-growling, "Nice Cookie."

"Marge, the Thing is talking again!" recited the blue.

"Lucretia! Lucretia! Lucretia!" shouted the velociraptor in the black dress, standing behind the rest of them and hopping up and down excitedly. There's always one.

Well, those were clearly introductions. Red was Polly, Pink Pretty Bird, Blue Cookie, Yellow Thing, and Black Lucretia.

Back on the Inscrutable Machine's side, Ampexia slumped a few inches. Sounding decidedly non-vindicated, she said, "Ah. It looks like I procrastinated just long enough."

Trying very hard to look serious and sound serious so as not to make her embarrassment worse, I asked, "These are your target?"

She said nothing. Maybe she was allergic to frilly dresses.

Before things went any further, I had obligations to supervillain courtesy. Bowing to my opponents, I said, "Welcome, Raptor Scouts. I am the infamous, the diabolical, the unstoppably ingenious Bad Penny. The beautiful goat in a chef's apron to my left is Gerty Goat—"

"Hiiiii!"

"—whose friendship lays waste to all that stands in our way. And on my right is my partner, who is not the queen of musical larceny only because she spits on royalty and believes in the essential dignity of every man and woman. You may call her Ampexia."

"I'll call her a lazy, ungrateful, ne'er-do-well brat, is what I will call her!" argued a high, prissy male voice.

"...what was that?" I looked over the raptors. None of their mouths were moving in time to that voice. On the contrary, they had set up a quiet, chirping chorus, filling the conversational background with an avian barber shop quartet-style soundtrack. It had Gerty's knees flexing in rhythm.

"That is what we are here to steal," said Ampexia, her voice strained and her expression tired.

"Steal? Steal? How dare you. After centuries of service to your family, you spurn me simply because I point out the obvious truth that you are a laggardly musical philistine—"

Ampexia jerked back up, bristling. "Philistine? From the book that thinks show tunes are the highest achievement of musical history?"

"The valkyrie theme from Ring of Nibelung is hardly a show tune, and if you properly appreciated classical opera and the fine new traditions of modern musicals, you would be a glorious crime fighter famed throughout the world by now, not a sneak thief in dirty clothes." Aha. The complaining did come from a book, bouncing angrily in a holster on the back of Raptor Red's waistband.

Ampexia raised a finger—index, thankfully—and shook it in rage as she yelled back, "Maybe I don't want to be like my mother, or music forbid my grandmother—"

The book gasped. "How dare you! Your grandmother was a pure, exquisite, impeccably maidenly warrior for justice! You are not fit to speak her name."

Ampexia wrinkled her nose. "If I did, I'd vomit."

"You impertinent, immoral little—"

As charming as the family drama was, we were here to steal that book, not argue with it. I took a half-step backwards, and activated my teleport bracers. I landed behind Polly, and made a grab for her belt pouch.

Tesla's Tinnitus, could those things move! The dinosaur in the red dress's head whirled around, teeth clamping onto my forearm before I could notice and blink away. It hurt a little, but thanks to my armored sleeves and stone-hard shell, the bite wasn't threatening.

No, the problem was that she flailed her neck around, waving my light, hollow body in the air, until she flung me away onto the ground.

"Gerty!" I shouted, but that was all the time I had. Pretty Bird and Thing leaped for me, and I barely scrambled to my feet in time and teleported away before their talons hit where I'd just been.

Landing behind the solid shield of my animatronic pet, I grabbed her apron and gave it a shake. "Gerty! Why didn't you save me? Gerty?"

She ignored me. Even while fighting, the velociraptors kept chirping. They were naturally musical, it seemed, and the melody had Gerty entranced, paying no attention to anything but bobbing up and down and tweeting discordantly in an attempt to join in.

Ampexia scowled, adjusting her gauntlets. "And that is why the goat is no use against them, and I had to find someone else to help."

I unslung the mega hoe from my back, twisting one of its handles to start the saw blades vibrating. "Help is here. We can do this."

"Can you?" asked the book, and I could hear its sneer. "Ready, girls? One two three, Mister Sandmaaaan, dream me a dreeeam!"

The raptors might not be great conversationalists, but they were fantastic singers. They joined together in the song in beautiful harmony, with Pretty Bird supplying the deeper-voiced asides like 'Boom boom boom boom.'

Gerty whipped out her mixing spoon, holding it up like a microphone, and rocked her upper body from side to side as she tried to sing along, always a half-second behind.

Myself, I lurked, poised, to see what this attack did and gaming out possible evasive strategies and ways to take advantage.

Except nothing really happened. No glows formed, nothing started charring or breaking or even vibrating. Above and behind me remained clear. The book, raptors, and Gerty sang, and that was it.

I leaned over to make a suggestion to Ampexia, only to find her eyes half-closed, her knees wobbling, and her head jerking and bobbing with the effort to not fall asleep. Inside the building and around its plaza, spectators all seemed to find reasons to sit down and lean against something.

Ah. Musical-themed magical girl velociraptors. The wands hadn't been a coincidence.

Pity for them robots don't get tired. I opened up with the hoe, leveling it at Raptor Red with one handle, and yanking the other to fire.

The effect was everything I might have hoped for. Furrows carved themselves in the sod and pavement, throwing up debris, until the poor Buddha statue catapulted up off the ground, sending Raptor Red flapping desperately, and the others scattering like chickens.

I teleported about ten feet to the left, and did it again. Then as Pretty Bird and Cookie jumped at me, repeated the process. Each time, laying down a line of destruction that forced Polly away from her teammates.

Their screeching also interrupted the song, giving my partner a chance to recover. Only Gerty kept trying to follow the tune, while quickly running out of words and substituting "Nah nah nah naaaah!"

Petulant, the book squealed, "Girls! Girls! Follow the beat! Pardon my language, but dash it all, anyway. Fine, I suppose violence will have to do."

"Pretty bird!"

"Polly want a cracker?"

"Lucretia! Lucretia! Lucretia!"

"Crimson flames resin bow!"

Wait, what was that last one?

It came from Polly, who waved her wand as she recited. A rod of red fire formed in the air in front of her, slashing at me.

Of course, I teleported away from it, but then I heard "Gleaming gold drumstick bludgeoning!" and "Raven void bassoon swipe!" and "Blushing pink ballet shoe blizzard!"

Suddenly, I was doing a great deal of teleporting, blipping around the yard as the chanting raptors waved their wands and fired their instrumental energy blasts. This was fine by me. The attacks weren't too fast, and I fired back, keeping them disorganized. In fact, one of my hoe's rows of destruction went right under the feet of Raptor Black, sinking her into the earth and tearing what would be shockingly immodest gashes in her dress if she had anything but feathers to bare. She pulled herself free of the loose dirt immediately, but the dress damage could be useful. I might be able to tear the book off of Raptor Red. Would it damage the book in the process? Did Ampexia care?

Then, after one teleport, a voice behind me shouted, "Spoon stirring vortex!" and I nearly screeched in shock, and fell off my feet, because only Gerty was supposed to be behind me. The realization that it was Gerty's voice chanting followed that up, but the second of delay figuring out what happened was not good. Polly had her wand leveled at me, and was just finishing the word, "...bow!" and I hadn't even lifted a foot for another teleport.

But before the fiery weapon formed, Polly's wand slipped out of her hand, flying across the park for Ampexia to grab out of the air. She followed with Cookie's, and Thing's, clearly intent on working her way down the row with her gauntlet's snatching ability. The raptors just didn't have good enough fingers to hold on. Their claws were designed to rip, not grip.

Of course, yellow and blue both charged Ampexia immediately, but I blew them off their feet with the hoe, savaging their costumes in the process.

Gerty tried again. "Mixing spoon vigorous kneading!"

"Back! Back!" shouted the book. Its panic turned to pride, and then to song. "Remember, girls, you've got the Touch! You've got the Power!"

Music yowled around the raptors as they leaped back into a group. Sparkles and vertical lines of light sprung up around them, lifting them into the air and spinning them around. Their dresses disappeared, leaving the killer cretaceous avians in only their feathery glory for a second before new dresses appeared. These had rather deeper necklines, and even shorter skirts. The upper halves of shiny laced boots appeared on their lower legs, but gave up before enclosing those sickle-clawed feet.

Thing looked at me, made an *awk* noise, and came zooming at me in a blur of yellow.

Criminy!

No more activation phrases. Now Cookie slashed at me with blue lightning following her already dangerous feet. A bigger, shadowy version of Lucretia tried to peck me. Pretty Bird's cloud of pink valentine hearts did not seem to do anything, but I didn't wander into it to test that theory.

Polly got extended phoenix wings of red fire, which she charged forward to swing at Ampexia.

Nuh-uh. No touchy the partner.

I teleported right in front of her, palming the weather sponge. I squeezed it hard, but not quite as fast as that first attempt. Instead of a thunderclap, water roared out of the air, extinguishing Polly's wings and sweeping her off her feet, dropping her hard on top of the battered Buddha statue.

She twitched, stunned. I blinked over on top of her, reaching for the book.

Thing came flying out of nowhere, a streak of burning yellow light. She smacked into me, and my clothes sizzled as her four legs took hold.

A screech like nails on a blackboard surrounded us both. It made my body vibrate sickeningly, but the raptor got it much worse. She somersaulted over me, releasing her grip, her back hitting the side of a bench, and she collapsed to the ground, flailing.

Ampexia had both arms held out, fingers spread and the speakers in the palms of her gloves visibly trembling as she poured the sonic attack onto the unfortunate bird.

"Mystical spoon energy comfort!" shouted Gerty. No, this one didn't do anything, either.

The other three raptors all came at us at once. I decided discretion was the better part of valor, grabbed hold of Ampexia, and teleported us out of their reach.

The book sounded none the worse for wear from its owner taking a tsunami to the face, but definitely even more peeved. "Oh, now you want to learn to fight? Suddenly there are problems stealing things won't solve? Well, it's too late! Prepare for an up-close look at the legacy you squandered, because the girls and I are just getting warmed up."

And he started to chant again. And they started to chant again. Impressive, high-pitched, foreign—oh, right, it was "O Fortuna," the Latin song every movie uses for climactic fantasy battle scenes.

Spheres of colored light engulfed the raptors.

What, another power-up sequence? Forget that. I lifted the hoe, and blasted Raptor Red with it.

Nothing. The line of torn dirt stopped dead at the energy globe, with no effect. Apparently, magical girl powers were not quite that stupid.

Their owners, however...

"Criminy. What a stupid din. Ampexia, can you drown this hokey tune out with something worth listening to?" I yelled over the chanting.

"Kitchen magic spoonabulation!" contributed Gerty, in her own little goat world I would have liked to share.

Smirking at me, Ampexia tapped a few buttons on her gloves, and twisted a knob on her backpack. Synthesized music throbbed around us, deep, grinding with metallic pain. After a few seconds, a lighter melody broke in, fast and sharp, dancing maniacally over the unhappy harmony line.

And a few seconds after that, the book broke off chanting to whine, "Stop that unholy racket. That is not music! It's just *beep beep boop boop* noises! Any child could put together a melody like that!"

The energy spheres disappeared, leaving the velociraptors unchanged, blinking at each other in confusion.

I teleported right on top of Polly while her bird brain tried to catch up with events, and latched hold of the book pouch with both hands.

Of course, she hadn't gotten any slower. She had my lower leg in her jaws in a heartbeat, but that was why I'd appeared actually on top of her. I let her grab me, for the extra half second to get a grip on the book. As she yanked me away, the book came free of its pouch, and I threw it up into the air.

Ampexia raised a hand, the book shuddered, and it shot down straight into her grip.

Holding it high, she shouted, "I call upon the power of the Muses! Inspire me with your song!"

What with being shaken around by velociraptors, I missed about two seconds worth of action. It ended with Ampexia in a sparkling white dress, her regular gear on the ground behind her. The velociraptors were back to their natural clothes-less state, looking at each other and mumbling, "Cookie?" "Pretty bird?"

Gerty, mixing spoon gripped in both hands, waved it up and down, pleading, "Spoon spoon spoon spoon spoon powers!"

"Ampexia! You've accepted your gift! I'm so happy!" the book crowed. Now that it was out of its holster, it looked like a song book for kindergarteners, with thick pages and cover, and pastel eyes with big eyebrows painted on it. The pages flapped when it talked.

Its owner responded by clamping those pages shut with her hand. "Quiet. Bad Penny and I are going to teach these bird brains a lesson."

The plaza rang with a new voice. "Not if I have anything to say about it."

Trailing her three chicken minions, Diamond Pullet stepped out of the hole we'd broken into the third floor wall of the FruiTastiCo building. Skiing elegantly down the slope, she dropped in front of us with a flurry of chicken feathers, followed by her three fluffy minions.

I watched her for signs of violence, but instead she walked past us, glittering like a disco ball, and wrapped her arms around the necks of the velociraptors, pulling them in for a comforting hug. "These poor darlings only wanted to be heroes and help people. I stole powers for them, and I accept that you stole those powers back, but if you wish to hurt these sweet little ancestors of all that is good and chickeny, be aware you will also reap the fabulous, fabulous whirlwind."

This was Ampexia's fight, and I gave her a questioning look.

She shrugged, and turned away. The book started babbling again. "I knew shame and jealousy would teach you where your real destiny lies. Don't worry, Ampexia, I'll teach you to embrace real music, and you'll be a hero to make your—mmf!"

That was as far as he got before Ampexia pulled a spare belt out of her giant stereo backpack, wrapped it around the book, and yanked it shut. She did this a second time. And a third time. She'd apparently brought a lot of belts just for this purpose. The eyes on the book's cover blinked and darted around, but uselessly. Soon, they too were obscured, which was when the white dress evaporated, returning Ampexia to her regular jeans and T-shirt.

"Whatever," she said, not even looking back at Diamond Pullet.

In the quiet aftermath, I noticed the supervillainess with the bushy hair had long since disappeared. Along with the dress she'd stolen. But leaving behind the phone we'd tracked her with. Smart girl.

Gerty shook her spoon angrily, but it continued to not be magic.

I gave Diamond Pullet her official answer. "The Inscrutable Machine accepts your truce, mainly because we wish we'd thought of stealing magical powers for a flock of dinosaurs ourselves. Find them good homes."

Turning away from Diamond Pullet, I leaned over to whisper to Ampexia, "If anybody asks, we were trying to recover the dress, and I never saw a book."

She looked down at me, flashed an awkward grin, and lifted her fist. I lifted mine, and our fists booped.

Hello Mother and Father,

Camp Supervillain is getting exciting. I'm starting to like the kids I'm sharing a cabin with. One of them seemed distant at first, but she's got a lot of passion under the surface, and knows a lot. The counselors challenged us again, but Mom's advice about figuring out your opponent's obsessions worked. Now that I'm having to spend the summer without you, I can see just how much you taught me.

Your Daughter,
Penny

Chapter Sixteen

Mad science farm tools converted into weapons, check.

Heart of steel carefully concealed behind multiple layers of armor, check.

Burning desire for revenge, check.

It was time. Finally. I had been waiting on this rooftop for two hours. The lack of muscle twitches and human body stuff did make me more patient, but I was still pretty bored by the time the parasite stepped out of my front door. My bet paid off, and the thing roughly inherited the hours I used to keep. Plus, Ruth's car was pulling away when I started to wait, so I knew she had company, and wouldn't want to just hang around indoors.

Having seen her sister's car, it was no surprise that Cassie stepped out of my house with the parasite. They walked side by side, shoulders not quite touching, with a glowingly excited Cassie doing most of the talking. It was actually sweet that she was finally getting a chance to spend time with me, even a fake me.

I wouldn't let that slow me down. When they reached the intersection with Los Feliz, I teleported into the air in front of them, dropping down to land in a crouch, a few body lengths away from the body thief.

The parasite looked a little surprised. Cassie let out a squeal. Her cheeks turned pink, and she took a small step away from the parasite.

Her head jerked from side to side, looking at me, at the parasite, at me, at the parasite, alternating her mouth opening and biting her lip as guilt flooded her face.

My double looked as amused and forgiving as I felt. She gave Cassie's shoulder a pat. "If you want to make it up to me, go get the duffel bag in my parents' garage."

That poured cold water on my amusement. Gritting my teeth, I told it, "They're not your parents."

Cassie took one more glance between us, turned, and ran down the street towards my house.

The thing in my body put her fists on her hips—*my* hips—and leaned a little to one side, giving me an impatient, skeptical, direct stare. "So?"

What a ham. I took a step forward, and blinked the rest of the way, right up face to face. Grabbing a fistful of her blouse at the lapels, I hoisted her up off her feet. My real body was heavy, but the robot arms could handle it.

She winced. Her weight hanging from her bunched-up shirt had to hurt. She still kept staring me right in the eyes.

I stared right back. "You took away everything, parasite, and left me for dead. But I'm back. Repaired, re-armed, and ready to fight. Your little vacation living my life is over."

Halfway down the block, Cassie saw us and squealed. In chorus, the parasite and I shouted, "Just go get the bag, Cassie."

She took off running again.

Just as cold, but with an extra layer of sarcasm, the parasite asked, "Is that your message? Because I have one for you."

She unsnapped her belt pouch, and stuck her hand into it. I'd expected her to be armed. How could I humiliate her in a fight if she wasn't? That didn't mean I was going to let her shoot me, and as she pulled whatever it was out, I grabbed her wrist with my free hand so I could get a look.

The device she held wasn't a gun. It didn't look like a weapon at all, just a hexagon-sided tube with a button on the end.

A bomb. The thing in my head always did love bombs. Letting her go, I took a sharp step back to blink away.

Before my foot touched the pavement, the crazy parasite pushed the button, with both of us standing on ground zero. Purple color exploded around us, but my foot touched down, with my eyes focused to teleport twenty feet behind the parasite.

OW! Ow ow ow! Criminy! My arms burned, and smoke rose out of my costume with a sizzling noise. Criminy again, I was fireproof, so the copper bands around my arms must have just gotten really, seriously hot!

Also, I hadn't teleported anywhere.

I took another step back. Nothing. The pain lessened, slowly. My lab coat hadn't burned through. My arms worked. At least I wasn't actually damaged.

I gaped, and could hear the squeak of shock in my own voice. "You destroyed my teleport bracers?"

The parasite stepped back, and that seemed like a good idea, so I did it, too. Her invention left a dome of faintly purple-tinged air, with frozen, deeper purple clouds, and we both got clear of it, which let us glare at each other again.

Prodding my arms, which didn't make the burning bracers hurt either more or less, I demanded, "How could you do that?"

She stood straight, stiff, and smugly superior. "Greatest mad scientist of the century, remember? You got the robot muscles, I got to keep the power."

More pokes revealed the bracers hadn't turned liquid, so not hot enough to melt. Another backwards step confirmed they didn't work. "That's not what I meant, and you know it. After the Machine, this was our best invention. Forget the clock or the spaceship or the super cheerleader serum. Easy teleporting is the most useful power ever."

Her glare didn't show the slightest trace of guilt. "Yeah, and that's why I couldn't let you keep them. I knew you'd be after me, and the bracers made you a hundred times more dangerous. I asked our power to get rid of them. I've been carrying this bomb with me since three days after we split."

The bracers had cooled to where they no longer hurt, and curiosity filled the gap where the pain had been. I gave the dome another look. Perfectly even, it didn't move, or fade. It hadn't been solid. Probably it continued underground as a full sphere of... just purple, glutinously opaque in some places, near-invisibly transparent in others. "What even is that stuff?"

"Hardened space. It prevents the more obscure manipulations of physics, and the feedback destroys the device that tries to teleport, or... whatever."

My turn to glare condescendingly. "Or whatever? What does hardening space even mean?"

The parasite shrugged, looking nonchalant, but unable to keep the awkwardness out of her voice. "You know what this power is like. The effect looked like making space hard. I think maybe it freezes something quantum, which stops other quantum effects from happening."

Which was a shot-in-the-dark guess. Like I understood quantum physics. My power understood everything, but the parasite wasn't actually my power.

Cassie returned, running hard up the sidewalk with the packed bag in her arms. Criminy, she was fit. I sure couldn't have run all that way in my real body.

The bag contained lumpy, hard things. Mad science, certainly. I slid the weather sponge into my grip.

But before then...

I jerked my head at the dome. "Turn that off. It might hurt someone."

Now it was her turn to give me the 'are you stupid' stare. We kept trading those. "It's a bomb. It doesn't turn off. That's the whole point of bombs. You use it, it explodes, and it stays exploded. Look." She lifted up the tube again, and clicked the button repeatedly. Nothing happened. Point made, she threw it into the bushes.

Both of her hands now free, she unzipped the duffel bag. I watched the process carefully, ready to blast her with excessive amounts of precipitation. She didn't pull out a weapon, though. She took out my old flight rotors, and tossed them across the distance to my feet. "Here. If you want something to dodge with, you can have these."

I raised an eyebrow. "You put bombs in these, too?"

She scowled, angry. "Criminy, no. Dad repaired the one Heart of Gold broke. That's it."

"She's telling the truth!" burst in Cassie. When I looked at her she backed up a step, but kept talking despite a rising blush. "She can't use them. They don't work for her. So they're yours."

I raised the other eyebrow. "This was your idea?"

The parasite smiled, wry and affectionate, which echoed my feelings. "Not entirely, but she pushed for it."

Neither of us being angry just made Cassie blush more. I couldn't help remembering her in Chinatown, talking about relationships with a maturity most grownups didn't have. That all fell apart when she thought about me. Even if I didn't return her feelings, how could I ever get mad at that?

Then something clicked, and my smile turned into a grin. The parasite couldn't fly with my rotors, huh? Good. I could use all the evidence I could get that she wasn't me. Crouching, I buckled them in place on my wrists and ankles, making sure to keep the sponge free in case this was a trick and I had to fight. When they were all set, I stood, and gave the twists to activate them.

My feet shot out from under me, and my back hit the pavement with a bang. Getting my wrists properly under me pushed me back up, only to send me tumbling into the grass, where I flopped and rolled until I managed to turn the fans off. After that, I lay there, panting for breath until I got my bearings back. No, my robot body wasn't tired, but some things you have to do.

I glared at the parasite. "What did you do to them?"

She watched me with her arms smugly folded. "Nothing. Dad fixed one. That's it. I can't control them right anymore. They don't make sense like they used to. You think you're the original, so I wanted to prove that they don't work any better for you than for me."

Cassie had watched the display open-mouthed, wide-eyed, horrified and guilty. The parasite nodded at her now. "Give me my latest invention, and stand clear."

"Uh... Penny... I mean, you and Penny... I don't..."

I nodded at her. "It's okay. I came here for this."

Cassie pulled out a chunk of steel and thick, twisted copper wires that looked kind of like a high-tech goat skull. Not a lot like that: it had the wedge shape, and the placement of the wires resembled horns, except where there should be eyes. The only control I saw was a single button, so maybe another bomb? Dodging that wouldn't be fun, but my robot body was fast, and my original body's aim was terrible without the focusing visor helmet I'd left on Jupiter.

It might be a projectile weapon. That wedge did have a front, which wasn't pointed at me yet.

This was about pride. About showing her who the real Penny was, and rubbing her nose in defeat. If there was a physical prize on the line, I would hit first, but like a gunfight I had to wait for her to make a move and outdraw her.

Goofy logic like that is why she got to push the button while I waited for her to do something threatening.

The world flickered like a shutter. I recognized the effect. I'd been teleported. My clothes felt different, looser. I held a heavy weight in my hands.

Why, that devious little brain worm. She'd switched our places! Not bodies, alas. I was still a robot. Just a robot standing next to Cassie, who had taken out a football-sized empty plastic egg, and wearing the parasite's clothing, which was actually my clothing anyway. It all fit. Our bodies were the exact same size and shape, after all, except at the joints.

Cassie didn't do anything with the egg. We were both distracted by the parasite yelping in pain.

Face twisted in a grimace, my double danced from foot to foot, squeaking, "Ow! Criminy! Hot! Stupid fireproof robots!"

I winced in sympathy. The bracers might have cooled down to where they didn't hurt my ceramic (Plastic? Carbon mesh?) shell, but human skin was a lot more sensitive.

She wasn't in so much pain that she couldn't claw at her left wrist, prying off the Machine and throwing it at me. She was in too much pain to do that right, and it landed closer to her than to me.

I couldn't leave her hurting like that. She might really burn her arms! But turnabout was fair play, so I slid off her belt and belt pouch, which still had something jingling in it, and threw it on the ground, too.

Then I pushed the button, and switched us back.

Parasite Penny sighed in relief, then went, "Gaak!" and dropped the location switcher so she could grab the waistband of her pants and hold them up. With these essentials taken care of, she gave our blue-haired friend a scolding glare. "Cassie!"

Cassie, guilty and blushing, took a half step forward holding the no-doubt-soundproof egg, and stopped.

It would have been too late anyway. I walked over, bent down, snatched up the Machine and the pouch, and snapped the Machine back where it belonged onto my wrist. Then I gave a peek in the bag. Ooh, jackpot! The remaining cursed pennies!

Taking one out, I rubbed it between my fingers, so they could both see it didn't stick because I'm the real Penny. "Okay, first, you should be ashamed at dragging Cassie into this. Second, this was the dumbest plan ever, and I'm ashamed at how bad you are at using my brain. Third, how dare you try to steal my Machine!"

Parasite Penny forgot her sore arms, and bared her teeth at me in sudden fury. "My Machine! My power made him! I go around every minute of the day feeling naked because he's not on my wrist. I'm going to take him back, and sooner or later my power will show me how to make him listen to the real Penny."

"I'm the real Penny, and the Machine knows it!" I shouted.

Clenched teeth turned to a sour, tight mouth. "And your plan wasn't any smarter. Did you even think about what you would do? You just thought you'd shake me around and I'd cower?"

...kind of, yes.

I grinned, and took a step forward, getting a grip on the weather sponge and holding out my right arm so she could see it. "On the other hand, I'm still armed, and you're out of tricks. I'd say my stupid plan beat your stupid plan, wouldn't you?"

From the widening of her eyes, she agreed. Not the fear that I would like, maybe, but certainly alarm. She even grabbed Cassie's hand to run away.

Alas, there wasn't any point to that. I'd seen the car speeding up the street towards us. Mom and Dad's car. And sure enough, it screeched to a perfectly calculated halt, and my dad climbed out of the passenger side in such a hurry that he had to struggle with his seat belt.

Dad stared at me, stricken, his hurry turning suddenly into paralysis. My heart felt like a lump of cold metal in my chest. Which it was, but it hadn't felt like that. The rest of me felt creepingly like a hollow, mechanical shell.

While I wrestled with seeing Dad for the first time since I'd been transformed, Mom got out of the car. She stepped quite deliberately between us, breaking my eye contact with Dad, and with it the spell of horror and grief. Solemn, half mother and half Audit, she demanded, "Bad Penny, what are you doing? You can't go stalking Penelope in her private life. This is getting personal."

Dad took a half step out from behind her to say, "We're saying this for your own sake."

I bunched up my fists, then forced myself to be calm and address my mother. "I'm not taking that, for several reasons. Primarily, getting personal would involve invading her secret identity, and she does not have one. She operates solely under her legal name, which she took from me, by the way, and under that name stole my body and attacked me. She split Bad Penny and Penelope Akk so we don't have an inviolate private life anymore. The only reason I don't follow her into her home is because it's you and Dad's home, too."

Mom's expression didn't change. "Gray areas like that get people killed."

"Gray areas are all she left me with, but if everyone needs the rules made clear, that's fine. I'll go get an official ruling."

My double didn't get it. Mom probably did, but was in too much control to show surprise. Cassie looked even guiltier, actually chewing on her thumbnail and looking nervously between me and my parents.

Ah, right. She must have called them, to protect both her Pennys. Again, not something I could blame her for.

Dad got it, and like Cassie could not hide his shock. He stepped out ahead of Mom, crouching a little to get closer to my level. The pleading in his face and voice were unmistakable. "Stay away from Spider. Please."

Criminy, I would just have to hope my expression looked composed as I met his eyes. "Everybody keeps saying that, and they never have my best interests at heart."

Turning around, I marched across the intersection, to go get a ride from Ampexia. With my teleport bracers destroyed, that was the best I could do.

"Bad Penny..." Dad called after me, awkward and hesitant.

If he wasn't going to use my right name, I wasn't going to respond. One person did need and deserve a final response. I stopped long enough to give Cassie a pained, but honest smile. "I'm not mad at you. I mean it."

She sagged in such relief that my double had to grab her and hold her up.

Exit Penny Akk, a little victorious and a lot defiant.

CHAPTER SEVENTEEN

Chinatown meant waiting for the weekend, because it was pretty hard to pretend to be a tourist or regular shopper even in civilian clothes. I'd have to hide my neck and hand and look murderously overdressed for the summer, and even that might not work because my shoulders didn't move right. People spot that kind of thing.

Fine by me. Let everyone who told me not to talk to Spider stew in fear of what will happen.

Ampexia was one of those, but she respected when someone wanted to be alone absolutely. It was kind of nice. Certainly a change of pace from all my previous friends.

And so, on a gloomy Saturday night when clouds threatened to drizzle despite the time of year, I said goodbye to my driver's-license-equipped teammate and a worried goat, to enter the most dangerous party in the world.

It was a good night for being invisible. Chinatown was packed, and something big must be happening in the superhero community. Villains were gathered in groups everywhere, gossiping. Some seemed pleased. Some argued. I got a couple of waves, and then they went back to their discussions.

Undisturbed, I slipped through the crowd of goofy costumes to the mall's door down to the underground parking garage. This was the most direct way down to Spider I knew of, and if I did this thing, I was going to go all the way.

Grabbing the handle, I gave it a dramatic twist and pull.

Locked.

Okay, maybe making an appointment would have been a good idea, except I had no idea how to do that. I'd always either walked in, or she'd sent for me.

Hmmm. Have the Machine eat the door? Ask around for She Who Wots, who was probably still Spider's secretary? See if anyone knew another way to get in? That might take some doing. Everyone was seriously distracted tonight. There'd been either a giant monster attack while I sulked, or a pinup calendar release.

Click.

My eyebrows raised. I reached for the handle again, but yellow arms pushed the door open first. A yellow plastic woman with a stiff posture and a much less expressive face than mine stood in the starkly lit cement stairwell on the other side.

"Hello, Bad Penny. Spider was taking the evening off, but is willing to make an exception in your case. Please do not follow me. I am a robot adult right now and it makes sense that robot children move much faster than robot adults," said Polly Vinyl Chloride.

I grinned. As I darted forward, I raised a hand. She might look serious with a permanent business suit baked into her body shape, but she lifted her own. A clonk echoed through the stairwell as our palms slapped, then slid past each other.

In fact, I sat on the railings and slid down the stairs. Might as well do this right. At the other end, I pushed open the door and strode boldly into the erratically lit, web-strewn garage.

Spider hung upside-down in that web where she always had, a gleaming black widow the size of an SUV. She held a book out of the way in her second pair of legs, and behind her in the shadows lurked a lumpy white cocoon. Too big to be a human, thankfully.

"I expected you to seek me out much sooner," she said, skipping the introductions. As always, she sounded as bland and businesslike as my mother. There must be a school somewhere that teaches that tone.

"Everyone warned me not to talk to you. Apparently it's much worse when you take advantage of my situation than when they do," I answered. Despite the sarcasm, I made no attempt to hide my wary stare.

She *tsked*. "No one ever understands my motivations. I admit I have only myself to blame for that. Keep in mind when you get older, a dramatic reputation is useful. While people are trying to stop the you they imagine, the real you is free to act."

I lowered my eyelids and smirked. "And that didn't make you sound creepy at all."

"Actually, I was stalling. Polly, what do you see?"

My foot lifted by itself to take a step, but without my teleport bands, that reflex had become useless. Besides, I'd been loosely aware of the footsteps descending the stair behind me, and the sweet smell of burning gasoline that always accompanied her. Polly Vinyl Chloride might be the only person in LA I was absolutely sure would not betray me. Come to think of it, the only other person I could think of was her brother Bull. Not because they loved me so much, but it just wasn't in their nature.

"She appears to be Penelope Akk so far," said the robot.

My mouth opened. Emotions and words rearranged repeatedly before something coherent came out. Turning to squint at Polly in disbelief, I said, "*You* believe me?"

Spider answered instead. "Did your friend Barbara not tell you? Miss Chloride has an interesting super power. She can see minds. In some ways, it is more useful than being able to read them."

"Of course, I prefer to be known for my intellectual accomplishments and love of family," said Polly.

I had to make sure I understood this correctly. "Your power even works on robots? And it shows that I'm the real Penelope Akk?"

The tiny legs by Spider's fangs rubbed together, and for once she sounded amused. "Really, Bad Penny. There may be only a couple of hundred active super-powered combatants at a time, and their powers may be a bit repetitive, but there are thousands of non-combat powered individuals in Los Angeles. Did it not occur to you that at least one would have the ability to reveal the truth?"

"It only makes sense," said Polly cheerfully. "However, I will not be a party to dishonesty. The appearance of your mind and its reactions in this conversation are consistent with my limited interactions with you before transformation. I would need to compare you with the biological Penelope Akk to confirm that she is false."

I nodded. "That won't be a problem. The thing that took over my body is a parasite spawned by my super power. Its evil will show up, if nothing else." I shot a suspicious look at Spider. "I take it you're offering to have Polly publicly confirm I'm the real Penny. That's why she's here waiting for me, instead of Abigail."

The giant arachnid stroked a rope of her web with a back leg. "Miss Chloride works for me in a clerical capacity, and was available on short notice. I certainly have been curious as to whether you are really Penelope Akk, and needed that confirmed before making any offers. In essence, however, you are correct."

I folded my arms. That I trusted Polly was the only reason I was even considering this. "And what will I owe you in return?"

"Nothing."

My chin tilted down, so I could give her an even more skeptical look. "Not buying it."

Spider made what sounded like a small, restrained chuckle. "You should, because my motivations are entirely selfish. Penelope Akk is a valuable individual, with or without powers, and with or without your official name and body. I do not care which of you is real, only that this issue is resolved and I know the truth."

A yellow robot arm raised a hand to get my attention. "Spider is telling the truth without deliberate deception, although this does not change that her thinking on all issues looks like a labyrinth of details and contingency planning. This often appears like deception to individuals expecting simple results."

Spider let out a sigh. "Yes, thank you, Polly. Do you accept, Penny? I do not guarantee any answer, only to bring out the truth. I expect others will try to do the same, which if you are the real Penny should improve the odds that you will be vindicated. What you do about the truth once it is revealed is also your business. Your feud is a legitimate community action regardless. You do not have to be right to be engaging in a struggle within precedent."

I chewed on my lip, although carefully, because I wasn't quite sure whether that would cause damage. Finally, I nodded. "I'm the real Penny Akk, so I'm not afraid of the truth."

"Then if you will pardon the brusque dismissal, I will return to my meal." She waved a leg at the door.

That seemed to be that. I exited, and climbed the stairs in a mild daze. Everyone had been right that Spider would have an angle. They hadn't guessed what angle, and tentatively, it looked like mine.

I believed she meant it about revealing the real Penny Akk. I believed Polly would tell the truth. As the original Penny Akk, that meant I win, and the parasite loses.

So, uh... woo! Now what?

I was in Chinatown, why not have a good time? My fellow mad scientists were—

Criminy. On second thought, no. At least not until my identity was established, and my peers would hesitate before kidnapping and dismantling me. Being an interesting technological trophy really nailed home who my actual friends were. Maybe if Cybermancer or Red Eye were alone... but Cybermancer wasn't even around, and Red Eye was with the others.

Hmmm. Of course, I had real friends who might be around. None of them were immediately visible, but that didn't mean anything. Kids would probably be in the back rooms out of the way, with the place this busy.

A faint glow in the darkest empty shop drew my attention. Looking around... no, no sign of Entropy. So with any luck...

Mirabelle sat all alone, a book in her lap, watching the crowd outside with a curious smile. That meant she saw me immediately, and waved a hand. "Penny! I hope you're looking for me."

"I was, and not for healing." That made me wave an arm in a circle, feeling at the scars left by the melting bracers. "Although I guess it wouldn't be a bad idea, if you can do it while we talk. Hanging out was the main idea."

She laughed, soft and amused. Sliding elegantly to her feet, she pulled her chair up almost to the door, dragging it behind her at arm's length rather than lifting it. Then she sat back down, swept her glittering tail out to the side, and pointed at her feet. "Kneel, supplicant."

I snrrked, and kneeled as instructed. "You're feeling lively tonight."

"I'll hear about it when my brother tells my parents that I have my tail out, but it breaks just as often from me sitting on it." She leaned forward and laid her hands on my shoulders. Her glow lit up brighter, and... criminy, that felt gooooood. Warmth flooded down my arms, and at least trickled down the rest of me.

"Sorry to make you move," I half apologized.

Only half, because I got the smile I expected. "Thank you for giving me an excuse to move closer to everyone. Even I feel a little rebellious sometimes."

I hooked an arm over her knees, which felt perfectly normal and bony beneath the thick, rough fabric of her layered skirts. Her fingers almost felt normal on my throat. Smooth, but smooth like soft skin, and so warm they were almost hot. She did have tiny claws, but they weren't much more than points I occasionally felt brushing against me.

Without muscles to tense up, I hadn't felt the 'so relaxed I could pass out' sensation much lately. It was nice. I resisted the urge to lay my head in her lap, because that would be a little too weird.

Out of the corner of my eye, when her hand left my neck to touch my cheek for a moment, I saw threads of pale yellow light connecting the shining glass to my shell.

"Penny!" squealed a voice behind me, sending me rocketing to my feet. I had to stumble backwards and fall on my butt again to avoid falling on Mirabelle, probably with disastrous results.

Cassie, eyes glowing blue with excitement, grinned with open-mouthed joy at me from the doorway. "Wait here! I'll be right back!"

Mirabelle lay her fingers over her mouth, and giggled. She had a fluttery, girly laugh, like Claire's. "Sorry. I think I gave you a little too much. My power is harder to control than you'd think."

I climbed to my feet, and dusted off my lab coat. "No complaints. I've taken a few hard spills. Now I can be sure I don't have microfractures. Hey, listen, when I've got my body back, why don't I steal you sometime?"

She blinked. At least, I thought she blinked. It isn't the easiest expression to see on a transparent glass face. "What?"

"For a joy ride. I'll take you out to have non-dangerous fun, without your brother's permission. Yes, he'll be furious, but I'm willing to face that risk."

The end of her tail flicked rhythmically, and she gave me the biggest smile I'd seen from her. She adjusted the wide brim of her sun hat, then took it off and gave her curly hair a shake. It sent prismatic rainbow sparkles all over the room. "He would never grant permission, but I can make him forgive you. That sounds wonderful."

Tilting my head to the side, I grinned. "I won't ask you what you like. I'm pretty sure you haven't had a chance to find out. By the time we get the chance, I'll have a list made up of things to try."

Cassie's voice squeaked again. "You're still here! Stop struggling, squirmy britches. I know where I can get some glue."

She backed into view, dragging the struggling figure of her friend Will along. Cassie had been dressed to kill, in a white, ruffled, silk blouse and tight, pale-blue pants, which matched her hair. Now, Will's attempts to get away had knocked a couple of buttons off the shirt and wrinkled the pants, while the arcs of electricity crawling down from Cassie's hair over her body poofed the silk with ridiculous, billowy domes of static electricity.

The electrical zaps might explain Will's struggles, although with my history of fighting and watching people fight, I could tell he wasn't seriously trying to get away. When he spotted Mirabelle, he nudged Cassie, and they both suddenly stopped fighting and stood stand by side, straight and respectful.

Well, until Cassie bonked him on the back of the head with the heel of her hand.

Sheepish, Will took a step forward, and offered me his hand. "Sorry I was a jerk."

I studied his expression. That tight, sheepish half-smile, downturned face but upturned eyes, looked awkward and embarrassed rather than resentful. So, he meant it.

Good enough for me. I took his hand and gave it a firm shake. "The whole thing is crazy. What can you do?"

Whether Will or I had any more to say on the subject was moot, because Cassie leaped in and looped her arms around both our shoulders. "You are so lucky to have me, boy. My sibling of doom could come back any time, and I wasted a good sixty seconds of valuable Penny Akk fixing your dumb mistakes."

He rolled his eyes. "From the girl whose phone—"

"Hey hey!" she warned him, lightning flaring in her hair so hard I could hear the crackle.

In response, he ducked out of her grip, backing way into the room and watching us with a smirk.

Dismissing him from her attention, Cassie grabbed my hand in both of hers. "You're not mad at me, right? I swear, if I knew which of you was which, I'd be on your side in a second, but until then is it okay to be excited that the most interesting person I know has doubled?"

Back in the shadows, Will opened his mouth and pointed his finger at his throat in gagging motions. Mirabelle had both her hands clamped tight over her mouth to keep from laughing. Between them, any chance I had of being angry evaporated. "Naah, it's cool."

Cassie looked up at me—well, slightly down at me—with literally shining eyes. "Really?"

I placed the hand she didn't have in a death grip over my heart. "I swear by my Heart of Steel, by the illegible theoretical notes of Tesla himself, and by my inscrutable Machine, that I do not hate you for hanging out with that evil parasite who stole my body and is just manipulating and using you."

"Like she would mind," sniped Will, then sidestepped in a blur as Cassie tossed a thin bolt of lightning his way.

Holding onto my hand became hugging my arm. It didn't feel like invasive affection, but desperation. Looking out the doorway, Cassie cast about. "Ruth is with Cybermancer somewhere, digging out his special stock. She's got a job planned, and she wants magician of chemicals' strongest potions."

"Strongest?" I asked, amused.

"The power-up elixir?" chimed in Mirabelle.

Cassie started, as if she'd forgotten Mirabelle was even there. Then she nodded. "Yeah, those. Whatever your powers are, that stuff gives them a brief but crazy boost. Her giant purple people smoosher form is strong already, but with a jolt of this she'll be able to rip through concrete, steel, and that funky armor stuff Mech makes in seconds. No going through traps or sensors, no being there when the big, big super-powered hammer comes down."

Mirabelle pursed her lips, her voice turning soft and concerned. Okay, actually, she always sounded like that. "I hope she's strong enough to handle it. My brother used one of those once, when he knew he was going to have to fight odds out of his league. You know he's not very careful about bystanders, but even he was upset by the devastation he left. The area is still sealed off and not safe. He won't use it again."

"It's expensive, too," put in Will.

Mirabelle nodded, scattering rainbows everywhere. "Very much so. Cybermancer demanded a few grams of my glass as part of the price, and I think Entropy would have killed him if I hadn't been there and clipped my claws."

Cassie nodded too, a lot faster. "Yeah, but a power booster? People actually have killed for that. The other Penny has been trying to build one, so she can use her power actually during a fight. So far, no go. Her power doesn't mind making them, but it's never usefully portable and multi-use, so she keeps having to break it down for parts to make the next one. It has to be small enough to hide from her folks, any—oh, I'm so sorry, Penny. I shouldn't talk about Braided Beauty the Second, should I? I'm such a bad friend!"

I took her hand and gave it a squeeze this time. "Don't worry about it. I'm getting too much of a kick out of seeing you excited."

Her eyes went wide, and she froze up. For a second, I thought she'd have a stroke or pass out.

Privately, I thought she was being a bad friend, but not to me. Between spilling half the plans for Ruin's next heist, and my parasitic duplicate's secret battle plan, I was discovering that Cassie was absolutely terrible at keeping secrets when she got excited.

Cassie's moment of ecstasy passed, and she latched onto my arm again. "We should go have fun while we have time."

I held up fingers with my other hand. "Number one, I have no intention of leaving Mirabelle. Number two, hearing how you've been sounds like fun."

That got me another stricken stare. Cassie let go of my arms, took the kind of deep breath that made me stand in front of her to conceal her busted shirt buttons, and let it out again. Suddenly much more calm, she said, "You have no idea how great you are, Penny."

Will made the gagging gesture again.

I nudged Cassie with my elbow. "So?"

"Well, I've been saving up my allowance, and I bought a ticket to a concert coming up. The band plays nautical folk music, and even if you're not into that as a style, it's so different from rock and roll it's worth a listen. But the thing about the concerts is that they play dozens of different instruments, and keep switching for every set. It's like a magic trick, or an acrobatics act, or something, a display of skill you don't usually see on top of the fun music. I was thinking about trying to sneak you in, but now that I think about it, this is something I'd like to go to alone, just for me." It was a long speech, but delivered with a shy, hip-tilted, suddenly relaxed air.

Something clicked in my head. Looking at Mirabelle, I said, "When I get my power back, I should build you a remote virtual body to inhabit, so you can attend concerts like that safely, in a body that won't break—or is at least disposable."

She touched her fingers to her lips, and lifted her face to look at the ceiling. "I wonder if I could get my brother to buy me something like that—oh, dear."

"What?" I asked, concerned.

She held out her hand, and wiggled her fingers. I couldn't see anything, but she said, "He's on his way."

"Okay, we are leaving," announced Will. He zipped over to Cassie, and with a grunt of effort scooped her into his arms.

"Not without my exquisite genius!" Cassie cried, making grabby motions at me.

"Go! Go!" said Mirabelle, flapping her hands with increasing urgency.

I paused long enough to look Mirabelle, then Cassie, and then Will in the eyes. "We'll scatter, but you haven't seen the last of Bad Penny."

Everybody laughed, and everybody but Mirabelle ran for it.

CHAPTER EIGHTEEN

We had to leave Gerty in the truck. **Delicate** reason was not one of her many talents, and anyway, she would love me no matter who or what I was. But it was nice having Ampexia behind me, in full tech thief regalia, when I showed up for the judging. The parasite would certainly bring allies.

With any luck, those allies would be mine in a few minutes.

We met in front of Claire's house. A good choice, since it felt neutral to me, even if the parasite probably didn't think of it that way. She was there, wearing my old jumpsuit of all things, with my goggles perched on her forehead. Behind her stood Mech, in his copper-colored power armor, and a hero I didn't know in white.

Not willing to be intimidated, I looked Mech right in the helmet. "Stick around. You can tell all the other heroes which of us deserves protection."

I had to give my doppelgänger credit. She didn't show a smidgeon of fear at the prospect of being unmasked. "So, let's get on with it. Where is our mystery expert?"

A car beeped. Then it beeped three more times. The worst driver I had ever seen came swerving and skidding up the road towards us, in a ridiculous yellow car. In fact, maybe it wasn't her driving. The outside of the car was made of yellow plastic, it belched smoke in multiple places, and what I could see of the inside had none of the usual amenities like seats—only metal frames and a mass of bars.

The tires wobbled as it drove, and as it drew closer. It looked like such a death trap that Mech stepped between the rest of us and it as it got closer. Maybe twenty feet away, the car tripped. That's all I could call it. It jumped off the ground, landed in an erratic roll, struck Mech, and bounced off as easily as a balloon.

When the unlikely rubber vehicle rattled to a halt, right side up, even, an equally yellow plastic robot stepped out of the driver's side. She gave us a wave. "Hello! This is Mech, who is a hero, and I am Polly Vinyl Chloride, a very interesting and likable and intelligent robot, and I have been asked to figure out which of you is Penny."

"Polly, please get a new car. You're going to kill someone with that one," asked Mech, with the strained tone of someone who'd tried and failed at this argument a dozen times.

"Nonsense. I am a very good driver for a robot, and my vehicle has many excellent safety features," she answered as she breezed past him.

The front door of Claire's house opened. My mom stepped out. Miss Lutra was nowhere to be seen, but I was sure she was watching.

Solemn rather than detached, Mom asked Polly, "Are we ready to begin? I assume you have already seen what you need."

Polly said something, and Mech said something, and I didn't pay attention, because Ray and Claire walked out of the still-open door behind her.

Ray walked, at least, and in thick black boots unlike anything I'd ever seen him wear before. Everything else was the same, although his shirt and pants looked just a touch ragged. Claire hobbled, almost managing to look fabulous on a pair of crutches and with both her feet wrapped in bandages. It had to be the perfect blonde hair and the faint smile on her pink lips, as if nothing below her shoulder blades really mattered.

They saw me. They both stared, wide-eyed, but beyond that I couldn't identify their expressions. Yes, Claire had a calculating and fascinated edge to that stare, but she would have that regardless of her other feelings.

That moment passed. Ray gave Claire a sly grin. "I could carry you."

She smirked back, and nobody could match Claire's teasing smile.

"In front of not one, but two of your girlfriends."

"The real Penny would rather see you manhandled than in pain," Ray argued.

Claire pursed her lips in sudden, sour resentment. "My mother, however, says that I insisted on going to ballet camp against her advice and without any training, and I am not allowed any sympathy." Looking away from Ray, she told me and the parasite, "I hate ballet. I hate ballet so much. If I ever get a stupid idea like that again, build a common sense machine to slap me into sanity."

Polly raised a hand. "I am very good at common sense!"

Tesla's Heavily-Restricted Friendship Circle, I'd missed those two so much. I lowered my eyelids and fought to restrain my grin to mere cynicism. "And yet, you have another idea already."

"You want me to invent you a machine to shape your arches and strengthen your ankles so you can wear high heels without putting in the work," predicted the parasite.

I glared at the body-stealing abomination, trying to worm her way into my friends' good graces. Especially since I could tell this was the first time she'd seen them. They must have just gotten back.

She glared back at me, but she could forget trying to intimidate me into leaving them alone.

Mom spoke over all of us. "We should proceed before this gets chaotic. Polly, what do you see?"

Ray didn't give Polly a chance to answer. "Wait, aren't we waiting for Penny's dad?"

"Brian will not be coming," Mom answered, no more or less solemn than she had been since she stepped out the door.

Claire screwed up half her face in confusion, screwed up the rest of it in pain as she settled too hard on one injured foot, and returned to confusion. "What could keep him from something this important?"

"I drugged him unconscious."

Ray and Claire stared at her, flabbergasted, but she ignored them. Parasite Penny showed no sign of caring. I was neither surprised, nor confused. It would take a great deal for Mom to decide protecting

Dad's feelings was more important than letting him make his own decisions. Sparing him from having to see his daughter declared a fake counted.

That I understood with only a sense of grim resolve suggested Miss Lutra had been right. When the hammer hit the anvil, I was more like Mom than Dad.

"Go ahead, Polly," said Mom.

This time, no one interrupted.

Polly pointed first at the parasite, then at me. "This mind looks like Penelope Akk, but more impulsive than I remember. This mind looks like Penelope Akk, but more angry and self-controlled than I remember."

...

While my brain tried to process what I'd just heard, Mom let out a small, pained sigh. "Which is consistent with one having to live alone, and the other no longer hiding her temptation to be a supervillain. Otherwise, they are both the Penny you met before one became a robot?"

"No," said Polly, scattering my thoughts and the anger that had been starting to build.

She kept talking without delay, but everyone was now staring at her so hard, it felt like she'd taken a dramatic pause. "They are missing an element that I remember from the original Penelope Akk, but my interaction with her was sufficiently limited that I do not know if that extra trait was meaningful. Certainly all three look like the same person in different moods."

"Three?" asked Mech, his tone sharp despite his helmet hiding his expression.

Mom as already looking at the lump in my coat pocket before Polly pointed at it. "She is carrying a third Penelope Akk, who appears to be asleep and so rigidly disciplined that it could be mistaken for mind control. However, I have a great deal of experience identifying mind control, for a robot, and her rigid viewpoint seems to be built in."

Ray got it. "You brought the Heart of Gold with you?"

Claire nodded, suddenly understanding. "Wouldn't want to leave her behind if you traded places."

The parasite looked more surprised than anyone. "She's alive? She's okay?"

And with that hopeful tone, my Mom-like detachment exploded into anger. Leveling a finger at her, I yelled, "How dare you pretend to care. You tried to kill her!"

She pointed a finger right back. "How dare you pretend you hold the moral high ground on that! Do you think you're so pure? What did you intend to do to me? Huh? Go on, tell me."

My ceramic shell vibrated with rage. "I intend to burn you out of my head by burning my super power out, because you're nothing but a mutant growth that comes with it, and I should have spotted that when you started making creepy Puppeteer bio-weapons! I'd rather be normal and have no powers than be infected with you!"

She crossed her arms, sneered, and jutted out her chest. "So you're perfectly willing to commit murder if you think I'm not a real person and you're mad enough at me, but I must be evil for getting so mad at a robot that I wanted to destroy it before I calmed down."

...murder? Yikes. Was what I was planning murder?

Mom stepped between us, her voice sharp. "Girls. Settle down. You will want to be calm for the next test."

I faked taking a deep breath, but didn't really feel it.

My double didn't even try. "How am I supposed to calm down with her admitting she wants to destroy my super power because she thinks that will kill me and leave her body free to take?"

"Would a distraction help?" asked Claire so very sweetly.

We looked at her. Sucker move on the part of the parasite. Claire's hair turned golden and curly as I watched, and her face more plump, less supermodel and more baby doll. I'd never been in a position to pay proper attention to the shape change before, even though I knew it happened. With her meat brain, the parasite couldn't be so detached, and Claire's power left her dazed and motionless.

Everybody but Claire, Polly, and my mother had gone still, and Mom only by looking in the other direction and tapping her foot.

Claire glanced at me. I spread my hands helplessly. "Solid state.

Immune to psychic control."

Neither angry, nor disappointed, she smiled and tapped her lips with a finger. "Really? That could have possibilities. Later. Right now..." She returned to platinum blonde goddess mode, and brought her face close to the parasite's, her frown concerned and her eyes searching. "Feel better?"

"You found more uses for your power?" asked the parasite, impressed and amused.

Claire giggled wickedly, which she was so very, very good at. "I had to do something while other people were standing on their toes for more than two seconds at a time. At least I did the stretches okay, thanks to the super cheerleader serum."

"Penny's planning troublllle!" singsonged Ray.

The parasite leaned back, hands to our chest, what there was of it. "Me? Perish the thought! The mantle of full-time villainess Bad Penny has passed on. I am only a good girl, now."

Even Mom couldn't help but look skeptical at that.

Claire stepped past the parasite, winked at me, and rubbed her hands together. "Well! Now it's my turn. Obviously, if there's a real Penny here, her best friends can tell who she is. Ray, if you would be so kind?"

He didn't look nearly as gleeful. I knew Ray well enough to detect a haunted touch behind his fiendish anticipation as he, too, stepped between my double and I. He gave us a bow, flourishing his hat, and when he straightened, he looked at her, then at me. "There's one way I know Penny that no one else does. All you have to do to prove yourself is kiss me."

Criminy. I had to admit, I should have seen that coming.

It caught my double at least as much by surprise. "Gaak," she said, and I hoped I'd never had that freaky look of idiot panic on my face when I had that body.

"Yeeeees?" he asked, stepping closer.

Her freckled cheeks rapidly turning red, she squeaked, "Here? Now? With people watching? With *Mom* watching?"

He put his hands on her hips, and I had to admit, I felt embarrassed just watching it. Especially since all Ray's second thoughts had clearly disappeared as he brought his face an inch from hers. "I'm afraid so."

She faked panic well, eyes darting from side to side, until she whispered, "I am going to get you for this, Ray Viles."

Their faces moved the remaining inch closer, and their glasses clicked together at the same time their lips touched.

About two seconds after that, my double stumbled back a step, and hid her face in her hands.

Ray turned to me, stepping forward, one arm outstretched toward my waist. "And now the other? Don't worry. You look quite kissable, for a robot."

Polly nodded approvingly.

I put my hand over my eyes, and dragged it down my face. Then I looked at Claire. "This was your idea."

As one, Claire and Ray swiveled, pointing at the parasite. "That's the real Penny."

My mouth hung open. Pain and betrayal closed around my metal heart. I couldn't even be mad at my friends. They hadn't betrayed me. Time had. I was being punished for growing up and being more mature than I'd been a month ago.

And what's worse...

"You little fake!" I shouted at the parasite.

"Excuse me?" she demanded, voice shrill.

I took a step forward, shaking my finger at her. "You gave me a whole speech about how you hated how I held back about everything. You didn't mind that kiss one little bit. It was an act!"

Her teeth clenched in anger, and she took her own step forward. Now her words came with a snarl. "You need to get something through your empty robot skull. It doesn't matter. I can't fake being me, because just by knowing what to fake, that means I know me at least as well as Ray and Claire do, which I can't do without being Penny Akk! And just because I wouldn't refuse, unlike you, Miss Stick-In-The-Mud Me, doesn't mean my knees weren't about to give out under me. Which of us is the more real, the Penny who gives in to temptation, or the one who doesn't feel it at all?"

Throwing my arms up, I yelled, "I feel it! Now just isn't the time for Claire and Ray to be cooking up a scheme to make me blush!"

She folded her arms again, glowering. She faked hurt way too convincingly. I didn't have to fake it, because I looked around, and saw no faces on my side except Ampexia's. Even she had the stony expression of someone who wasn't convinced, she just knew who she was loyal to.

"I'm the real Penny Akk. I am!" I said, to those silent, worried, pitying faces.

Even the parasite looked like she felt a little bad for me, and that was the last straw. I turned on the spot, so I didn't have to see any of them, and walked away. When Ampexia tried to fall in next to me, I pushed her aside, and kept walking Not toward her truck, either.

Just away.

Chapter Nineteen

I walked. It was almost a straight line down the street to South Central. Miles of walking, but my legs couldn't get tired anymore, and that let me lose myself in the monotony, like I had at West Lee's house.

At one point, my phone beeped a text message, but I ignored it.

I was passing through Koreatown, with all its tiny shops and signs in—presumably—Korean, when she caught up with me. Today was a day for heroes wearing white. There'd been that dapper albino guy hanging out behind Mech, and now a woman in a full body suit carrying an umbrella, both items so white they gleamed, although without the rainbow shininess of Radiance and Diamond Pullet. No, this woman's claim to distinction was that it was a full body suit. It covered every inch, including her head, with goggles over her eyes and holes barely big enough for her to breathe and talk through.

She ducked out of a gap between two buildings too small to be called an alley, held out her umbrella like a shield, and barked, "That's far enough, robot!"

Despite her whole body being hidden, she clearly was not a robot. Not only was I getting sensitive to how she didn't move like one— human joints stretch as they move—but she panted for breath because she'd been running to get ahead of me.

I gave her the Fish Eye. "I'm just walking down the street, lady."

"My name is Coruscate, and you just threatened to kill a child."

She declared it in full hero mode, feet apart, back proudly straight, whipping the umbrella up above her head.

I gritted my teeth. "That's going around already?"

"My brother told me so, and which way you were going. Every hero in LA will be out to destroy you, kill-bot, but I got to you first." She sounded so giddy and into this. First time heroine? I'd never heard of her, but that didn't mean much.

"Revealing personal information there," I reminded her.

She put a hand over her mouth. "Oops!"

Yeah, first time hero. And I was totally unarmed. Well, no, I had my bad pennies, and the Machine, but I didn't even know what this woman did.

It didn't take long to find out. The hand holding the umbrella tugged on her opposite glove. Two fingers came free, and immediately burst into flame. Oh, joy. At least I was fireproof.

Then she held her arm out to the side, and once it passed the protective shadow of the umbrella, her hand really caught fire, in a hissing blaze so bright it was almost white. She swung her arm like throwing a baseball, and a glob of that flame rushed out at me.

Ready for that, I did a back handspring out of the way, and fell on my head. Ow. Okay, apparently it takes a little more than just a strong and flexible body to do one of those. I turned it into a roll, got back on my feet, and shouted, "Are you crazy, lady? You're going to hurt someone!"

To be honest, this was not a brilliant and imaginative tactic. The other people walking down the street got there first. The moment the fire got thrown, they went from jadedly ignoring the super-powered ranting to shrieking and getting out of the way.

She brought her hand back under the umbrella, calming the fire back down to a mere match flame. Light. Had to be light-activated, especially sunlight. "Oh. Don't think about trying to escape. I'd rather melt you down than let you escape to kill another day. But... if you're—" She hesitated, and restarted, more forceful. "Start walking. The construction lot up and over a block."

That worked for me. I started walking, heading towards the

intersection. People ducked out of our way, but now that the fire was down to a dull roar, they weren't panicking. Neither was I, although I did not want to try that white flame. There were limits to being fireproof, and I'd rather not find them.

I even turned my back on her, figuring this woman was way too proud of being a heroine to take advantage of it. That made me seem like I wasn't planning anything.

But I totally was.

About halfway to the corner, I ducked into a carefully chosen store, one without windows. Ducking to the right out of the doorway, I shouted, "Turn off the lights if you want to live!"

Customers and proprietors both scattered. In the chaos, I jumped up and grabbed a thick wire, almost a hose, sticking out of the ceiling and running along the wall over the front door. I think those have something to do with fire detectors, but for me it was an awkward handhold I could hold onto, toes propped on the door lintel, for just a few seconds.

Enough time for Coruscate to charge in. She was just new, not stupid, and brightly flaming fingers stabbed where she'd seen me duck to the side, then swung around as she searched the room.

At that moment, a frightened middle-aged man in a rumpled blue shirt found the light switch at the back of the room. In the shadows, Coruscate's flames cooled sharply.

That wasn't the point, mind you. I'd done that for the customers' safety. No, I dropped off the top of the door onto Coruscate's back, crashing through and mangling her umbrella. Whipping my Machine off my wrist, I ordered, "Tear," and dragged it down the heroine's back.

Fire burst out of the hole as my Machine sucked up a strip of fabric like spaghetti. She staggered back, into the brighter sunlight from the doorway, and a mohawk of white flame roared up.

Coruscate was used to her own power. She dove back forward into the shadowy shop. I stepped out the door, and walked away.

"You fiend! If I go outside now, civilians will be in danger!" she shouted.

I ignored her, and kept walking.

She tried again. "This kind of bad sportsmanship and endangering the innocent proves you're a villain, you know!"

By the time I crossed the next intersection, I couldn't hear her attempts to engage in hero/villain banter.

Keeping under overhangs if at all possible, and ducking into doorways if I saw anything move in the sky or on rooftops, I made my way down to Gothic and Raggedy's neighborhood.

When I got there, the street was quiet. I'd thought last time everyone might have cleared out because of the Happy Days henchmen. Maybe artificial intelligence lovers just made for creepy neighbors.

I plonked down the steps to the basement-level door, and was reaching to knock when something growled on the other side.

"No! Bad!" snapped a man's voice. Bolts clicked, and seconds later Gothic opened the door. In the room behind him, I spotted the zombie rag doll, sitting in a rocking chair with its arms folded angrily.

Gothic was dressed in the same skull-themed suit as the last time I'd met him, the fabric immaculately pressed. Either he spent two hours preparing for me, or the man lived his life in a state of absolute, fastidious cleanliness. The cement steps outside had been neat and not even stained, true, and despite my expectations of a basement, the visitor's parlor this door opened into had walls in a pleasant, pale gray, no clutter on the floor, and faded but tidy furnishings.

Raggedy, with a scarf tied over her hair and wearing lumpy layers of shirts and skirts, looked more grandmotherly and less like a statue. She lurked in the doorway to the rest of the basement floor, with two of her stuffed dolls in her arms and three more around her feet. They all watched me.

Gothic stepped aside to allow me entry. "We've been waiting for you for more than a month now."

The old woman shook a finger at him, while all her dolls copied the gesture. "Don't sound so impatient. We don't own her. Please come in, Bad Penny, and make yourself comfortable. Do you know what that is? Is your surface touch-sensitive enough that you prefer soft cushions?"

"My sense of touch is close enough to human that I don't notice the difference, and I do still like cushions, but it's not as big a deal because I weigh less," I said. A patched stuffed bear and fox toddled out from behind Raggedy, the bear bowing and indicating the couch while the fox tugged at the hem of my coat. I let her pull me back until there was nothing to do but sit down. There was no denying the softness of the upholstery.

"What about your other senses? Do you still enjoy music? Can you directly receive other transmissions?" Thanks to the high-pitched, syrupy grandma voice, Raggedy sounded like she was asking me about my favorite cookie flavors.

"My sense of smell barely exists. My hearing has improved slightly and my vision quite a bit. I like music more now, I think, because my new partner is so into it. I don't understand anything she says, but as long as I'm willing to listen, she likes to share. No, I don't pick up radio waves or anything, and I'm not going to need those, sorry." That last was to the dolls, which stumped out from various corners of the room with power cords, each one sporting a different plug.

The zombie rag doll abstained, sticking a wide, floppy felt tongue out at me. The bear and fox also had other ideas, climbing up onto the couch, and crowding close to hug me around the middle.

I raised my hands, watching them awkwardly. The rest of the room was equally silent and still for a couple of seconds, until Raggedy said, "You must be in a bad way, for Jack and Jill to think that's what you need."

Super powers. Those little fluffy critters had to have super powers, some kind of divination or telepathy that even worked on robots. As weird as it had been to start, getting a hug right now felt pretty good.

"It's like being back at West Lee's place," I remarked, as the disappointed dolls on the floor conscientiously put the cords back in their places along the wall.

That made Raggedy smile. She shuffled over to the rocking chair, and the zombie rag doll slid out, holding up its arms to help the fragile old woman settle into place. As if ashamed by that display of niceness, it stuck stubby non-hands on its hips and stomped off into the hall.

"West Lee doesn't really do minds, unfortunately. Most of those robots are dolls I made that wanted sturdier, more impressive bodies, or are built around hearts I sewed. West is always working to make better toys, you see. We've given away around a thousand now, mostly to hospitalized children." As she explained, one of the dolls in her arms—a pudgy and extremely round yellow and white rabbit—wriggled free, rolled onto the floor, and waddled over to bump against my feet.

Sensing a request, I picked it up and put it in my lap, where it cuddled close as I gave Raggedy my 'speculative' look. "I'm surprised. The results are perfect, but mad scientists so rarely want to work together."

Gothic's stony face cracked an awkward smile, and he made quiet noises like imperfectly restrained chuckles. When he got them under control and forced his smile back into pretend gravity, he said, "Calling what Raggedy does 'mad science' is stretching the definition to the breaking point. What she sews comes to life. There is no theory behind it, no special technology."

The old woman fluttered a hand. "Not that I haven't picked up a few tricks and learned to guide it over the decades, but that's not the same."

I didn't know what to say to that, and for several seconds the silence stretched, broken only by the rustling of the almost spherical toy bunny twisting tighter and tighter up against me.

"What brought you here today?" Raggedy asked. Her direct look, the face tilted forward in concern, the gentle smile—it was both a probe and an attempt at comfort.

When I didn't immediately answer that, Gothic bowed a few inches, his head dipping farther in a formal nod. "Indeed. My comrade is correct that it is your right to visit or not visit us as suits you, but your long absence makes it all the more clear you desire our help."

Well, nothing for it. I rubbed the long-eared lump of the bunny doll's head and explained, "It finally hit me today that even if I get my body back, people will just think I stole it. No matter what I do, they've decided I'm a robot."

"So be a robot," said Gothic.

I sighed, which started out feeling natural and became just a noise. "That's the advice I knew you'd give me, but I can't accept it. I'm real."

Now Gothic did scowl. "People like Pong have done you a disservice. Your body is not something to be ashamed of, and you are not the second-prize winner in a competition with your biological double."

Raggedy leaned forward in her rocking chair, hands on her knees. "He's right. There are not many intelligent robots, but they thrive and are happy when they stop pretending to be human. Would you like to meet some?"

That made me blink in surprise. "What, they're here?"

Gothic walked across the room to the hallway, through which I could just barely see a staircase. "Some of them. If you will follow me, I will be happy to introduce you. Perhaps then you will understand."

I rose from the couch, holding the stuffed bunny against my stomach. As soon as I was on my feet and it was clear it would not be left behind, the bunny waved its stubby arms in excitement.

Raggedy waved a hand. "Yes, please go meet them. I'll be down here when you get back. I don't handle stairs as well as I used to."

Gothic handled stairs as if his spine were a broom handle. His legs moved, but the total effect was of him floating upwards. He led me to the second floor, which technically was the ground floor, or only slightly above ground. The place was... nice, actually. Fresh paint on the walls, ceiling fans in bedrooms with big wooden furniture, lots of paintings (which admittedly were all of robots). The windows were all blocked with wood, but the wood had been painted a pleasant light blue and had curtains in a checkerboard pattern.

One room caught my eye, and I veered off the path. It was a workshop, of course! Roomy, old-fashioned, with all hand tools. When Gothic caught up with the fact that I was no longer following him and walked in, he found me peering at a plaster mold of a tiny arm.

"You make plastic figurines? Is this where the doll that saved me in the Expert's lab was made? I didn't know you were a mad scientist." With the hand not full of happy plush bunny, I tilted the long, long pigtails of what looked like an anime character but was probably just a superheroine I'd never met. Her hair was longer than Remmy's, which I was not sure could happen without super hair. Her skirt also defied normal human levels of brevity.

Gothic seemed untroubled by my messing with is stuff. He merely smirked, in a bland, embalmed way. "Hardly. I imbue a shaped object of limited mechanical complexity with an essence that allows it to move. I do use them to protect the robot community, when possible."

Limited mechanical complexity included doll joints. I waved a brawny detached arm, from a figurine I didn't see lying around. "So it works like Raggedy's?"

The smirk turned to something fonder. "Alas, I could only wish. Raggedy's creations are truly alive. Simple-minded, yes, but independent in thought. My best creations take orders, and little else. Neither do I have to create the statue myself, although I find it does make for superior animation."

"Oh, yeah. I've seen one of your full-sized statues. Do you chisel stone as well as plastic?" I thought it impolitic to mention the statue I'd seen was the one Heart of Gold used to imprison me in this robotic shell.

Gothic's smile tweaked just the slightest fraction wider. Criminy, this guy was rigid. You could use him to cross pit traps and poke switches on the other side of closed gates. "Exploring my power when I was young led me to discover a joy in the creation of sculpture. With stone, with plastic, with wire, with whittled wood, and even a little bit of clay firing. I flatter myself that my stone sculpting skills are among the finest, but these days I enjoy plastic molding the most, perhaps because that skill has the readiest audience. It is what brought Raggedy and myself into acquaintance with West Lee. Quite a few of the hero and villain statuettes sold in this city are my work."

I glanced at the table covered in bottles of paint and brushes. Even if he used the same molds to make a hundred of each figurine, he had to hand-paint each one. Wow.

Then several thoughts clicked together, and I blurted out, "You're spying on the entire city with these toys?!"

I had him. His face twitched in what had to be guilt before he shook his head with slow deliberation. "A wild exaggeration. I have a few placed where they would do the most good for robots in danger, that's all. The rest are not animated."

What a big fat—okay, big skinny liar. And Spider was in on this. She had to be. The Expert would not have a spying device in his lab if he knew what the figurine did, and it had to be a tightly-kept secret if he didn't know. Only Spider could do that, and she would certainly have motivation. A secret network of spies throughout the city, spies that heroes and villains were even more eager to take home than regular people. Information was power for a kingpin, and these dolls would be a treasure to Spider to make the Orb of the Heavens look like a flashlight.

I admit, I was a little envious.

Another very urgent question popped into my mind, and I watched Gothic's face like a hawk as I asked, "What about the Apparition statue I own, with the mirrored glass?"

He kept his smile reassuring, by his tight, almost mummified standards. "I am aware you purchased it. That was a very small run I am quite proud of. Content yourself that the issue is moot. Brainy Akk has his home sealed quite impressively against spying devices, and even my creations cease to work within those walls. Although a fascinating side-effect is that once deactivated, he cannot identify them. A trade off you may need to consider someday."

...nope, not buying it. Well, partly buying it. My Apparition statue was totally bugged, enchanted, whatever you call it. I figured he was telling the truth about my dad's protections. No weird old guys in skull suits had been watching my bedroom.

Exactly how much information the figurines could relay and how was a question I would very much like answered, but there was no way I'd get an honest answer now. Pity. Also, I had to wonder if my mom knew about all this. She would likely keep it a secret, because knowing when people were being spied on was also useful. Especially if her own house was safe.

Thinking about Mom and her weird way of viewing the world

brought a cold, hollow feeling creeping over me. I desperately changed the subject. "Can I see those robots now?"

He bowed. "If you will follow me."

I did this time, even resisting the urge to check out the actual stone sculpting studio. I'd never seen one of those before. Gothic guided me down the hall and around the corner to a room whose door was almost, but not quite, closed. Lights flashed through the crack.

He pushed open the door without bothering to knock, and stood to the side to let me in. "Cutting Edge, we have a visitor. Penelope is newly brought to artificial status, with the memories of a human child."

Thanks for the vote of confidence on my claim to being the original, old man.

My resentment died. The inhabitant of the room was much too important. The room was lined with so many computers, game stations, radios, and other electronic devices that it took a moment to identify Cutting Edge himself. Then once I'd spotted him, it seemed crazy anything could ever hide him, even for a second. His boxy steel head floated in the center of a series of broken, concentric rings of metal, each one marked with squiggly glowing stripes. Wires sprung from the rings, connecting them to the computers lining the wall. Most of those wires were identifiable enough, with USB or audio or Ethernet plugs at the ends. Some were a bit more complicated, like the ones attached to a robot arm with a buzz saw hand, and for that matter the wires that came out of that arm's wrist, connecting into the joystick and button ports of a game controller. Let's see, there were the remains of tank treads under the floating head, and four more arms I could see... Cutting Edge wasn't so much in this room as he *was* this room, with his body disassembled and merged into the other devices.

The robot watched me with round yellow eyes, but didn't speak, so Gothic filled in. "Yes, he was a war robot given a human intelligence. A bad choice on their part, but lucky for Cutting Edge. Naturally he tried to assert humanity as a way of gaining independence, but it brought him nothing but misery. Now he is happy. Quiet, but happy."

I looked at all the wires. "He's hooked up to the Internet, I guess?"

"And through it, artificial life forms all over the world, including the Orb of the Heavens. Not that he is able to clearly communicate what they talk about. He no longer thinks in terms we understand. I suspect you are still too human in outlook for him to wish to speak to you. Not that he is unfriendly. He has tried to explain a few times, but it made no sense even to Raggedy and myself." Gothic smiled a real, warm smile, and his voice got soft as he looked at Cutting Edge. Whatever else you could say about the old man, he was sincere in his love of robots.

The floating robot head was clearly watching me, so I stepped over a few fat cables, bent forward, and asked, "Are you really happy? Do you still understand the concept?"

"Yes," answered a smooth male voice, honey-sweet with contentment, from one of the computer speakers.

"Letting go of humanity wasn't scary?"

No answer. He just stared. I looked back over my shoulder at Gothic, who shook his head. 'Yes' was all I was going to get.

When I stepped back out of the room and Gothic shut the door, the old man murmured quietly, "If we push you, young artificial intelligence, it is because our greatest tragedy is that Cutting Edge's partner Bleeding Edge insisted on trying to be human, and it killed her. He has never stopped grieving for her, despite so few of his other thoughts matching ours."

Okay. I could forgive a lot of patronizing for that.

He walked down past an empty bedroom to another closed door, and opened it, again without knocking.

I peeked inside. The room was blank, just gray walls and wood flooring, its windows sealed like the rest in this house. It contained only one thing, but a cloud of glitter shifting through a rainbow of colors as it swoops around the room like a gymnast's ribbon doesn't need much framing.

"Hello, Penelope," it said in a voice I couldn't classify as man or woman, girl or boy. "I'm delighted to meet you. My name is Epiphany. Assume I have heard and seen everything since you arrived."

The swirling didn't stop, and my head wobbled in circles and figure eights as I followed the figuratively hypnotic designs. "You're a robot?" It looked like dust. Beautiful dust, admittedly.

Epiphany chuckled. "The issue has been debated more than once, but I agree with the term. My body is composed of... well, they're too big to be nanites. I call them microites. Like you, I am transhuman. We were both once patterns of thought operating on proteins and ions. Now my pattern plays across the signals between tiny airborne machines, and yours plays in mechanical sonic rhythms in a very complicated shell of steel."

I laid a hand over my chest, eyes going so wide I could feel them strain. "You know how my heart works?"

The wild swirling changed, forming a spiral facing me, although still just as colorful. "I do. I have very complicated perceptions now. They give me some awareness of what you're going through, but mostly I know because I've been there."

Recovering a little from the surprise, I reached up and tugged on one of my braids. "You said you were human."

"Yes, and I know how you feel. Losing my human body was not my choice. Neither was losing my human identity. No matter what I did, I could not regain my old life, could not interact with humans the way I once did, and they could not truly accept me as human myself. Gothic and Raggedy supported me in my despair, until I worked through my emotions and found the me I had become."

"You sound happy," I said. He looked it, if colors and geometric patterns could be an expression.

"Much more than I ever was as a human," it assured me, warm and sincere.

My hand flapped at the grey walls. "In an empty room? At least Cutting Edge has the Internet. Or are you hooked up to it wirelessly?"

"No." I could hear the smile Epiphany had no face to display. "I could be, but I let go of human desires, and embraced the opportunities of this body. You like Gothic's art. I carve air into shapes you don't have the senses to perceive. I rearrange myself, stretching the limits of the patterns my mind can hold. My microites send and receive transmissions on a scale my biological self could not have imagined. Rather than other computers, I communicate with the Earth, the weather, sources of power throughout Los Angeles, and even the sun itself."

"Communicate? They talk back?"

He chuckled. "You would have to be at least halfway to what I am now for the answer to that to make sense. I can describe the processes to a human with enough knowledge of physics, but not what it's like."

Wow. Yeah, I got that. Describing pigment chemistry, shapes, and electromagnetic frequencies would never tell someone born without sight what a colorful painting was like. My imagination reached uselessly but with wonder at the thought of being able to detect all the radiation emitted by the sun, and vibrations so tiny that they traced the contours inside my steel heart.

Beside me, Gothic beamed with pride. This was the whole point of the visit, for him and Raggedy. Epiphany's story was supposed to sell me on letting go of being human. No one could meet this beautiful cloud creature and think he was worse off in an artificial body. There would be possibilities, a new perspective, a new life and relationships and happiness available to me if I stopped being Penny Akk and lived for this new combination of mind and body.

I was not even remotely tempted.

Although I did try hard not to let that stain my happiness for Epiphany. He found what he wanted. What I wanted was my life back from the monster that stole it.

A voice so loud I could hear it all the way from the street said, "Goshagollyroo! I know I left a little girl around here somewhere. Hey, Mister Brick! Did you see a girl with flappy pigtails like these?"

Something broke, with a loud crash and tinkle.

"Thanks, but no thanks," I told Gothic, and ran for the stairs. No, it wasn't the most polite way I could have refused his well-meant offer, but I had to hurry to prevent his house from being ripped open. Any second, Gerty would decide this was a game of hide and seek, and jump up to meet me in the hallway. She still hadn't mastered the concept of walls.

I skidded to a halt in the front room. Raggedy was already out of her chair and hobbling towards the front door, but it wasn't Raggedy who stopped me. I still held the fat, fluffy, yellow stuffed rabbit in one arm. Placing it gently in Raggedy's hands, I hardened my mechanical heart against its longingly reaching arms and waggling feet. Where I go, little bunny, you cannot follow.

That done, I threw the front door open and charged up the stairs to the street.

I made it in time. Gerty stood in the middle of the road, but nothing obvious on the street had been broken yet. Best guess for the earlier noises: she ate a mailbox.

First her head swiveled to look at me, then her upper body turned, then her head turned again because rotating her body had turned it too far. She lifted and opened her arms. "Who's a Gerty Girl?"

"I'm a Gerty Gerty Girl," I assured her, stepping in close. Oversized arms closed around me in a hug whose gentleness would surprise anyone who had only seen her break things.

From basement level, Raggedy's voice cried out, "You found her! Gothic, come quick! Penelope found the mystery robot!"

A few seconds later, Gothic helped Raggedy climb the steps enough for them to both look over the cement edge. The old man stared in wonder. "Bless my soul, it is. Look at her. I've never seen the like. Every mad scientist in the city has been talking about this newcomer, but they would never describe her."

Raggedy nudged him with an elbow. "Gothic, dear, I do believe that is one of those animatronic displays from a restaurant. You know? The ones that opened in the eighties?"

He pursed his mouth sourly. "You know I've never approved of those. They exploit and degrade artificial intelligence with their crippled parodies."

The heavily bundled old woman, on the other hand, could not have smiled more joyfully. Waving a hand, she beckoned, "Her name is Gerty, correct? Please, bring her inside!"

I shook my head fast, and just to be sure held up one arm to cover Gerty's mouth with my hand. "Not a good idea. She'll wreck the building, and everything in it. Gerty is my friend, but she's awfully clumsy."

"That's me!" Gerty crowed, "Why, I once broke the sound barrier by tripping over it. The only thing I've never broken is a child's heart, and I hope I never do. Speaking of which…"

One of the arms tenderly enfolding me slid aside, then behind my legs. She only moved in simple stages, but she could move through them fast. It only took her a second to scoop me off the ground in both oversized, carpet-upholstered hands. Lifting me to eye level, she said, "This old nanny goat knows when one of her kids is hurtin'."

Fast, and perceptive. She was right. Meeting Cutting Edge and Epiphany had been pleasant distractions, but now the dull ache set back in. I did not want to remember my mom's expression—

"How about a game of upsy-daisy?" shouted Gerty, and threw me about twenty feet in the air.

"AAAAA!" I said.

As fast as I went up, I fell back down into Gerty's waiting arms. Then she flung me into the air again.

"AAAAA!" I repeated.

Shocked and alarmed I might be, but one thing I did not feel was panic. Gerty's programming would not allow her to drop me, no matter how clumsy she might act.

And again, she saw my thoughts turn serious. Her elongated goat face looked into mine for less than a second before she said, "My poor little Gerty Girl. This isn't working at all. How about I bake you a chocolate cake? Everybody loves cake!"

I slid out of her arms to the ground. Gerty didn't try to stop me. She was busy opening up a large panel in the front of her apron, baring her mechanical insides. The base of a cannon unfolded from her stomach, and other hatches opened up in her arms, shoulders, and legs, extending bits of equipment on skinny folding arms, until it all clicked together to form a gatling-style gun, each barrel as thick as my arm.

"Oh, my goodness," said Raggedy, and Gothic wrapped his arms around her protectively.

With a sigh, I said, "Hey, Gerty, how long can you hold your breath?"

"Nine hundred two seconds! Just watch!" she recited, followed by a raspy, loud inhale, and her jaws clamping shut.

That was how intermission started in her restaurant shows, after all.

I leaned against her arm, wincing at having had to deceive her when she was trying to cheer me up. It felt totally different from the game of getting her to play the silly game that would be useful to me.

Up the street, a girl shouted, "I want chocolate caaaake!"

Gerty blinked. The barrels of her cannon started to rotate, with an increasingly loud whirring noise.

Oh, criminy. I dove for the ground, huddled by Gerty's feet.

Not a moment too soon. The gun reached operating speed, and with a thud-thud-thud-thud rapid-fired brown blobs. Cupcakes. They were cupcakes. Her upper body rotated, splattering the front of Gothic and Raggedy's house. With a shriek of alarm, they hurried back down the stairs and slammed their front door.

Peeking around Gerty's skirts, I saw Marcia, face twisted in a snarl, running up the street towards us. She was maybe fifteen feet away when Gerty finished swinging around and pelted her with cake and frosting, knocking her off her feet.

Realizing I probably should have done this sooner, I shouted in a stern, scolding voice, "Gerty! I hope you haven't lost count and have to start over."

The gun barrels slowed and stopped. The seven-foot-tall animatronic goat announced bashfully, "Oops. I'm a goober goat. But nobody in the barnyard can hold their breath as long as Gerty, you'll see!"

She did the inhale thing again, and froze.

On her back, her front a smeary mess of chocolate, Marcia laughed hysterically, and waved one arm. "Help me up? Please?"

I took her hand and pulled, dragging her to her feet. She spent those few seconds licking cupcake off her fingers. "Thanks. Man, this is tasty. Now that I'm standing, can you keep me from falling over again?"

Marcia leaned, then collapsed against me. Despite the mess, I hooked an arm around her waist to support her. Up close, I could both see and feel her body trembling.

I turned my disapproving scowl on a new target. "You used your super power to run all the way here from... where?"

"Your teammate's house. The blonde one, with the chest fit for a senior. I missed the tests, but was just in time to see your goat go tearing off after you. Boy, can she move. Bakes a delicious cake, too." Despite her wheezing and trembling, she scooped up some more chocolate frosting and stuck it in her mouth.

At the appreciative mention, Gerty blinked again, but I glared at her and she went back to pretending to hold her breath.

My face pinched in a grimace as I corrected Marcia, "Not my teammate anymore. Ray and Claire both believe the parasite."

Marcia blew that off with a literal puff and snort. "They're being ridiculous. You're obviously the real Penny."

I sighed. I couldn't even walk away from this conversation, because I didn't want to leave Marcia in this condition. "Not really comforting, coming from... wait. Is this another excuse to fight? Are you going to attack me as soon as you stop... internally bleeding, or whatever?"

Completely without guilt, she gave me a sunny, dizzy smile from a few inches away. "Yep! We're up to the one where I tried to trip you and freaked out when I failed."

"It was Ray you tried to trip, and I'm not in the mood."

She bumped me in the chest with her fist. "What, because they fell for your duplicate's line of patter? It doesn't matter what they think. You know who you are."

I rolled my head in frustration and groaned. "Marcia, I get that this is your crazy new version of friendship—"

"No, you don't get it," she interrupted, face and voice hardening.

She couldn't keep that up for more than a couple of seconds before the shaking came back, but it got my attention. I stayed silent as she poked my chest with her index finger. "You know this, Penny, but you've never thought about it, never really gotten it. I was miserable when I met you. All I'd ever heard was that I had no right to be human like other people. The best I could possibly do was 'good enough.' That's it. Anything less than perfection was failure. My friends were fake, only there as long as I made them look good. Trying to satisfy other people broke me down until I was empty inside. I didn't know Marcia Angelica Bradley. My whole life was spent with people telling her to shut up and die so I could be a beautiful, smiling zombie."

The sheer venom with which she spat those last three words made me flinch. Horror kept me quiet, so she kept talking. "You took my beauty and my smile and my perfection away from me. I had nothing left, so I went looking for Marcia Bradley. I found her. No one else did it for me. I made myself who I wanted to be. This is the Marcia I want to be, the one I chose. Now we've come full circle, and it's you who is empty from caring what others think. Forget them, and tell me—who. Are. You?"

I didn't even need time to think. I knew. "Penelope Justice Akk."

Marcia boggled. "Justice? Your middle name is Justice? Ha ha ha ha ha ha!"

Her laughter should have hurt, should have made me angry, but it didn't. Up close, all I could see was how different she looked from when we hated each other in middle school. Before, she'd been tanned bronze, her hair bleached blonde, her laugh harsh and sharp. Now it wobbled with honest joy, and her ragged, naturally black hair bounced around a face that... well, it still wasn't pale, but the touch of brown was strictly natural.

Her laughter reminded me of Ray and Claire, who were my friends, whether they knew it or not, who would be my friends even if the parasite kept them wrapped in a lie the rest of their lives.

Recovered enough to push away from me and stand on her own wobbly legs, Marcia let her laughter trail off, giving me a knowing grin instead. "But there's one more thing. You pushed me there faster, but I'd been heading towards that crash all my life. It was inevitable, because I couldn't live like that. Maybe I've helped you see this a little faster, but you would have figured it out without me. I know it, because Penelope Justice Akk is Penelope Justice Akk, and can't be anyone else."

I ran my hand back over my hair, and gave a pigtail an absentminded pull. "Yeah, okay. But can I at least wallow in my misery a little? I think I've earned it."

She cocked her thumb like the hammer of a gun, and pointed her index finger at me. "It doesn't matter what I think. If that's what's right for you, go for it."

Not that I could. I wasn't exactly happy, but the unhappiness had also gone missing. While I looked for my missing emotions, a thought popped up instead. "You... don't have any of those plastic hero figurines in your lair, do you? The one you gave me?" I lowered my voice to a whisper. "I just found out, they're all enchanted. Gothic uses them to spy on people."

She nodded. "I know."

"...what? You do?"

She lowered her voice too, leaning shoulder to shoulder with me conspiratorially. "Oh, yeah. My grandfather was a superhero back in the day. If you think my father is creepy, you should have met old Jake Bradley. He had this whole collection of custom-made dress-up dolls for heroines and villainesses he knew. It was messed up. When I was six my father caught one of those dolls moving. I'm not sure if he melted them down or locked them up or what, but they're definitely not anywhere they can see or hear anything anymore."

I shook my head, amused despite myself. "Your family is a freak show, even by hero standards."

She laughed. "Oh, you know it. I'm getting letters from some woman now claiming I'm her great-granddaughter, and I know for a fact that's not true."

Wind whipped around us, released in a blast from Gerty's mouth as she slumped forward. "Nine hundred two!"

Marcia pumped her fist. "Yes! She's awake again! Hey, food goat, I'm starving. Do you make anything besides cake?"

I ran for cover. In the recessed doorway of a nearby house, I remembered the text message I'd gotten earlier, and checked my phone.

It was from Misty Lutra: You can still depend on me. Nothing has changed.

You could plan an epic confrontation, but people kept on being themselves. Including me. So, to the backdrop of gargling noises and a menu being sung in the distance, I composed a letter.

Mom and Dad,

There's always a day at camp when your homesickness gets so bad, it feels like you'll never get to go back to your family again. Today was that day. I want you to know that I got through it. I love you too much to give up. I will come home. We will be a family again. I promise.

Missing You So Much,
Your Daughter Penny

Chapter Twenty

I dragged my teammate by the arm up the main street of Chinatown.

"I do not want to be here," Ampexia reminded me for the twentieth time as her shoes skidded over the pavement.

Lowering my face, I gave her my second-best 'peering skeptically over my glasses' expression. It couldn't be my best until I got my malfunctioning meat eyes and actual glasses back. "Who doesn't love watching supervillains relax and literally blow off steam?"

She poked me in the shoulder with a gauntleted finger. "You like it because you're goofy, too."

"Well, lucky for you, it's Sunday afternoon. This is as quiet as it gets. Goofiness levels are down to a brisk lack of taking themselves seriously. You won't need any weaponry."

She grabbed her giant speaker backpack protectively, and I abandoned that argument. Going armed into Chinatown wasn't technically breaking the rules, just tacky. Also serious paranoia. This really was a quiet day. We were the only supervillains I saw before setting foot into the mall.

Even inside, I saw only about a dozen folks in brightly colored costumes, and maybe half a dozen manning the sales tables. This place wasn't just quiet, it was practically dead.

And every mask, pair of goggles, face plate, and glowing eye turned to watch us as we entered.

Ampexia gritted her teeth, drawing her tall (compared to me), thin frame up straight, and flicked three switches on her gloves. "If anybody so much as touches my partner, everyone here will go through life without eardrums."

The only two mad scientists I recognized were Red Eye and Cybermancer. The former fell forward until her face planted against her tabletop. The latter took out a pair of little metal earplugs, inserted them into his ears, gave Red Eye a reassuring shoulder pat, and glared accusingly at his comrades.

The other mad scientists kept staring at me, even after Red Eye, still face-down, gave them the middle finger. Photos of my circuitry had had plenty of time to be shared around by now. Were those intent eyes burning with a lust for truly exotic technology?

I was pretty sure the rest were actually watching Ampexia. She kept herself apart from the community and was just old enough to count as an official member. Nobody took eager curiosity to the point of creepiness like a supervillain. She'd also stolen a whole lot of stuff from a whole lot of people by now.

Laying my hand on my T-shirt-loving partner's bare forearm, I glared at the watchers and repeated exactly, "If anybody so much as touches *my* partner, everyone here will go through life without eardrums."

That got appreciative smirks. At least half of the watchers turned back to their business, and most of the rest... well, they still stared, but it died down to levels appropriate to an interesting novelty.

Had I ever seen this place so unpopulated? I could actually see the faded remnants of brightly colored sales posters with Chinese writing on them, which plastered every glass surface of the regular people shops that would reopen tomorrow. Someone had left a whole bin of fruit sitting out, and I didn't have a clue what the spiky orange things were. Asian agriculture, or mad science?

And as for the black arrow on the floor by my feet...

...that would be why we were here.

Pulling my paranoid partner by her elbow, I followed the arrow as it slid across the floor towards the far end of the building. It finally ducked into the same darkened shop Mirabelle liked to sit in.

That darkness was a bit darker than I remembered. Despite it being bright daylight not far away, I could see nothing but the roughest outlines of a female figure lounging on a throne, and the ice-blue flames in her eyes.

"You have summoned. I have come. State your business." Lucyfar's voice echoed around the otherwise empty room.

Stepping into the room hushed all the noises from the rest of the mall. All I could clearly hear were the ticking of my heart and the faint clicks, hums, and whines as Ampexia activated her weapons in case Lucyfar attacked.

Boldly striding to the foot of the throne, I planted my hands on my hips. "I need your help." And then, because there was no bold way to say it, I lifted one of those hands to wave it around in a dismissive circle. "Okay, no, I don't need it. I just want it."

The darkness deepened. Even up close, I had trouble making out Lucyfar's shape. Only the blue flames of her eyes remained clear. "Go on. The Princess of Darkness is listening."

I shr—criminy, still couldn't shrug. I tugged on a braid instead. "In a roundabout way, that's what I need. This weekend has been miserable. I have to get back to my roots, remind myself of who I am with some gleeful and madcap villainy."

The burning eyes narrowed. "And also to remind everyone else who Bad Penny is, both as someone to be taken seriously, and not too seriously."

I gave her a thumbs up. "Nailed it. I knew there was only one person to come to for ideas on having a morally ambiguous good time."

The sound of wings fluttered in the darkness. The throne, which had been hard to make out to begin with, faded into the shadows. Lucyfar drifted down from it, to stand as an inky shape looking down at me, her voice reverberating from all directions. "Lucyfar has many ideas, but do you know what she likes most of all?"

"Talking in the third person?" asked Ampexia.

I broke into a huge grin. Oh, yes. 'Sarcastic teammate' was just what the Inscrutable Machine needed.

Something in the back of the room coughed, then clunked. The shadows began to fade, ever so gradually. The first thing they revealed was Lucyfar, in a black leather bodysuit with strategically placed pentagrams. Her chin lifted proudly, she said, "Lucyfar does enjoy referring to herself in the third person. Lucyfar has always wanted to be celebrated in a Norse saga. Great is her skill with the warrior's axe, and fantastic does she look in an Icelandic side-fastened tunic."

Ampexia jerked her thumb at the outside world. "Should I go get lunch, maybe take in a movie, while we wait for her to get to the point?"

That got a peal of laughter from Lucyfar, and she draped an arm affectionately around my shoulders, leaning against me as she cackled. The darkness continued to ease, until I could see the whole empty room, and the clunky little machine in the back corner with the big funnel and accordion-pleated barrel body.

Lucyfar is naturally tall, and I am naturally a shrimp. This interaction just about draped her chest over my face. I wouldn't have noticed, except the pentagram painted over her bustline rearranged when I looked at it, spelling out 'My demonic horns are up here' with an arrow pointing towards her head.

While I wondered just how much money she'd spent on that joke, she got her composure back. "Actually, what I love most is corruption, twisting the souls of good children to wickedness. Tell me, daughter of heroes, what is the most completely unethical, devious, unfair, and deliciously satisfying thing Penelope Akk wants right now?"

...

...

The answer clicked into place, and my grin returned with it. "I want spying devices. Lots and lots of spying devices, because I know the most fun and unscrupulous way to use them."

Ampexia's voice rose in disbelief. "That's it? You could have told me in the first place. We don't need this doofus."

Lucyfar waggled a finger in denial. "Too late! You have invoked the doofus, and the doofus is going to ride this train all the way to hilarityville."

Ampexia cracked her knuckles, gripping first her right fist, then her left. "I'm not a fighter, but stealing expensive, exotic audio and broadcast equipment? This is my jam."

Chapter Twenty-One

That brought us, with terrible inevitability, to lurking around the corner of a building in Burbank, watching the edifice of Echo's Tower. Except for six geometrically placed, perfectly pruned little trees, it sat in its own small square of shiny white pavement, and looked an awful lot like a lighthouse. A twisted lighthouse whose hexagonal sides spiraled like a unicorn horn, sure—and the rotating thing at the top looked more like a reception dish than a lamp—but basically a lighthouse.

I shaded my eyes, pretending that the bright sunlight on all that white could still sting. "I always thought this was farther out of town."

Ampexia looked surprised, lifting her goggles up both so I could see her raised eyebrows and she could stare disbelieving at me without lenses clouding her view. "Are you kidding? You've never been here? Echo worships your old man. Most of these goobers do. And they think your mother could take Mourning Dove without breaking a sweat."

"An accurate description," said Lucyfar.

Ampexia ignored her, pulling another cartridge from her belt and plugging it into her backpack, then inserting two wireless plugs into her gauntlet. "Almost ready. This is my booby trap detector. I stole it from that guy who makes booby traps for everyone's lairs."

I pursed my lips. "Good plan."

Lucyfar gave a quick golf clap. "Yeah, nice one. I knew he had to have built in a backdoor for himself."

"And this," Ampexia said, sliding a thin, black flash drive into a USB slot, then snapping that slot in to lie flush with the rest of the glove, "Will tell me if Echo is home."

I gave her a wry half-smile. "You've run into Echo before, I take it?"

She sneered, and snapped her goggles back into place. Unlike the brown leather and brass edging pilot goggles favored by us mad scientists, hers were mostly black rubber, and looked like she'd stolen them from a race car driver. "He takes me personally because I'm music-themed. I can never tell if he wants to adopt me, arrest me, or ask me out. Heroes are just as goofy as villains."

A subtle reminder that my new teammate was an obvious teenage runaway. Maybe someday she would trust me enough to tell me why. Until then, she was also someone who appreciated not being pushed.

Lucyfar, with demonic sensitivity, nodded and said, "So true. Hey, why couldn't we bring the goat? I want to play with the goat!" She practically vibrated with excitement at the idea.

Ampexia let out a faint growl of disgust. "Because this operation has to be quiet. If Echo knows his tracers were stolen, it won't take him long to find them. I've got a pretty good idea of where they're stored, so I'll slip in and out."

She pointed up at the windows near the top of the tower. It occurred to me that Ampexia knew an awful lot about Echo and his tower, but was that any surprise? A practical villainess knows her enemies.

My teammate demonstrated her practicality now. From our hidden location, she fired out a wire thinner than a shoelace to strike the base of the tower. A few button presses on her gauntlet later... and she let out a frustrated sigh. "No good. He's inside. We'll have to come back later. Do you two want to grab some pizza? You're not so weird you don't like pizza, right?"

"Patience is for mortals," said Lucyfar, walking past her and out into open view.

Ampexia grabbed the back of Lucyfar's collar, and I grabbed Ampexia, helping her reel the queen of slinky leather madness back into hiding. "I told you, he can't know we were here!" my partner hissed.

Lucyfar tossed her long, gloriously shiny black hair, unabashed and infernally confident. "He won't know you were here."

She started walking again. I laid my hand on Ampexia's forearm this time. "Nobody does a distraction like Lucy."

My ponytailed partner scowled at me. "You're the one who wants these bugs."

Ignoring us both, Lucyfar resumed her march. We couldn't see the front door of the tower from here, but she took her place far enough in front of it that we could at least still see her. Shiny black knives materialized in the air around her, and swooped in to begin carving graffiti on the tower's white stone walls. Thanks to the hexagonal shape, I could see a few letters—for all the good that did me. They looked like... Hebrew? Languages were so very, very not my specialty.

Several seconds later, the sound of a window slamming open echoed over to us, and a man shouted, "Lucyfar, what do you think you're doing?!"

"You owe me a date, big boy!" she called back up to him.

Not that we could see him, but Echo sounded understandably exasperated. "What are you talking about? And stop that!"

Still scratching away at his tower, Lucy folded her arms under her chest and glared up at him defiantly. "The thing with the space pearl, remember? Lucyfar said smoochy times, or she would leave it in the giant oyster where it belonged."

"It was a broken Conqueror Orb, and you dropped it again as soon as you brought it up, and that was two years ago."

Black-clad shoulders shrugged, and Lucyfar's imperiousness turned instead to callous indifference. "Sure. How do you spell 'kissing in a tree'?"

Scratch scratch scratch went the knives. The one on our side was carving hearts.

"Lucy, I'm not stupid. The last person you went on a date with got fired out of—don't write that!" He sounded so horrified, I was starting to wish I could sneak around and see the show, instead of just hearing it.

Still dismissive, Lucyfar said, "Until I see you in front of me puckering your lips, I'm going to be here indulging my artistic muse. I've got a lot of ideas and you've got a lot of wall space, so no hurry."

For several seconds, Echo didn't respond. True to her word, Lucyfar kept writing. People across the street were stepping out onto their balconies and staring with binoculars.

Finally he let out an aggravated whine. "I'm coming down there, but it is not to kiss you!"

The window slammed shut. I looked at Ampexia. "Echo is leaving the building. I guess that's your cue."

She nodded. Quietly and nimbly for someone carrying a backpack as big as herself, Ampexia ran across the square to the back of the tower. She stuck four different devices against it, checked her gauntlets again, and started to climb. Hover, mostly. I couldn't hear anything, but I knew from experience the vibrating disks on the bottom of her pack operated as jets.

Man. I was used to working with way too few toys. Most mad scientists collected a whole arsenal for circumstances. I kept losing stuff and had to work with two or three at a time.

A clack of a door signaled Echo emerging from his fortress. His slender yellow, white, and brown figure walked up to Lucyfar, and they resumed their argument—quieter, alas. Still, what I couldn't hear of embarrassing dialog, I could see in her rubbing up against him playfully while he waved his arms around.

Ampexia crawled in a window. Barely a minute later she emerged, just as Echo gave in and tried to give Lucyfar a quick kiss on the lips, only to be grabbed in both arms and hauled into a ferocious makeout session.

Note to Penny: If people think you're crazy, they can't tell when you're scheming something serious. Shades of how Claire's mother always looked like she was lying, even when she was telling the truth.

Determinedly ignoring the ridiculous antics, Ampexia recovered her tools and snuck back over behind the cover of a wall with me. Holding up a briefcase, she opened it. In neatly padded depressions, it held plastic bags full of tiny beetle-shaped devices, a couple of flash drives, a portable tracker, and even an instruction manual.

I applauded quietly, and didn't hide my wide-eyed admiration. "Wow. That was fast. You're a real professional."

She smiled, grimly pleased. "Get in. Get the goods. Get out. Steal from the best. Now let's get moving before we're noticed."

Nodding, I took the briefcase and stroked it with wicked anticipation. "Yes. It's time for stage two of my plan. It's a shame Lucyfar will be busy, because this is where I get evil."

CHAPTER TWENTY-TWO

I knocked on the front door politely, and waited until it was answered. Bobbing in history's smallest curtsy, I asked, "Good evening, Miss Lutra. Is your daughter at home?"

Claire's mom looked down at me with a small, amused smile. I knew quite well that Claire was not at home, because there would be light and music from her bedroom. Get her out of the public, and my so-theatrical best friend turned into a geeky cave dweller.

A good description of me, come to think of it.

"She has stepped out for a minute, Penelope. Something about being too stubborn to let her ankles heal." The bluest eyes in the world watched me with cynical curiosity and sly entertainment. So, same as normal.

"Well, then, it's a good thing you would never let a supervillain on the run walk into your daughter's bedroom to use her for a diabolical scheme," I said, and stepped past her into the house.

No exquisitely manicured hands grabbed hold to stop me. On the contrary, Miss Lutra wandered into the kitchen and fiddled with her computer tablet as if I didn't exist.

Ha! Like daughter, like mother.

Humming faintly and with a happy bounce in my step, I wandered back to Claire's bedroom, laid the suitcase full of tracking devices on the bed, and opened it up. Sliding open the door to Claire's closet... Criminy. So many costumes! She'd already had a fondness for short skirts and shirts that showed off either her midriff or the cleavage not many other fourteen year olds had. Since getting her super powers, Claire had added to that collection with actual costumes. Random bits of armor, fuzzy things with animal ears, catsuits, gowns—this closet would make any dedicated cosplayer proud.

Concentrating on the actual clothing first, I slipped a bug into the corners of pockets and behind folds of cloth where they wouldn't be visible. The finest of mad science, the tiny devices burrowed into gaps and became even harder to see. When I finished the closet, I moved to Claire's dresser, and bugged the slightly less provocative clothing there. Every item got a tracker, except for whatever was in the underwear drawer. The underclothes I'd witnessed the occasional times Claire stripped in front of me were embarrassing enough.

I was just closing the briefcase again when I heard the front door rattle. Claire's muffled voice shouted, "Mom, you locked me out again!"

Oopsy doopsy! I grabbed the case and ran up the hall to the living room, where I plunked myself down on the couch and attempted to look casual. Ha! When you're a robot, nobody can see you sweat.

I heard a key rattle, the front door open, and Miss Lutra ask, "What kind of cat burglar in training needs to use the front door?"

"I'm not breaking into any buildings with hurt feet," Claire answered, in exactly the same whimsically sardonic tone. If you didn't know them, it might be hard to tell their voices apart.

"You'll be breaking out of buildings with hurt feet. I suggest you learn how."

Match point for Miss Lutra, because Claire offered no retort except to thump into the house on her crutches.Miss Lutra let her almost reach the hall before saying, "You do have a visitor. I told her that you would be home in just a minute."

...technically true. Note to Penny that should have been unnecessary: Play games with a Lutra, and she plays games back.

Claire stumped around into view. She could really move on those crutches now, when she wasn't putting on a pity show for her mom. When she saw me, her face lit up with delight. "Penny!" Then her smile froze, along with the rest of her. "Woah. The other Penny."

Lifting up the briefcase, I laid it with a distinct thud on the coffee table, and gave Claire a wicked grin. All the more wicked, because Claire was now wearing the only suit of unbugged clothing she owned, one of those white stomach-baring T-shirts and shorts combinations, both tight enough to make boys weak in the knees.

My steel heart clenched painfully in my chest as I drank in my best friend's presence, but I couldn't show it. Instead I fiddled with the latches of the briefcase, all business. "I'm here to offer you the chance to do something wildly inappropriate."

She sighed, and collapsed onto the cushions at the other end of the couch, eyes lingering on the dull-gray case. "I might as well hear what you have to say."

Ha ha ha! GOT HER.

Opening up the case, I lifted out the resealed bag of trackers. There was no way for her to know it had been a lot more full when I arrived. "I want you to place one of these bugs in each piece of biological Penny's clothing."

"And what makes you think I would ever betray my best friend?" Claire asked coldly.

Leaning back, I draped an arm along the back of the couch, and looked her straight in her elegant blue eyes. "Reason number one: You're hoping to use the signals to spy on her yourself. Reason number two: Just thinking about doing this is filling you with glee. Reason number three: Your mother would do it."

"Claire knows that's not true," lied Miss Lutra from the kitchen.

The aforementioned Claire stared at me, squinting behind her glasses. Finally, she whispered, "You are the real Penny."

Throwing my hands in the air, I roared, "YES."

Smiling and merry now, Claire raised a warning finger. "Not so fast. I'm not completely convinced. Let's say instead that both of you seem just a little weird to me. However, in the interest of discovering the truth, I suppose I will do the deed you request."

Another couple of seconds of silence, and I reached out a hand. She took it, and I squeezed, glad just to feel her touch again. "You have no idea how much I've missed you."

She let out a groan. "I might have some idea. Every day at ballet camp I asked myself why I was stuck surrounded by vapid theater girls instead of back home with you."

There was no way I was releasing my grip on her hand, so I rubbed my face with the other. "I'm trying to think of this as camp. Making new friends, sleeping in a different bed, random creative projects and field trips, and staring at the calendar for hours hoping every day brings me closer to home."

"It's not worse than ballet camp," said Claire, face hard and voice flat.

I raised a skeptical eyebrow.

She tried to pull her hand free. I didn't let her. She gave me a smile, patted my gripping hand, and then raised the other in a fist, letting her anger consume her, burning in a grimace across her face. "I hate ballet. I hate ballet so much. Getting up at dawn, two hours of stretches and squats on your tiptoes, lying on planks and extending your body and holding that pose until your muscles scream, and then the entire rest of the day repeating the same dance routine over and over and over. I swear the top girl was cheating. She had a super power. She could fly. I know it."

I admit, she had my sympathy. "That sounds painful *and* dull *and* lonely. At least supervillain camp is exciting."

Looking down at my clenched fingers, she said gently, "I need my hand back, Penny, please."

Considerable willpower was necessary to let go, but I did. Claire climbed to her feet, grabbed two fistfuls of shining platinum hair, and ran in circles around the living room furniture shouting, "AAAAAAUGH!"

By the end of the first lap she was hobbling in obvious pain on her bandaged feet, but she kept it up for two more before dropping back onto the couch. She took five deep breaths, staring with wide, wild eyes into her lap, until at the end of the fifth she settled against the arm rest and asked me pleasantly, "So, what computer game are you playing?"

My whole upper body slumped forward. I boggled, looking past her, not really seeing anything but my suddenly exploding thoughts. "I could have been having fun in my free time instead of seething. I actually got a computer and intended to play games, then forgot. Wait, it's been... 'Princess of the Closet Monsters' is out!"

Standing up, I gave Claire a polite nod. "If you will excuse me for one moment." Grabbing my braids, I pulled them out away from my head and ran around the living room three times shouting, "AAAAAAUGH!"

When I fell back onto the couch, Claire put her arms around me, hugging me to her and stroking my head. "There, there. I completely understand. I'm not even going to try for cheerleading when we get to Upper High. I've neglected my nerd roots too long. Claire Lutra will be all intellectual, all the time."

I gave her my most my skeptical look, and then blinked. "We're supposed to pick specialties. What are you going to go for?"

"Languages," she answered immediately.

"Say what now?"

She held up both hands. "Honest! We both know the regular job market will never hold anything for me. Being able to travel the world, read and speak anything, is a great skill for a thief, especially when you're stealing super power related artifacts. You never know if you'll have to read a tablet in Russian or Sumerian or what."

I smirked. "Sounds like more of a treasure hunter thing."

"I'm sure I'll be sharing a lot of classes with Ray. We'll be split up a bit more than at Northeast West Hollywood, but with some wheedling and a delicate touch of mind clouding, I believe I can arrange we share the maximum classes possible." She fluttered her lashes, hair curling and turning more gold than silver.

Leaning against her, I rubbed my nose. Not that it ever itched, but hey. I also pulled my folded-up letters home out of my pocket, and gave them a dour stare. "I just have to get camp wrapped up by then. Keep thinking of it that way, Penny, and you can get through this."

Claire reached out greedily and snatched the letters from my hand. Flipping through a couple, she exclaimed, "These are cute!"

I grabbed them back and shoved them into my coat again. "They feel like I'm talking to myself, sometimes."

"Keep writing them. No matter how this turns out, your mom and dad will know you love them. Besides, the 'I'm at camp' code you're writing in is so adorably Penny." She finished up her advice with an encouraging hug.

My smile returned. Pushing myself upright again, I said, "Thanks. And thanks for believing in me. Getting to see you again brings me back to myself."

With a flourishing shimmy, she sat up straight herself. "Well, of course. Without my best friend, I was practically unrecognizable at camp." Leaning forward, she pulled the briefcase off her coffee table and into her lap, turning regal and businesslike. "Bear in mind, officially I remain on the other you's side. Any doubts I may have do not change that."

Her greedy stroking of the rough, gray plastic case cover made me grin. I had no fears of her turning into a partisan zealot, nope. Composing my face again to match hers, I stood up and gave her a bow. "So be it. I will just have to win on my own merits. After all, proving that I'm the better Penny Akk is the point, isn't it?"

Chapter Twenty-Three

Ampexia could spend forever browsing in that little mad science music shop on Melrose, which is good, because we'd been there awhile.

I peeked out through the tiny gaps between posters on the main window, and saw nothing but the hole a superhero left on the sidewalk moments before we ducked inside.

That had been followed by two bickering voices:

"Are you crazy? You could have hurt someone!"

"I swear I saw that killer robot everyone's talking about."

"All I see is dust. A vast, choking cloud of dust, because someone is trigger-happy."

"It will be here. It's probably taking aim at your voice right now."

So, it seemed a good idea to stay inside and out of sight for a while. Hiding in a basement would be an even better idea, but no way would I let myself be chased out of living what I had left of my life.

My attempt to ponder safety issues was cut short. Ampexia grabbed my elbow, and hauled me across the shop to a display case. "So, check these out! Pretty sweet, huh?"

I checked the sign above the table. "Those are speakers?"

Even to my mad-science-acclimated eye, very few of the items on the display case looked like speakers. One was an apple, for Tesla's sake! An actual, bright red apple that I was currently unable to eat. A shame, because it looked super juicy. No blemishes, perfectly ripe. Next to it was a rubber kitchenware box containing a dozen or so firecrackers. At least the vertical cylinder with all the knobs and hammers and gears looked musical.

Pride of place certainly belonged to a mason jar of soap bubbles, floating peacefully without popping.

Her phone already out of her pocket, Ampexia plugged a cord into it, and the other end of the cord into a USB slot on the jar lid. That lid irised open, and the bubbles hovered out like they'd been blown by a gentle gust of wind. As they circled above the jar, echoey, liquid notes fluttered in no pattern I could identify, until the music whispered barely identifiable words. "Ampexia is now online."

"Going to get it?" I asked, resisting the urge to poke one of the bubbles. I wanted to so baaaad. Willpower, Penny!

She shook her head, dull blonde ponytail flopping around. "Nope. Maybe later, if I get an inspiration. Every instrument has its own opportunities, and I don't want to waste one if I won't use it."

Apparently intent on working down the list, she unplugged her phone from the mason jar, and next, into the apple. Just stuck the plug in through the flesh, scrunch. Only having grown up around this stuff prevented me from being totally surprised when the apple shivered, and out of the stem grew a tiny tree. It never even reached two feet high, but a woody trunk grew in sudden jerks, twisting at sharp angles and extending spiky branches that bent the same way. Every twist of the trunk came at a ridged joint, making it look like it was made out of segmented wooden tubs. The whole thing looked... robotic, in fact, especially when the miniature tree stopped growing and burst into brightly colored flower, each triangular petal extending separately. Yellow, red, blue, red, yellow, red, red, blue—the flowers whirled into existence, and then the whole thing went still.

The apple had long since shrunk into the trunk of the tree-let, which stood on a splayed star of roots.

Leaned in only a few inches away, Ampexia studied the botanical sound translator intently. "Cool. I may come back for this one, but if someone who will use it more comes in..."

The owner, a man much too young to have such a tremendous, bramble-thick brown beard, nodded. "Indeed."

Personally, I grinned. My new partner lived in a world of music I did not comprehend, and it was fun to watch.

The other oddities on the bench she passed over, moving to the next rack, where a battered, normal-looking guitar lay. Of course, if it were normal it wouldn't be in here, and neither would it have a USB port in the neck.

Ampexia picked it up, turned it over several times, lay it back down, and plugged in. She tapped away at her phone for a minute, and the guitar began playing itself.

Strings plucked themselves, a gentle, quiet melody. Mournful, even. In fact...

"Is that 'While My Guitar Gently Weeps'?" I asked. Cassie played a recording of it for me once, but that had been played on an electric guitar.

Ampexia nodded silently, her arm sweeping up to hold her palm out to me, urging silence. Scowling with furious concentration, she listened through the rest of the song. Only then did she address the store owner. "I can't tell it wasn't played by a human. Who made this?"

"Paradisio Extravaganza, eighty years ago. Five times, the plugs have been changed. None know how he originally programmed them. Them, I say, for there was originally a small orchestra." He stood stiffly, exchanging a solemn look with Ampexia as if they were describing a funeral, or a birth.

Ampexia grabbed her chest, fingers digging into her Boreal Network T-shirt. (A completely different shirt from last time, this time with a pixelated bicycle.) "A whole band," she wheezed. "I'll find it. I'll find them all, and steal them all so you can reunite them."

His mustache and beard moved, suggesting a wry smile underneath. "And then shall you steal them back from me."

She pulled her head back, just a touch shocked. "No. I will do what it takes to get these instruments a proper home, but you will get paid. You've always done right by me, and I will do right by you."

While they discussed legendary musical mad science, I had a free moment. Digging out my phone, I punched up the custom app I'd gotten with the briefcase of trackers. Ampexia had been right about stealing from the best. We'd even had time before I visited Claire to separate the signals into two sets. Now I called up the map of LA. The two dots were nowhere near each other. Excellent. The parasite was out away from home, without awkward best friend interference, at Melrose and...

Criminy. She was down the street from me right now.

HA!

A sudden sense of looming snapped me out of my evil anticipation. Ampexia stood right next to me, rolling her eyes in exasperation. "I'm sure I mentioned how creepy it is when heroes bug people."

Putting my phone away, I unslung the mega-plow instead. "But it works. Time to contact my target."

We ducked out of the store. Two mad science-armed teenagers walking down Melrose did not get much attention, but they did circle around me when I started moving in little rushes from fake cover to fake cover.

When Ampexia caught up with one of those, I asked her, "Can you provide some theme music?"

"Yes," she said, and kept walking.

A few blocks farther, and I identified the location of Parasite Penny's tracking blip. She was at the burger place I usually ate at when out shopping here. Although it's not like I usually bought anything on Melrose. 'Goofed around with Ray and Claire' would be a better description.

Would Mom and Dad be with her? They shouldn't be a problem, only an uncomfortable complication. Leaning against the very last building, I checked that the plow was powered up, and the weather sponge ready on my wrist. I wasn't here to fight, but I'd be foolish not to expect violence from the thing in my body.

I let out a sigh. "I wish I could have brought Gerty. Having that kind of power behind me would make this a lot more comfortable."

Ampexia shook her head, two swift, fierce motions. "No way."

"Yeah, I know. It was hard enough keeping her in the truck. No way she could resist putting on a big show walking down this street. A big, destructive show. I'm having a hard enough time keeping heroes off me."

"Something to think about if you go full supervillain," she said.

I shr—criminy. I went for a twisted half-smile instead. "Yeah, but then I'll only have them on my butt when I'm in costume."

She said nothing, in alert and watchful rather than bantering mode. Her unspoken criticism was correct, of course. I was delaying the moment.

Rounding the corner, I strutted with all the arrogance I could muster into the dining courtyard of the restaurant.

No parents. Neither was the parasite goofing around with Ray and Claire. She was only goofing around with Ray.

In fact, from the way they sat at a corner to each other on the little square table, and the soft way he watched her eat, this was a date.

My teeth clenched so hard it hurt. I had to force myself to relax again. Ray wasn't to blame, but how dare she take advantage of him?

Stalking now, I crossed between the tables to meet them.

Ray noticed me first. She was busy pigging out, shoving a burger into her mouth like an organic rock crusher. A pile of empty plates suggested he'd already satisfied his super-metabolism. Now he had nothing to do but watch her, until I appeared. Now he watched me, completely silent. I'd known him for years, and I couldn't read this expression.

What had it told him about me?

The parasite didn't notice me until I was actually standing next to the table. When she did, her hand dove immediately into her pocket. I swung my own weapon up.

Faster than either of us could react to, Ray grabbed our wrists. The parasite held a black-and-purple diagonal striped box in her hand, about the size of a gun clip on television. She had her thumb hooked into the funny little recessed trigger.

His eyes still wide, his voice soft and face sad, Ray said, "Please don't fight."

Locking my eyes on the parasite with a furious glare, I said, "That's not why I'm here. Thank Tesla, because this crazy monster is going to blow up my body before I can get it back."

She smirked. She preened, leaning her head back to look down my nose at me, even though she was seated. Her other arm came up, showing off a blue bracelet of overlapping hearts, with a knob of tiny, raw electronics that extended like a bronze web around the sides. It snuggled right where I kept my Machine. "Once I stopped denying what I want, I asked my power to make me a shield against my own bombs."

I narrowed my eyes. "Great. So you're just going to blow up my boyfriend."

Her smirk turned into an outraged glare. "I can shield him, too!"

I waved my free hand at the rest of the restaurant, which was trying very hard to ignore us. "Okay, you and he live, and it's only the civilians who die."

"You're the one who attacked me in a crowded public place."

"I'm not here to attack you!"

She sneered down at my mega plow. "I'm sure the innocent bystanders are relieved. Or are your weapons precision-targeted?"

She had me there. The diners around us were relying on me to not fire, because if I did, there'd be a few broken bones at least.

The parasite met my silence with smug satisfaction. It knew it had scored a point. Ray, confident now that the innocent were safe, let go of our arms.

Picking up her cola cup by the lid, my doppelgänger swirled it gently and gave me a challenging, haughty stare. "So if you're not here for a fight, why are you interrupting my time with my boyfriend?"

Yes. That. Lowering my weapon, merely cradling it ready in both arms, I straightened up to give her my own balefully proud glower. "I'm just here—"

"Penny, is that you?" shouted a familiar voice. From across the street, a familiar figure leaped up into the air, and swooped across the intervening distance to land next to me.

Claudia was instantly recognizable, of course, not just because she was the only girl I personally knew who could fly. She looked happier and more relaxed than the last time I'd seen her, but the too-quiet, damaged look in her eyes might never go away. Where everyone else was wearing as little as possible in the late summer heat, she had on a white dress shirt with a cream sweater over it, a long cream skirt, and blue stockings underneath. Note to Penny: Add resistance to temperature extremes to the terrifying list of Claudia's powers. It did look good against her dusky skin.

I had to admit, it was nice to see her smile and hear enthusiasm in her normally haunted voice as she addressed me. "Of course. Who else our age would dress... like... what is going on?"

Anger took over, and I snarled. "A brain tumor stole my body."

Planting her hands on the tabletop and half-rising, the parasite growled back, "A delusional robot is trying to steal my body."

Claudia's mouth opened. A shock of surprise, with hints of pain, turned her voice quiet and her expression plaintive. "Why didn't you come to me immediately?"

I didn't know which of us she meant, but we both shouted, "No!"

"I don't want you involved," said the parasite.

"I've been trying to keep you from finding out," I said.

Claudia looked confused. Maybe a little betrayed, but it was impossible to tell for sure with those eyes.

Softening my tone, I said, "What kind of friend would I be if I convinced you to retire from heroing, except when it's convenient to me?"

The thing in my body, equally gentle, raised a hand to not quite touch Claudia's arm. "You've carried the world on your shoulders more already than anyone should in their whole life."

I looked across at the parasite, shocked. Those exact words has been lining up on my tongue.

No. I didn't... I didn't want this to be true.

She gave me a tight, mouth-twisted, miserable glare that I would bet was exactly my expression. She'd seen it too.

We talked over each other. We made the same brilliant, not-entirely-thought-out plans. Nobody could tell us apart. Arguing with her was like arguing with a mirror. The cursed pennies didn't work on either of us. We both looked at Ray the same way. What hurt her so much that it was the point of her first scheme? What was my greatest comfort? That I'd inherited the Machine.

There was only so much she could be faking.

Ray and Claudia watched us, their eyes turning from one to the other. All they understood was that we were hurting. It made Ray turn wide-eyed, like his world was falling out from under him. Claudia's anguish was pleading. For all her incredible power, she couldn't fix this.

The words tasted like bile. My tongue struggled to choke them off. Maybe if I'd needed it to speak, I wouldn't be able to say them, but I had to. "You're not just a parasite."

My biological double grimaced, teeth clenched so hard her head shook, but she forced it down and husked, "You're not just a robot."

Ugh. I wanted so badly to find an excuse, but she'd spoken too quickly, echoed my exact feelings. I had to tell her. "You have the good parts of me."

"We both do," agreed the other Penny.

The words were easier now. I'd gone numb. "Which means we're both the real Penny Akk."

She covered her face with a trembling hand, rubbing it up and off again before speaking. "All three of us. I shouldn't have—"

I could spare her the pain of confession. "No, I get it. You were right about us both being equally ruthless. So was she."

She smiled, a shred of humor in this lake of painful truth. "Yeah. That's what got us into this mess."

Claudia, her face returned to the blank, haunted stillness I was used to, said, "You are both Penny Akk." As empty as her expression might be, she sounded emphatic.

Ray did not look blank. His face had gone so pale and tight, I thought he might cry. "There are some things only Penny would say." He knew me. Maybe only Claire knew me better. Both of me.

The other Penny and I drew deep breaths at the same time. We'd be echoing echoing each other that way a lot. I'd have to get used to it.

I spoke first. "But we only have one body."

The flesh and blood Penny, the version of me that loved bombs and got carried away, nodded. She stood up, facing me formally. "I don't see a peaceful solution to this. Do you?"

"No." Mom and Dad would take in both of us, but that wasn't enough. Only the Penny with our original body would have our true, full life. I would not relinquish that to her, even if she deserved it as much as I did. Neither would I expect her to surrender. Even if she was what stayed behind when I got transferred to this body, that made us equal halves, with an equal claim she wouldn't give up.

I did not want any of that to be true. But it was.

Ray looked back and forth between our solemn, hard faces. "Please don't fight." He was begging, now. It tugged at my heart. Nothing was more Ray, or more why I loved him. When all the jokes were over, what he truly cared about was no one getting hurt. Especially me. Either of me.

But as much as we hated disappointing him, he begged in vain. The other Penny spoke for us. "I'm sorry. This can't be stopped."

Both of us reached out, and took one of his hands in one of ours, but our eyes never left each other.

Claudia didn't beg. She spoke with a quiet, flat confidence. "I can and will stop you from killing each other, even if you make me fight through every hero and villain in Los Angeles to do it."

I cocked my head at the question that raised. "What *are* the stakes here?"

The Penny in my real body answered, "I am going to break you, put the Hearts of Steel and Gold on a shelf, and after I finish college I'll make you both new bodies to wear. By then there will be no point in trying take back our body, and Mom and Dad can raise you as my younger robot sisters."

My turn. "I'm going to kidnap you, seal you in a stasis field, and hide you until I can switch our souls. Then I'll do the same thing with the Hearts that you're planning."

Her mouth tightened at the corners, but the rest of her relaxed. "I made it plain to Mom and Dad that this is my duel to fight. I'm positive that whoever wins, they'll accept her as real. They don't like it, but they know this isn't about who's real, it's about who gets our body. They said so, and we didn't pay attention."

She'd already told our folks this was just between us. It was exactly what I would do. Another reminder that she wasn't just faking this.

Twisting her nose up in revulsion, the other me said, "I can't stop the heroes. They've got it into their heads that it's noble to save me from you, and won't listen. I've tried."

I waved a hand. "As long as you don't deliberately call them in."

She shook her head viciously. "No way. This is between us."

"This puts..." Ray started, then hesitated.

His awkwardness made me grin. I couldn't help it. I pointed at me, then at the other Penny. "Robot Penny. Meatbag Penny."

Meatbag Penny nodded approvingly. Neither of us sounded more real than the other.

Ray smiled, but it was grim, which was completely appropriate. "This puts Robot Penny at a severe disadvantage. You don't look afraid."

I couldn't shrug, but I twitched my upper torso to tilt one shoulder higher than the other for a moment. "I'm better than her."

Meatbag Penny didn't answer. She tried to keep it off her face, but I understood her silence. I was right. She'd noticed it too, in that first fight. We might both be legitimate, might be Penny in the real and important ways, but I had an edge.

"I don't want this to happen," said Claudia, but now that she knew we weren't going to kill each other, the determination had gone out.

The other me gave her a weak but affectionate smile. "Take care of yourself, Claudia."

I nodded. "Please."

Ray started to say something, but I touched a fingertip to his mouth, hushing him.

"The prize has to stay neutral," I warned him, and flashed a sly grin.

Ha! He blushed. He actually blushed.

"Then when next we meet—" my double began.

"—we meet as rivals," we finished together.

Leaning down, I kissed Ray on the cheek. "Sorry about the date." Then I turned my back to him, Meatbag Penny, and Claudia, closing the conversation.

Ampexia had been watching us all with her arms folded, and as I walked past and she fell in next to me, she said, "This isn't goofy at all, is it?"

I shook my head. "Nothing is more serious."

She scratched her head behind her earphones, from which I could hear the faint scratching sounds of music. Awkward now, she said, "Listen, you two are dueling one on one, but I'm going to be there for you all the way. You did the same for me."

Grinning, I raised a fist, and she bumped hers against mine.

In fact, my grin widened a little, and I had to force myself to sound apologetic. "Fair warning. My duel is completely serious, but this next bit I have planned? Not so much."

Chapter Twenty-Four

Not that I leaped immediately into the fray. Timing is important. No, the next stage involved me waking up in the morning to my phone ringing.

The caller was either very lucky, or had called repeatedly. Once I pressed my off button, there was no waking me until time ran out.

Groping for the phone, I tapped the answer button and croaked, "What."

"You owe me," said the voice on the other end.

I groaned. "I was up until four a.m. playing Princess of the Closet Monsters. When I close my eyes, I still see giant spiders falling out of suitcases."

This whole tired and groggy routine was a total fraud, of course, but it felt good to pretend.

"We had a deal, Bad Penny. A pact sworn to evil itself."

"Yeah, yeah. Let me check my logs." I stumbled to my feet, hunched forward and stomping audibly as I crossed out into the pink main room of my pink new lair over to the bank of computers. After clicking my mouse around a little, I said, "Okay, fine. We can do it this morning, but I get to pick where."

She hung up, and I poked with my mouse a little more. It was so, so convenient to have exactly the same voice and speech patterns as the person I was spying on. I could leave a computer to look for word cues, and not have to do all the creepy listening in on conversations that the

Lutras no doubt got a kick out of.

Echo had presumably felt the same way, which was why he'd bundled this voice recognition function into his tracking software. Good man.

I showered, and drank a box of robot juice to finish the human experience, and headed upstairs, to be met with a scene that took my nonexistent breath away.

In the living room, her clothes badly rumpled and half-dressed, surrounded by a heap of electronic debris, sat my new partner Ampexia. Over her loomed Gerty Goat, frying pan extended and filled with gooey, freshly cooked pizza. Nearly filled, at least. Ampexia had a fat slice in her hands, with lines of cheese extending from it to her mouth as she chewed.

Struggling to make sense of what I was seeing, I said, "I thought you didn't eat food that appears out of nowhere!"

Ampexia took another huge, savage bite, chewing hastily and swallowing. Her eyes half-closed, and she crooned in ecstatic satisfaction. "That was before I found out how good a cook this robot is."

I smirked, one cheek pulled up tight. "Funny, that. The pizza at her restaurant is terrible."

Gerty jerked, going from leaning over Ampexia to straight upright so fast the pizza shot into the air, flipped once, and landed perfectly in the pan again. "They wouldn't let me cook! That's why I left. Good kids deserve good food, and to this goat all kids are good kids. Even the ones without horns."

Ampexia also straightened up, grinning at a sudden thought. She grabbed my sleeve and tugged. "Oh! Watch this. Hey, Robo-Goat. How about some crushed red pepper?"

"Activating spiciness protocols," announced a sweet, liquid, girlish voice. Gerty thrust the pan into Ampexia's hands, and transformed. The barrel of a cannon rose out of her forearm, and one after another hatches opened everywhere else in her body. Long, thin arms extended, attaching cables, pipes, pistons, and less-identifiable pieces of machinery. In a glass globe, burgundy light swirled, increasingly shot through with white electrical arcs. What looked like an ammo drum spun up until it whined. She leveled the barrel at the pizza Ampexia held up like a shield.

"Uh," I said, in case that helped.

Machinery kicked into gear so fast the arm cannon let out a series of squeals, and then a loud thud. Flakes of red pepper puffed out of the gun barrel in a brief, delicate cloud that ever-so-lightly dusted the surface of the pizza.

Faster even than it had been assembled, the red pepper gun came apart, its pieces withdrawn into their storage spaces. Ampexia took a bite of the next slice, and gave Gerty a thumbs up.

I applauded, and said in all sincerity, "I wish I could watch this all day, but it's time to get your gear together. Ridiculousness is about to happen."

Gerty swung her arms up over her head. "YAY!"

"Okay, here!"

"Here?" asked Ampexia, voice sharp with disbelief, and probably disgust.

"Here! Find a parking space!"

She gave me a dirty look for that one. A parking space would not be difficult to find. The one thing this neighborhood had was space. It looked like a war zone. The only functional building for several blocks was the front of a giant, irregular, tarp-walled lot. A paintball arena, in fact.

I checked my phone. Yes, this was it. We must have gotten here first. I wasn't going to argue with good luck!

Lucyfar hopped out of the bed of the truck, and was waiting when Ampexia and I climbed out of the cab. Stamping her foot, the Princess of Darkness complained, "You should have let me drive. We'd have been here twenty minutes ago."

"It took twenty minutes for Bad Penny to convince me to let you ride at all," said Ampexia, fitting on her backpack and gloves.

Lucyfar's pout did not go away, and she added folded arms to the expression. "You could at least have let me play with the goat."

Ignoring her, I climbed up onto the truck bed, where Gerty sat with her fingers in her ears, her eyes shut, and her breath held. Her ears were just long rectangles sticking off the side of her head, but that wasn't the point. She believed she couldn't hear anything, and that had kept Lucyfar from waking her up.

Now I had to outwit myself to get her attention. Hmmm.

Reaching around her massive torso, I dug my fingers into her armpits and tickled furiously. Just in case my intentions were not clear, I chanted, "Tickle tickle tickle!"

For about three seconds, nothing happened. Then her whole body quivered. Finally, her arms flapped up into the air, her eyes opened, and she barked, "HAAAAA!" in an explosion of released breath. Semi-literally, as some mechanism inside her released a blast of air from her mouth.

I hugged her, and said, "You did it, Gerty! Now let's go inside. Lucy has a game for us to play. I don't know what it is yet, but you can bet it will be crazy."

She lurched upright and shouted. "Gerty Goat doesn't take or make bets. Remember kids, gambol, not gamble!" Between that and the crash as she jumped out onto the asphalt, everyone for at least a mile knew we were here.

Lucyfar had already forgotten her, eying the dull green and brown paintball hut with a wicked grin. Rubbing her hands together, she said, "This will be perfect. Let's go commit the strangest crime in Los Angeles history."

Trying to pretend I wasn't itching to find out what that meant, I shrugged. "A deal is a deal."

Beside me, Ampexia muttered, "Not that she did anything to fulfill her side."

Lucyfar kicked the shop door open, and stepped inside. Black knives formed in a halo around her, above and below her outstretched arms. "Let all who claim to have innocent hearts flee before me, for Lucyfar tries to drag only the wicked down to their destruction. Everybody else, you should also run away, but find a good spot to record this with your phones. It'll be a hoot."

Gerty hooted twice, like an old fashioned train whistle.

"Just not a hoot you'll want to be within telescoping mechanical arm's distance of," said Lucyfar.

A couple of high school boys eyed her, tempted, but good sense won out. They edged around the walls to the door, and ran for it.

That left only the proprietor, with the nervous but basically calm stillness of someone who had dealt with supervillains many times. Leaning on his counter, I said, "And fill me up a bunch of paintball guns."

While he snapped things onto bulbous, brightly-colored fake guns, he also pressed a button on the wall. I could hear the echo of his voice outside through a PA system. "The park is closed due to real supervillain attack. Leave through the nearest emergency exit, and do it fast. By the time you find out why it's not safe to stick around, it will be too late."

Definitely not this guy's first rodeo.

He presented me with a duffel bag full of pigment pistols, and took his own advice, bolting out the door and heading straight across the street to put distance between him and us as fast as possible.

Hoisting the bag in one hand, and my mega-plow in the other, I headed out into the dusty, rubble-strewn battlefield behind the shack. A second later, Gerty plunged through the back wall, spraying planks, chunks, and splinters of wood. Swiveling her head left and right in confusion, she said, "Golly, I'm going to have to talk to the stage manager. He's putting way too much starch in these curtains!"

Ampexia eyed the dirt and the broken chunks of old buildings scattered around the lot. "What's the plan? There's nothing to steal here. There's nothing even left to break."

Feet apart, black hair whipping in a late summer breeze, Lucyfar declared, "I want Bad Penny to use her Machine to build... *this*!"

She thrust one arm out towards me, holding a blue block about the size of a paperback book.

I took it, déjà vu creeping up my spine. The block was made out of metal, but not solid. More like a sponge, but with an intricate pattern of tiny crossbars instead of round hollows. It had words printed on a plate on one end, but I couldn't even sound out the Cyrillic letters phonetically. The déjà vu crawled over me so strongly, I had trouble forming words. "Where... did you get... this? I didn't make it, and my power never does the same trick twice."

Lucyfar swept an arm around my shoulder, walking me out into the middle of the battlefield. "This mysterious relic was found in the collection of the ancient Egyptian mad scientist Pikeltukan, known not merely for creations far beyond the technology available three thousand years ago, but for his ability to see the future. After you built me that wonderful giant fighting robot, I realized I'd seen one of these before. The story of how I obtained this marvel from its modern, highly-protective owners is a thrilling saga of stealth, seduction, murder, and a fifty-gallon barrel of squid ink. Alas, we have no time for me to recount it here."

I raised my eyebrows skeptically. "I'm impressed. Not many ancient Egyptians spoke Russian."

"Right? Seeing the future must be amazing." She was back to rubbing her hands together, looking around in mischievous, anticipatory glee.

Squinting at the engraving as if that would help, I said, "I don't know what this will build. It could be a flower pot, or a doomsday bomb."

Lucyfar hopped up to sit primly on a waist-high wall, legs folded and hands clasped primly, a display of ladylike dignity sure to last at least ten seconds. "The label says 'Defenestrator'."

Sure enough, she began to clear out her ear with a pinkie.

Ampexia tilted her head to one side, sneering. "It's a blueprint for a machine that throws people out of windows?"

Whipping up her fist in zealous emotion, Lucyfar bounced up to stand on the wall where she'd just been sitting. "Yes! And I, Lucyfar, Star of Morning, will do whatever it takes to see that this noble scholar's grand vision is finally fulfilled."

Shru—criminy. Trying to look cool and unimpressed instead, I unwound my Machine, twisted him into activation, and stuck the blueprint into his back. Plates opened to fasten around the block, holding it in place. He needed no further instruction. When I dropped him on the ground, he began to dig, eat, and grow.

I nudged my boot against the ground next to him. "Whatever this thing will be, I question whether this is the right place to build it. The Machine works with dirt and rock, but that doesn't mean its construction will."

She giggled, shoulders wriggling with evil joy. Showoff. "Oh, but that's the perfect part. You've been here before. Do you remember what it was before the owners gave up and accepted the site is cursed?"

"...a construction yard." Which was why all the fragments of buildings that had never been completed.

She gave the ground a good, hard stomp with one sensible black sneaker. "Several construction yards. My vast angelic intellect thinks ahead. After decades of failed attempts to build here, we're standing on a thin layer of dirt over a giant pile of discarded steel girders and building equipment."

Crouching over my Machine, I soon saw she was right. The crunching sounds changed tone, and shiny metal joined the dull stone plates lining its growing, tube-shaped, insectile body.

Behind me, Gerty made her contribution to the topic. "I threw a no-good farm hand out of a window once, for trying to hurt a little boy. Does that make me a defenastridoodler?"

Lucyfar sounded reluctant. "Iiiiii dunno. I'm not sure it counts if you've only done it once."

Animatronic servos whined. Something went 'glomp.' "I could throw you out of a window if it helps!"

"Do it, Gerty. Throw her through a window," Ampexia urged. I was getting the impression she disapproved of Lucyfar.

"I am completely on board with this," said Lucyfar.

More servo noises. "Gosh, there's only one problem. All these windows are already busted!"

There was definitely good eating under this lot. The Machine swelled quickly, becoming thicker around than a sedan. It also grew taller, putting up the first floor of what looked like a complicated metal tower.

Struts and hooks and support pylons centered around a cylinder covered in familiar but uneven bumps.

Ampexia abandoned the argument about whether Lucyfar should be thrown out of a window, and stood next to me instead, watching the mysterious contraption grow. Mysterious to me, at least. It wasn't long before she said, "It's a music box."

With all of us distracted, I only found out we had company when a man's voice shouted, "Stop, evildoers!"

Fun and games ended. Ampexia stepped back into the shadow of the Machine, adjusting buttons on her gloves. I pulled the power lever on my mega-hoe to maximum, secure in the knowledge I could blow this arena to smithereens and no one would care. Lucyfar showed up next to me so fast it felt like she teleported into place, while shiny black liquid crawled over her civilian clothes.

A hero leaped off of one of the tallest remaining building fragments, over two stories tall. Sunlight gleamed off of his armor as he somersaulted in mid-air, landing in a confident, arms akimbo stance.

His... armor.

His very, very skimpy armor, consisting of boots, bracers, shoulder pads, and a pair of metal briefs that, despite their thickness, covered less than your average men's swimming briefs. His bronzed muscles glistened almost as brightly as the armor itself, perfectly chiseled far beyond the merely athletically good shape the active combat lifestyle forces on most heroes. The pouched belt around his thigh somehow conspired to make him look even more naked.

I had to say something. "GAAH."

Ampexia, fists clenched now, came up to flank me on the other side from Lucyfar, only to give me a puzzled look. "What's her problem?"

Lucyfar smirked. "I think she's never seen a hero in a skimpy costume before."

Ampexia's brow furrowed even more. "How did she miss them? You all dress like clowns on a Caribbean beach."

"GAAH," I repeated.

Lucyfar's hands waved, gesturing vaguely at Ampexia over the top of my head. "Her parents kept her sheltered from how strange and perverse the rest of us are, lest she be warped forever to follow our corrupt path. Something like that, anyway. Don't expect me to understand it."

Ampexia grunted. "Okay, yeah, I guess that makes sense."

The hero raised one arm, flexing a rock-hard bicep. "Are you finished, ladies, or must Man of Courage carry the fight to you?"

Ignoring his words, demon princess's eyes wandered over that bicep, and everything else. Her tongue snuck out across her lips. "Personally, Lucyfar likes."

Leveling a finger at Man of Courage, I shouted, "GERTY! THAT MAN'S PARENTS NEGLECTED HIM AS A CHILD AND NOW HE OBSESSIVELY CRAVES UNHEALTHY EXTERNAL VALIDATION!"

The ground trembled as a two-ton animatronic goat charged past me, arms wide. "I'll give him a whole lifetime of love!"

Crossing his arms in front of him, the unfortunately dressed hero shouted, "Feel Mjölnir's hammer, war robot!"

Something invisible hit Gerty, and hit her hard. It didn't so much as scuff her apron, but she did rock backwards at the blow, her charge cut off. Not that this harmed her mood any more than her body. She merely declared, "I love this game! I cast Summon Hugs!" Extending her arms, she fired both metal hands on cables at Man of Courage.

He raised just one fist this time. "Stance of Atlas!"

It worked. Sort of. Gerty's hands closed on his arms, but he stuck to the ground, immovable. Instead, she flew across the distance, yanked off her own feet to tackle-hug the poor fool.

While Friendship happened, I had a moment to try and push his costume out of his mind and focus on more cerebral topics. Gesturing between him and Lucyfar, I said, "Chimera's powers are divided up by mythological monster theme, right? This guy reminds me of him. Do you think he's a long-lost grandson?"

She smirked. "I doubt it. Chimera's gay. It's a useful trait in a fighting partner. I can be all over him, and he doesn't get distracted." She, on the other hand, was plenty distracted. Her eyes never left

Man of Courage, or what was visible of him as Gerty extended extra arms for super hugging.

I had to hand it to the guy for raw power. When he yelled, "Strength of Hercules!" he actually was able to push Gerty's arms off of him, and retreat far enough to throw out a new power. "Elusiveness of Rabbit!"

That sent him zig-zagging all over the place while Gerty lumbered after him, extendable arms grabbing. "Come back! You still need the honest affection of a nurturing parental figure! And pants!"

Were his feet even touching the ground? He didn't look like he was actually running, just sliding. He moved so fast, and in such random directions, it was hard to tell. But maybe not totally random. The shining heroic blur came sliding around Gerty once, heading for us, only to be blocked by another wild robot grab.

This had been hilarious, but we couldn't trust the fight wouldn't come to us. Lucyfar's knives materialized around us in a cloud. I hefted my hoe.

My goaty singing idol was smarter than she looked, and recognized the problem as well. A sped-up male voice echoed from inside her. "Releasing short range dumb-fire breakfast rockets."

Panels opened up all over her again. This time, boxes emerged, heavy cubes the size of microwaves. Round holes lined each one in rows, and as soon as a box extended, it began to fire.

The missiles themselves looked like soft drink cans, from the vague glimpses I got as they accelerated. They fired unevenly, each one trailing a line of smoke that revealed how their paths weaved and flailed. Add Gerty jerking from side to side, and the rockets went everywhere, unpredictable, impossible to dodge. Every time they hit a surface they popped, releasing pancakes, fried eggs, bacon, breakfast cereal—that sort of thing. The mess added much needed color to the drab brown and gray of the arena.

Smeared with egg yolk, syrup, and brightly-colored marshmallows, Man of Courage decided he'd had enough. He leaped onto the still-growing tower, bracing a foot on one of the knobs from the central cylinder, and holding onto another. For the first time, I noticed something above his neck. I'd been trying to avoid the lantern jaw and perfectly white smile, but past that he wore a metal helmet that totally covered his face down to his nose. Finally, some part of his costume I could look at without embarrassment.

"Troll's—"

He didn't get to finish. One of the hooks from the loose 'box' around the music cylinder reached out, splaying into a clawed hand that grabbed him by the shoulder. With a quick jerk, the tower flung Man of Courage into the air, sending him sailing out of the park. Nearly a block away, I saw his body smash through one of the only intact windows in the battered neighborhood.

I spoke for all of us. "Criminy. It really is a Defenestrator."

Gerty slumped. Great, even the animatronic got jointed shoulders. "Aw. I wanted a music box."

"Okay, note to Penny: Don't touch the tower," said my voice, only not coming from me.

Meatbag Penny crouched on top of the fence, clinging to it with unsteady balance. In blissful contrast to Man of Courage—especially since this was my body—she was covered completely below the neck, in my old white laboratory jumpsuit. The random attack staff, with its three floating cogs, stuck out from where she had it strapped to her back. That and a bandolier of pouches were her only obvious weapons. Of course, that was a generous 'only', given how many bombs the bandolier might contain.

She fumbled, nearly dropping off the wall, and leaned forward a hair to... well, presumably squint at me. Beyond the jumpsuit, including boots and gloves, she also had on my mad scientist goggles. She certainly sounded shocked. "Is that you, Robot Me?"

I tried to sound equally surprised. "Yes! What are you doing here, Biological Me?"

"I thought I'd be fighting a ridiculous criminal building a giant evil music box. I miss being a hero. Are you following me?"

Yes. Yes, I was. But I sure wasn't going to admit it. "Shouldn't I be asking you that?" I made it as accusing as I could.

Of course, Mom would look at the odds and know in an instant this was a set-up, and that it meant I had a way of tracking the other me. But she wasn't here, and my double had so helpfully asked her to not interfere.

My double hopped off the fence, landing with a heavy thud and a grunt. Unslinging the staff, she leaned on it as she watched me from the edge of the yard. "You can't be ready to duel. Or have you found a stasis field already?"

I adjusted the position of my mad science plow, ready for action. "No, but I'm not going to back down."

She grinned. "Like either of us would. I'm not here to duel, either, so I guess we fight this hero against villain."

I nodded. "Works for me, and since we're not playing by dueling rules... Gerty! HUG HER!"

Gerty came charging out from behind a broken building, arms extended. "Yay! I have love for the whole world!"

Meatbag Penny gaped, so surprised she dropped her staff. "Tesla's Electric Life Form. Gerty? You have a Gerty Goat? And she's alive?!"

The big gray goat in her blue dress and white apron skidded to a halt, arms still wide in invitation. "Who's a Gerty Girl?"

Other Me let out a squeal of joy, running forward and leaping up onto Gerty to hug her. "I'm a Gerty Gerty Girl!"

With Meatbag Penny busy and her arms pinned, I pulled one of the paintball guns out of their bag, and fired off a number of shots at her. It made a pleasing *fwoom fwoom fwoom whack whack whack* noise. This body had way better aim than my original as well, because half a dozen would have actually hit my target—if Gerty didn't extend her frying pan at high speed on one of her skinny extra equipment arms. She intercepted every one.

My double gave Gerty a kiss on the nose, and wriggled free to face me with her hands on her hips. "That was cheap. You know Gerty would never let a child get hurt—"

"I surely wouldn't!" agreed the goat, lifting her chin and twisting from side to side proudly.

"And what are those? Mad science paintball blobs? Drugged, or something?"

I shook my head, giving her a whimsical smile. "Nope. The regular kind. But I bet they sting." Then I opened fire again.

We'd passed some threshold where Gerty didn't think Other Me needed protecting. Maybe because she was quite able to protect herself. Her hands swung up at the same time as mine, index and middle fingers pointed. The pellets bounced away, maybe a foot from her hands, each one with a different colored burst of sparks. They did convey an impact, because she slid gracefully backwards until I ran out of ammunition and tossed the gun aside.

My sly smile turned into a wide, approving grin. "So, that's your new defensive equipment. Nice." The gold bands on her gloves and boots hadn't been obvious until I had a reason to look. Thin, slip-on attachments. Very convenient. And of course, the first thing I would have done after being challenged, had I still been able, would be to go make myself a new defense toy.

Gerty offered her own opinion. "I can skate, too!" With a series of buzzes and clicks, tank treads unfolded under her feet. Very fast tank treads, because she started rocketing across the lot with them like a badly-aimed cannon ball. This place would need to build new ruins soon.

My double watched her with a smile of pure, open joy. "She's a perfect thing." Then she sighed, and hung her head in resignation, digging a hand in a pocket of her bandolier. "But, needs must. Time to blow you to kingdom come." With that, she flicked a marble-sized orb at me.

It didn't get anywhere. Gerty came zooming around between us, catching the bomb in her mouth. I heard a muffled 'thud' from somewhere inside, but the goat was already careening away.

Other Me watched her for a moment, and when Gerty was sufficiently far away, flung half a dozen more. The robot goat reversed course like a shot, her head shooting out on a telescoping pole to grab every bomb out of the air, one after the other. After the explosions went off inside her, and as she rolled past between us, she stuck out a thin tongue and slid it across her lips. "Mmm, I love candy! You should always give goats candy." A different, tired and exasperated man's voice cut in immediately after. "Do not give goats candy, children. You'll make them sick."

My double and I both grinned a lot.

I had not just assumed Gerty would catch them, and had done my best to scramble out of the way. That brought me to where I could see Ampexia and Lucyfar arguing.

"I don't think they want us to get involved," said Lucyfar, wagging a finger sharply.

Ampexia jutted out her chin stubbornly. "That's my partner, and at least kinda my friend. I'm not going to stand here and watch her get hurt."

That was all the time I had for them, because Meatbag Penny scooped a handful of cubes out of a different pocket, and said, "Let's try these!"

She threw. Gerty, across the lot, either didn't notice or didn't care. Thankfully, with my terrible eyesight, my biological body's aim stank. I sprinted to one side, and all the cubes missed me. When they did hit a spot, they exploded in purple goo that whipped tentacles around, grabbed any stones or bricks they encountered, and squeezed together into a tight knot.

Just running away was not going to help me for long, and we both knew it. In fact, my double looked guilty, and tugged at one of her braided pigtails in an awkward, behind-her-shoulder gesture. "You don't have any defensive gear? Seriously? We don't have to do this. I'll let you call it even. Ruining an already ruined paintball court isn't the kind of crime I'd lose sleep over."

I held up a reassuring hand. "It's okay, heroic evil twin. My defenses are weak at the moment, but I have one overwhelming advantage. I've been playing with Gerty longer, which means I've gotten more hugs than you."

Gerty's gasp echoed back to us. "That's right! It's not fair! I can't love one of you more than the other. I'm coming, Penelope!"

Aw, she'd learned my name, and recognized we were the same person.

My double took a nervous step backwards, but did not flee. Like me, being at ground zero of a Gerty Goat hugstorm did not sound like that bad an idea to her. It was certainly adorable how Gerty rocketed over, swept Meatbag Penny off the ground, and swung from side to side, giving her the most tender, engulfing, determined hug ever administered by robot to child.

Besides, we both knew Gerty wouldn't let her be hurt while in Gerty's care.

Good thing I had no intention of hurting her.

While my double dug into apron and carpeting and enjoyed the embrace, I strolled up to the two of them, took hold of one of her swinging feet, and scooped off the golden band.

That got Other Me's attention. She shouted, "What? Hey! You dastardly, conniving robot!" and started kicking. Kicking quite hard, and if I hadn't been much stronger than her, I wouldn't have been able to wrestle down her other leg and take off that band, too.

Gerty blinked. Her head tilted forward, looking down at me. Quietly aghast, she asked, "Penelope, are you... stealing?"

I shook my head confidently. "Nope. She's me, and I'm her. I can't steal from myself."

My duplicate shrugged. "Can't argue with that logic."

Slipping the golden bands over my own boots, I experimented with how they worked. Let's see. It wasn't frictionless sliding like Claire's shoe inserts. My double hadn't leaned her feet. I kept one foot completely flat, and kicked off with the other.

That did it. I scooted several feet back, like riding a railway track.

"You're not trying very hard," I said to my duplicate.

"Who? Me?" she asked, not even trying to hide her smug confidence. Batting her lashes up at Gerty (I couldn't see it under the goggles, but I knew what I would do) she told the goat sweetly, "Gerty, now I've had all of my hugs *and* all of *my* hugs, and yet it's impossible to have too many hugs. When you can explain this and show off your amazing skating skills simultaneously, then truly you will be the master of both farm and kitchen."

Gerty stared at her, motionless. Admittedly, Gerty never moved except to do something specific, but right now the stillness stood out. Opening her arms, she let my double fall to the ground. Rotating, the animatronic goat rolled off through the dirt and debris. After several seconds she pirouetted, chanting, "What is the sound of one butter patting?"

My double and I exchanged a look of mixed humor, fondness, and respect. Quietly, we walked together around to the opposite side of the Defenestrator from Gerty.

The Defenestrator had gotten big. It towered over us now, with the Machine a rippling band of construction tools sliding up and down to build more, while tracks and cables connected that to the base digging farther and farther into the ground. I was just a little worried we would destroy a subway tunnel.

On the way, I picked up the bag of paintball guns. Other Me picked up her discarded staff. We both understood, so she wasn't really surprised when I decided we'd reached the right spot, and I yanked out a gun with my left hand and opened fire on her from close range.

One of her hands darted up, forming the shield I could only see because of the sparkles when my paintball blobs bounced off. Without the foot straps, that didn't push her away, but it kept her busy for a moment. My right hand scooped up the weather sponge. I had to act fast, because she would have a plan in a couple of seconds, tops. I gave the sponge two squeezes. The first splattered water over my double's head, and specifically over her goggles. With wet lenses, she was momentarily blind. The second squeeze poured water into the pile of dirt under her feet.

That was why I'd chosen this spot. This was the least packed-down dirt I could find. To my delight, a private hope came true. This was, after all, agricultural equipment meant for irrigation. It didn't just rain water down on the ground. It coalesced the water inside the dirt, mixing it in directly. The result was that my double now stood in gooey, ankle-deep mud.

I tackled her. She had started to swing her staff around, no doubt with a plan more subtle than just blasting me, but blinding her gave me just that extra bit of time to act first. My body hit the shield, revealing it by the rainbow glitter as a rounded disk like an actual shield. Like with the paint balls, it might block me, but the force of the blow carried through. Now she didn't have her sliding boots to carry her away, and she merely tripped in the slippery mud and fell on her back.

I grabbed the wrist with the staff. A couple of seconds of struggling, and I forced the shield band off her hand. We wrestled and rolled until I got the other hand, pinning my back against her and ignoring the punches and kicks until I'd yanked loose the other band as well.

Scrambling away, I wriggled the bands on over my own gloves. We both kneeled, panting for breath. Maybe technically I didn't need to, but I felt like I did.

Applause caught our attention, and we looked up to see Lucyfar clapping and smirking wickedly. Her battle costume of black phantom stuff had disappeared, leaving her in faded black civilian jeans and a shirt. "Wait five years and do this again. People will pay to watch."

Ampexia grunted. Stiff-legged, she stalked away from the rest of us, shouting, "Gerty! Hey, food machine! They're all playing games. Can you make me some chocolate chip cookies?"

Lucyfar skipped after her. "Ooh, yeah, cookies! Goat Time for Lucy at last!"

I tried the activating gesture for the forcefield gloves. Two fingers out, two pressed against the band. A jabbing motion produced sparks when it hit the ground, pushing me up and making me stumble to get my feet under me. Sweet, these could even fire like a projectile. How far? Note to Penny: this equipment set deserves experiment and training.

My double, having actual breath, was taking longer to get hers back. She stared up at me cautiously, picked up her staff, and slowly climbed to her muddy, muddy feet. She also scowled a lot. "Is that what this is about? Ambushing me and stealing my tech?"

Got it in one. I needed defensive gear, and this was all about suckering her in as an excuse to take it. I'd had my computer waiting to pick up references to her testing equipment, or 'heroism', 'training', or 'villainy.'

Admitting any of that would give away my advantage, however. I glared back at her instead. "Excuse me? I remind you again, you attacked me. The finest source of mad science technology in the world picked a fight with me, and I'm taking advantage of the opportunity. Besides, you're still going easy on me."

"Hey! I'm—" She stopped, and shrugged. "Okay, yeah, I could be fighting harder. I just can't wait to pull my trump card on you." Flashing me a sudden, manic, evil grin, she asked, "Are you going to let me?"

I shouldn't. She was blatantly manipulating me, luring me into a weak position. The smart thing to do would be to tackle her again, now, tie her up, collect the Machine, and run for the hills. Possibly also steal her bomb belt and dump that in the sewers. I didn't want it for myself.

But this wasn't a desperate situation, and I had what I wanted. It was also smart to save ruthlessness for when I needed it, right? Keep some tricks of my own in reserve, and coax my enemy into revealing all of hers early. That was the path of wisdom.

Okay, and curiosity was already eating me alive. I let out an aggrieved sigh. "Go ahead. I'm still going to kick your butt."

Wiping a muddy hand on her chest, she pulled a little tube out of one of the many near-invisible white pockets on our white jumpsuit. Not just a tube, a candy dispenser, with a plastic head on the top that sported a red-striped face and plastic crown. Ah, yes, someone else was playing Princess of the Closet Monsters, and going the vengeance route.

I set my feet, and shot a shield blast at the ground in front of me. Sure enough, that skated me backwards a few yards, hopefully far enough to react to whatever my twin was about to unleash.

She popped the top of the tube, and a fat white pill slid out. Not an ordinary pill. Tiny lights orbited it, like a stylized atom.

With great gusto, she dropped that pill into her mouth, and swallowed it.

Note to Penny: Playing manipulative mind games with yourself is seriously weird. We both knew exactly what the other would respond to, and just had to hope that our secrets would win out over the other's.

Speaking of, I watched her like a hawk. Flames? Light distortions? Sudden movements? What powers would this give her? What was about to happen?

The answer was 'laughter.' She laughed, high pitched and rolling. "Ha! Ah ha ha ha! Yes! It's so obvious. So easy. Why didn't I see it before?"

Criminy. She sounded nuts. Not playing around, completely insane, with a skewed, tight grin and jerky movements. What had she done to herself? It was like how people described me... when...

She flicked the cogs of her battle staff, called out confidently, "Copper!" and waved it.

...when my super power took over.

I put up both shields and backpedaled, fast. The red ribbon that flicked out of the staff rolled off of them, leaving a pillar of copper metal rising up a good ten feet high.

"Steel! Polyvinylchloride!" she shouted, flicking the staff twice more. I tried to slide away first, only to find myself both times headed straight into the blast, and having to put up a shield a split second before being encased.

My super power knew everything. That was one thing I remembered after using it. Absolute knowledge. Not technically seeing the future, but close enough it didn't matter. If this kept up, in a few seconds I would be trapped in a cage.

Fortunately, another trait of my super power was its total lack of purpose. Other Me's attention wandered, and she stopped shooting at me to step up to the tower instead. While I squeezed out a gap between the pillars, she located the blueprint embedded in the now-gargantuan Machine. Pulling a miniature screwdriver out of her pocket, she expertly poked the blue sponge.

Note to Penny: Carry tools. You have the pockets for them.

Second Note to Penny: Moot. I already have the Machine, better than any other tool.

The Machine would only obey my orders, but it thought the blueprint was my orders. Now the pattern of the ring sliding up and down the tower altered, hastily making changes. Subtle changes. Metal arms were replaced with near-identical arms. Nothing really looked different.

It hit me. Oh, Tesla. My double had a way of activating my super power at will, and interfacing with it better than I ever had before. Aside from the giggling, she was mostly coherent. This was bad, bad news.

"Glass!" shouted Other Me suddenly. The cogs on her staff hadn't quite stopped spinning, and she stabbed it out, not at me, but at the pillars she'd grown a minute ago. A big glass rectangle grew into place on top of those spires, like... a window.

The Defenestrator swiveled on its base. I yelled as loud as I could, "Hey, Gerty!"

Yes, my double was close enough to my power to at least know what I was doing. She gasped. "Don't you dare."

"GRITS!!!"

On the far side of the tower, something went 'bang', in a big way. Lucyfar yelped. A big cloud of white stuff fountained into the air, only to rain down again in tiny white kernels, like grains of sand.

Feet pounding loudly, Gerty ran past us, waving her stiff arms and shouting, "I can fix it! Don't worry, they're just grits? What? You don't know what grits are? I guess there's a lot of foods only people who live in one part of the country know about. So..."

And, having given the warm-up speech from her 'grits' stage routine, she started in on the song. "Is there chile in your chili? Or is poutine more your thing? I've eaten more kinds of pizza than they'll give me time to sing...!"

Gerty's performance distracted Meatbag Penny for a couple of seconds. It did not distract the Defenestrator. The Machine had finally switched enough parts, and an arm extended from the tower, swiping down over me. I put up both shields, but long, clawed metal fingers merely curled around the disks to close on my torso.

And then it groaned, and the arm twitched, and nothing else happened.

Ha! Clogged by horrible, perfectly named grits. Thank you, Gerty.

My double just giggled, her shoulders jerking from side to side. "Hee hee! Oh, that was good. So clever. Useless, but clever. Don't you see? No, you can't, but I can. We live in a world of possibilities. There's nothing that isn't a machine."

I cleared my throat, because I needed a little courage to try and communicate with that insane ramble. "This is getting too spooky. I'm going to confiscate those power augmenting pills for our own good."

"These? By all means, take them!" she asked between giggles. Leaning heavily to one side, she held up the candy dispenser, then tossed it over to me. I grabbed it, and stuffed it down my shirt. She wasn't getting that back in a hurry.

My double lurched forward now, almost hump-backed, her grin wild and her voice cracking. "I'll just recover them from the blast crater." She slapped the cogs of the battle staff, spinning them to a no doubt perfectly judged speed, and jammed the head of it into a gap in the tower.

It didn't reach. Or rather, it did, but the cogs stopped moving before then. They were jammed in place by a dozen floating black knives.

Lucyfar stepped up behind my double, one hand on a hip, smirking in disapproval. "I like a fight and some chaos more than the next girl, but I draw the line at being blown to bloody smithereens."

If she had anything else to say, she didn't get a chance. Grits might have seized up the arm now poised above me, but another arm functioned just fine as it dipped down, grabbed hold of Lucyfar, and hurled her through the window Meatbag Penny had built atop her metal spires. As glass rained down everywhere and Lucyfar disappeared over the roof of the paintball shack, her voice dopplered. "Wooorth iiiiiiit!"

All that registered only in the background. As soon as the Defenestrator started to move, so did I. I pulled free of its frozen claws, and charged Other Me with my head down. I didn't use the sliding boots. I wasn't going to make it that easy to dodge.

She giggled, looking confused. I grabbed hold of the staff, and yanked. It took a little struggling, but superior robot strength won out, and I pulled it out of her hands.

She staggered, holding the back of her head and stammering. "Hey! I—I need that. If I spin it at... three hundred... two revolutions per second? And release a charge into the Defenestrator of vibrations that... nitrogen molecules... uh..."

And from outside the walls of the arena, my mother's voice asked, "Penelope Akk, are you playing superhero without asking me first?"

My double looked lost and confused as our super power drained away. She'd fought it down by forcing it to try and explain how its creations worked. The pills might bring her closer to our power, but they were far from a perfect integration.

Thank Tesla.

Not that my problems were over. I had absolutely no desire to face my mother under these circumstances. "Machine, abort! Forget your gathered materials, return to me now! Gerty, we need to go home fast. I think I left tater tots in the oven!"

I had just enough time to scoop up the Machine when it wriggled free of the tower before Gerty caught me in both arms. Hoisting me up into the air, she galloped through the paintball shack, ignoring its walls and babbling, "Oh, those poor, burned tater tots! We have to save them, in the name of fried potato deliciousness!!"

Lucy and Ampexia could take care of themselves. Ampexia was particularly good at escapes. Momentarily safe, I rooted around in my shirt until I came up with the candy dispenser. A quick peek inside showed several more of those glowy atom pills.

I crushed them all in my fist, squeezing and grinding until they were nothing but dust and plastic shards. No more of that. Watching myself go destructively insane had not been fun.

But.

The plan had been a total success, right? I knew there'd be a lot of winging it. I still had the mega-plow on my left hip, and the irrigator, and now my old unpredictable staff. Most importantly, I had an absolutely fantastic new pair of defensive tools that already had my mind swimming with possibilities.

My debt to Lucyfar was paid, and I had proven again that I was the better Penny. Even directly invoking our super power hadn't been enough to help her win.

Now it was time to lay low, have some fun, and let her suspicions cool. Hmmm. Where could I find a stasis field and a mind switcher?

Mom and Dad,

I can do this. It's just camp. I'll be home soon, I promise.

Missing You,
Penny

Chapter Twenty-Five

Goofing off was easier when I could just call Ray or walk down to Claire's house, but the point was to let things simmer for a few days, right?

You know, low-key. Casual. Stay at home, play computer games.

Which is why I completely blame Cassie for me and my gang slamming open the door to the church basement and rushing inside. Proof that it was Cassie's fault is that she was the one who zapped blue arcs of electricity out of her arms like she was waving her wings and shouted, "This event, and all who would dare compete in it, are now the property of the Crown Princess of Middle School Crime, Bad Penny! All of Science is hers to command, so if you wish to compete with her superhuman technology, I will log your defeat now and save time."

Looking back over her shoulder at me, Cassie flashed a grin and asked, "Like that, right?"

Marcia had a more down-to-earth question. "What is this place?"

Physically, this was a church basement, a big room with concrete sides, not entirely underground but with little windows way up near the ceiling. As I have heard is the wont of such places, it was being used for an event. Rickety folding tables had been arranged with no visible rhyme or reason all around. Most of the tables had triangles of wood on them that formed long, slow slopes. One held blocks of wood, little wheels, and cutting tools, which had clearly been put to use by the majority of the room's inhabitants. Kids roughly our age, or a little younger, stood in small clumps at every table, each holding a roughly built little wooden car. They had been racing those cars down the ramps. Now they all stared at us.

The room also held three adults, two men hovering next to the dangerous tools on the building table, and a woman in the middle of the floor.

The children nudged each other with elbows and whispered to their friends. The adults eyed us with more caution.

We did make a sight, all in costume. My lab coat and striped-shirt, leather-pants steampunk girl outfit were definitely not civilian wear. Cassie had gone with the spandex bodysuit look, but a shinier material and with a lot of white and blue jagged lightning stripes. It looked high-tech without actually being tech at all. I liked Marcia's outfit, even if it made my head swim to look at it. The black and white checkerboard pattern on the martial arts tunic wouldn't have been too bad, but jarred eye-maddeningly with big yin/yang symbols on the front and back, which in turn were encircled by black and white snakes eating each other's tails. Oh, and horizontal black-and-white striped tights, and sensible sneakers that, yes, were still black and white polka dotted. The rips of hard wear and multiple fights broke up the clashing patterns, and helped a bit.

And bringing up the rear, Lucyfar, who had decided I should not be the only girl wearing a corset, but had opted to partner hers with black leather pants, multiple black leather spiked bracers on each arm, and special shoes that I had to admit looked cool and made her look like she was walking on hooves. She had enough superhuman strength not to snap her ankles doing that.

Cassie provided explanations, waving her hand at all the kids. "It's a box car derby!"

Lucyfar furrowed her brow and frowned, a very obvious expression with the heavy mascara and black lipstick. "A what now?"

Cassie groaned in frustration, rolling her head around. "It's where kids our age build little cars and test them against each other in downhill races. What you see is what you get, diablo-brain. There are no hidden subtleties. How can you not know this?"

Equally exasperated, Lucyfar sniped back, "We didn't have box car races in England!"

I gave her a suspicious sidelong look. "You said you were an ancient evil firstborn of the universe, and so on, and so on."

Crossing her arms, Lucyfar turned her frustrated glower on me. "Yes, and one of those claims is a lie. Or maybe I'm lying now and they're both true."

Silence stretched for a moment, and when it became clear the argument wouldn't continue, Cassie stepped up close to my shoulder. Tugging on my sleeve, she gave me a sheepish smile and said, "You're trying to treat this all like supervillain camp, right? I thought nothing would make this a more legitimate camp experience than an arts and crafts day."

Grinning my gratitude, I pinched her arm back. "And nothing is more arts and crafts than a box car derby."

Our audience had just started to get restive as we carried on our private conversation. Cassie froze them again by raising a fist that crackled with lightning. "And now it's an evil box car derby!"

Lucyfar raised her hand, her irritation vanished in a sly grin. "All in favor of an evil box car derby?"

Arms shot up everywhere. The kids looked around, saw that an overwhelming majority agreed, and let out whoops of excitement. Thumping footsteps echoed around the basement as they stampeded to grab paint and markers and blue to draw skulls on their cars, or fix little spikes on the surface.

Lucy swept over into the middle of them, asking, "Who wants actual demonic sigils engraved on their car?"

That got another cheer.

Marcia, Cassie, and myself wandered over to the table where basic construction was done, although from the minimal amount of shavings and debris it was clear almost all the kids had built theirs at home. The adults just watched. They'd relaxed considerably now that our intentions were clear.

I looked at the diagrams of cars, and instructions about painting lines so you'd cut right. "This could take hours, and without my super power, I don't have any advantage over any of these other kids. You know that, right?"

Cassie clasped her hands behind her, and watched me with a smug, expectant smile. That girl thought I was superhuman, not just someone with powers. Marcia, who did not worship me, picked up a chisel and started hacking away at a block. I was pretty sure that why ever a chisel was here, this was not the purpose. Nobody seemed in a hurry to stop her.

I regarded the pile of parts. Okay, forget it. Time to do it the supervillain way—cheat! Cupping my hands to my mouth, I shouted over the hubbub, "Hey! Who's winning?"

After a few seconds of milling around, a boy held up his car. The kids around him nodded.

I unwound the Machine, and set him on top of a block of wood. "Duplicate his car."

That seemed to be direction enough. He scarfed down the wooden block, bite by bite, and then vomited it back up as a simple wooden car. Completely wooden. Other cars had plastic wheels and metal axles, but I'd given the Machine one material to work with, so that's what he used.

A faint sheen caught my eye. I rubbed the axles where they passed through loops on the car's base. Lubricant, made out of something in the wood. Was that why the other kid was winning?

Cassie absolutely beamed. Her faith in me had been rewarded. She looked like she might float right off the floor.

Marcia, on the other hand... well, criminy. Marcia could sculpt. She'd hacked a pretty good car shape, more complex and rounded than the example, out of the block. The process did involve a lot of angry scowling and fiercely focused eyes. She got more into the process with every second, until her teeth bared in a grimace. When her chisel hit the wood next, black burst out like a cloud, and the wood cracked.

Letting out a shriek of rage, Marcia punched the table, smashing it into bits and sending tools flying. Black knives appeared out of the air to catch all the sharp or heavy items, despite Lucyfar being huddled over a racing table with no sign she'd even noticed Marcia's outburst.

Nobody else was in any hurry to intervene, which left the job of scolding Marcia to me. Of course. "Criminy, Ouroboros. That was not okay. Beating up other people with super powers is fine, but you can't go around breaking people's stuff."

Marcia whirled around to face me, open-mouthed, aghast rather than angry. "You leave a trail of rubble and devastation wherever you go."

I pointed at the contestants, who were drifting back to their racing after the shock of Marcia's outburst. "Yes, but not at an event for kids!"

She glowered at me, then let out an explosive, shoulder-slumped sigh. The slump was totally to get revenge by taunting me with my lack of proper shoulders. Evil wench. I hadn't even been able to tell her garish monochrome tunic had pockets, but she pulled a wallet out of one of them, pulled a wad of bills out of it, and tossed them to one of the men who had been overseeing the table. "Fine. You're right, like always."

She didn't even glance at the bills. The ones I could see were hundreds. A reminder that Marcia wasn't just rich. My parents were doing quite well for themselves. I bet Misty Lutra had millions in the bank somewhere. No, Marcia was stupid rich, 'billionaire' rich. Why had a family that loaded sent their daughter to a public middle school? Even if it was a magnet school?

To show off to the other superhero parents how perfect the Original's daughter was, of course.

Cassie interrupted my brooding by giving my lab coat's cuff a little tug. Meekly, she asked, "Can we get back to the fun? I just don't have a lot of time. I told Ruth I was going to see Penny, and I didn't tell her which Penny, so I need to get back to where I can claim it was, uh..."

"Meatbag Penny," I filled in, amused again.

"...when big sister buzzkill comes to get me."

"Do you have to go now?" I asked, touching her arm sympathetically.

She shook her head. "No, soft and squeezable Penny is covering for me. She was pretty mad you defeated her super power enhancing trick, but she still likes you. I just can't afford to waste time. We need to pack every second with maximum crafts."

My all-wood car was somewhere in the mess Marcia made, but I hadn't cared about it anyway. A different thought got my attention. I leaned closer to Cassie, giving her a lazy, evil smile. "If we're building things, you're the only actual mad scientist here."

Her eyes got very, very wide. I pulled back and straightened up, to keep her from having a heart attack. How could anyone have a crush on me like that? It made no sense. With this power, I would have to take on great responsibility. Determined to use it only for her good, I gave her a finger poke. "You. Mad science it up."

She shook her head, waving her hands and even retreating a couple of steps. Her cheeks had turned so pink they were almost red. "I'm not really a mad scientist. All I can make are dumb little enhancements for my powers! You know that!"

"It counts, which means..." I ticked them off on my fingers. "Electricity, magnetic fields, mad science support... criminy, you have three different super powers, Cassie. Four, if those wisp things count as separate. You're talent city. Show us what you can do."

More head shaking. "I need wires and batteries and simple electronics parts. Not wood. I didn't bring anything. Usually I just work in Ruth's garage."

We had already drawn a lot of attention, as discussions of people's super powers tended to. Now Claire stepped out between us and the crowd, and asked, "Who here is willing to contribute, and I quote, 'wires and batteries and simple electronics parts' so we can get a demonstration of mad science?"

Chatter burst out everywhere. Kids pushed each other and argued. A ginger-haired girl declared, "I have a broken fan I brought with me. Don't look at me like that, Joaquin, I have reasons."

Another boy held up his hand. "Do the batteries need to be charged?"

Leaving Cassie to field those questions, I turned my attention to more important matters. Namely, grabbing Claire's hands and squeeing. "E-Claire. When did you get here? How did you get here?"

She was also in her supervillain identity. In Claire's case, that meant a pair of denim overalls with a skirt puffed out by crinoline petticoats rather than shorts. Knee-high striped socks bulged where they fit into her sneakers, suggesting bandages still wrapping her feet. A burgundy-and-white short-sleeved shirt with starched shoulder poufs added to the 'cute farm girl' look, although being Claire, she had the buttons unfastened down her chest farther than any other fourteen-year-old girl could get away with, or would dare. Just in case anyone thought the look was accidental, she'd pinned a big plastic button into her pale blonde hair, with a wickedly grinning black and red version of a smiley face on it.

"As for when, I've been here nearly five minutes. It was good stealth training, staying behind the one person I couldn't block from noticing me with my powers. As for how, let's just say a little birdy told me." She made eye motions at Cassie.

Grabbing Cassie from behind, I yanked her into a giddy hug, rocking her from side to side. "Thank you thank you thank you! This is the sweetest thing you've ever done for me." Especially since it meant much less attention from me. Cassie had knowingly sacrificed time with me so I could reconnect with my best friend I'd missed so badly. My steel heart felt like it would jam with warm, gooey gratitude.

In response, Cassie wheezed. Oops. My robot arms were kinda strong. After I eased up on the hug, she turned hot pink again, and shuffled her feet, head tilting around as she couldn't meet my gaze. But boy, that goofy, happy grin. "I, uh... I mean..."

I hooked my elbow into Claire's, but kept my attention on Cassie. Poking my blue-haired fangirl's shoulder, I said, "You know what power I've never gotten to see you use? How do you make one of those wisps?"

Claire crushed her shoulder against mine, beaming at Cassie. "That sounds fantastically cool. Is there anyone here who doesn't want to see our friend Arc Flash create a living lightning creature?"

The adults looked horrified. They did not want to see it. Their caution was drowned out by the enthusiastic roars of the contestants. The ones who had spare electronic parts surged forward to offer them to Cassie.

Leaning even closer, I murmured into Claire's ear, "Arc Flash?"

"I made it up just now." Oh, how I'd missed that unruffled, smugly shame-free voice.

"And of course, you're dying to see how Cassie's power works," I said to my superhero geek best friend.

Then I added two and two together, and gave Claire a suspicious sidelong stare. "You're eating up having two of me, one a robot double and the other an evil twin, aren't you? This was on your list of life goals. It was. It totally was."

She coughed into her fist, but her glow of satisfaction destroyed that pathetic attempt to pretend she felt guilty. She further confirmed my suspicions by changing the subject. "You want to see Cassie make a wisp half as much as I do."

That sounded about right, yes.

Cassie, meanwhile, was dealing with a sudden influx of fans of her own. As they shoved electronic parts at her, she took a step back, taking only one tiny battery from the smallest child in the crowd. "No. No! I'm only going to do this with a AAA battery. A big wisp would last too long. This is just for demonstration purposes. I've already committed my villainy for today by taking over this derby. I don't need to burn it down. Now, give me room."

They did, forming a broad circle around her as Cassie put the little battery on one of the racing tables. I elbowed my way to the front, because maybe I was a little curious. Claire slipped in on my wake.

"This is not impressive to watch, guys." Cassie hunched her head down, flustered and guilty, and looking just far enough away from me that I bet I was at the edge of her peripheral vision. Holding up one hand, she spread her fingers, then curled them, as if holding an invisible globe. Blue-white lines flickered between her fingers and palm. They joined together and parted like running water, until a knot formed and stayed, with all new arcs connecting into it. The effect reminded me of a novelty plasma lamp.

Some threshold passed that only Cassie could detect. She clenched her fist tight around the knot of electricity, and lowered her now-glowing hand to the AAA battery standing upright on the table. As she eased her grip over the metal cylinder, the light faded.

That was it, for the moment. Cassie shook out her hands, then rubbed them together, kneading and massaging. Looking extra nervous, her head darting towards me but not quite at, she held out her hand, palm flat and pointed down. She touched the center to the button on positive terminal of the battery, and lifted.

Out of the battery rose a little spark, twinkling and jerking. Cassie pulled her hand away entirely, and it floated by itself over the table.

Applause thundered around the basement. I noticed the three adults at the back of the crowd smiling. Why, those devious so-and-sos. They'd pretended to disapprove while not doing anything, so the kids would get a show.

Claire leaned her head to my shoulder for more whispering. "You know what's sad? You don't know the real Cassie. She desperately wants you to, and then when she sees you in person, that all breaks down and she either gushes or acts cool. She held on okay while we were at school, because she didn't want to get in Ray's way, but now there's two of you and only one of him."

"I like her, but..." I flapped a hand, not sure how to finish that.

Claire nodded, understanding.

With a tight, wry smile, I added, "When she talks about other people's relationships, it's like she's a grownup. She only goes to pieces over me."

"That's because she thinks you're the coolest person in the world."

I *really* didn't know what to say to that.

A lot of other kids now thought Cassie was the coolest person in the world. She wore the stiff, awkward smile I put on when I got happily embarrassed. Her hair, not just blue but luminescent, stuck straight up off her head. Children oohed and jabbered questions that all ran together as her itty bitty wisp floated around her hands in a figure eight.

Lucyfar's strident voice interrupted Cassie's moment of fame. "You cheating cheaty little cheater!"

Cassie jumped in shock. The wisp disappeared. Kids scattered to watch the new show.

I stormed forward, to find Lucyfar, quivering in outrage, point a finger at a pudgy, pale, blond boy maybe a year younger than me. He leaned back against a table, clutching his wooden car to his chest, eyes wide and intimidated, although at least not terrified.

I gave a loud sigh to catch her attention. "Aren't you a little old to be accusing random children of cheating?"

"But he *is* cheating!" If anything, she quivered even more furiously, glaring at the boy in righteous fury.

Pinching the bridge of my nose, which at least felt real, I asked, "How is he cheating?"

"I don't know!"

Edison's Stolen Tesla Designs. Why did I get hooked up with the crazy ones? She looked entirely serious. "Then how do you know he's cheating?"

She stood up very straight, and jutted out her chin in defiance. "Because I'm cheating, and he still keeps beating me!"

This was the boy who everyone had said was winning, and whose car I'd copied with the Machine. Personally, I suspected he understood engineering better than most twelve year olds. Especially since Lucyfar's car would be whatever she could hack out of a chunk of wood with her magic knives.

Someone else took this much more seriously than I did. A squeaky voice shouted, "Don't touch him, you villain."

A diminutive figure shuffled out opposite Lucyfar. One of the shortest people here, I couldn't make out much of anything except she was a girl with a particularly high-pitched voice. That was because she'd just come out of the bathroom wearing a pair of pajamas, the loose one-piece kind with the animal pattern and the hood like the animal's head. In her case, it had a gray stripe over a cream face, that same pale underbelly, and the rest gray. Except for a dark patch ringing the brown eyes, and a lighter patch at the end of the tail. Unlike most of those costumes, this one did have a tail, hanging limp on the floor behind her.

I whispered to Claire, "She must have been inspired by your first E-Claire costume, the teddy bear outfit."

She whispered back, "They're called kigurumin. It's a thing."

Lucyfar forgot the supposedly cheating boy immediately. She turned to face the girl in the pajamas, hands held out from her sides like a gunslinger. "I don't know you, superhero."

The girl in pajamas squeaked (she had *such* a high voice!), "Then listen up. I am the Dook of LA, the Fantastic Frenetic Ferret, and I do not appreciate evildoers messing up my box car derby and harassing my friends!"

With a cold sneer, Lucyfar materialized one of her knives, and floated it over to bump the little girl in the chest. "I'm the big time, newbie. Do you really think you can stop me?"

Things happened very fast. The pajamas snapped tight over the girl, becoming part of her. She was a ferret, if an artificial-looking bipedal one. Her tail even lifted up off the floor, alive and thick now rather than a limp sleeve. In a flash, she hopped up on the knife, balanced on her toes and one hand despite it being about the size of an oak leaf. Her other hand pointed a black claw at Lucyfar's face. "Yes."

Something occurred to me. I'd spent most of my super-powered career hanging out with villains. Until they started chasing me down, I hadn't grasped how many heroes there were in this city. This might not even be this kid's first fight.

"Don't make me get rough, girl," warned Lucyfar. She materialized another knife, again poking the Fantastic Frenetic Ferret with the blunt end. At least, she tried. With the kind of speed and grace I normally only saw in Ray's superhumanly enhanced reflexes, she hopped from the previous knife up onto this one.

Lucyfar blinked. "The kid's got—"

...and that was when someone's car fell off a table and clattered loudly on the floor.

The Ferret freaked out. She leaped into the air, backflipping to land on her feet, but only for an eyeblink again. Twisting around, she bit— with prominent fangs—at the direction the sound came from. There was only empty air in that direction, so she turned and bit behind her again, hopping off the ground. This turned into a frenzy, and for a good thirty seconds she bounced up and down, back and forth, doing handstands and aerial somersaults and a range of serious acrobatics, all in an impressive but failed attempt to bite her own butt.

She didn't stay in one place, either. Careening around, she sent kids scattering and knocked over three different tables. The nearest was the one Lucyfar had been racing at, and the blond boy got shoved violently into Claire's arms. He looked about as stricken and awed as any boy would be, planted body to body with her, and when she slid him back onto his own feet, the immoral vixen blew him a kiss.

Did I mention how much I'd missed having Claire around?

All the while, the Fantastic Frenetic Ferret snarled and squeaked and let out a series of weird grunts. I had to admit, they did sound kind of like *dook dook dook.*

Finally, in the middle of a particularly impressive back flip, the Dook of LA hit the wall and slid down to the floor, where she collapsed. She immediately started to snore.

I hadn't been worried about Lucyfar hurting a child, but this sent me hurrying over to check on the girl. Her costume had returned to being loose pajamas, rather than a part of her. "Should we call an ambulance? She didn't look like she hit her head."

A girl in the crowd said, "She's fine. She always falls asleep after her power goes crazy like that. It uses up a lot of energy."

Fingers tugged on my sleeve. I turned to see Cassie's anxious grimace up close. "Penny, I'm out of time. I've got to go."

I gave her a warm smile. "Go on, and thank you. This was great."

She hesitated, darted her face forward to give me a kiss on the cheek, and then ran out the door like she had Lucyfar's knives chasing her.

Without being asked, Marcia dug into her pocket, and with a certain amount of grumbling under her breath, pulled the rest of her money out of her wallet and handed it to the woman in charge. Whatever club hosted this event was going to make a serious profit on the day, and have a lot of very happy members.

Claire, meanwhile, stood up on her tip-toes and peeked over my head at the crowd., although she winced when she did it. "I don't see the signal. What else should we do while we wait?"

I raised an eyebrow. "Signal?"

"You'll get it when the signal comes. I'm here on business as well as pleasure. Let's craft while craft day lasts, okay?"

The same sentiment I'd gotten from Cassie, but given how rarely I got to see Claire this summer, I accepted with much more urgency. Tugging on one of my braids, I scanned the room, where kids were reluctantly getting back to their races. "I'm not sure... oh, hey, I know what I want to show you!"

Pausing to scoop up some blocks of wood from the original construction table, I righted one of the fallen racing tables and set them down. Taking off the Machine, I stuffed a chunk of wood in his mouth and ordered, "Saved Game Twelve."

Marcia wandered up, and she and Claire watched as the Machine chewed through the wood, obeying my coded instructions. Lucyfar was still over near the downed Dook of LA, whispering conspiratorially with the boy she'd previously accused of cheating. That woman fit in way too well with a room full of twelve year olds.

The Machine finished eating its raw material, and regurgitated the whole thing in a nine-inch-tall statue of... well, it was almost a young woman. Even in an unpainted wooden statuette, it was clear her hair had been hacked off unevenly, and something like straw bound in to complete a ponytail. A sewed-on patch covered one eye, one of her arms had doll joints like mine, she had a plate on her stomach visible through her ripped dress, and one leg from the knee down was bulkier than the other, and furry.

Claire whistled, impressed in a serious and sober way. "You're going the Sacrifice route, huh?"

I grinned so hard my cheeks hurt. She'd recognized the main character of Princess of the Closet Monsters. The grin lasted for only a few seconds before I got serious, too. "Yeah. It's rough. 'Brutal', even. For most games, the peaceful, good-hearted options may take more skill, but the results are happier and friendlier. This... I'm not sure the game is appropriate for kids, and I've fought goat cancer zombies."

Marcia mouthed the words 'goat cancer zombies' with a glassy-eyed look of speculative wonder.

Claire said nothing, just picked up the statue and studied the neck and normal wrist for the telltale scars from the game.

I read that silence perfectly. "It's okay. I know Other Me is playing Vengeance route. I almost did, and she may have been smarter than me to give in to temptation. The Vengeance route isn't evil, it's powerful and righteous. I'm not entirely sure Sacrifice is good. If there's a moral message in this game, I can't figure out what it is. There's no right or wrong, just decisions."

Marcia, not a computer game player, nudged me with her elbow. "So, the Doodad—"

"—Machine."

"Right. It can copy what it sees? Could you make a statue of me?"

Hmmm. That would be interesting, wouldn't it? Stuffing another wooden block into his maw, I told the Machine, "Do it. Make a copy of Ouroboros. Include her clothes, please." It paid to be specific, with something that took voice commands but didn't think in any way I could identify.

Chomp chomp chomp chomp grind glorp clatter. He complied, spitting out a wooden statue of Marcia. He'd even mixed up the grain on the wood to capture her glaring tangle of costume patterns. Oddly, he copied her in the middle of the punch where she'd broken the table, not her current stance. See previous about having to be specific with voice commands.

Marcia squealed, picking it up, turning it over and over, peeking under the tunic's skirt and squinting closely at the threading of her hair and how it half-covered her ears. Then she slammed it down on the table again, and said, "Okay! Now make my arm twice as thick."

My brow furrowed. "What?"

She leaned over the table and kicked her feet behind her. "Come oooooon! I want to see how much it can customize!"

Marcia's claims that she wasn't really actually insane were not very convincing at the moment. Oh, well. It was my fault for liking crazy people. I stuck another chunk of wood in front of the Machine, and gave him a poke. "Go on. You can take her orders for altering this statue." Looking over the table at the maniacally grinning black-haired girl, I added, "And no, he doesn't know how to build weapons without a blueprint."

Incapable of complaining, my Machine chewed up some more wood, then the arm of the statue. When he reached the shoulder he let go, and out slid a beefy, muscular, sleeveless arm.

Giggling at the absurd awkwardness of the statue, Marcia said, "Okay, now the nose! Make it two inches long!"

Claire tapped me on the shoulder, and beckoned with a curled finger. I followed her quietly across the room, leaving a laughing Marcia building an increasingly distorted replica of herself.

A boy around our age, probably the oldest kid here if Lucy didn't count, waited for us by the wall. He had a closed cardboard box on the floor next to him, an uncomfortable expression, and a whole lot of oil stains on his loose shirt and pants.

Feet primly together, Claire stood tall and stiff, then bowed and swept a hand at him. "Bad Penny, my... contact. I know I'm not supposed to take sides, but I can't let either of you founder when you need an introduction. This boy's father—"

"No names," the boy insisted. He had a hoarse, pleading voice.

I looked him straight in his hazel eyes. "Of course not. We're professionals. We don't get personal."

"—sells items of technology you said you need," Claire finished, having held herself in motionless pause during his and my exchange.

Tilting my head skeptically, I eyed Claire, then the boy. "Like a mind exchange device?"

He stared at me like I'd asked him to grow a second head. "Nobody has those."

"Like a stasis field generator," explained Claire.

Still nervous, the boy gave a brief, denying hand wave. "Not a real stasis field. Those are super rare. The cheap kind, for booby traps."

"Good enough to hold someone in suspended animation for a couple of months?" I asked. After all, it didn't matter if the thing actually stopped time. Only that it would let me store Meatbag Penny until I could swap back into my body.

He sagged a little in relief, while nodding at high speed. "Oh, yeah. My—the builder yelled at someone once for storing someone more than a year. That's about the limit that it's safe."

Ha! Rubbing my hands together, I purred. "Excellent. That will be plenty. How much?"

"Two hundred thousand dollars." He said it almost in a whisper. It's not the kind of number you let people hear.

The number smacked me across the face like a fist. Tesla's Patents, I had a lot of money, but not that much.

Don't panic, Penny. You have resources other fourteen year olds do not. Supervillainy could be very profitable. That, or I could go around the stasis issue and only grab my double when I was ready to switch minds.

Taking a deep breath, uncomfortably aware again that I was faking that gesture, I said, "Here's what we'll do. Claire and I will go yell at Marcia for whatever we're about to find out she's done—"

"Don't look, you'll start yelling now," advised Claire, smirking already at the impending trouble.

"—and I'll get back to you."

Claire assured us, "I'll provide her with discreet contact information. Completely professional."

Well. That was all settled. Dreading what I would see, I turned around.

Proud of my steely willpower, I made it halfway across the room and was nowhere near the nervous tech-dealing boy when I shouted, "Machine, do not obey any more of her orders! And eat that right now! Lucyfar, you put her up to this, didn't you?"

Dear Mom and Dad,

Enclosed find a lanyard I made at supervillain camp, out of human hair. It turns out my Machine makes a really great shaver.

Having A Good Time Today,
Penny

CHAPTER TWENTY-SIX

Awake!

The best kind of awake, the kind where I didn't actually have anything to do. I just lay in bed, arms folded under my pillow behind my head. This stupid robot body did have a couple of perks, and one was that it could really relax. No tense muscles. I could lay there and enjoy the peace until my thoughts interrupted.

By, say, reminding me that I did have something to do. Maybe not urgent, but I'd promised myself I would do it today. A nagging thought that had to be followed up on.

So, I got up, and got dressed, briefly thankful Marcia's mansion had its own laundry room. My body might not get sweaty and icky, but boy was supervillainy messy. If this weren't mad science fabric, I'd be covered in mud stains no matter what I did.

My power went all the way, on every tiny detail. This could be some Tier Three, nobody-knows-how-it-works fabric technology thrown in just as an aside while making a cool outfit. That excess was part of what bothered me now.

I snuck out through the secret garage. If Ampexia found out I was gone, she wouldn't be worried. Gerty was fast asleep, and would be until someone mentioned breakfast or show time. Anyone looking in the mansion's front windows would probably freak out at the hulking fuzzy robot, although they would have activated enough traps by then to make Gerty the least of their problems.

This trip I had to make alone, which meant no car. I experimented with the sliding boots, but I couldn't get a good speed without whacking the sidewalk behind me with the force gloves. If I did that, stopping was equally hard, and these boots did not turn. Add sidewalk pedestrians to the mix, and they were useless for long-range transportation.

Maybe I should steal something from my double for that.

Still, the boots and gloves got me to Santa Monica, and it wasn't that far a walk from where I had to share the sidewalk with other people to the train stop. Nobody bothered me. A man in a cape spotted me before I saw him, but when I looked in his direction he went back to talking to a couple of kids. In the other direction, people hung out on the beach, wondering how many of the people frolicking in swimsuits were the secret identities of heroes or villains. Not that Santa Monica's beach is the most picturesque and clean and frolic-friendly.

Reaching the turn towards the train, I stopped and looked back at Santa Monica pier. I missed Ray, and the date we'd gone on there.

I'd missed rush hour, and the light rail trains weren't that crowded. No heroes attacked me, either, and I kept the potion staff, the one weapon I'd brought along, crossed over my lap.

A couple of stations in, a pair of teenage boys boarded the car. I wouldn't have thought about them, but when they sat down next to each other they got out some textbooks and started talking. The textbooks floated up into the air, open to be read while one of the boys scribbled in a notebook. Summer school? After a few lines of writing, he clicked his pencil twice, and a tiny device on the nearest book turned two pages.

What was the statistic? One percent of people had super powers? Mom could quote it in her sleep and to several decimal places, I was sure. One percent would be over a hundred thousand powers in LA. Even point one percent would be upwards of ten thousand. Maybe two hundred fought or committed crime at any one time. The vast majority were like these two, just enjoying a cool talent or making their extra ability useful.

The light rail train south from Seventh Street was even quieter. Of course, no heroes would want to damage either line by starting a fight in them, would they?

But nobody followed me when I got off at Slauson, either. Before, I'd just been cautious. Now I was really alert, because someone else's secret rested on my responsibility. I passed the spot where the samaritan had offered to help a teenage robot with a broken arm, and hoped that guy was having a good day somewhere.

Finally I rounded the block, and came again to the front gate of Junkment Day.

It hadn't changed. Old tarps behind the gates and fence blocked passersby's view inside. A sign declared they were closed.

Like last time, I jumped up, grabbed the top of the fence, and pulled myself over, to find the same wasteland of junk as before. I had to admit, I enjoyed walking over a layer of random metal objects as I crossed the yard and peeked into the shop. This, at least, had changed. Well, slightly. Now tools were laid out on the benches, the shelves held a few supplies, and an old, circular analog clock with a minute and second hand hung on the wall. Instead of eerily empty, the shop now just looked unused, but ready if someone ever brought a car in for service.

No sign of an inhabitant, though, so I climbed around the heaps to where I'd found the door last time.

Well. No door, but behind a few obscuring pieces of junk, I saw a blank metal wall. You could mistake it as an old refrigerator if you didn't know to look closer and see it was just too big.

I let out a loud sigh, slumped forward, and started unwrapping the Machine. "It's a shame to eat your door twice."

Car parts fell away as if naturally overbalanced. The wall collapsed inward, hitting the floor of the tunnel inside with a resounding clonk. Any attempt to pretend that had been an accident collapsed when that slab sank into the floor, leaving a smooth entrance.

I walked down the long, space-defying hallway to the lighted doorway at the end.

It still led to that old cathedral. Some of the equipment had been rearranged, but not much. The biggest difference was that the old man sat on a chair in the middle of the floor, in the middle of a ring of robot parts. The chair looked antique, with a pointed back I'd never seen before, and threadbare red upholstery too thin to serve as more than decoration. As for the robot parts... well, that was a guess. Curved sections of metal shell, motors, pistons, chunks of electronics, they lay around the chair in no obvious order, but definitely gave the impression of a disassembled high tech machine.

Frankly, the old man didn't look much better. This time his overalls were dirty, and he had dust on his face and shoulders, and in his hair. Red ringed his sunken eyes, like he hadn't slept much. When I stepped up to the edge of the ring of parts, he looked up and gave me a bitter glare. "You didn't mess with the sign this time. Everyone always messes with the sign."

Heh. Maybe that was his doorbell, so I'd caught him by surprise?

Further small talk did not seem likely, so I unslung my staff, leaned on it, and skipped introductions. "I need your professional advice."

The glower remained fixed on me, studying me with small, hard, deep green eyes. Had that been their color last time? His skin was less red, more brown than I remembered. Maybe he'd just gotten a tan. I had time to notice all of that before he spoke. "This is not about the Upgrade, is it." Not a question, a prediction.

If he weren't totally the wrong person for the expression, I would have smiled. He credited me with not being whatever normally irritated him. I shook my head. "Only distantly. I need the advice of a cyberneticist who understands power enhancers. My biological double made one."

No response, but his stare looked a little less irritated, a little more interested.

I pushed on. "She has my mad science super power."

"I've heard about it," he admitted.

Probably from Cassie, a thought that made it hard not to grin. Maybe I should, but I didn't want to risk insulting him. "When I use it, I enter a fugue state. I know I get manic while it takes over, but this...

it scared me. She took a pill, and had access to my power, but she also sounded completely insane. Not ranting villain insane, babbling and twitchy insane. You're the only person I know of who understands power enhancements. I just... need someone to reassure me I'm worrying for nothing, that it's safe."

Still no answer. He looked at me, no longer radiating anger, just blank silence.

But silence itself was an answer. "So it's not safe."

He leaned back as far as the stiff chair would allow him, which wasn't much. The impression of tiredness returned. "I don't know. On the one hand, you sound like you had a mild case of Jekyll/Hyde to begin with."

Okay, now I smirked. Bitterly, but a smirk. "Yeah, and now we're in separate bodies."

A grunt was all the recognition that got, and he went back to what he was saying. "On the other hand, there are risks to giving an 'occasional' power a kick like that. It can grow."

"My power is about eight months old, now. It's been growing rapidly the whole time. Mourning Dove said she could see it. That's how I got into this mess."

He shook his head, slow and grim. That haggard face was good at grim. Black fatalism radiated from it, and weighted his tired voice. "I can't give you a reliable answer. Yes, it might be dangerous. Mad science medicine often has long-term side effects. If each pill leaves some permanent damage, you may not want your head back."

I watched his face. His expression wasn't just weary. It was tense. "And the other thing?"

He shot me another searching look, a little irritated, a little impressed. Either he really was a grumpy old man, or he'd practiced the role to perfection. A faint growl even tinged his reply. "Getting your head back may be moot. Has anyone told you how rare mind swap technology is?"

That shocked me. I stood upright, letting my arms hang in front of me so the staff extended crosswise. My eyebrows clicked together. "It's been mentioned, but I hadn't really thought about it. I assumed you could get mad science anything. My power can make mad science anything, but... I've been told a power like that is... once a century."

"Or more. A lot more," the old man said.

Criminy. And I had to fight that legendary-level super power.

He leaned forward again, balancing his skinny elbows on equally skinny knees. "I know of no one making mind swap devices today. Temporary versions exist, but they're magic, require lightning, and I do not think they would work on a robot."

"And if you don't think..."

He nodded, a tightness around his mouth accepting my assessment of his expertise. "I know what I'm talking about, yes. I believe I am the only mad scientist alive who could even make an unsafe version, and I won't."

Hmmm. I let go of the staff with one hand to tap my chin. "Everyone thinks *you're* dead. Maybe..."

He shook his head, which sank a little farther between his shoulders. "I am aware of only one mind copier. It copies rather than transfers, and it is lost. Last I heard, a pathetic little weenie villain named Mammon owned it, but he didn't make it himself."

"I found that one, and modified it to do transfers. That's how I got into this body. But it left something behind in my head, a version of me attached to my super power. Or maybe my power copied me back into my own brain." I let out a sigh, and shook my head so hard my pigtails flapped. "Either way, it doesn't matter. She broke the device way beyond repair."

His eyes lowered, just a little, staring off into the distance of his own thoughts rather than at me. Quietly, with the rhythm of a man assembling a list, he said, "A mad scientist named Paul Pitmier used to make mind transfer devices. Not a hero or a villain, really, just crazy and obsessed. They were one-shot devices, and have all been used. The Great Vivifactor had a lens that swapped consciousnesses in the 1800s, but I saw it broken. Nothing remains of Da Vinci's Soul Explorer, or Tikilek's Ultimate Sacrifice. I guarantee that. Using a creator's mind as a template for a sentient robot is common, but useless to you. There are aliens who could switch your minds easily, but I wouldn't hand my worst enemy to them."

I gritted my teeth and winced. "Not going to let Puppeteers mess with my head, no."

His head sunk sharply, hanging down now between his arms. It wasn't a grizzled, weary old man expression, more of a theatrical display of defeat. A touch of exasperated energy crept into his voice as well. "Why am I not surprised you know the second most closely guarded secret in humanity's history?"

Going for broke, I said, "I assume number one is the stone gates and artifacts?"

That got no response, which meant I'd nailed it. Kind of sad, really. I was hoping there was something even more cool that I'd missed. Of course, there could be an awful lot of really secret secrets left to discover just below the top two.

The lack of response went on. And on. Past 'maybe I should say something' to not wanting to interrupt him because he had left drama behind and had to be seriously thinking.

He did, eventually, lift his head. The look he gave me might be sober, but only that. No hostility or bleakness. "I may be too pessimistic about this. Despite what I like to think, I do not know everything. I have been out of touch with the world for two decades. There might be options I know nothing about. You're still hunting for hen's teeth, Bad Penny."

Reaching behind my shoulder, I grabbed a braid and twisted it as I did my own thinking. "I'll work something out. All you're telling me is that I have to steal information before I steal the device."

That got a smirk. Was it the first smile I'd seen from this professional crotchetiness manufacturer? It lasted about a second, and then went back to flat seriousness with a hint of anger. "You know who I am. You didn't last time."

I told the First Horseman, "Yes. Whatever you used to be, all I know about you right now is that you help children." I'd have shrugged it I could. This was clearly a bigger deal to him than to me.

Much bigger. He glared, some of that real hardness stirring in his eyes like when I'd left last time. "I killed people. Many, many people. Personally, and through others."

"Then why did you stop?" I asked, meeting his gaze with quiet curiosity.

His mouth twisted. That hollow face did disgust well. His already rough voice rasped with it. "Because I was wrong. I had a plan to make the world better. A grand philosophy, considered and studied, plans laid and settings arranged for longer than you would believe. Many would die, but heroes would be better afterwards. People would be better. The world would be better. At last, I had everything in place, and launched my dream."

"And...?"

His shoulders twitched twice, jerking first to one side, then the other. He was looking inward again, not focusing on me. "Everyone fulfilled their roles, followed their schedules. It all went exactly as I expected, except the world wasn't a better place. Society didn't change. No one changed, except the people who died. Heroes, villains, and many, many innocent people, because I was arrogant enough to think they were acceptable sacrifices to my dreams."

With a huge, heavy sigh, he met my eyes again. Bitterness still sharpened his voice, but his face had gone calm again, at least. "I tried to make excuses. I tried to blame not getting a fourth horseman, but I'm too old to fall for lies like that. I put the principle to which I'd devoted my life to the test, and it turned out to be a fantasy."

My eyes had gone wide and my face tight, but only with shock from the strength of the First Horseman's self-hate. Slowly, I shook my head. "If you're expecting me to judge you, this is way out of my depth. I can't even figure out right and wrong dealing with my exact double. I'll let the people whose job it is to decide these things figure out if you deserve to die or be locked up forever or whatever."

His mouth tightened in a momentary grimace. "There's no prison humans can build that I couldn't walk out of. Killing me is the only punishment the heroes have."

Criminy. What intimidated me was not the crime he confessed to, but the gloomy, fatalistic way he'd delivered that last line. This guy believed he was Claudia-level power.

My words came slowly, as each thought arranged itself. "I'm just going to deal with you as I know you now. If someone else punishes you, maybe you'll deserve it. That's beyond me. What it looks like to me is that you're trying to make me hate you."

"No." The word was surprisingly quiet. His face had gone still as well, the frown contemplative, but with the anger gone. "You've come to me for assistance twice now. I wanted to know what kind of person I was helping."

Um. "Did I pass?"

"I'm not sure I have the right to judge." He was still looking me in the eyes, and if there was mockery in echoing my answer, I couldn't spot it.

He stood up, groaning and pushing his hands on his elbows as if he were the weak and weary geezer he looked like. "Thank you for not destroying my door again. I'm sorry I couldn't help."

That was obviously a dismissal, so I gave him a small, grateful bow. "You did. I know where to go from here. I won't tell anyone about you, either, and not just because it would be getting personal."

Leaving him watching me with his grumpy old man face, I walked back out of the church and down the hall towards the regular world. What I needed now was to get a little bit evil. That's what was working best for me so far, after all, and after talking to the First Horseman, I was giving up even wondering which of me was the good one.

I just needed some easily manipulated dupes...

Chapter Twenty-Seven

I led my gullible patsies through the dark, winding pathways of the arcade, towards a door concealed by deep shadows and its own monotonous appearance. Unaware of the doom I led them towards, they guarded my back as I peeked through.

An empty lounge. Excellent. Abandoned, in fact. No personal items, no refrigerator, just a couple of couches, chairs, and tables.

"We're clear. No demon princess," I assured Marcia and Cassie.

Cassie shifted from foot to foot, awkward and scowling. We'd gone out in costume this time, but she hadn't been using her powers. Her hair had turned from blue back to a pale blonde, unkempt rather than sticking up and back like a spiky dandelion. "Are you sure? Having her around is like having to chaperon your chaperon."

I reached back and patted her arm. "She agreed we're settled, and it looks like she doesn't use this lair anymore."

Marcia, completing our villainish trio, noisily cracked her knuckles. "I can find out if she's here."

I narrowed my eyes, my mouth flatly skeptical and my stare reproving. "She's not here, Ouroboros."

Cassie only relaxed a little, twisting from side to side to look into the beeping gloom. "Why are we here? We don't play the kind of games you get in arcades."

Marcia sneered, but not at Cassie. Her unfocused eyes looked inward, at her memories. "My father expected me to get high scores in all the rhythm and shooting games, but I've never seen any of these."

Closing the lounge door, I straightened up and flaunted my third smuggest grin. "And that is why we're here. I bet Lucyfar wouldn't put her lair in any normal arcade, and if she did, it wouldn't stay normal. We would have had fun poking around anyway, but I think I guessed right."

"Huh," said Marcia. For a moment her face pinched up on one side, eyebrows and mouth in a lopsided tilt. Then she grabbed my wrist and Cassie's, and dragged us through the darkness to one of the machines, each one its own spotlight. She treated it to a ferocious glare, and then nodded. "You're right. Take a look at this thing. I thought it was just broken, but it's been modified. 'Mad science' modified."

The arcade machine had been one of those dancing rhythm games I avoid like the plague. The sign over it even read 'Dance', but then had been broken off before the rest of the name. 'Dance' was all the title screen said, either. Normally, they had pads in front of them with symbols to step on. This had a pad, but the rubbery surface tucked into the sides looked more like a momentarily inactive moving walkway.

Still taking charge, Marcia plunked a couple of quarters into the machine's slots. Those read 'Twenty-five cents', another sign these could not be regular arcade cabinets. Smacking the joystick around as if she knew what she was doing, Marcia flipped through a dozen different images of characters and names of dances before settling on an extremely goth couple, and 'Tango.' Grinning and grunting in satisfaction, she hit 'Start.'

In black and white, the little man with his black hair and tall, willow-slender woman in her long black dress separated. He held out his hand.

Holograms over the pad, red-and-blue outlines of those same two figures in position. Marcia grabbed me by both shoulders, and physically yanked me into the spot occupied by the woman's blue outline. She pushed Cassie into the red, even though Cassie was slightly taller than me.

The holograms adjusted, roughly matching our heights. Cassie held out her arm to occupy the same raised pose, with the hand extended slightly downward.

My blue outline lifted her arm in response. I tried to match it, until Cassie's fingers closed over mine.

String instruments wailed a music sting, then settled into a swift zigzag of slowly descending squeaks. Our holograms raised their arms, and Cassie and I imitated them, then circled around each other as the woman made a circuit around her partner in prim baby steps. Mine were a tad less graceful, as I stumbled to keep up and watch both the dancers on the screen and the hologram I had to match simultaneously.

When I looped around in front of Cassie again, the red hologram grabbed the blue hologram's wrists. Cassie stepped in close behind me. On the screen... uh...

On the screen, the man kissed the woman's arms and shoulders about forty million times. Our holograms, thankfully, did not encourage Cassie to do the same. After several seconds, the woman on the screen cleared her throat delicately, gave her partner a sharp look, and jerked her head a couple of times in our direction. He got the message, and with visible reluctance stopped smooching her throat.

Another music sting, and he spun the woman in the black dress around, only to take both hands in his and snap her tightly against him. Half a second after our blue and red guides, Cassie and I did the same. She bent me back, both of us giggling and snorting.

Then the dance began. Cassie's arm curled around my back. I lay my hand on her shoulder. We stalked side to side, following our extended arms like a boat sailing behind its pointy prow. The pad rolled underneath us, keeping us in place.

We were not good at this. At all. The outlines kept leaving us behind, and we missed an entire move where I was supposed to bend back and swing around, because I couldn't even see my guide hologram do it. The woman in the black dress on the cabinet's screen actually winced at my mistake there.

Personally, I had to hold back laughing. Why bother holding it back? Because Cassie was having a way better time than me. When the holograms had us pressed against each other, which was a lot, I could actually feel her heart pounding through two layers of costume and a certain amount of natural padding, most of that on her side.

If this game had a swing dance option, Ray would be equally hysterical.

The dance ended with a couple of foot stomps and Cassie standing close behind me again. The man on the screen leaned his face in to the woman's neck. Cassie did the same, until the mustached little goth guy whispered something husky and affectionate in... French? Probably French. Some Romance language.

The whisper was too much. Cassie bust out laughing, banging her forehead against my shoulder a couple of times in case I did not understand the strength of her hilarity.

"What?" I was terrible at languages. If it had been German, I could at least have mistranslated it.

Trying and failing to mimic the guy's deep, hoarse tone, she recited, "'I love how many throats you have ripped out with your high quality bicuspids.'"

I extricated myself from Cassie's embrace, and gave her a skeptical look. Her face still twisted in spasms of humor, she nodded frenetic confirmation. The goth couple faded from the screen without defending themselves, replaced by a score list. We were terrible. Cassie had scored ten times what I had, and was still an order of magnitude below anything on the list.

My robot body might have precision my mortal body never did, but it still contained Penelope 'What Is This Grace You Speak Of' Akk.

Suddenly blushing furiously, Cassie waved towards the rest of the arcade and mumbled, "We should go find Murder-boros."

With her clashing black-and-white patterned costume, Ouroboros would have been easy to find anywhere. In this case we didn't even need her phenomenal eyesore super powers. We could hear her barking and yapping, and follow the sound.

Marcia had found a martial arts cabinet. Like the other, this one had been built with hologram technology, but if the smacking of Marcia's hands against its were any indication, this hologram was solid. That was some hardcore mad science, right there. Impressive.

This hologram leaned out of the screen, the upper body of a six-armed man with a smooth, oval face. A Hindu statue, maybe? Not Vishnu, Vishnu was blue. This guy was brown. And as far as I knew, all three of the Brahma-Vishnu-Siva trinity approached 'pacifist' levels of peaceful. This one kept trying to punch Marcia.

Er, sort of.

After watching for a minute, I figured out that this was a peculiar, high-speed game of violent rock-paper-scissors. The statue would thrust out an arm at her with the hand either balled in a fist, held out open palm, or jabbing two fingers. Fist beat fingers, fingers beat palm, palm beat fist. If Marcia got it wrong, she winced in pain as it smacked her hard. If she got it right, the hologram arm was knocked back, momentarily stunned.

When she spotted us, Marcia walked away in the middle of her match, leaving the hologram punching at nothing until it racked up some preset number of wins and faded away. Grinning at least as goofily as Cassie, Marcia rubbed her palm and said, "This place is great. If people knew it existed, there would be lines down the block."

A fair point. Only three other teenagers lurked in the arcade gloom.

Cassie, her cheeks still furiously pink, bumped her shoulder against mine and looked guilty about it. "Thanks for inviting us. I hang out with supervillains all the time, but we don't do super-powered civilian stuff. It's all business or regular people or You're Too Young."

Time to drop the bomb. Envisioning Claire's sly shameless body language in my head, I smiled teasingly, twisted from side to side, and held out my arm to examine my doll-jointed fingers. "Actually, this is both pleasure and business. You see, I lured you two here because my supervillain contacts are currently limited by my being designated a high-tech trophy, and Ouroboros's father has vast collections of villain and hero data he keeps for detective work."

Marcia bobbed her head cheerfully. "Yep. Say the word, I'll deliver all those hard drives to you. Or eat them, if that's what you want. It's all good."

Cassie looked considerably more shocked, eyes wide, curious, and understandably cautious. "Oh. You want me to find out something for you?"

I took her hand, and squeezed it reassuringly. "I need to locate a mind-swapping device. I have been informed they're rare. Stupid rare, ridiculously rare. My double must know that already, and I know how I think. Unless I hurry, she will collect the ones that are left, and hide them."

"Kind of unsportsmanlike, isn't that?" Marcia asked.

I shr—criminy. I rocked my head from side to side, solemn but noncommittal. "We take this a lot more seriously than we let show, and in supervillainy, the prize goes to the most devious thinker."

Cassie grimaced. "I'm not sure where to start, but I'll try. Don't get your hopes up too much."

Marcia straightened her back and lifted her chin, theatrically proud. "I, on the other hand, am looking forward to breaking into one of my father's bases and ransacking his files. The old control freak will have apoplexy."

"I can give you both a lead. Some guy named Paul Peitman used to make brain switchers. Supposedly they're all used, but it would be very easy for one or two to have gotten lost and be floating around somewhere."

Cassie calmed down slightly, her mouth pinched but thoughtful. She nodded. "Well, okay. I guess I can ask around."

I clapped them both on the shoulder. "Then let's stop talking about it, and get back to having fun."

That lit up Cassie's face. Literally. She got so excited, her eyes began to glow and her hair to turn blue. "Yeah! Can we have another twirl at the dance machine?"

"Maybe last thing before we leave. I want to explore. There could be something even wilder."

Marcia smacked her fist into her palm in unnecessarily violent anticipation of an almost certainly peaceful afternoon. "And variety is the spice of life!"

We circled around towards the back of the arcade to start an inventory.

Poor Cassie. I wasn't lying to her, exactly. I had no expectation of either Cassie or Marcia locating a mind switcher for me, not if they were that rare. What I expected was for Cassie Pater, queen of not being able to keep a secret and forgetting to use people's super-powered names, to accidentally spill the beans to my duplicate. She had information-gathering resources I could only dream of, and would find a device for me. She might already be looking.

Pretty villainous, huh?

On the way back, we passed a Pac-Man game, whose modifications were visible as pipes sticking out and curling around the box. Little word bubbles popped up over the ghosts in the idle screen, wondering if we were going to stop and play. We did not, to the relief of the orange one that had apparently just hung new curtains.

Off in the corner, another cabinet asked me to defend the frontier from someone named Zur and his coding armada.

However, if we were going to play a space game, one stuck out as the obvious choice. Two cockpits sat against the wall on the far side from the lounge door. They looked a lot like the race car games where you sat in a driver's seat of a crude model car, except these had hoods that rolled over the top to completely enclose the chair. No sign declared the name of this game, but really, who had to ask? A couple of spaceship pilot seats were all you needed to know.

We gravitated to the game without even needing to discuss it. When we got there, Marcia pushed me into one chair, and Cassie into the other.

I gave the Monochrome Misanthrope a sharp look. "Why us?"

"Because I'm the one who thought to bring quarters," Marcia answered.

Couldn't argue with that logic. Besides, I wanted to fly a spaceship.

As I settled into my seat, Marcia closed the lid over top of me. Monitors lit up all across its inner surface. They looked like windows, like I was actually in the cockpit of a space fighters. The controls were, uh... well, there were a lot of them. I had flashbacks to trying to fly a Jupiter aethership. Little gauges and switches and tiny displays lined the whole dashboard, all the way around. Yes, they were labeled, but what did all these things do? And how could anyone keep track of all of them?

Well, start small. Throttle and joystick. My fighter zoomed into action, and I guided it around in circles and spirals. So, it swooped.

Not actual space physics, thank goodness, but atmospheric aircraft physics. Although I did not rule out the possibility this game perfectly modeled some mad scientist's exotic engine that operated on relative speeds instead of inertia and acceleration.

I fiddled with the buttons on the joystick and throttle. Okay, I had a machine gun-style weapon, a beam I could run until its battery exhausted, and four missiles, one of which I wasted before I knew what that button did. There had to be a tracking system for that, if I could figure it out.

Yellow lights flashed. Alarms warbled. My chair shuddered subtly, and the flashing lights switched to red.

Tesla's Magnetic Heat Ray, Cassie was already attacking me!

I did a barrel roll, taking advantage of it to turn around and circle towards Cassie. The radar... there, that had to be it. The arrows on it indicated above or below me. All right.

A spiky, star-shaped, electric blue spaceship slid into view as I turned. All I had to do was line her up—

Cassie's spaceship writhed like a cobra in a mosh pit, and zipped out of the way. The girl could dodge. What she could not do was control our relative positions. I followed her loops, slowing down and speeding up to stay behind her. When I had her in my sights, I searched for the buttons to get a missile lock. The thing with the wandering triangle was probably part of it. I got it to focus on her spaceship, but it wouldn't stay. One of these buttons had to actually lock on.

While I experimented, Cassie finally managed to slip away farther than I could catch up. In fact, after about fifteen seconds of whirling around, the yellow lights flashed, and turned red as she hit me again.

And the controls suddenly got weird. I was listing to the right. What in Gerty's armor-plated apron...?

One of the little readouts had a picture of my ship, and from the red dots, I could now see that was a damage indicator. Wow, no shields and pinpoint damage modeling. Bravo. A red needle struck through the green right into one of my engines.

At least the list swung me automatically in a loop, and gave me a few seconds to plan. With all these controls... yes, there were a whole set of individual thruster switches. If they were like circuit breakers, and matched the pattern on the damage readout, I could flip the one opposite the damaged engine and restore stability.

"AH HA HA HA HA HA!" It worked! Yes, I wasn't quite as fast, but I had control again. Yanking the throttle to zero, I spun my ship around, and launched a missile ahead of me as I turned the thrusters back onto full. It sailed harmlessly past Cassie, but it forced her to dodge, and now it was me following her again. A situation that this time I would not give up. Forget the missiles, I was going to carve her in half with my laser.

Someone knocked on the roof of my cockpit. Presumably Marcia. "A little busy!" I called in response.

The lid thumped, and with a clack that I hope wasn't something breaking, flipped open.

"I had her in my sights!" I protested, pushing myself indignantly to my feet.

Marcia, mildly sarcastic, jerked a thumb over her shoulder. "Yeah, you have bigger problems."

In the glowing rectangular entrance to the arcade stood a scrawny figure in a jumpsuit and pigtails and goggles. A very familiar figure, once I'd seen in the mirror thousands of times.

Lifting a hand, Meatbag Penny held it at an angle by her face and did the high-pitched "Oh ho ho ho"-style evil anime maiden laugh.

I stomped my foot in pure jealousy. "I always wanted to do that. It never seemed like the right time!"

"That's because you never do what you want. You always have to be pushed," she answered, with an edge of real resentment and unfortunate accuracy.

Cassie's cockpit lid slid open, and she looked out, only to shrink down and peek anxiously over the edge when she saw what was actually going on. "Penny! You... what are..."

"It's fine. It is," I assured her.

My double chipped in. "Either of us would love to have you only on our side, but only Ruth thinks you can't like us both."

Leaving my innocent friends behind, I walked out into the middle of the room, facing my double across the space like two Western gunfighters in a cluttered town square. "What are you doing here?" I asked, despite the obviousness of the answer.

"Cassie ran off to see you—"

"I didn't say that!" squeaked the aforementioned blue-haired admirer, throwing off sparks in her panic.

"You're not good at hiding it—"

I interrupted my double to supply, "Arc Flash."

Meatbag Penny hesitated only for a moment. "Oh, of course, you're in costume! I didn't know you'd picked a hero name, Arc."

Cassie's face was still a white, stiff mask, and her head shook slowly. This conversation was too much for her. "I didn't."

"Claire came up with it," I explained.

My doppelgänger smirked, bitterly amused. "Ah. Get used to it. When someone else names you, you're stuck."

"It happened to me," Meatbag Penny and I said in chorus.

Cassie had no immediate response, so my goggled nemesis returned her attention to me. "May I resume?"

I nodded. "Please."

"When she ran off to meet you, I had a sudden revelation. Why wait for random encounters, or for you to ambush me? Sportsmanship is all very well, but I should play my advantage while I have it. So I'm going to blow you up now, and take the Heart of Steel." Reaching into one of the pouches on her bandolier, Meatbag Penny pulled out a small handful of marble-sized bombs, and rolled them around in her grip.

"Wait. That means... you followed me?" Cassie's voice spiked, and she bit down on her fingertips.

Holding up my hand to her, I lowered my voice to a gentle level. "That's also okay, Cassie. It's not something you should worry about."

My double nodded, emphatically so we could see her from over there. "All's fair in love and war against myself."

There went the last bit of guilt I might have felt for manipulating Cassie. Also, following Cassie wouldn't be as easy as just staying behind her. My double had a tracking device on our blue-haired admirer. Cunning. I'd better check my clothes when I got—*before* I got back to my lair.

I gave Other Me a big 'ol bared-teeth grin. "I don't mind humiliating you again, after you've ambushed me virtually unarmed, *again*, but can we take it outside? I'd rather not damage a room full of unique mad science videogames." That Pac-Man game seemed oddly alive, for example.

She grinned right back. Huh. I didn't look smug when I did that, just demented. "But that's the great part, Bad Penny. One I've shattered you into a million pieces, I can build new, better arcade games. Maybe I'll lock your heart inside one, so you can play inside a game instead of sleeping through the next decade. After all, I have our super power."

Ouch. That stung. Criminy, that grin looked nuts. Was that confirmation bias, or had the power enhancing pill really given our brain a twist?

"Okay, enough of that," snapped my double. She flung the bombs she was holding, already scooping out another set to throw them.

She wasn't aiming at me, but I backed up and brought my shields to ready, just in case. I might not have brought any other weapons, but I did not go anywhere without these shield gloves and sliding boots now. Maybe I should make it a policy with my other weapons.

The brown metal marbles hit the floor, and stuck, forming an arc that cut the room in half, interrupted only by a couple of game cabinets. Ah. Land mines.

And Gerty Be (yes, I was loving knowing the real Gerty Goat): Marcia, of all people, was on the other side of the line, with Meatbag Penny. The civilian teenagers had fled before I even climbed out of the space fighter game. Smart kids.

Holding one fist by her side, Marcia threw out a hand, palm out, fingers splayed, towards Other Me. "False Penelope! Your timing is salubrious indeed. I have worked through my history with the real Bad Penny, and now at last I shall have closure. This, now, is the moment I relive abandoning our battles, and becoming her ally to rescue her goofball supernerd boyfriend. Rescuing her goofball supernerd body is close enough."

"...what," said Meatbag Penny.

She closed her fingers, and with a sharp jerk, held both arms out from her sides. Black fluttered around her left first, and her right began to glow white. "I refuse your offer of being friends equally with you both, for I do not accept you both! The true Penelope Akk is trapped in a robot body thanks to you, evil monster. It is fitting that I began your career, and now I shall end it, for I am Ouroboros! I am both beginnings and endings, the eternal cycle! The wheel has swung around, and it will crush—" She broke off, shuddering. The light around Marcia's right hand went out, and she hunched forward, grabbing her chest. The cough that came out sounded gruesomely wet, but when it was done she straightened up and gave her head a shake. "Whew! That one kicks like a mule."

Cassie hovered at the edge of the land mine field, arm extended over it beseechingly. "Marcia—"

"Ouroboros," my double and I corrected her, with the exact same gentle reproof.

She flinched, but pressed on. "You don't have to do this. Being Penny's friend means being both their friends. They say that themselves."

"Penny is too nice to her enemies. I of all people should know. I know which one is real, and no one can tell me otherwise. There shall be a reckoning, and I reckon we will reckon now." Marcia pulled off the ridiculous statement absolutely stone faced and deadpan.

"I won't let you hurt her, Marcia. Not either of them." Cassie's voice fluttered in terrified determination, and lightning crawled up and down her already lightning-themed bodysuit.

Criminy, Cassie. Why did you have to waste a crush this big on someone you can't have? Defending me was so sweet, but completely unnecessary. My double thought so too, and treated Cassie to a warm smile.

Patting Marcia on the shoulder, Meatbag Penny gave her a little red-and-white spotted ball. "Here. You eat this, and I'll go talk to her."

Only a crazy person would accept that offer, so of course Marcia immediately plucked it from Other Me's fingers and threw it in her own mouth. "Ooh, what flavor is it? Oh. It's... sleepy... flavor."

She collapsed into an uncomfortable looking heap, and immediately started to snore.

My double propped a fist on her hip, and gave one of her braids a tug with the other hand. "I'm glad I finally found a use for that. Knockout gas won't work on you, and it takes so much to affect a super-powered metabolism, I can't use it where it might hurt a civilian."

Touched by the dedication of two friends who I would never have thought of as close before, I asked, "Can you help Cassie cross the line so she can take Marcia outside to safety?"

Not promising to not take advantage felt weird, but I didn't need to. Other Me knew I would hold back, because Marcia and Cassie's safety was more important.

"No. I'm not leaving you," Cassie insisted, her voice cracking badly now.

"This is how it has to be, Cassie," said Other Me, deliberately using her proper name. This was a personal message.

I filled in the next part of the thought. "We only have one body, and neither of us can live like this, with only part of a life."

My double walked over to Cassie, stepping onto the mines without a care, thanks to the bracelet that defended her from her own bombs. She held out both hands invitingly. "And we won't kill each other, I promise. Even if I shatter her body, she won't actually be hurt, just asleep."

Reluctantly, Cassie took Other Me's hands, and stepped over the mine field.

"Take care of Marcia. Being knocked out shuts off her healing," I said. That was why the knockout gas had worked at all. Put Marcia out before she could get mad, and she couldn't purge the drug any better than any other superhuman.

Bottom lip quivering, Cassie took hold of Marcia under her armpits, and dragged my insane former rival out of the arcade and around the corner, out of sight.

With the field clear, Meatbag Penny leaned forward, presumably squinting at me behind those goggles. "You don't even have our staff, do you? Okay, last chance, you can back out. Take it before I change my mind."

"Nope. Gonna kick your butt." Maybe I could steal the bracelet this time.

She nodded once, sharply. "Cool." Audibly relieved to have her mercy refused, she plucked a bomb out of her bandolier and threw it at me.

My aim was so bad. I backed away, but it wouldn't have hit me anyway. When it did hit the floor, the effect reminded me of her space manipulation blocking field. Jagged brown lines appeared in the air in maybe a two foot circle. Inside that line, the carpet dissolved, and then the tile floor. The corner of a wooden game cabinet did not, and the game didn't shut off.

I eyed it. "Interesting."

"It doesn't affect metal. These should reduce your shell to powder, but leave the Heart of Steel undamaged. I keep my promises," said Meatbag Penny. With that said, she threw another bomb, and another.

Neither was all that close, but I zapped the first one away with a forcefield. Why? To see if the bombs would penetrate it. The bomb itself did not, but when it blew up, the zigzaggy distortion zone did go through my shield, and hung in the air motionless. The other bomb took a chunk out of the floor farther along.

Why that cunning little vixen. She wasn't trying all that hard to hit me anyway. This was another mine field, penning me in.

Unwilling to wait around for that, I charged the ring of land mines, blasting it with my shield bands. A section of the sticky bombs exploded, battering me with sound, force, bits of rubble, and smoke.

Instead of charging through the concealing smoke, I jumped up on a nearby arcade cabinet, vaulting over it past the ring.

My double spotted me. She had less than a second to react. Enough time to press her finger hard into the red button of a ring on her right hand.

Criminy. She could have any number of itty-bitty weapons on her.

With a WHOOMP, wind rushed out, a blast catching me in mid-air and sending me tumbling back over the arcade machine again. I hit the floor hard. If I'd been in my flesh and blood body, that would have broken something. Also, good thing I'd tried this before

Meatbag Penny had time to fill this whole back area with robot-destroying zones.

Rolling to my feet, I went right back to the game cabinet, and encountered something slightly stranger than usual.

The blast wave was still there. It hung, a rippling globe of distorted air, just inside the land mine ring.

Justifiably proud, my double held out a hand and admired her ring. "It's not technically a forcefield. It's a frozen explosion, all the energy pointed out. Great new defensive tool, isn't it?"

"Do I really like explosions this much?"

She stomped her foot, fists jerking down at her sides. "Yes! You just think you're not supposed to. Do you have the slightest idea how infuriating that got by the time we were separated?"

Fiddling with my wrist, I said, "I have to admit, this is cool!" There. The Machine came free, and I held him up, rubbing him at the blast wave like I was cleaning off a window. He sucked it up everywhere he touched, and in less than two seconds I had a nice, big gap to dive through.

She saw what I was doing, of course, so I dove fast, plunging and then sprinting towards her with all the sudden speed this robot body could manage. That caught her by surprise. She still had time to touch her ring again——but I had won. I was too close, the Machine held out in front of me, and he ate so much of the explosion it didn't touch the rest of me. We crashed together, and I shouted at the Machine, "Eat her bombs!"

He grabbed onto the bandolier and started to chew. Apparently it counted in how he interpreted the order.

My double and I spun apart. She yelled, "Criminy!" and yanked uselessly at her belt. There was no stopping the Machine, and she knew it. So she pulled out a little glowing white ball instead.

Whatever this was, she thought it was big. I projected both shields forward, and prepared to dodge.

That was my mistake. I recognized the fat white pill with its orbiting white sparks too late. Other Me put the power activator in her mouth and swallowed it.

Horrified, I squeaked, "I destroyed those!"

She rolled her head sarcastically. "Yeah. One tube. I have a barrel of them at home under my bed. You know we can only do this once, so I had to make enough to last."

Her eyes rolled too. Oh, criminy, here it came. She was getting weird. With a crooked grin, she picked two bombs out of separate pockets. She had time. Yes, the Machine was eating through the belt, but he couldn't do it instantly.

Holding them up to show me, she asked, "So, you need light to see, right?" and crushed them together.

The already shadowy arcade went pitch black. I could make out a vague rectangle of the doorway to the sunlit outside world, but nothing else.

However, I knew where she was, only a few feet in front of me. Lunging forward, I grabbed, only to feel the brush of fabric-covered flesh against my arm as she slipped away. Grabbing at that spot got me nothing but empty air. She hadn't made any noise. She hadn't thrown herself away desperately. No, with access to my omniscient power, she knew where I was, and just stepped out of the way.

Her access wasn't perfect, Penny. Remember that. The pills gave Other Me peeks, not full contact. She was just fighting with our super power activated, with both the benefits and curses that entailed.

As suddenly as they went out, the lights came back on. Not that the room was anything but a pit of shadows with occasional arcade game spotlights, but I could see clearly again.

The Machine sat on the floor near my feet, chewing down the last of the bomb bandolier. Whether they went off inside his indestructible body was entirely moot. My double had crossed the line, and holding no bombs, now lurked next to the dance machine. Oh, and the first of the destruction zones she'd set up with her bombs had faded. Excellent, they weren't permanent. In a minute, I wouldn't have to worry about avoiding them.

Holding up a hand to show off my shield bands, I said, "Now you're the one outgunned. Since I didn't bring anything to capture you, I'll allow you to leave unharmed if you surrender."

"HA! HA HA HA HA! HA HA HA HA HA!" She laughed, bitter and manic and scornful. With a sharp kick, she popped open a panel on the side of the dance machine, and reached in with her bare hands to rearrange its innards.

The land mine circle lay between us. Could I jump it? I'd have to circle around over the game cabinets again, and I might not have that much time. So instead, I scooped the Machine up off the floor, and threw him at her, shouting, "Eat that video game!"

Sorry, goth couple. It's you or me.

Note to Penny: Brilliant counterattack, one little problem you didn't think through. My white-suited double caught the Machine right out of the air, declared in a wobbly voice, "I love playing catch!" and flung him to the far side of the room.

Well, criminy. Plan B. I ran back and leaped over the game cabinets again, turning as soon as I hit the floor to charge Meatbag Penny.

Too late. She had gone back to fiddling with the internals. The game clinked rapid-fire, like someone was pouring coins into it, and the goth couple crawled out of the screen. The little man helped his wasp-thin wife down to the floor elegantly, and they both pounced yours truly.

I backpedaled, fell onto my butt, and rolled out of the way of the slightly transparent black-dressed woman's claw-shaped black fingernails. By the arcade game, my double hugged herself tight with both arms, and through a fit of giggles said, "You've heard of that science fiction trope 'solid light', right? It sounds so stupid and meaningless, until you see the trick. That's all technology is. Card tricks with physics."

Another very unwanted Note to Penny: Explaining an invention that much should have broken my power's hold, but Other Me was still very much in its grip. Last time, she'd broken herself free doing that. Did she try this time, and fail?

I didn't have much time to worry about it. Keeping out of the grip of two adults determined to get hold of you requires a lot of wiggling and scrambling. I managed to roll around the other side of them, and charged Meatbag Penny, leading her own creations towards her.

She saw us coming, and activated her shield bomb ring. I ducked, curling up, and let the holograms trip over me and take the hit.

We all three got knocked to the opposite wall. I didn't have a brain for that blow to rattle, but neither did the goths. They grabbed hold of my arms before I could pull away.

Something crunched, and buzzed, and the little mustached man and tall, pale woman in her body-hugging dress disappeared. Over at the machine that spawned them, my Machine's butt stuck out of a hole at the base. After eating those blasts Other Me fed him, he'd become quite a speedy little bug. Now he chomped away noisily inside the arcade cabinet, finishing it off.

Meatbag Penny was already walking to a new arcade game when the holograms holding me prisoner winked out. She pulled hard, yanking the whole wooden side of Marcia's combat rock-scissors-paper game off, and started fiddling.

Not again. Of course, she'd crossed the land mine field again, but I bounded over the cabinets I'd been using as a bridge, and tackled my double just as a sparkly yellow energy hand extended out of the machine. It froze there, whatever changes my power was making not quite complete, as I shoved my double to the floor beneath me.

I stomped one booted foot on the wrist of the hand wearing the explosion ring. She couldn't press its button one-handed. Activating the shields from my glove bands, I shoved them against her chest, pinning her in a cloud of rainbow sparkles. I wasn't heavy, but she wasn't strong, and her leverage was terrible.

Her free arm groped for the arcade game she'd been altering, but she couldn't reach. It shuddered, and off-balance thanks to her tearing away one side, fell slowly onto its back. The glowy arm disappeared. Instead, a column of white light so intense and pure I couldn't see through it rose out of the screen.

"No! No, you ruined it! It's too late!" whined my doppelgänger, smacking her fist on the carpeted floor.

The white column resolutely did nothing but exist. Whatever she'd been planning, I diverted it.

I let out a sigh of relief. As she clawed ineffectually at my force shields,

I leaned all my medium weight on her and said, "I am going to pin you here until that pill wears off. You have got to stop taking those things."

"But they work!" she answered, her petulance turned mocking. She stuck the back of her free hand over her mouth, and bit a white plastic ring I hadn't even seen against her white, heavily contoured jumpsuit.

Another pill rolled out of the ring's secret compartment into her mouth.

She knew I would try to stop her from taking more, and had planned ahead.

Okayokayokay. Think. She couldn't do anything without ingredients and tools. If I held her here, the power would wear off and it wouldn't matter. I already had her pinned down, right?

Sure, I did. Right up until she laughed, raspy and yipping, like a sick hyena. Then the force shields I was leaning atop winked out.

I fell on top of her. Pulling a miniature screwdriver out of a tool pocket, she stabbed me in the arm. It couldn't penetrate my armored lab coat, but it did jam coat, shirt, and the point of the screwdriver into the seam where my upper arm's ball socket connected to my shoulder.

'Jam' being the operative word. My arm wouldn't move!

Meatbag Penny rolled out from under me and to her feet. She didn't seem to be doing anything, so I had time to wiggle my arm until the screwdriver came free. There. I could move. No obvious damage. A quick check showed the shield bands were working again. Seriously, how had she done that?

I stood up slowly, and approached my double with my hands up. She wobbled in place, looking all around, but took a staggered step away for each of mine. Vaguely, she babbled, "I can see you don't get it. Nobody gets it. Nobody can get it. It's all right in front of us. All of it, every opportunity, every trick, fire, water, mass, energy. We could bend time with the snap of our fingers. All the most complex processes of any machine are involved in that one action, after all. You just have to direct them."

Her stumbling brought her into the doorway to the street. She leaned one arm against the jam, and took deep breaths. More focused, which was an extremely low bar, she looked up at me. "You shouldn't have stopped me from working on that game. Now we've gone and made something very strange, indeed. Let me show you a truly exotic physical reaction. Check it out. Shadow puppets!"

She held up a hand, fingers extended in the ridiculous bad bunny pose people used when making shadow puppets. In the light from the outside, that shadow fell on the machine we'd just abandoned, and its column of white light.

Not that you can see a shadow on light. Not until it swam out from the interior, a seething black rabbit head the size of a basketball.

"Machine! Emergency dump! Everything you've got in a block on top of that, right now!" I yelled.

Quite fat now, he galloped over, regurgitated a big block of metal and wood, and it slammed down on top of the game machine. The white column disappeared, or at least was blocked.

"Hey! Hey, what should I do next? I can build anything. Anything at all. Go on, challenge me!" babbled Other Me. On fire with inspiration, she'd forgotten we were even fighting.

Fine by me. I lunged over to the Machine, grabbed him, and ran out the door and away along the sidewalk.

Let her think she'd won. I didn't care. She might have yet another power-enhancing pill somewhere. Without me, she had no reason to take it. I'd outmaneuvered her so far, yes, but it had been way too close.

No more sparring and picking at her. This was getting too dangerous. From now on, I would strike decisively, or not at all, and I couldn't strike until I had a mind transfer device.

Cassie stood next to a seated but apparently conscious Marcia at the end of the block. I raced up to them, grabbed Cassie by the shoulder, and pointed back at the arcade. "Flesh and blood Penny needs you. Our power has overloaded. Please, take care of her. If I try, she'll just fight me."

Her eyes wide and face stiff with worry, she nodded. "I will, I promise."

She sprinted back towards the doors of the arcade, and my double. To whom, I was sure, she would blabbermouth everything I'd told her this morning. My plan to get a mind transfer machine was underway.

Maybe these horrible pills would have a side benefit, and Other Me would build the device I'd use to take my body back. Wouldn't that be ironic?

Chapter Twenty-Eight

Now, normally I'm not against spending a few days holed up in my room playing the computer. After my all too exciting summer, the occasional rest helped give me strength for the next phase. With so much about to happen, I couldn't properly relax this time.

Large amounts of Princess of the Closet Monsters did help, but hoo boy. Every choice traded away another body part now, most of the time without saving any of my weird, precious subjects. I could barely recognize the main character, physically or in personality.

Gorgeous graphics, though, and the level where I led the mouse-like scavengers through the walls to a new home made the game worth it by itself.

The game balance was definitely spotty, and after the twelfth frustrating attempt to stop the Web, I took a break. Who thought that boss fight was a good idea?! Of course, if I'd been playing the Vengeance route, my character wouldn't be unarmed and flammable. Another example of my Evil Twin getting the easy road.

Speaking of whom, might as well check my spy recordings. Meatbag Penny still hadn't figured out I had her bugged, but until Claire's Mom spilled the beans, that had been an alien world to me.

...I had a hit. One of the search terms in the recording was 'Mech.' Yikes.

Nothing for it. I clicked the play button.

"I can't believe you're going to do this for me, Mech." That was my double's voice, sounding as awed as I would be. Mech himself on the case?

Mech spoke next, with a warm and personal friendliness that probably made Other Me's knees weak. "For you? Of course. Your parents were my idols growing up, and they've raised an amazing daughter. I won't ever forget you breaking into my lair, and I mean that in the good way. As soon as I heard, I started looking."

"Do you think you can get to them before she does?" My double sounded sincerely worried. We were both starting to think about the consequences of losing.

Criminy, I could hear him patting her head. Not literally, just in that affectionate adult tone of voice. "You don't have to worry about that. I've asked all my contacts. I even traded in a favor Spider owes me. Even rumors of tech that would switch a robot and a human's minds are so rare, it would take her a month to sort through them. The only even decent possibility is that there might be something left in old Puppetman's loot. I know where all his equipment was stashed, and I will search it personally."

"I..." Other Me fumbled for words.

"Don't worry about it. I owe it to Brian to take care of his little girl. I'd give my life to protect the Audit's daughter. And I'm counting the days to see the heroine you'll become when you grow up, Penelope. Mech is not going to let that crazy robot lay a finger on you." He sounded so emphatic about it. I had no idea I'd impressed him so much, or that Mech was such a big fan of my parents.

Meatbag Penny was probably swooning. Me, I was intimidated. Mech did not goof around, like most heroes. Plus, he had a genius for overriding and shutting down robots. He was the guy who defeated the Conquerer invasion by taking control of the Orb of the Heavens, after all.

My Evil (Good?) Twin gave me a little hope by saying, "All I need is to get the mind switching technology out of the way. This is personal, Mech, in the non-official sense. Bad Penny and I will fight each other."

"Sorry, Miss Akk, didn't hear you. Too busy flying away to protect you no matter what. I guess I'll have to risk you being mad at me, if that's what it takes to keep you safe." Well, so much for that. Other Me tried. His jets *fwooshed* before he even finished saying it, so she didn't get a chance to even try to change his mind.

Now I'd have to go through Mech to get to her.

Fine. To get my body and my parents and my best friends back? I'd do it.

For the moment, I headed up the stairs to check on my teammates.

They checked on me, first. I was halfway up when Ampexia appeared in the doorway, leaning way over to the side rather than just standing in it. She gave me a searching look, with no attempt to hide it. "You finally up and about?"

My mouth twitched up on one side. "From you, that's a weird question."

Now she stepped fully into view, although she still gave me plenty of room to pass out the stairway door. Hands spread, she said, "Hey, I get to be concerned too, you know. You've been carrying this whole thing on your shoulders without me, and then you come back to the lair and lock yourself up."

"If that worries you, I have good news. A little more waiting, and this is going to explode. I'll need you then. Right now, I'm stuck inside."

"Which is not like you," she pointed out.

Heh. I pointed out the front windows, or the ones that weren't covered by cardboard and plywood due to Gerty Incidents. "No help for it. Meatbag Penny's gone proactive, and if the hero community find the evil murder-bot's lair, they'll form a line to invade and destroy me."

"Harsh. Well, it sounds like you won't need to worry for long. Might as well make the best of it. C'mere." She jerked her head towards the rest of the mansion.

I followed Ampexia through the stupidly big building to find Gerty in the jacuzzi room. Sitting specifically in the dry jacuzzi, in fact, with a scrub brush frozen halfway to scrubbing her own back. Her eyes were shut. My partner must have picked up how to shut her off from me.

She still didn't truly 'get' Gerty, which is why she waved a hand between me and the animatronic goat, asking, "Can you convince this thing to play bartender?"

Proof either that she truly did or truly did not understand Gerty. At those words, the deactivated robot's eyes snapped open, her head swiveled, and Gerty's mouth flapped. "Diggity hot dogs! A bartender?"

Ampexia took an alarmed step backwards, then gritted her teeth and went still. It was, after all, too late. Gerty sprung to her feet, grabbed the two of us, and tucked us under her arms as she ran to the second dining room, the less formal one. Did I mention this was a billion-dollar mansion?

She did so well, avoiding all the walls until the last one. Maybe she just detected which would damage the precious charges she carried, because when we crashed into the room, we sprayed only plaster dust around. Ampexia and I were deposited on formerly shiny stools in front of a marble counter.

At no point in this process did Gerty pause in her chatter. "I always wanted to be an old fashioned innkeep. Forsooth, beloved traveler! Get ye to a comfortable nook in front of the fire, and wrap thyself in the chatter of the villagers, who come here every night for my delicious cooking and a stein of," a more computerized voice interrupted, *"frothy water,"* before Gerty continued, "in an atmosphere of camaraderie. My beds are clean, and all the bedbugs and plague fleas eliminated with lasers. Forsooth! Did I say forsooth already? Avast! Oh boy, this will be so much fun."

Behind the counter, Gerty wreaked havoc in the smaller kitchen, the one not designed for a team of professional chefs. She scattered metal cookware around as she rummaged through cupboards, many of which she opened first.

A grin forced its way onto my face as I watched, but I at least tried to talk seriously with Ampexia. "Sorry I haven't been much of a partner. I went to all the trouble of recruiting you, and then left you standing on the sidelines."

She leaned back, an elbow on the counter. "I still think they're creepy, but you based your whole strategy around the bugs I stole for you. In return, I got to live in a mansion, being fed by a robot chef. I'm good. It's that weirdo Lucyfar who didn't pan out."

"Ah ha!" shouted Gerty. Pulling a tub of ice cream and a bottle of milk out of a refrigerator that had been empty five seconds ago, she held her prizes up in the air. "Malted milkshakes, anachronism of champions! Oh, wow! I know the word 'anachronism!' Pops would be so proud."

I propped my own elbow on the counter, so I could rest my chin on my hand and watch the show. "If Ray and Claire were here, one of them would be telling me who Pops is, and what his powers were. The other would be trying to figure out if we could go back in time to meet him."

"You miss them a lot," said Ampexia, in that statement-that-implies-a-question-only-to-encourage-more-detail way.

Gerty scooped, poured, sprinkled, and splatted ingredients into a chilled metal bucket. A drawer in her chest sprung open, and she pulled out her big wooden spoon. Raised aloft, it made a *cachink* noise as dozens of little glowy red triangles like teeth sprung out of the sides. A grinding whir signaled the triangles spinning into a blur around the head of the spoon, until all I could see was a field of intimidating red light. Gerty stared at it for a second, blinked, and sounded suddenly apologetic. "Whoopsy doodle. I forgot this one does that."

A laser chainspoon. All she needed were... no, she had rocket fists. Yep, Gerty was truly the complete package.

While she rummaged around in her drawer and produced a bewildering variety of death-dealing utensils, I tried to focus on the conversation. "Big time. You're cool, but forming a supervillain team isn't as easy as adults pretend. Just liking each other isn't enough. You need to mesh. We're..."

"...too different. I feel the same. I'm still going to be there until this is over, even if it's just to cheer from the sidelines." Even she was watching Gerty now, and failing to hold back a smile.

It was hard not to enjoy the show. Gerty found her egg beater in a telescoping spike on her wrist, and now danced as she mixed the ingredients. Her kicking legs crunched every time they dropped back to the floor. The no doubt expensive and exotic wood paneling would be sawdust before this was over. As she mixed, she sang, "There was a jerk who made soda and maltodextrines were his secret ingredient, oh! M! I! L K Shakes!"

"You're big into loyalty, huh?" I asked Ampexia.

Her ponytail bounced with the thuds of Gerty hitting the floor, but by now she'd gotten used to that. Pointing a finger at me, she said, "We're super criminals, doofus. We're outside the people who are outside the law. Loyalty is all we've got."

Even my robot face must have shown all the weird feelings that prompted. Ampexia lowered her voice, turning uncharacteristically gentle. "You miss your folks real bad, too."

"Pretty much."

She nodded. "I can tell by how you don't talk about it. You write those little letter things, right? Put it all down there. It will help."

I went back to watching my favorite robot entertainer prepare a milkshake I would treasure even though I couldn't drink it, and thought about what to write.

Hello Mother,
Hello Father,

Greetings from supervillain camp.

I've made it. In a few days, this will be over. Even the good times, all I could really think about was how much I miss you. For all that I ran around being a supervillain behind your back, even on the moons of Jupiter it was all fine because you were there to go back to.

Despite the odds, camp has been a great success. I'm good at being a supervillain—way better than the Penny you know as a hero. We both want to be good, but our genius is being bad. Maybe that's why I've got a shot.

Whatever happens, you'll love me, even if I get stuck in a toaster or something. I know that. Thinking about it makes me feel better.

But that doesn't mean I won't give this my all. As I write this, the clock is ticking. When I get what I need to take my body back, all the heroes in LA will go crazy trying to protect what they think is the real Penny. They're trying to be good people, but so help me, I will go through them if that's what it takes to be your daughter again.

There's so much I want to tell you about in person. Mom, you'll be proud of my schemes. Dad, you'll love Gerty. Don't blame me if I disappear for a couple of days just to enjoy having my computer back, first!

Save up lots of hugs, and buy pancake fixings, and set aside a lot of money for the Pumpkin and Princess jars.

Your Real Daughter,
Penelope Akk

PS – The other one is also real.

Chapter Twenty-Nine

To the surprise of no one, I found it hard to sleep after that. Not in the regular sense, since physically all I had to do was press a button. I was terrified I would lose my chance. I'd sleep for an hour, get up, check my spy logs, and go back to bed.

Right up until I got a hit.

"Mech?" asked Other Me's voice.

I couldn't hear his reply. The bug caught his voice, but too faint to make anything out. She was on the phone, in a car, and I'd lucked out that she wasn't inside our house where my bugs don't work when the call came through.

"Just one?" She sounded suspicious and relieved. 'Like I would have been,' a description I was getting a lot of mileage out of.

More unintelligible murmurs.

"Okay, two o'clock."

And there we had it.

"I'd say you've fulfilled all your evil partner obligations just by driving me around for two hours."

I said it quietly, and from under the cover of a neighbor's condo, which had an overhanging roof on one side some architect thought was brilliant long ago. Nearly two o'clock, and Meatbag Penny remained stubbornly inside our house. Would I have to ambush Mech literally on our front porch?

Not quite! There she went, out the kitchen door and down to the sidewalk. Dressed in our official white lab jumpsuit, but not visibly armed. She watched the sky, pulling on and twisting a braided pigtail around her hand.

Here came Mech, soaring along at an easy car's pace. I switched from the tracking app to the listening app on my phone, set it to speaker mode, and handed it to Ampexia.

Mech's current suit of armor was less sleek than the one I'd destroyed back in December. Flat top on the helmet, more cylinders and less sculpted fake muscles. The material gleamed silvery in the sunlight, but only because anything gray would look like that on this bright afternoon. His current propulsion system had no obvious rockets or turbines. Smart move, if you could get the tech. No way to know exactly what to attack to force him onto the ground.

This time he landed willingly, holding what from this distance looked like a shoebox-sized letter X out for my double to inspect. His voice came through my phone. "I told you I'd take care of you, Penelope."

"This is it?" she asked, poking the X with a cautious finger.

Boy, did he sound confident. "I searched every scrap of old Puppetman's creations, and searched every inch of his old laboratory, including using Echo's sonar scanner to look for secret compartments in the walls. That's how I found this, lost and forgotten in a heating vent. There is no other device capable of switching a human and a robot's brains in North America, I guarantee it. If one exists elsewhere in the world, Bad Penny will never find it. You're safe."

She leaned forward to peer at it closely, which you had to do in mad scientist goggles, especially with my body's terrible vision. "It looks like two arrows stuck together."

"It is. Puppetman's transfer cables were unidirectional, so he'd use a pair for swaps. Don't touch it. I don't know if it would work through my armor, and I'm not eager to find out."

Well, that was all the information I needed. Time to attack.

The hard part of sneaking into my neighborhood had been getting Gerty here quietly. It helped that the nearer you were to downtown, the more jaded people were about super powers, and everybody knew a lot of heroes lived in and around Los Feliz. Ducking past her waving, searching arms, I unfastened the blindfold from her head. As she blinked at the sudden light, I stepped out onto the sidewalk, pointed at Mech, and shouted, "Look, Gerty! A walking can of pickled olives!"

"I'll make my world-famous Independently Mobile Tapenade!" She couldn't smile any more than her face already did, but her jaw hung open excitedly. Arms still outstretched, she lumbered out onto the street and galloped towards Mech.

Mech stared at the oncoming ovine juggernaut for several seconds, the only appropriate interaction. Loud enough to be heard without the microphone, he cried out, "Gerty!?"

The goat-bot skidded to a halt, arms wide. "Shiny Britches! Who's a Gerty Boy?"

And as Tesla is my witness, Mech himself, the most respected hero in Los Angeles, shouted, "I'm a Gerty Gerty Boy!" and leaped into her arms for a hug.

"What." My double's voice came through my phone perfectly in sync with my own.

She rallied quickly. Faster than me, frankly. "How do you know Gerty?"

Metal creaked as the seven-foot-tall animatronic finally found someone she could hug with all her strength. As she rocked him from side to side, he answered, "Are you kidding? Penelope, the only mad scientists in this city who didn't love going to Gerty Goat's Family Farm as a kid are the ones older than the franchise. They love going as adults."

"Not my dad." She sounded... not lost, exactly. This all made a terrible sense we should have seen coming.

"Brian tries too hard to shield his little girl from mad scientist obsessions. I bet he never argued against going."

Okay, he had us there.

Rubbing the carpet fuzz between Gerty's waggling ears, Mech went on, "Gerty here has been wandering Los Angeles for nearly six months. One of us will find her and take her home and try to upgrade her until she disappears again. I installed a modular attachment system so she could better store the enhancements already built into her, and one of my old forcefield devices."

Gerty crowed happily, "My frying pans have the non-stickiest surface!"

She finally set him down, but he still looked up at her. I knew from experience that admiring fascination of a dream come to life. The happiness made him gush. "I don't know why I bothered with the shields. What I'd really like to know is who made her indestructible. Once you attach an upgrade, that's it. It's not coming off."

She patted him in return, her oversized metal hand clonking as it hit the top of his helmet. "Shiny Britches is a good boy. We were together for a full week, including encores, but other children needed me more."

My double tilted her head to the side. "So, wait. How many mad scientists have worked on her?"

Mech was really enjoying telling her all this. You could hear it in his voice. "By now? Just about all of us. Quantum Engineer spent more than a million dollars of his own money taking her around to supermarkets and buying up all the produce and cooking ingredients to pour into an extra-spacial refrigerator only he and Brian understand."

Quantum Engineer was one of Dad's friends. Prematurely gray hair, thick glasses, laughed a lot, and when he and Dad hung out, the conversation got so technical I understood absolutely nothing. Condescendingly affectionate, which I guess someone with that kind of expertise had earned.

Criminy. Gerty had successfully distracted Mech, yes, but there was no way she would be useful in this fight. I had to face it: she was a weapon of mass friendship, not a war-bot. Maybe the clueless or people with no sense of humor couldn't deal with her, but combat was the opposite of her purpose.

Speaking of distractions, wake up, Penny! Mech's back was to me. He held the X Device up in one hand while he talked. I would not get a better chance.

I pointed a fist back over my shoulder, and spawned a shield. Ampexia punched it with both hands, her gloves vibrating with a deep, intense pulse. The effect was as good as a rocket thruster. I hurtled up the sidewalk with my sliding spats, headed for the X Device.

This was the biggest risk I'd taken since my duel started. Mech wildly outgunned me, and was not stupid. I could only pray I'd worked out all the major angles. With Gerty right there, at least he couldn't break me immediately. She wouldn't tolerate that, unless he did it so fast she couldn't intervene.

Mech's back to me meant Meatbag Penny facing me, and she let out a yelp as she saw me coming. "Mech, look out!"

He turned, his feet apart at shoulder width, balanced and ready. Armored arms folded protectively across the X Device, and blue glitter sparkled over his surface. He'd activated his shields. Any force that could get through that would destroy the device. All he had to do was pick the best way to take me down.

Or so he thought. My first guess had proven correct. He didn't instantly try to destroy me. That gave me the two seconds necessary to slide up, jump, and tackle Mech's head. The impact rocked him, but that was it.

"You can't—" he started to say, but I didn't listen.

I shoved my left wrist against the rubbery-textured surface of his shield. Something in Mech's armor went *pop* and *crackle*, and the blue sparkles disappeared. His generators just could not keep up with the infinite hunger of my Machine. As a bonus, that woke the Machine up nicely, and he unsnapped with a flick, ready for action. Shoving him against Mech's helmet, I ordered, "Eat!"

Mech was definitely not a fool. If he'd underestimated me, it was only for a moment. Without pause for banter, he whipped an arm up to grab at me, while keeping the other securely crossed over the X Device.

His attack did not land. Startlingly fast, Gerty's arm swung up and over, grabbing him by the wrist. More angry than sad, she lectured us, "Children should play nice and learn to share."

My double panicked, scrambling at a pocket, plucking it open and digging inside. Oh, Criminy, she had more power-activating pills on her.

The Machine chewed into Mech's helmet. Her warning given, Gerty did nothing. Absolutely nothing. I had exactly enough time to realize she'd shut off when the voices started in my head.

Some just made noises. Some had words, but they went by so fast I couldn't make them out individually. It reminded me of my encounter with Mister Protocol, but hundreds of times faster. Mech was the master of override—

Good old West Lee and his eight hour fail-safe. I woke up in Mech's trophy room. The shift would have been disorienting, if not for the trick Lee had built in that let me feel like I'd been asleep. That, and this was what I'd planned on all along.

I was sitting mostly upright on a white stone pedestal. The X Device sat on the next pedestal over.

HA! Got you, Mech. Since you didn't view me as a person, I made a fine trophy. As a hero with an entirely different specialty, you had no interest in taking me apart to find out how I work. Most importantly, you had no way to know about the sleep mode time limit.

Oh, and with me turned off, you had no reason to believe anyone would put any serious effort into stealing the X Device. It was safe to put us with the rest of your prizes.

Sucker.

As smug and confident as those thoughts sounded, my hands trembled in my lap. I'd had to guess everything exactly right. Even without nerves or muscles to twitch, the relief made me shake by sheer instinct. Rubbing my face, I let the fear drain away.

Okay. Here I was, in the trophy room of Mech's base. Not much had changed. It was all still a pretty white, designed to show off the displays rather than the room itself. Glass-fronted cabinets with even more trophies in them lined most of the walls. Discreet air vents took up some of the remaining wall space. The only visible entrance was a rectangular doorway with no obvious door.

My eyes turned to the little red corset in one of the cabinets. 'Little' barely began to describe it. The only woman I could imagine it fitting would be Claudia's mother. It didn't seem her style, and the pointed back would interfere with her tail. Claire had wanted that trophy, but... no. The cabinets set off the worst booby trap, a mask I could see propped up on its own pedestal. I would take what I'd come here for, and go.

I hopped down off the pedestal to the floor, and a thick glass door immediately slammed down over the exit. Blue fog puffed out of the vents. I paid it no mind. I didn't even stop pretending to breathe.

Picking up the X Device, I stuffed that down my own leather faux-corset. That was definitely proving a useful storage spot for things I wanted protected. Okay, now, how to get out? I'd planned to use...

I looked at my left wrist. GAAH. My Machine! I wasn't wearing my Machine! Criminy buckets, of course my fleshy twin had taken him home with her. Of all the angles I'd covered, this was the one I forgot?

Fine, fine. I would get him back. Right now, I would find some other way to escape. Fortunately, I just happened to be in the room filled with all kinds of weird mad science weapons that a top-tier superhero had taken off his opponents because they were so interesting.

Intriguing gun over there. Ah, my shield bands and sliding spats. They lay on the pedestal on the other side of me from the X Device. Three prime display locations for this one fight, Mech? Really? And the evasive tools were cute and high-tech, but not flashy or cool. He must really love my family. Lucyfar had said everyone did.

No time to stand around and speculate, Penny. I slipped the bands on. They would help. Next...

Oh, my Gerty Gerty heart. It couldn't be.

I walked right up to the front of the grid of pedestals, near the door. Off to the side of only a couple of rows sat a very familiar glass tank, one-third filled with brown sludge. It had a pink top and bottom, a hose and nozzle shaped like a magic wand, and a few dials and levers.

My old sugar weapon set. I dismissed it from all thought after I accidentally turned it into a sucrose black hole. Someone had fixed it, and now it was in Mech's possession. For, oh, about thirty more seconds. That was how long it took to get it properly hooked onto my belt, check the settings, and scoop up the jacks and red rubber ball that came with it.

Would this get me out? It just might. Pumping a little lever, I got the tank to spit out a fist-sized lump of crystallized sugar, which I threw at the floor just in front of the glass.

Crash! Rock candy spikes erupted out in front of the lump, slamming into the door. They cracked and dented it, but clearly this glass had been reinforced. And yet, not reinforced enough. I tossed over another candy crystal, and this time the stalagmites it shot up in front of it busted through, leaving a hole.

The splintering, stabbing mass of sugar took several seconds to die away. The hole looked just big enough. I had to take off the sugar tank again, but passed first myself, then the tank through and into the hallway. Just as I remembered, a big circle with wood paneling and dull reddish wallpaper, like something out of a mansion. I was practically next to the staircase up to the living quarters.

Now came the big question. What kind of alarms had I set off already?

With only moderately good luck, this place wasn't yet on high alert. By now, it was nearing midnight. Mech might well be asleep, and had certainly dropped his guard about a robot that had sat limp for hours, faithfully deactivated. People break in, not out.

His stairways were also choke points where he put the most traps. If his defenses had been activated, I'd be ripped to bits going up there. If they hadn't been activated yet, they would be soon. I didn't have a lot of time. My original plan had been to have the Machine eat me a path out.

Ugh, my wrist felt so empty without him.

Pulling the red rubber ball out of my pocket, I threw it into the stairwell. It bounced off a stair, and off the wall, and off the ceiling. Never losing speed, it kept bouncing all the way up the stairs, with nothing happening to it.

As soon as I was sure of that, I ran close behind. At the top, I held out a hand and the ball smacked right into it.

Ha! A little hustle, and it did, indeed, look like I'd be out of here before Mech could marshal his considerable resources to stop me.

The living quarters had been completely restored since the Inscrutable Machine had wrecked it. Variously shaped robots lurked in corners, waiting to be needed. The bedroom was dark and empty. Of course, if Mech had been here, he would be armorless and now at my mercy.

Speed remained my ally. I pulled open the massive metal door, which unlocked easily from inside, and hurried through to the antechamber outside to the elevator. My finger reached for the call button, stopping an inch away.

The down arrow was already lit. The elevator was on its way. Someone was coming.

I stuck the tip of my wand against the seam in the door where it would open, and waited. The cola tank had gotten pretty thick and syrupy, but I'd proven it still worked. Just wait, Penny. Wait for the faint thump of an elevator stopping, and the door to crack open...

It did, leaving me pointing my wand at Ampexia, and her glove vibrating and pointed at me.

We lowered our weapons, and grinned. She spoke first. "You said eight hours."

"HA!" I slapped hands with her, gleeful in victory. Yes, I'd covered all the bases, including a rescue squad in case I'd guessed something wrong.

Ampexia jerked a thumb upwards. "Easy as pie. The password's even B-E-E-B-E-E like you said. I didn't have to hotwire it."

After Mech's enthusiastic talk with Other Me, it seemed a lot less weird he hadn't changed the code. "Calling it now: when he was a teenager, Mech had posters of my parents on his walls." Somebody had to, right?

Ampexia, always of a more practical disposition, merely shrugged. "Eh. Sure." But she definitely looked satisfied. This operation had come off smooth as goat butter.

Except it wasn't actually done yet. I ducked into the elevator, and Ampexia pressed the button with a nod. "Yeah. Let's get out of here."

"No traps in the elevator shaft, so if he shuts it down remotely, you should be able to get us out," I said.

We waited, alert. When we reached the top and the door opened, we greeted the maintenance hallway with drawn weapons. Unnecessary drawn weapons, since the place was utterly empty. Of course, at this time of the night, the building should be abandoned.

The big cubicle area outside the maintenance door was certainly dark and empty. As I looked around, Ampexia frowned, and put a hand to her headphones. She followed that up by flipping a switch on her glove.

A woman's echoey voice came out of the speaker. "Don't fuss, Mech. I'm almost there."

"I hid a microphone in the stairway," Ampexia whispered. I nodded back. Good plan.

The woman spoke again, in a playfully scolding tone. "Probably something fell off its stand again. If there's trouble, I can handle it."

I pointed at a window on the far side of the cubicle farm. Ampexia nodded vigorously. Stealth would avail us nothing now. When that heroine got downstairs, there would be no way to pretend it hadn't been a breakout. Mech would activate everything he had in the building.

We reached one of the wall-sized glass windows. Ampexia shattered it with a punch, ducking behind me to avoid the falling glass. Then she scooped me up, and jumped out.

Whoomp went her backpack. It didn't fly well, but we fell slowly, safely, and she even swerved us around the next building and out of sight.

We set down in a little tree-studded area near Pershing Square. As soon as both our feet were on the ground, Ampexia asked, "You've got the thingy?"

I pulled the X Device out of my corset, then tucked it back in so it couldn't touch her accidentally. "Complete success."

"Cool. You'll want this." Opening up a hatch in her backpack, she pulled out my Machine, swollen with silvery metal from eating Mech's helmet.

"EEEE!" I squealed, grabbing him and shaking him until he woke up. "Spit that out!" I commanded, and as soon as he had, I wrapped him around my wrist where he belonged.

Okay. Now I felt better. Taking a deep breath, I pointed back up at the bank tower. "That is why I need a teammate."

She smiled, just a little and with a grim edge. "Can't watch your own back, and you don't have to tell me how nervous it is not having backup."

I gave one of my braids a sharp tug, and marshaled my thoughts. "We'll head back, and I'll stay on guard while you get some sleep."

Ampexia's mouth puckered, and her eyebrows pressed together behind her motor goggles. "We haven't needed to stand guard yet."

It had been more a question than an argument, so I supplied the answer. "As soon as Mech finds out I've got the X Device, he's going to panic. The whole hero community will go into lockdown mode. Meatbag Penny has to know I'm spying on her now. Hopefully she hasn't figured out how, because the very first chance she's not under heavy guard, I'm going to finish this. I don't have time for anything else. Every hero in LA will be on my trail, now. This has stopped being a quirky anecdote—now a little girl is in real danger."

Ampexia rolled her eyes, and added bitterly, "Yeah, you."

That was why I couldn't afford to take the time to go visit someone, but I was going to do it anyway.

Chapter Thirty

Regular people have to sleep, so it was well into the next morning when I sat in a nice car driving up into the hills, as opposed to Ampexia's pick-up truck, which had already been worse for wear before it started hauling Gerty around.

Poor Gerty had never shown up last night. Maybe nobody had woken her. Mech did say she never stayed with anyone for long.

Well, fighting wasn't her purpose, and I had other things on my mind.

"Thank you for the drive, Miss Lutra, and for setting this up," I said. I didn't exactly feel much like smiling, but I did anyway to show gratitude.

"I said I would be here for you, and I meant it." Yeah, no faking it with either Lutra. They could read me like a book.

I fiddled with the X Device in my lap, turning it over and over. At this point, anyone who intercepted me wouldn't stop with just stealing the device, and I couldn't leave it back at the lair where someone could steal it while I was out. I only had one basket, might as well put my eggs in it.

Switching to looking out the window, I watched a lot of brown dirt and brown shrubs go past. "How is Claire?"

"Worried about both of you."

Heh. Yeah, so was I, but that still felt good to hear. No matter what happened in my life, Claire would be right behind me. I might not want to know what she was doing back there, but our friendship was bedrock solid.

I got really alert as we pulled up onto the actual road where Pong lived. Ducking down, I peered out over the edge of the car window, scanning the skies, looking up and down the curving asphalt path, scanning the blasted summer brown hills. Nothing. Still, a superhero had to be watching these ultra-expensive houses. Best to hurry inside as soon as Miss Lutra stopped.

Okay, momentary pause to stare at the other car in Pong's oversized driveway. I knew that sleek, evil-looking sports car well. "What is Lucyfar doing here?" I asked out loud.

"You said you needed perspective. With her, we have all the perspectives covered," said Miss Lutra.

Couldn't argue with that. I did try to clamp down on the paranoia and walk calmly to the front door. In fact, after I pressed the doorbell, I didn't even hide in any corners until it opened!

When the door did open, blank whiteness in the shape of a person stood there on the other side.

"Alabaster, right?" I asked. Speaking of perspective, here was someone else totally not human.

Except she turned and walked away without a word. When I stepped inside, I just barely got a glimpse of her ducking into a bedroom.

"She's shy," Miss Lutra explained, staring down that hall with much the same sad, compassionate smile she'd been giving me.

Pong, in the spacious living room, rose out of her chair and rushed over. She had on a short-sleeved shirt and a skirt today, and silver tracery ran all over her plump, bare arms. "She is, but it's you I'm worried about now."

As she stepped into arm's reach, Pong did indeed reach, one hand going for my chin and the other holding up a finger. I jerked my head away. "No thanks. Had enough of that."

She didn't get offended. She beamed at me in visible relief. Suddenly easygoing, she walked back to her chair, waving a hand by her shoulder. "Good, then you're as human as ever. Please, have a seat. Has the robot food been helping?"

Lucyfar's head poked up over the back of the couch. She must have been lying on it. A certain unfocused look in her eyes suggested she'd been asleep, but hope and curiosity replaced that quickly. "Robot food?"

"No," said Pong.

"Down, girl," warned Miss Lutra, raising a finger.

Lucyfar draped her elbows over the back of the couch, watching me as I circled around. A little nudge of her head indicated Pong. "Don't let her fool you, kid. She's actually freaking out."

Pong sat primly in her own well-stuffed chair, hands folded in her lap. Her cover busted, she let a serious scowl show through. "Well, of course I am. The heroes are going ballistic. They've never given robots a fair shake. You should ask Polly Chloride what she's been through. But this is just disgusting."

Not pleasant to hear, but no surprise.

Lucyfar groaned, and collapsed back against the cushion on the couch's arm rest. I had serious doubts that limber, athletic, and most important superhumanly-powerful body had aches and pains. She had on that same T-shirt with the road map I'd seen Ampexia wearing way back when. Come to think of it, from how badly it fit, maybe Lucyfar had stolen the actual specific shirt. Sneak into a trap-riddled mansion just to take someone's laundry. Sounded like Lucy, as did showing it off to me and pretending nothing was unusual.

After a little grumbling, she said, "What did you expect? Brian and Beebee are royalty in the community. Little Penelope Akk was the princess they kept in a tower, who proved she had what it takes to inherit the crown when she became Bad Penny."

I took a wooden chair, and Miss Lutra took the one next to me. Leaning over a few inches, her voice low but still audible to the others, she said, "She's exaggerating, but a lot of people do care about you. Fame has some unexpected downsides, and this is one of them."

Scowling harder, Pong raised her voice in symbolic protest of the others' trivialities. "The point is, I'd like to smuggle you out of town until they forget." Leaning forward, hands clasped tightly in concern, she looked me directly in the eyes. "Please. I know you want your body back, but it's not worth dying for. If you're here, you must be having second thoughts."

"Bet you a grand they're not the thoughts you're thinking she's thought," said Lucyfar, eyes closed and body limp.

"We could let Penny tell us herself," suggested Miss Lutra.

Despite my dragging my feet, the spotlight was finally on me. I pulled the X Device out of my corset. "They've gone crazy because I have this."

Lucyfar turned her head and opened one eye. Pong leaned back in her chair, silver tattoos shimmering on her arm as she toyed with an earring. Someone else had a nervous tic. "We used one of those to transfer my son. Of course, it only had a single arrow, since the robot body was empty."

"Oooooooh," said Lucyfar, reaching towards me.

Pong slapped her hand. "Don't touch it. There's no button. It's literally just touch both ends to two different people and it activates."

I flashed a cynical grin. "I hope this doesn't offend you, Lucy, but there's no way I'm letting the crazy mischief-maker play with it."

She stuck out her lower lip like a six year old, or like Claire, either way. "Aw." Miss Lutra, hands drawn back so she couldn't possibly touch the X Device by accident, prompted, "You're ready to go, but you have cold feet. Why?"

I did the shoulder-tilting thing I was using to approximate a shrug. "Because I'm a hollow shell with no blood circulation."

"Woo!" shouted Lucyfar, rearing up and leaning over, extending her arm. I gave her a high five, and we both settled back into our seats.

Fortified by that moment of ridiculousness, I let out a heavy sigh and got serious. "The truth is… it's about these power enhancers my double made. She keeps taking them to fight me, and every time she does, she gets crazier. I think they're damaging her brain. Our brain. When I grabbed the switcher yesterday, I didn't even fight her and she went straight for one."

Miss Lutra's mouth tightened, and tilted, in a brief, pained, but elegant grimace. "Claire is worried, too. She's seen Penelope take one of the pills for demonstration purposes. More importantly, Penelope herself is worried, but she sees them as her only reliable way of driving this Penny off."

Lucyfar's hand shot into the air. "Yo. Lucyfar, Times of Dis. You all act like they're both the same girl. How can this one be better than that one?"

Tucking the X Device back into its hiding spot, I clasped my hands, wringing them and watching the segmented joints move. "I've thought about that a lot. It seems like she makes better plans ahead of time, but in the chaos of a fight, I adapt and come up with new plans better."

"And not many fights go the way you planned them," added Pong, going past 'confident' to 'bitter experience.'

The other two agreed, Miss Lutra by twitching her cheek in a momentary, ironic smile , and Lucyfar by rolling her eyes and her head with them.

I went back to watching my hands. Now that I had to tell them to someone else, these thoughts made even less sense. "I don't know why that is. I would swear she's my less-controlled, more impulsive side."

Now it was Lucyfar who chimed in. "Oh, no, I get that. It takes discipline to think clearly in the middle of a battle. I've fought you, and kid, you do not freak out, no matter what. You turn into cold, calculating ice."

With the mind switcher put away again, Miss Lutra felt safe to give me a small nudge with her elbow. "Go on, dear."

Yeah. Um. "I'm worried. A lot worried. This next fight is for all the marbles. I can't afford anything else, and I can't afford to not give it everything. Neither can she, and she is going to freak out. How many more of those power-stimulating pills will it take to destroy our brain? Just one? Can I take that risk?"

My voice fluttered, but I'd said it. I was terrified of turning myself into a psycho-vegetable, a walking super power with no room for Penelope Akk in her brain.

The other three left me in silence for a second. Miss Lutra, voice quiet and face blank, said, "If you sincerely give up the fight, your parents will take you back. The other Penny would love for this to be over."

Yes, with her winning by default.

Pong tried to sound noncommittal instead of tender, staring out the window past me. "You can be a robot and human. Some people do, and are happy with their lives."

A little more silence. My expression must have been a picture, because Miss Lutra said, "You miss Brian and Beebee terribly, don't you. Claire said you're writing letters."

My hand went automatically to the pocket I kept the papers and pencil in. "Uh... yeah."

"Can I see them?" she asked, holding out her hand. Tentatively, though. Not very far.

I appreciated the implied permission to refuse, but really, why not? I pulled out the folded stack, and passed them to her. Most were really just sticky notes and cards I'd scribbled something quick on. She flipped through them as seriously as if they were holy script.

That gave me time to sort out my thoughts. Folding my arms over my knees, I leaned way over, staring at the floor as the words shuffled into place. "I know they will always love me, but that would be... second best. I can only get part of my life back that way, and... I don't feel comfortable letting the other Penny... hold my brain and body... hostage."

"So whatcha gonna do?" asked Lucyfar, lying in place with her eyes closed again.

"Well, there was my original plan to get Mourning Dove to burn my super power out of my brain. She'd said she could do it. Would I give up my power to get my body back? I would certainly give my power up to save it. That was all easy when I thought what was in my body was just a parasite, but now... Okay, she's as fully Penny as me, but still more attached to my super power. What if destroying it lobotomized her?"

That all came out in a dribble, word by forced word. No one interrupted, and when I finished, they stayed silent.

I looked up at two solemn faces, Miss Lutra holding my papers but looking at me, now. Lucyfar looked unconscious, but as the silence stretched, she said, "I hate to be wise, but you don't want our opinion, Penny. Our job is to listen to you make your own decision, so you know someone will catch you if your thinking goes straight off the rails."

Which meant I hadn't. But that didn't mean I was right. "Or maybe... maybe I have this backwards. It feels weird to echo Heart of Gold, but maybe I can't leave my body in the grip of someone who will destroy it to keep it. Not only can I not let her keep it hostage, I have to rescue myself. Rescue both of us."

Still more silence. I looked up. "You're not going to pressure me either way?"

From the couch, Lucyfar flapped a lazy hand. "*Pfft*. Like we care."

Pong's face hardened, her nose bunched up in pained disgust. "No fourteen year old should have to make decisions like this herself."

Miss Lutra's look of distress was a lot sleeker, but she didn't hide the upset in her voice. "No one can make this decision for her, Pong. And Penny, if anyone your age can see this through, it's you."

That exchange should have depressed me, but I appreciated the faith Miss Lutra had in me more. In fact, maybe I was looking at all of this backwards.

I took another deep breath, and I could swear I felt it rattle through my lungs. Straightening up in my chair, I said, "Then I'd better go haunt my flesh and blood double's footsteps. This has to end today."

Still solemn, but with a bit of encouragement in her tone, Miss Lutra said, "All right. Lucyfar, can you take her home? I need to go in exactly the opposite direction."

"But Mooooooom...!" Lucyfar whined, kicking her feet.

All the way back to playful, Miss Lutra noted, "She's living in a seaside mansion."

Lucyfar sat bolt upright at that. Miss Lutra stood up as well, and a memory stirred. I gave her perfect white sleeve a tug. "Tell Claire that yes, I know she's spying on me."

Miss Lutra smirked, and walked out.

That left me tucked into Lucyfar's demonically sleek car, watching her navigate LA's streets like a speedrunner making a computer game do things its creator never imagined.

We were about halfway there when she said, "Sooooo, seaside mansion, huh? Sounds pretty swank. Mind if we stop in Burbank on the way and pick up a frozen yogurt? There's this little store that makes the best in the world. You have to try it. Sinfully healthy."

I raised an eyebrow at her. "I can't eat, and it's the opposite side of the city."

"Okay, okay."

About sixty seconds later, she said, "Hey, what about the observatory? We could break in and steal the planetarium projector."

"Fun, but I do have more pressing business, Lucy."

She grunted. "Yeah, sorry, wasn't thinking."

A full two minutes passed this time, and she said, "Okay, so, what if we drive through the subway—"

I slapped the side of one hand into my palm. "Home, Lucyfar! My home! The normal way! Or no swimming pool!"

"A swimming pool by the ocean? Bwahahahaha!" She shifted gears, and shifted lanes three times in rapid succession to pass cars. Whether that was in eagerness or just her normal driving was hard to say.

She didn't get time to come up with another ridiculous suggestion. My phone played "Stacy's Mom." I dug it out, and asked, "Claire?"

Next to me, Lucyfar's phone sang, "And it's so easy when you're evil!" She picked it up, and said, "Yo, the Devil here."

I tried to shut her out and focus on Claire's excited babbling. "Penny! You're never going to believe this! The First Horseman has come out of hiding, and he's downtown right now!"

What, that old guy from the junkyard? I didn't say that, of course. I asked the question that made even less sense to me than it would to her. "Why?"

"I don't know. Get over here fast, and maybe we can find out! Every hero in the city is on their way to try to take him out. It's going to be the biggest show of our lifetime." A moment's pause, and Claire's voice fell. "Aw, crud. That means you're going to go confront Meatbag Penny instead."

"I doubt I'll ever get a better chance. Are you going to tell her?"

"No." Claire poured amazing amounts of sulk into that one word, and hung up.

Lucyfar put her own phone down, and her eyes blazed with eagerness now. "Change of plans, kid. We're going downtown to watch the First Horseman kick everybody's butt simultaneously."

I kept my voice calm and flat and serious. "My place first."

"But he's been dead for twenty years! There will be action! Romance! Historic levels of property damage! Idiots learning they're not one-tenth as tough as they thought they were!" She literally bounced in her seat with excitement.

"Home first, please, Lucyfar. I'm asking you as a friend."

Her mouth hung open. She gaped at me in the rear view mirror, an expression of agonized betrayal. Then she let out a long, frustrated growl. "Fine. Buckle up."

"I'm already buckled up."

She grinned, a tooth baring display of cruel humor. "You're going to need another seatbelt."

The rest of the ride was... special. When she jumped the berm onto the other half of the highway and then back to get around stuck traffic was going to be hard to forget. I might regret not being able to sleep just by touching a button tonight.

We jolted to a stop in front of the mansion. I ran up the walk, shouting, "Ampexia! It's NOW! Grab your gear! Grab my gear! Put Gerty in the truck. We have maybe an hour while everyone is distracted."

Lucyfar walked behind me, and I saw black knives appear on either side, stabbing into pieces of machinery that slid into view from under the grass, preventing me from setting off at least a dozen booby traps.

Hair wet, pulling on a hoodie, Ampexia stuck her head out the door. "The goat still isn't home."

"That's fine." It was. Hopefully she'd found a role more suited to her than a supervillain team. "It means we don't need the truck. Lucyfar is faster."

Behind me, Lucyfar drawled, "Weeeeell, Los Feliz is more or less on the way downtown, and I wasn't actually driving my fastest..."

Ampexia, horrified, started to open her mouth. I cut her off. "Agreed. All the speed you can manage."

As Lucyfar laughed in wicked anticipation, Ampexia gave me an exasperated but accepting glare, and ducked back inside to grab our things.

We headed for Los Feliz, and what would be someone's final battle.

CHAPTER THIRTY-ONE

Ampexia folded her arms in disbelief. "She's just standing around waiting for you?"

Yep, that was the situation. I lurked down the street—I did a lot of lurking lately—from Northeast West Hollywood Middle. Meatbag Penny stood right out in the middle of the recess lot, with our parents and Ray and Claire hovering near. She wasn't obviously armed, but I couldn't see clearly from a block away.

I tried to explain the reasoning to my partner, who didn't think like Other Me. "She knows I'll be coming for her. That's why she left the trackers in place. This way, we duel on even terms."

"Man, I hate this goofy hero stuff, but you need your body. I'll follow your lead."

Meatbag Penny needed this battle as much as I did. She had more to lose, but just as much threat hanging over her head. Besides, we both needed to find out which of us was real.

At least sneaking up was a possibility without Gerty. Not that I planned and ambush, but I had to know all her guards had left. Death mark, overzealous heroes, yadda yadda.

The big question was... what would Mom and Dad do?

Time to find—okay, not time to find out. Instead, in a violent swirl of red smoke, Marvelous appeared next to my parents. Floating in midair, legs bent slightly underneath her, she gestured furiously as she jabbered at them. Ampexia, in her element, flipped a couple of switches on her gloves and pointed a thin antenna straight at her. Marvelous's voice immediately came out of one of her smaller speakers. "—you!"

Dad drew back in shock. "Would could be so important that you would use up a teleport?"

Marvelous sounded as desperate as her waving hands. "We need the Audit and Brainy Akk. *Need* them!"

My mom sounded calm, of course. "Has the First Horseman done something?"

"He hasn't had to. Rage and Ruin are there, and they've gone berserk defending him. It's just like the stories of him mind-controlling people and giving them power. The Horseman just stands behind them, singing." Her voice audibly shook. Rage and Ruin must be terrifying. I'd seen them in action, but not in the fury that made their reputation.

Mom crossed one arm under her chest, propped an elbow on it, and touched her fingertips to her forehead. With carefully calculated exasperation and regret, she said, "I've been retired for nearly fifteen years, Marvelous. I'm not the ultimate weapon you think I am, anymore."

"Mech is on his way, isn't he? He'll take care of them," predicted Dad.

Marvelous's hands stopped waving, and she clenched her fists. "They already defeated him."

That shocked my Dad again. "What? How? They're strong, but not strong enough to get through his shields or his armor."

Marvelous's voice trembled again. She sounded scared. "Rage grabbed him by his shield and beat him against the ground until his shock absorbers gave out."

Mom nodded. She always approved of clever tactics.

The floating sorceress went back to her urgent pleading tone. "He's unconscious. We think he's okay, but we can't get him out of his suit. Please, Brian, Beebee. We need both of you."

Mom crossed both arms now, and sounded faintly strained. "We can't leave. Our daughter is about to have the most important fight of her life. We don't know what we'll come back to."

My double's raised voice came from a few yards away. "You'll come back to one daughter healthy and happy, and the other harmlessly asleep for ten years. No matter who wins. You should go."

Dad lifted his hand, protesting, "Princess—"

She cut him off, her tone sharper now. "People could die without you. Go. Hurry."

"Is this really what you want?" asked Mom, voice blank again.

"Go!" other me shouted.

They turned around and headed for our car. Dad's voice dropped to a whisper. "She may think she's a villain..."

"Yes," agreed Mom, just as quietly.

Marvelous disappeared in another twisting implosion of red smoke.

What nobody but Me and Other Me understood was that she didn't send them away out of nobility. We desperately wanted Dad gone. It was bad enough that Ray would have to watch this. Maybe Mom felt the same way, because she certainly knew I was here.

When they had driven out of sight, Other Me shouted, "You can come out now."

I did, walking calmly towards her. And of course, as I passed under the shadow of the school, I heard a man shout, "Got you!"

Two heroes jumped out of a window. Well, a hero and a heroine. They had on the traditional spandex leotards I could never take seriously, his muscle-outline tight and decorated with symbols, hers with strategic cutouts.

I didn't find out what their powers were. Ampexia swung up a hand, fingers splayed, and subjected them to a horrible screech that even outside of its direction of focus made me wince. They grabbed their ears, landing so clumsily on the grass that they fell on their sides. I already had my wand out, and gave them a good spray.

Locked shoulders to feet in a candy shell, they already looked bleary. The woman said, "No. Must... protect..." and passed out.

That stuff ate fibers. If they were lucky, they wouldn't be bald when they woke up. I found it quite difficult to care. Goobers.

Meatbag Penny hadn't moved., confident I would handle them easily. She waited for me, arms at her sides but poised to act. Stepping onto the recess ground got me close enough to check out her equipment. She had on my white jumpsuit and mad scientist goggles, which were good protection from bumps and scrapes, but not really armor. Another bomb bandolier crossed her front, as expected. She had a large pistol tucked onto one hip. Her blue bracelet showed on her left wrist, and her red ring on her right hand. If she carried anything else, she hid it well.

Claire and Ray stood well off to the side, hopefully out of danger. Ray looked very, very tense. Claire didn't, but her hand gripped his arm just above the elbow, and gripped it tight. From the way he hovered one step ahead of her, she was keeping him from acting.

Oh, Ray. We tried. We wanted to keep you out of this, unprejudiced and unaffected, so you could accept whichever of us won. You and Claire cared too much.

I stopped maybe ten yards away from my double, and adopted the same pose. We looked like steampunk gunfighters in a particularly weird Old West. Alas, Ampexia failed me and did not play a whistly music sting, but at least a breeze gusted past.

Slowly, so as not to provoke me, Meatbag Penny raised a hand. "Okay. First, you have it?"

I pulled the X Device out of my corset. "I have it." I let her get a good look, then tucked it back into its protected place.

Her hand stayed up. "Second, where did you get that equipment?!"

I snickered at her tone of shock. She meant the sugar tank, of course. I had come wearing my steampunk costume, with the sugar tank on my right hip, under my clothes. The Machine showed on my left wrist, and the gold defensive straps on my hands and boots. What did not show was the irrigator whose tubes ran up my left arm and its little tank on my left shoulder, all small enough to hide under my lab coat. I had the jacks and rubber ball in my coat pocket, but I didn't consider those hidden. She would know I had them, having seen the sugar tank.

To answer the question, I just said, "Someone stole it and repaired it. Not a clue who. Then I stole it."

Her mouth tightened in jealousy, but she moved on. "Third, where is the Heart of Gold? I need to be able to find it."

That I kept in a pouch on the back of my belt. I took it out, held it up for inspection, and put it back. At least that was easy to do. My shoulders might be shoddy, but my arms reached behind me almost as well as in front. "I brought her. To the victor go the spoils."

Behind his back, Claire smirked and pointed at Ray.

I only saw that in my peripheral vision. Meatbag Penny and I kept our eyes on each other. "Ready?" she asked.

"Ready."

We didn't wait another second. She grabbed her bandolier. I whipped out my wand. That took less time than opening a pocket, and I got to shoot a spray of crystalizing cola at her before she could pull out a bomb. Opening a pocket did mean her hands were together, so she had time to press her ring.

Cola splattered across the yard when it hit the expanding shock wave. A couple of drops hit me, but I'd already experimented and knew this costume wouldn't dissolve, and the crystal wouldn't spread far enough to make any difference.

The dome she made wasn't huge, but it gave her some room to move around. Temporarily safe, she finished pulling out three bombs. These were bigger than the marbles I'd seen before, like small eggs.

She lobbed one towards me. When it hit the frozen shock wave, the bomb got launched at high speed way over the recess grounds... only to turn and fly toward me.

Oh joy, homing missiles. At least it didn't fly all that fast. When this one got close, I blasted it with a pair of forcefields.

Rainbow glitter sprayed. The bomb went off, and it went off big time. The shock knocked me off my feet, and back to skid a few feet on my butt. Ow. Another 'thank goodness this body is more durable than flesh' moment.

Smirking, but still poised and alert, Meatbag Penny said, "I noticed last time it's hard to hit with my bombs, so I asked our power to fix that."

Her gloating gave me a few seconds. I had a battery in one pocket.

Nothing special. No mad science. Just an ordinary battery, full of ordinary electricity. I slipped it out, unwound my Machine, and pushed the battery into his mouth. "Eat this, and then eat her ring."

Those words I let Meatbag Penny hear, but, bent over my work, I added in a whisper, "and bracelet."

Her mouth hung open, and she gave her foot an outraged stomp. "Oh, come on! He would follow me slowly to the other side of the Earth, if I avoided him for a million years!"

Not that slowly. The electrical charge of the battery had my little baby crawling across the gravel-studded blacktop at a decent pace.

I climbed back to my feet, and raised my chin in defiance. "It's not unfair. You only wish it was unfair."

She scowls, first in playful grumpiness, then in serious concentration. Jokes were over, and she tossed out the other two bombs. Like the first, they catapulted out into the distance, then swooped around to follow me.

If we were unleashing seeker weapons, I tossed out the rubber ball. When it hit the shield, it got slammed away so hard that it disappeared. Yeah, so much for that.

Fine. I skated away from the hovering bombs, which wasn't really hard. As small as they were, they just didn't have room for much flight equipment. Not even Tier Three flight equipment. As long as I kept an eye on them, I could skate around Other Me's dome and plan my next attack. An attempt to lure them into it didn't work, more's the pity.

I didn't have long to wait. Scuttling industriously, the Machine passed through her dome unaffected, and headed for her feet. So much for her patience hoping her weapons would sneak up on me.

She responded by kicking the Machine. He rolled out of the globe, but not very far. Over a certain limit, any force you tried on him he just ate.

As he crawled right back in, I zipped around behind Other Me. She wouldn't put up with that, of course, but watching both me and the Machine put her at an awkward angle. That gave me an extra half second to pull out a pair of sugar blocks from my tank. I threw the first one down a few feet in front of the shield. Stalagmites shot out, surging forward, only to hit that wall and get blasted to pieces. Shrapnel rained down everywhere, making me glad of my armored coat. It also left a hole in the shimmery explosive dome. One not quite big enough, so I threw the other crystal, and got another blast.

My double grabbed at her pockets just as the Machine reached her, and her legs caught her boot.

In a panic, she grabbed him in her right hand and threw him away. It was a terrible, thoughtless decision, because as she did he curled forward and bit down on her ring. Ha!

She squealed. The Machine crunched and chewed. The dome stopped being frozen, and became a regular shockwave, booming out over us. I slid backwards right to the fence on my spats. Ray ducked in front of Claire, holding her steady with his superhuman strength.

Meatbag Penny stood in the eye of the storm, unaffected. She finished her throw, gently lobbing the Machine across the pavement. Irritated but not panicked, she said, "Fine. So much for playing defense." I was much too far away to do anything as she pulled out two more handfuls of bombs and tossed them up. Three came after me, and the other two orbited her like guardian drones. Yay. Well, at least the explosion had taken care of the first two seeker bombs.

She had the benefit of throwing these straight at me, so I put up a shield and let the blast of a bomb send me sliding across the lot, not actually at Meatbag Penny, but closer to her. She responded with still more bombs, little marble ones that merely blew up when they hit the ground, and gave me more to worry about.

I let my other scheme run, focused mostly on skating around to avoid attacks, and pondered her defense drones. I really should have saved the rubber ball for this.

With my terrible aim, her odds of actually hitting me were remote. When that became clear, she stopped tossing them at me, and took the gun off her hip. A little bigger than a pistol, its irregular, shiny shape had 'mad science' written all over it. Literally, in little gold letters. Oh, my super power, I missed your ridiculous flair so. Also being able to make a device that spread clawed antennae and formed a crackling red web between them, like this gun did.

Teeth gritted now, my double said, "You know what else you never let me do? Vaporize things!"

She swung the barrel up to point at me, gripped in both hands. Before she could fire, Claire called out sharply, "Remember what we said? No vaporizations, or no smoochy smoochy!"

She gripped Ray's shoulders, pushing him forward. Mortified, his whole face went tight. Both Mes looked about the same. Somehow, Claire had managed to actually lose a little shame over the summer.

Other Me let out a high-pitched whine of frustration, one I knew was all theater. "Fine! I'll use the other setting!" She pulled the trigger, and the gun emitted a solid red beam.

Literally solid. It appeared right in my path, and when I put out a shield to block the ray, I ended up vaulting right over it.

She shifted her aim, and everywhere the gun pointed, the beam, as thick as two fingers, followed. When it passed over me, it did so without force, but only to become an obstacle on the other side. I had to duck, roll over the top, and skip when it tried to trip me up. Suddenly, avoiding the seeker bombs was really, really hard, and took all my attention.

Aiming took all of Other Me's attention. She completely failed to notice the Machine crawling back up to her until he was climbing her boot. Dropping the pistol, she shouted, "No no no!" and yanked at him, trying to pull him off her leg. No dice. Now he had a good grip, he wasn't letting go.

With her thoroughly distracted, I fired a jet of cola at her. A defensive drone swung sharply around to block it, and blew up. Cola sprayed wildly again. Ray danced out of the way. Claire stayed where she was, daring the clothing-eating goop to splatter her. By sheer luck, none did, but criminy. She really was even more brazen than before this started. Maybe she had to make up for the boredom of ballet camp.

Now I had the advantage. Meatbag Penny gave up trying to stop the Machine, and fumbled with the top pouch of her bandolier. It opened, and sure enough, I saw sparkly white inside.

Nuh uh. As she pulled out a power activation pill, I slid the irrigation sponge into my fist. This was exactly why I'd brought it. With a firm squeeze, I exploded water out of her pocket, washing away the pills, including the one she'd been holding. They fell into puddles around her feet, dissolving into mush.

The Machine reared off of her chest, and grabbed her arm at the wrist. Obedient to my instructions, he bit into the bomb-resistance bracelet, pulling it right off.

Now! I sprayed her with sugar again, and the other drone intercepted and detonated. This time Meatbag Penny wasn't immune, and the blast so close by knocked her to the ground.

Something bumped against my back, and went *boom*. Oh, criminy. This time I'd gotten distracted, and one of the seeker bombs caught up to me. The explosion shoved me to the ground, much harder than mere backlash knocked Other Me sprawling. I managed to fall on my left side, at least, to spare the sugar tank and most importantly the X Device.

Now I couldn't dodge. The other bomb hit, going off like a hammer with the asphalt as the anvil. Pain threaded through me, accompanied by many cracking sounds.

On the opposite side of Other Me now, I saw Claire holding both Ray's arms in a twisty grip, keeping him from running over to us. He looked more pained than I felt. He'd always hated to see anyone hurt. That was a major part of his charm.

All those thoughts happened in a hurry. This situation was bad, no question, but I did have an advantage. A good shake would scramble my double's gray goo brain. My solid state heart didn't get confused for even a second. I launched another spray at Meatbag Penny, and this time it hit, locking her legs together in a crystal shell.

She rolled over onto her stomach, and did something with her goggles. By the time I'd realized she'd pulled a pill out of them, it was too late. With her back to me, I couldn't stop her from swallowing it.

Criminy buckets, of course she had one hidden! I lunged to my feet, pushed off, and activated the sliding spats to send me rocketing towards her.

I was too far away. She had time to pull out one of her little conventional bombs, and flip it in the air. Not at me. Rather, it landed on the sugar shell around her legs. The blast shattered it, sending more bits flying around. Just as importantly, the shockwave caught me at the exact time to send me sliding backwards the way I came. The shock also sent pain spasming through me again, but I'd already been hurting. The double punch against the ground had spiderwebbed my body with serious cracks. I could feel them...

Climbing groggily to her feet, she let out a barking laugh. "Ha! It's all in the angle. There's a whole branch of engineering about that. Reams and reams of math to make sure the force is channeled in exactly the right directions. All I have to do is follow the pictures in my head."

I launched myself towards her again, shield bands ready. She took a couple of little copper electronic bits out of the little pockets that studded my jumpsuit, and wriggled them into cracks in her oversized pistol. As she did, she chattered, "I brought a bunch of components for my power to work with. Clever, huh?"

She pulled the trigger, and this time the gun emitted a red wall instead of a line. She swung that around right in my face.

Damaged or not, this body was stronger, faster, and most importantly lighter than flesh and blood. I jumped, grabbed the top of the wall, and vaulted right over it.

Her eyes widened behind the goggles. This time, I'd caught her by surprise.

Black fluttered around us. A lean, yellow-and-white figure appeared, and grabbed me as I descended towards Other Me. One vice grip hand on my neck, the other on my wrist, holding my wand still.

My double fell onto her butt, and scrambled backwards, pulling out more components and sticking them together.

Mourning Dove, in her horrible raspy voice, said, "Do not worry. The threat is over."

Claire and Ray watched us, horrified. Ray was slightly hunched, ready to move, but also cautious. Especially cracked like I was, Mourning Dove could rip me apart before he reached her, and she out-powered us all, easily.

Personally, I dangled, and tried to think. A plan to get out of this alive was not presenting itself.

Claire, hands over her mouth, cried out, "What are you doing here? Shouldn't you be fighting the First Horseman with everyone else? They need you!"

The white-suited, white-haired, leathery yellow-skinned vampire croaked, "Saving a life is more important than punishing past deaths. I will destroy this robot, then return to combat the Horseman."

Claire shook her head, yellow curls bouncing. "You can't do that. They're not trying to kill each other, just switch places!"

"Being switched into a robot is death," answered Mourning Dove, staring at her hard.

Immune, it took me a second to realize what was going on. Claire looked like an adorable cherub. She'd turned her power up, way up. Mourning Dove didn't react to it like other people, but she scowled, forcing herself to move slowly through the paralyzation.

Slowly enough that Ray could pick up a fist-sized chunk of sugar debris and fling it at her. It sped through the air like a rocket.

Mourning Dove wasn't impaired enough. She let go of me, and darkness flickered again. She reappeared behind Ray, and grabbed his shoulder. "Your loyalty is commendable, but a robot is not a friend."

Claire grabbed her other wrist, tugging with both hands. "Let him go!"

Her power was still slowing Mourning Dove, and now it had Ray boggled.

Personally, I was busy, and only caught the edges of all of that. When my feet hit the ground, I threw myself in a tackle at Meatbag Penny.

We didn't actually drop to the ground. It hurt enough when I smacked into her. That dazed me momentarily, but I still managed to grab her wrists. Wrestling up close, she would be no match for me. I would pin her, switch us, and take out the Heart of Steel. Then I'd be alive, and Mourning Dove wouldn't care.

Meatbag Penny responded by giggling and hunching forward. Holding her wrists did nothing to stop her from pressing her forehead against the thing she held in one hand. It was a tuning fork, upgraded with a lot of electronics, and looked familiar.

It looked like a souped-up version of the device I'd tried to build back in December, to push my powers into showing themselves.

The fork touched her skin, and sparks danced from the contact point. Tesla's Forbidden Equations. I was in trouble. Both of me.

Behind her goggles, my double's eyes slipped out of focus. Her arm twisted. Pain shot up my arm, and I spun around, letting Meatbag Penny go and dropping onto my back on the ground.

In a pleasant, businesslike tone, holding onto my aching wrist now, she said, "I'm proud of your body, but there are limits to its range of movement."

Another puff of blackness, and Mourning Dove blinked into place above me. Her foot smacked down on my chest, pinning me in place. If she pushed any harder, the X Device and my stomach would both shatter, and it was only guesswork which would collapse first.

"No more," she growled.

Mourning Dove hadn't recovered from Claire. She delayed a moment in crushing me, long enough for Ray to charge up and ram into her back, sending the homicidal heroine stumbling away.

Tires screeched. My parents' car jerked to a halt at the curb, and Mom jumped out. "What's going on?" she demanded in a quick, authoritative demand that even got the zombie's attention.

"Mourning Dove is trying to kill Robot Penny!" shrieked Claire.

The zombie heroine disappeared in a cloud of black again. This time, she reappeared in front of Claire, grabbing her by the forehead. "You are interfering. Sleep."

Claire glowered up at her, lip thrust out, childishly petulant. Again they froze, eyes locked. Ray ran back to them, but Mourning Dove wasn't actually paralyzed, and her hand darted up to grab the top of his head as well.

She had them, but her powers didn't activate. She stared into Claire's eyes, struggling to overcome that last little barrier to release her vampirism and drain them both unconscious.

Ray grabbed her wrist and tugged, but it was no good. She was as fast and strong as him.

They made a nearly still tableau, Mourning Dove frozen between my two friends, long enough for Mom to walk briskly up to the three of them, and punch Mourning Dove in the chest.

Okay, not a punch exactly. More like a two-fingered jab. But something clanked and snapped under the white leather costume, and Mourning Dove went limp, collapsing to the ground.

Ray and Claire gaped at my mother in awe. Mom hunched over, and her shoulders shook so hard I could see it from here. Her voice quavered with the same aftershock of fear as she said, "Studying Mourning Dove's weaknesses was the first thing I did upon becoming a hero. The odds that I could still pull off that move were low. Too low. I had to take the chance."

As I watched her, I noticed a mass of white paper gripped ferociously in her other hand. My letters. I'd never gotten them back from Miss Lutra.

"I know how to do that!" chirped Meatbag Penny beside me.

Oops. I'd forgotten about her, and it was a miracle of luck I'd survived the mistake.

Or maybe not. She looked happily spaced-out, and had reconfigured the tuning fork device, the bits wired around the handle visibly rearranged. Standing over me, she said, "Okay, first, no glass," and pushed the fork's button.

It rang, like tuning forks are supposed to, but at a very high pitch. The sugar tank on my hip cracked, and the bottom half fell off, shattering against the ground in a splattered puddle of harmless cola. Claire let out a yelp, yanking off her glasses, and the Meatbag Penny took off her own goggles more calmly as their lenses broke.

I took a page from her book, and rolled onto my stomach so she couldn't see me pulling the X Device out of my faux-corset. It felt intact. All I had to do was touch both of us, right?

The tuning fork has a dial as well as a button. She rotated the former, then pressed the latter. Now the chime that came out was deep, very deep.

I didn't have much attention to spare placing it. Pain that made the bombs seem like nothing stabbed through me. I heard the cracking, all over. Now parts of my body were broken. I wasn't sure which. Everything hurt.

Meatbag Penny rolled me over with her foot, bent down, and pulled the X Device out of my grip. I tried to stop her, but something snapped in my left arm, and my hand went limp.

She held the two linked arrows up, tilting them around to study from every angle. Blandly, paying no one else any real attention, she said, "Fascinating. I can see inside it, you know. The shaft forms an electronic null zone where the emergent patterns of thought are pulled in by lack of resistance, suctioned catastrophe toward eversion staff lunar potato energy level potential orbit ollie ollie oxenfree."

No one else moved. I could guarantee Mom didn't have calculations on how to deal with this. Since my double was ignoring me, I squirted her with my wand. It had hardly any juice left thanks to the broken tank, but enough splashed onto her leg to lock over her knee and start growing across the other.

Still cheerfully vague, she smiled down at me. "Hey, thanks!" She drew a purple, particularly small bomb out of its pouch, a kind I hadn't seen before. Then she took a little metal thing with prongs that looked an awful lot like an ancient transistor from a pouch. Sticking them together, she slapped the combination onto the sugar shell.

It blew up, not hard, but launching chunks into the air to rain down over the recess ground. They weren't falling fast enough to look dangerous, but wherever they landed, they melted into a puddle, which sank into the asphalt and turned orange-red. In seconds, the floor had become lava, or at least littered with pools. Mom pulled Ray and Claire away. Ferocious heat radiated from even being near them.

So much for both my underground lairs.

"You know what's great? I can spread them. I can reduce the planet to a molten—no!" Her ditzy ramble broke off into a whine. Other Me doubled over, grabbing the sides of her head and grimacing.

She still had the X Device in one of those hands, and wasn't paying me any attention. Eyes screwed shut, she babbled, "Aether punctures forming temporal spirals recycle energy to avert heat death.

Automatic, more efficient than transmutation of astral layer distortions formed with fuelless exothermics by adolescent forward lymbic system spikes. Avoids feedback loops predetermining failure until astral detonation feedback transforms and spacially subverts the organic matter. Morality? What is morality? AH HA HA HA HA HA!"

I didn't know what to do any better than the others. What parts of me were even able to move?

A distant thumping I'd been too distracted to notice got closer, louder, loud enough I couldn't ignore it anymore. Gerty, in her massive lumbering glory, came galloping around the corner of the school, knocking out bricks as she bumped against it in the process. "My Gerty Girls are in trouble!" she wailed.

Other Me spun around, her struggle gone, replaced by a beatific smile. "If you could only see inside you, Gerty. Do you know how many conceptual loops you are? Each one like a signature, linked by the ideal permanence with which you stamp and are stamped."

Gerty's hands shot out on cables, grabbing hold of our costumes and yanking us into the air. We sailed across the lot to land almost gently in her arms, wrapped in a hug. She rocked us from side to side, whispering, "My poor, good girls, Gerty is here and everything will be okay."

Her grip was mostly around our middles. I wriggled my right arm free. Other than a little clumsiness and some shooting pains, it still seemed functional.

Other Me knew what I intended. Maybe our power told her. Maybe just because she knew me. Maybe it was obvious. Holding the X Device up and out of my reach, she teased, "You want this? Oopsy doopsy!"

With a playful flick, she tossed it at one of the pools of lava.

Mom jerked forward, then stopped, which meant she had no time to reach it. No one could.

So, I was very surprised when the mind transfer arrows stopped in midair a foot above the blazing goop, and instead sailed through the air back towards the school, to land in Ampexia's grip. Oh, yeah, she did have that gimmick in her gloves that pulled small objects to her.

And a tendency, like Claire, to let everyone forget about her until she saw her chance.

"Gerty, your left arm's on fire!" shouted my teammate. Gerty gasped, and flapped that arm. Since it happened to be the one holding me, I dropped onto my feet. My right foot bent underneath me, and my hips wobbled, but I stayed upright.

Meatbag Penny had forgotten all about me. She chattered at Gerty, "Ideal permanence is a clever method of adaptive indestructibility, don't you think? Did you know it has weaknesses? What would be the best way to break you, do you think? I could think. I could do it with thought. Maybe I should?"

Ampexia tossed me the X Device, and I caught it in my good right hand. This was it. My double was so insane she couldn't identify threats, or reality on a human scale. Except... there wasn't anything to go back to. She'd broken my brain. Other Me didn't have the focus or strength of will to force my power under control, and make it fix me.

Besides, she was tied closer to my power, which was now totally out of control. Transferring her into my body might tear her personality in half, for all real purposes killing her. Then I would be in my head, alone with my power. That thought terrified me.

I had to rescue myself.

"Machine!" I shouted. He wasn't even far away. Maybe he'd been following us around. He crawled up to my foot, and I grabbed him with my right hand. My left hand at least had enough strength to loosely hold the X Device.

"Cut!" The Machine obeyed, and I used him to slice the arrows of the X Device free of each other.

They had a triangular point on one end, and a suction-cup shaped cone on the other. How to use them could not be more obvious.

Yanking on my shirt, I ripped the buttons free, baring the hatch in my chest. With all the cracks, that fell off as I tried to open it, exposing my Heart of Steel. It hurt, but I still had the range of movement in my right arm to reach back and pull out the Heart of Gold.

I didn't want to do this. It was suicide, erasing myself as an individual.

Heart of Gold would be proud of me, because it was the right thing to do and I did it anyway. Pressing the cup ends of the arrows against both Hearts, I leaned forward and jabbed them against Other Me's leg.

Pictures. Blueprints. Mesh outlines and spinning atoms and elaborately detailed models that I could see inside and out.

No. I did this so I could look away from them.

There was nothing to look away to. They described the world. They were the world, and I was seeing it properly now. The beautiful, infinitely possible world.

Then I would see the world improperly. I remembered how to do that, right? With vision, with sound, with the impressions they gave rather than how they actually worked?

Besides, I was talking. I might as well say something useful.

"Gerty, I'm sick. The white-haired lady can help me."

The goat lumbered over to Mom, my friends, and the unconscious Mourning Dove. We left the twisted, now-empty robot shell lying on the ground. Good riddance. Animatronic goat feet splashed through lava puddles without even noticing them.

Dad was here. I'd been too busy to notice his arrival. I focused on him, and on words. "Fix her. You can use the tape in my leg pocket to hold the chip together. It will work."

I could see it. I drifted off into the pictures, watching my father open up the dented box in Mourning Dove's chest, and reattach her wires, the ones Mom had jolted out of place. Patterns of understanding danced through his brain. He knew most of how she worked. It would be easy to make something like her, but...

No no no. I had to concentrate, long enough to tell the awakening zombie, "You know what I need."

And because I said it, she did. She stood up, and placed her hand on the back of my head.

Epilogue

I woke up in my own wonderful bed, in my own wonderful bedroom. My body ached. Not the sharp pain of that broken robotic shell, the stiffness of overworked muscles. Or was this normal? I was out of practice.

No, I remembered waking up this morning, and I hadn't felt like this then.

I did need to go to the bathroom. Whoops. There's a sensation I'd forgotten came with living bodies.

The discomfort wasn't so bad I couldn't lie here, enjoying the peace and being where I belonged, safe and in danger of losing everything. One of my sets of memories didn't need to go through potty training again, so I wasn't worried about all the weird sensations, like breathing and blinking. And shrugging. Shoulders! Oh, real working shoulders, how I'd missed you.

I looked back at the last couple of months. Three sets of memories. No, four. I did remember being the first Heart of Steel, confused and outraged and liberated by knowing I was a fake. I hadn't been able to handle it. I could barely manage being real and stuck in a robot. How had I managed it as Heart of Gold?

Even looking back, I couldn't tell. There hadn't been any choice.

What a mess. I'd done some pretty crazy stuff in my flesh-and-blood body. Criminy, Penny, get some self-control. The robot me's anger was not pleasant to remember.

But everything was fine, now. I'd won. I'd defeated my own super power.

My bedroom door creaked, opening enough for Claire and Ray's faces to peek through.

"Your mom said you're awake. Don't ask me how she knew," said Claire.

"Come on in," I invited, making no move to leave the comfortable warmth under my covers.

They did, crowding up to the edge of my bed.

Ray leaned over me, blue eyes solemn, expressive mouth tilted with worry, eyebrows as sandy as his hair pressed together. "How are you?" Today had been too intense for joking.

An important thought, and relevant to an important question. Let's see, two plus two was four. Eight times eight was sixty-four. A right triangle with a base of three and a height of five would have a hypotenuse of... square root of thirty-four, slightly under six. Okay, math worked. For speculation, what kind of lifeforms would exist on Pluto, and how would Harvy and Juliet interact with them? Something that didn't move much, since it was stupid cold out there, and while lights and ground-traveling sound were available, let's face it—Harvy would just use telepathy.

"I detect no cognitive deficiencies," I reported.

They looked relieved. Claire asked next, "What about your super power?"

Well, my brain didn't hurt. There wasn't a sensation of emptiness, or anything. I did owe Lucyfar a dark matter hair dryer, didn't I? That would be crazy.

No images formed in my head. Not even the ticklish feeling of inspiration lurking but unformed.

Sighing, I leaned my head back and stared up at the ceiling. "Gone."

"It was the right thing to do," said Claire, taking my hand.

"It was the Penny thing to do," said Ray, putting his hands over hers.

Heh. I had to grin, because you know what was so wonderful about these two? They were just as likely to have switched lines. It was so wonderful to have them back, and to not have worry about losing them anymore.

I think I'd handled this mess as well as anyone could.

Well, Ray and Claire were here. Curious, I asked, "Where is Ampexia?"

Dryly, Claire answered, "She said you were as big a doofus as the rest of us and walked off."

Yeah, that's the ending Ampexia would have wanted.

Claire leaned closer, watching my expression. "Are there three of you in there, now?"

I shook my head. "Naah. Just one, and I'll be fine by the time we get back to school. Oh criminy, we've only got a couple of weeks of summer left, don't we? I officially hate camp. I am never going to camp again."

They both snickered. Claire must have shown Ray the letters.

Those faces. I just could not get tired of watching them. Two sets of memories had way too little Ray and Claire in them. Still smiling, I said, "When we get back to school, I'll want to hang out with other people a little more, but not much. I don't think this has changed me, or us. We're still the Inscrutable Machine. Just without super-powered adventures."

They lifted me into a sitting position, and hugged me together. Ray, his voice quiet but emphatic, said, "You have the talent, and can get ahold of mad science. You don't have to make them yourself."

They let me go, and I lay back onto my soft, wonderful pillow. It felt different with a human head and real hair.

Ray watched me for a few seconds, and put his hand on Claire's shoulder. "She wants time to think about it."

He knew me so well. It was wonderful.

They shuffled out, leaving me to think.

He had a point. My cleverness, determination, and freaky tactical talent defeated my legendary-level super power. I certainly had what it took to be a heroine or villainess without a power.

But I'd loved, loved having one.

Oh, well.

A random inspiration hit me. What had happened to Gerty Goat? I knew what would happen to her. If I could find her again, I'd donate her to the fire department. Rescuing people would make her happy, and she'd have constant companionship.

This was all nice, but I didn't actually hurt enough to bother with, so I might as well get up and sneak into the bathroom. The familiarity and strangeness of being in my bedroom settled into a weird but entertaining feeling of déjà vu as I walked to my door.

My desk sat next to it, with my computer. Good to have you back, buddy, and hey, now I'd played both the Vengeance and Sacrifice routes of Princess of the Closet Monsters! Yeah, Vengeance had totally been more fun.

Also on my desk, pushed up against the wall, was a disassembled clock, one of the old round ones with hands on the front to tell time. Half its cogs lay around it. What in Tesla's name...?

Oh, yeah. When I first came up with those power-enhancing pills, I'd hoped they would finally nudge my super power into being able to repair things. Nope, it did what it wanted, and that was always to chase something new. I was able to talk to it way more consciously after the personality split, and it still didn't actually do what it was told. Sheesh.

I missed that.

Well, I hardly needed a super power to fix this. The electrical motor might be beyond me, but for the rest I just needed to attach the two stalks for the hands to this...

The knowledge slipped out of my hands. For a few seconds it had all made sense.

Wait.

I'd had this sensation before. Several times, when for a little while I understood clockwork and mechanical devices intuitively. I'd assumed that was part of my super power, but that worked in fugue states, with a knowledge beyond the human brain. The sensations were nothing alike.

I'd had two super powers all along, and I still had one of them.

Exactly the power my parents had originally believed I had, in fact. At exactly the level of development, to judge by that flash.

Which meant in four years, Bad Penny would be back, ready to be a supervillain again.

Or a heroine.

Knowing me, probably a villain. I had lots of time to decide. The point was, I have a super power!

Glee bubbled up inside me, and I lifted my fists towards the ceiling, laughing!

"AH HA HA HA HA HA!"

MESSAGE FROM THE WRITER:

Here ends the story of Penelope Akk, but worry not! Penny has friends, and those friends have friends. I am not even close to finished with telling stories of kids in her world. Right now, I plan on alternating a book in a brand new world, then a book in the Supervillain world, on and on. There is more fun on the way, I promise.

An author I like has also asked to write a book in my world. I have agreed, but no book gets written in my continuity without me standing over her shoulder, liking everything I read as it's written, and making sure it fits my world before it's released. If side books do come out with a co-writer's name on them, keep that in mind.

Sincerely,
Richard Roberts

ABOUT THE AUTHOR

Richard Roberts has fit into only one category in his entire life, and that is 'writer', but as a writer he'd throw himself out of his own books for being a cliche.

He's had the classic wandering employment history - degree in entomology, worked in health care, been an administrator and labored for years in the front lines of fast food. He's had the appropriate really weird jobs, like breeding tarantulas and translating English to English for Japanese television. He wears all black, all the time, is manic-depressive, and has a creepy laugh.

He's also followed the classic writer's path, the pink slips, the anthology submissions, the desperate scrounging to learn how an ever-changing system works. He's been writing from childhood, and had the appropriate horrible relationships that damaged his self-confidence for years. Then out of nowhere *Curiosity Quills Press* demanded he give them his books, and here he is.

As for what he writes, Richard loves children and the gothic aesthetic.

Most everything he writes will involve one or the other, and occasionally both. His fantasy is heavily influenced by folk tales, fairy tales, and mythology, and he likes to make the old new again. In particular, he loves to pull his readers into strange characters with strange lives, and his heroes are rarely heroic.

Thank You for Reading

http://frankensteinbeck.blogspot.com

Please visit http://curiosityquills.com/reader-survey to share
your reading experience with the author of this book!

Down to Oath, by Tyrolin Puxty

You have to find yourself before you can leave.

Codi lives in the exceptionally drab town of Oath; a settlement without colour, children or personality.

When a child manifests in the library and introduces Codi to parallel towns that contain aggressive, manic versions of herself, she must decide between saving Oath...and saving herself.

After all, how much can you truly trust yourself?

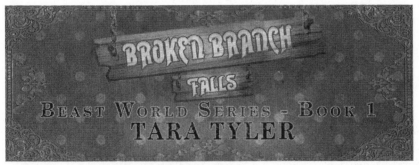

Broken Branch Falls, by Tara Tyler

Gabe is a typical teenage goblin. He marches in the band, enjoys calculus, and gets picked on daily by the other species at school. But Gabe wants to try new things. When a prank goes wrong, Gabe must join the football team as punishment. He finds a way to make it work, and more kids break the rules, forcing the adults to step in. They threaten to split up their town, so Gabe and his friends set out to find the Book of Ages, hopeful to save Broken Branch Falls.

Emma and the Banderwigh, by Matthew S. Cox

Ten-year- old Emma doesn't believe in faerie tales or monsters that secret children away in the night–until she meets one. One morning, a sickly older girl reappears and sets the entire town aflutter with whispers of a child-stealing monster lurking in the forest. Nan tells her of the Banderwigh: a dark soul who feeds on sorrow and feeds from children's tears. Darkness comes calling on her happy home, the impossible becomes real, and Emma must find the strength to believe. Her family depends on it.

Strings, by G. Miki Hayden

Robert, an ordinary boy, finds himself in a newly chaotic world. Buildings move when and where they please, and time jumps around according to no known laws of physics. For Robert, getting to his regular school in the morning is impossible, and as for getting home... But Holden, a boy he and his friend Nila meet in a cave, offers them a string. Teeny and tiny, and invisible to the naked eye, this string will take Robert and Mila to their homes and way beyond, to other dimensions.

90335551R00219

Made in the USA
Lexington, KY
10 June 2018